THE FORGOTTEN STONE

E.A. WINTERS

DRAGONLEAFPRESS

Edited by Tahlia Newland
Cover design by Covers by Combs
Map drawn by Tania Gomes at MysticWingsArt

ISBN-13: 978-1-958702-00-0

DRAGONLEAFPRESS

DragonLeaf Press
https://www.eawinters.com

To Grandma, for your endless patience and encouragement, for our phone calls after reading the rough draft of every chapter, and for always being there.

1

———

Enouim had complained just that morning about how her life was going nowhere, but she would rather be serving drinks than running for her life. She swung herself over a rock fence and catapulted forward with all that she had, afraid to look behind. Never to turn. That was the precept of her people, the rallying cry on every battlefield and at every bar where the tales were told. Today, she found the adage loathsome rather than inspiring.

The grass gave way beneath her leather footwear, and the familiar smell of horses welcomed Enouim to the pasture. *Idiot,* she chastised herself. *And of all the people to enrage, you just had to pick Chayan.* Enouim ducked between the horses, vaulted the fence on the far side, rolled to the end of the plateau, and dropped five feet to the level below.

Gorgenbrilders were excellent friends and allies, and, even more, dedicated avengers. The stereotype felt wildly out of place with Enouim, but Chayan was the epitome of brute revenge. Crouching low enough to keep her head out of view, Enouim took a moment to gather her breath. Images of the young woman filled her mind, her brown hair permanently in a messy braid and tossed over broad shoulders. She had earned respect in the community as a lethal warrior, formidable hunter, and for having a shorter fuse than most. Her legs were like oak trees, her arms seemed functionally to be made of steel, and she appeared to have little time for human connection. She cared far more for blood, sweat, and —well, Enouim wasn't sure Chayan had tear ducts, but blood and sweat anyway.

Enouim flexed her slender arms and sighed. She had a sort of wiry strength, but Chayan was rarely challenged even by experienced warriors. Gorgenbrild settled almost all scores through physical means, and Chayan never let anything go. She was nearly undefeated, and though she'd been brought to Justice Hall on three separate occasions for extreme force beyond what was due, she had been able to weasel out of it every time. This left Enouim two options: face Chayan and take her chances, or try to make it to Deliberation to state her case.

She definitely wasn't ready to face Chayan. She had to move.

The land of Gorgenbrild was characterized by rolling green hills sprawling across largely uneven ground. Ahead of her Enouim saw stone houses, some standing alone and others built into the sides of steep hills. Enouim glanced around, searching for anything helpful, and caught an image reflected in the window of one of the houses. Her blood ran cold. Chayan, her face fixed in a grimace, flew effortlessly over the horse enclosure fence and landed without a sound. She ran low to the ground, holding her right arm—bent at an unnatural angle—close to her body.

Gorgenbrilders were known for their values of bravery, strength, honor, and minding of their own business. Debts were settled with physical retaliation, with only the most egregious injustices being taken to Deliberation. And after that morning's debacle, Enouim technically owed Chayan at *least* one of her bones.

She shuddered. A single broken arm was hardly a handicap for someone as accomplished as Chayan. Facing her simply would not do, and the more Enouim thought about it, the more desperate she was to avoid it.

Enouim ran as quickly and quietly as she could, head low, along the wall up and to her right. Not thinking, she kicked a pebble, and it rolled down the slope behind her—*tsk, tsk, tsk* —as it hit the rocky way. The sound mocked her, echoing her thoughts as Enouim chastised herself for the mistake. Panic welled up in her chest, and she launched herself up the rise, round a bend, and off the ledge, aiming for the roof of a house the next level down. Halfway through the air, she realized— too late—that the roof of the house was more uneven than she'd thought. Panic rarely brought the best judgment or the most delicate movements, and Enouim found herself tumbling over the house and plummeting to earth on the far side.

In a stroke of luck she caught a rock partway down on the opposite side of the house and came to an abrupt halt. Enouim hung there, over a window, for a moment, taking in ragged breaths of air. With those breaths came a steadier mind.

Her feet found purchase on the window ledge, and Enouim almost laughed aloud at her relief to discover that it was open. She swung through the window into the house and dropped to the floor, finding herself in a circular entry room with a wooden table built rounded to hug the wall—the house of Bondeg Polenko. The door stood further down, and hooks for weapons hung on the far wall. Various furs and skins adorned the wall opposite her, along with the host's second-best weaponry. The best would be kept close at hand, and if the quality of those on display was high, company could be assured that the owner could afford to show it off because even greater pieces were secure in their possession. Today, however, most of the hooks were empty. Two passages extended to her left. One led to living quarters and one to a dining area.

Bondeg, a gruff, seventy-four-year-old warrior with many achievements, was a highly respected leader in the community, so his home was larger than most. It was said that Bondeg had slung nearly thirty zegrath over his broad shoulders in his time, a record none had threatened in as many years. Most notably, Bondeg had led the charge next to Quarot of Kalka'an against the Iyangas in the Liombas-Katan Campaign. No significant endeavor was undertaken without his knowledge, and if it was important enough to garner his attention, Bondeg himself would be orchestrating it all. In fact, Bondeg was heading up an important excursion that very moment and was expected to return that same afternoon. An alarm bell rang somewhere in her mind at this, but it couldn't compete with the overpowering mental picture of Chayan's unpleasant face.

Bondeg was the great warrior who'd restored Gorgenbrild's autonomy and maintained its reputation. When she was a child, she heard that Bondeg had once skewered an ill-willed intruder by throwing a lance through the very window she'd come through. The shady bloke never saw it coming. The more she thought about Bondeg's unflinching stare, the louder that warning bell rang, but she reminded herself that it was secondary to a more pressing need. For now, she was safe and could consider her next move.

Enouim let out a heavy sigh and sunk back against the rock wall beneath the windowsill. Chayan undoubtedly heard the pebble she kicked and would be bearing down on her any moment. Come to think of it, her less-than-graceful fall over the roof was likely seen by someone. That someone might point Chayan in the right direction. As if on cue, low voices wafted in through the open window. Enouim heard the sinister *swish* of a blade slicing through the air as if to practice before it made good on a promise to slice through her flesh. Enouim winced.

Soft, hurried footsteps approached, and then stopped as a distraction came up the slope. Distractions were good, very good. The quick *clip-clop* of trotting horses and the excited clamor of men returning from a perilous venture filled Enouim's ears like soft grass receiving weary feet. Urgent, animated voices called for further action and discussion raged over which "further action" was best. One popular fellow declared that the best thinking happened over drinks, to which a chorus of praise and laughter went up and the group began to disperse. The low, gravelly voice of an authoritative man demanded they meet him at Mangonel Mornings in no less than twenty minutes. Well, what a manure pile to be in. The voice belonged to Bondeg Polenko, and his heavy boots hit the earth with a *thud* of finality as he dismounted his horse right outside.

With Chayan almost certainly outside the window and Bondeg at the door, Enouim had nowhere to go. She briefly considered begging Bondeg to hear her out and keep Chayan at bay, but according to Gorgenbrilder custom Chayan had a right to her revenge. To make things worse, Chayan and Bondeg were on good terms—*as good of terms as a person can be with a walking boulder*. But boulder or not, Chayan had enough relatability to develop a mutual respect and even some jokes with Bondeg over excursions they'd weathered together. Chayan would likely wait until Bondeg left for the Mangonel, being wise enough to know not to interrupt a man like him in such a state. He clearly had earnest business to attend to, and jumping in with such a trivial matter would not bode well for her.

Enouim lifted herself up and craned her neck to look back through the window. Chayan stood a mere fifteen feet from the window and looked directly at her with a sneer. Enouim dropped back down and flattened herself against the wall, but something jutted uncomfortably into her back. She reached behind her and grasped what felt like a rock—not helpful— then realized that if Bondeg was particularly distracted, he might not see her if she was under the table. She twisted toward the table to crawl under it, but the wooden floor beneath her gave way and swallowed her whole.

2

About four feet down, Enouim hit a dirt floor with a jolt, and a nearly imperceptible *click* sounded above her. Light came in through narrow wooden slats above her head, but the tunnel into which she'd fallen reached into darkness. It appeared that the rock she'd touched was a mechanism connected to a trap door that, when rotated, released a hinge that dropped the portion of the floor on which she'd been sitting. It must have been well camouflaged with the rest of the flooring to need no rugs to conceal it.

The natural response to a self-governing policy dominated by violence was that people established strategies to give them an edge in moments of need—hidden tunnels and entrances, and go bags prepared in advance with tools and resources for survival. Any self-respecting Gorgenbrilder had at least one hidden doorway in their home, on principle even if they couldn't afford to make them overly creative. If Enouim could reach one of her own family's house entrances, she could be safe for a while.

Footsteps crossed the room above her, and she heard Bondeg set a shield and other pieces of weaponry back in their places on the wall. He called to Chayan to join him and the others in their discourse at Mangonel Mornings. The main hall for drinks and merrymaking, Mangonel Mornings—named after a catapult designed to destroy rock walls—was the prime location for people to share any news of interest.

Most Gorgenbrilders didn't find drinking in moderation a realistic or understandable suggestion, and tolerance of strong drink ran thick in their blood. Anyone drinking a satisfactory amount, and any visitor experiencing Gorgenbrilder brews for the first time, was likely to wake the next morning feeling as though something had socked them. Employed there herself, Enouim had many opportunities to watch the dedication of Gorgenbrilders to their fermented drink.

Enouim didn't wait to hear Chayan's answer. Since the Polenko family's tunnels, such as the one she'd stumbled upon, would lead to safety, she struck out for wherever the end might lead. On hands and knees, Enouim crawled through the three to four feet high tunnel carved from the earth and supported with intermittent wooden supports. About half an hour later, she came to the end. Taking a deep breath, she reached up and pushed on the wooden door in the ceiling.

It gave way and flipped up, and she saw branches overhead. She clambered out of the hole and took stock of her surroundings. She'd emerged at one edge of the community, among several trees. Footpaths wound through the rolling terrain, dotted with enclosures for horses, goats, and pigs, which stepped down multiple levels, like cosmic stairs. The land reached up to meet a clear blue sky, save for a dreamy wisp of pure white cloud. The scene was set against a backdrop of mountains in the distance, and sheer cliffs dropped away behind her. She was struck by the peaceful alternation between green grass and gray rock—green and gray, green and gray.

The light was soft in the descending sun, but the world would still be illuminated for several hours. Enouim drank in the familiar sights and soothing colors, allowing the peace in the view to steady her heartbeat. Her mind regaled her with the day's events. How could she have been so stupid? And why had she built it up so much in her mind? It was an accident, after all. Surely it wouldn't be so bad. And yet, Enouim could not stifle the shudder that rippled through her body when her mind conjured up Chayan's contorted face and imposing musculature. Enouim was slender with lanky arms and legs. She imagined the only creature she might truly intimidate was a rabbit.

Drawing her gaze back to her immediate surroundings, she took in the few trees behind and around her and the brush beneath her feet. Nothing moved or made noise except the occasional bird, and no one was around to have noticed her sudden appearance. She might easily reach the community unhindered. Surely, the tunnel had bought her some time. A rabbit with soft, mottled brown-and-gray fur stared back at her, its large, innocent eyes unconcerned. Making fun of her. A rabbit? Honestly?

Enouim shook her head to clear it and started down the incline. Her house wasn't far from here. Though her family home didn't have any tunnel entrances on this end, she could probably make it without them. And if Chayan took Bondeg up on his offer to join them at Mangonel Mornings, well, all the better! She hurried into the town toward her house, a modest, stand-alone dwelling not incorporated into the landscape like some of the others. The ground was flat here, so there was no need.

Although their house style was more exposed, Enouim

thought it felt friendlier, due in part to having windows allowing natural light in from both sides rather than just one. A small pen around one side held the goats and pig, and the pony shared space with several other families' horses in a larger plot nearby. The pony, a dutiful twenty-nine-year-old mare named Pinky, stood about thirteen hands high. Her coat, though interspersed with several colors, looked pink from a distance. Though affectionate and willing to work, at her age she simply couldn't do all that she used to.

Enouim entered the house and dashed past the kitchen down the hall to her room. She grabbed a small knife off the wooden end table next to her bed and slid it into the built-in sheath of her boot, then checked the dagger she always carried at her waist. She hardly used it, save for chores, but all Gorgenbrilders carried at least a couple of weapons. She hadn't been in any real physical altercations before and avoided conflicts that might lead to one.

Voices drifted toward her from the kitchen—her mother, Qadra, and brother, Pleko. Pleko, five years older than her nineteen years, no longer lived at home, so he must be visiting —or, more likely, returning something he'd borrowed.

"Enouim?" her mother called. "Come in here for a minute. Where are you rushing off to?"

"Just a minute!" Enouim threw on a fresh green tunic and adjusted her wrapped belt over it. Light and loosely fitted to her body, the tunic had long sleeves with intentional holes that hooked over her thumbs. She wadded up her old tunic, still covered in dirt from her tunnel crawl, and tossed it under the bed, then she snatched a hooded mantle off her bed and tugged it on over her tunic as she headed to the kitchen. Her mind spun in circles. Should she tell her family what had happened? She rarely kept anything from her family. But she didn't usually do such stupid things.

Enouim slid sheepishly into the kitchen doorway. Her brother leaned against the far wall and took her in with a quizzical look, while her mother faced away from her, preparing the evening meal. The pig stood at her feet, snuffling on the ground for scraps.

"Get back, you!" her mother said to the pig, nudging her sharply with her foot. "Honestly, what is the point of you?" She shook her head. "Always wanting scraps, overfed, but still skinny! What's the point of a pig that doesn't get fat?" Turning to her son, she added, "I swear Jilka Monkin only gave it to us to get rid of it. Worst gift ever."

Enouim's brother made eye contact with her and rolled his eyes. They both knew their mother had grown rather fond of the pig. It kept breaking through the pen to be next to her, and now she didn't bother fixing the fencing.

Enouim cleared her throat. "Afternoon, um, I'm late for the Mangonel. Supposed to help out this evening."

Qadra turned around, wiped her hands on a rag, and placed them on her hips. "There you are. What's that on your face? You can't go to work looking like that. Where have you been?"

Enouim shifted her feet. Lying was wrong. "I sort of ... had an accident." She glanced up at her mom and Pleko, both now fully engaged.

Her brother raised an eyebrow. "An accident?" he said in disbelief. Enouim's mother cast a look of annoyance his way, which he ignored.

"I'm sort of panicking. I'm supposed to go to the Mangonel, but I'm already late and Chayan is supposed to be there, and earlier I sort of, kind of, broke her arm. I didn't mean to!" Her words tumbled out in a rush. "She's going to kill me, isn't she? I can't go there now!"

A beat of silence. They exchanged dumbfounded looks. "You *WHAT?*" Her mother finally managed.

"Hey, your first engagement! If you're going to jump in, jump in with both feet," Pleko joked, cracking a grin.

Enouim saw zero humor in her circumstances.

"How did this happen?"

Enouim explained that she wasn't exactly *late* for the Mangonel; she was missing. Except everyone who was there earlier would have seen her tear for the door and make a run for it. Chayan had been there, discussing the mythical weapon that could change everything for defending Gorgenbrild against the mountain tribes, who threatened their land and livelihood once again. The weapon was called the Ecyah Stone. Well, in truth it was called a number of things. Whatever the pronunciation, the stone was said to carry a formidable power giving strength, vitality and success to all who wielded it. Whether or not it was real had been debated for years, and though most chalked it up to old legends, a few maintained that the legends had to originate from somewhere.

The mountain tribes were not particularly dangerous as small bands of warriors and historically spent their energies destroying one another—which was fine by all in Gorgenbrild. However, splinters of the Iyangas tribes that Bondeg had led Gorgenbrild to soundly defeat years ago had grown back like an ugly weed. A young man called Malum Khoron-khelek was sweeping through the tribes like a blight, stitching them together into an imposing new force called the Sumus. His power grew by targeting and defeating tribes one by one and assimilating them into a swiftly expanding empire. As the ruthless reputation of Malum Khoron-khelek went ahead of him, tribes became far more pliable, preemptively offering themselves to his service. In return, he protected them—from himself—and rewarded skilled leaders with position and power.

Sumu scouts had been seen in the last six months, though never caught, and rumor had it they would soon push in on Gorgenbrild. Their position on the cliffs was enviable, and Gorgenbrild was the only threat to the tribesmen's total domination of the northern mountains. Already two trade routes had been attacked and tensions were rising as Sumus drew near and Gorgenbrild refused to stand down from control of the ever-popular Carnat Route. Some in Gorgenbrild whispered that these barbarians desired the Ecyah Stone for themselves, and those believing in its existence demanded Gorgenbrild find it first.

Enouim continued to share with her mother and brother how the discussion among the warriors in the Mangonel had become heated, and Chayan had stood up. Insults were thrown, mugs were slammed on the table, and it looked as though things might get physical. Meanwhile, the meal orders of Chayan's company came up, and Enouim was charged with taking them over. Balat, one of Enouim's friends and a coworker, had dared her to take the food and refills to the group on Chayan's side of the table, and when Enouim hesitated, he'd given her a hearty shove. Enouim stumbled, doing her best to keep the wobbling tray upright, when her feet landed in slick beer-soaked floor and she fell.

She threw her hands out to catch herself, but the heavy tray and its contents flew through the air and collided with Chayan, knocking her off balance and sending her toward the wall. An instant later, Enouim careened into Chayan with surprising speed. She wasn't sure exactly what happened as they fell, but when Enouim collected herself from the ground and examined the damage, she realized she'd landed on Chayan's arm, which was now bent in an unnatural manner.

Chayan had screamed at her, declaring that Enouim had done it on purpose, that it would take weeks for her to recover, and would limit her ability to co-lead the mission to find this great weapon for Gorgenbrild.

Chayan had held out her good hand expectantly, wanting Enouim to offer her own arm for retribution, for Chayan to break it then and there to even the score. Sheer panic had risen up in Enouim and logic took swift flight. The next thing she knew, she was tearing through the kitchen, out the back door, and through the town like all the fury of the First Morthed War was descending on her small frame.

"I thought maybe if I could make it to Deliberation and explain my case ..." Enouim's voice dropped away, hearing how unrealistic that sounded now.

Her mother's response confirmed her fear. "It's a broken arm. Deliberation isn't going to hear you out, and Chayan is friendly with the board anyway."

"You don't think she'll kill me?"

"What you did was stupid, but it's just a broken arm," Pleko put in. "What's the big deal? You made it all worse by running, and now she might even have grounds to claim more, but your life seems extreme even for Chayan. Just go explain it to her in public at the Mangonel and let her break your arm. Maybe if you offer her your arm, rather than waiting for her to spring on you, you can pick your non-dominant side."

The reasoning was definitely sound, but it didn't seem too sensitive of her fear of pain. But then, neither was Chayan. Pleko's suggestion was likely the best course of action, but Enouim was still reluctant to hand over her bones. What could possibly drive someone to purposely enter a physical altercation, she would never understand. Of course, on her part, there was also size and skill to consider. Gorgenbrilders praised bravery and glorified the fearless, but Enouim had always thought ambitious bravery without acknowledgment of one's own limitations was just gussied up stupidity. If a person was daring and lucky, they were hailed as conquering heroes, but if daring and unlucky, their airheaded decision-making was ridiculed.

An impressive outcome earned respect, but what was the point of aiming for an impressive outcome if you knew the odds condemned you from the start? Going about her own business had been effective until now, until her own business had tripped into Chayan's. At this point it was more strategic to let Chayan restore the status quo and continue with her life. Enouim was glad her mother had called for her and given her an opportunity to slow her thoughts, share what had happened, and consider sensible options.

Enouim bit her lip. "I've never broken a bone ..." she said quietly. Lamely.

Pleko's face softened. He tried again. "You'll be okay. There's nothing to be done about it now, and if you wait too long, she'll claim another bone as interest."

Qadra sighed. "I'm sorry, but I think Pleko might be right. You can't run forever or she could claim you owe her more than a broken arm for dodging. Maybe you can wait briefly to catch her in better spirits and explain what happened then. Who knows? Maybe she will allow you the mercy of strength."

The mercy of strength was an exception for carrying out vengeance blow for blow. If the victim who had the right to retaliate was stronger than the attacker, the person may consider the assailant no more significant than a fly. The person relinquished his or her right to vengeance by crossing arms in an X and pressing it into the torso of the undeserving wrongdoer in a gesture communicating power restrained. This mercy allowed the Gorgenbrilder to save face, as it showed strength and insulted the wrongdoer, yet avoided expending the energy to return force with force. Although she didn't like the idea of humiliation and the condescending looks that would come along with it, Enouim was attracted to her mother's hopeful words.

"I guess I don't really have any other options."

"Your other alternative would be to ask for a real fight to earn respect and end the matter that way ... but that might be counterproductive," Pleko chipped in. Seeing her disheartened face and the real fear remaining there, he added, "Look, you'll be fine. I've broken bones and it is painful for a while, but it's not the end of the world. And that's how I learned to juggle with one hand!"

Enouim gave him a sarcastic, "Thanks," and let them know she planned to talk to Chayan. Maybe Chayan was at the Mangonel and distracted by battle plans. That should cheer her up. Either way, Enouim should probably talk to her superior at the Mangonel and let her know that after meeting with Chayan, Enouim might be rather impaired for a while.

After that, she would offer herself to a furious warrior to be broken.

nouim struck out for Mangonel Mornings, skirted the main entrance, and sidled up to a small window to peek inside. Gauging by those in attendance, it was quite the important gathering. Bondeg, Pryan, and Twedori were all present, each of them influential community leaders. Chayan had apparently accepted Bondeg's invitation. She sat near him at the table, her back turned to the window, but her outline was unmistakable. Canukke was leaning in and saying something ardently to his companions. Several others she couldn't identify faced away from Enouim.

Canukke spoke with all the confidence of a man who knows he cannot fail, and unlike those whose arrogance is hollowed by defeat, he seemed rarely to taste those bitter dregs. He stood tall and imposing, broad-shouldered and well-muscled, and a glance at his face removed all doubt that he knew it. Despite his marriage vows, the women of the town rarely kept their distance. The men were equally taken with him, dreaming of being as impressive. Like many in Gorgenbrild, Enouim found him intimidating. Yet she also found his egotistical assertions and elaborate, inevitable retellings of his feats more obnoxious and off-putting than charming.

Enouim left the window, rounded the corner, and entered through the back door. Pulling her hood up, she ducked past the kitchen to peek into the large, one-room hall serving guests. It was amazing how a group of such accomplished people could be so captivated by one man. Canukke clearly still had the floor and had slipped back into refreshing everyone's memory on a particularly harrowing exploit. From what Enouim could gather, he was making a point about how his idea for the current problem was the best option.

"... and from its peak, I saw the intent and positions of our enemy as clear as the dawn. I tossed the savage over my shoulder and brought him halfway down the mountain to the very mouth of a zegrath lair, and in my hands, he told me everything he knew. He lost all respect, betraying his people's secrets. But then," Canukke said, laughing, "men who were once daring have turned to fumbling oafs upon encountering me." With this he pulled back his shoulders and flexed his muscles, throwing a self-assured look toward a small woman delivering drinks to a table nearby.

Enouim followed his glance and took in the familiar frame of Edone, a stunning maiden who had caught the eye of every young man. Five years ago, Canukke had come along and swept her off her feet. He had not won her over as quickly as the others, and he'd liked that, identifying her as a challenge. Over time he'd won her, and she'd fully embraced the delight of young love. Now, all intrigue and luster seemed long since to have been sucked dry. Enouim had spoken with Edone on occasion and learned a little—she was tight-lipped. Despite Canukke's objections, Edone had continued to run the Mangonel after her father unexpectedly passed away, and she had poured herself into her work. Seeing the look pass between them, Enouim felt a bitterness toward Canukke for the isolation Edone felt, and she silently cursed his empty, haughty words.

At the same time, Enouim suspected there was something deeper in that moment. Canukke exalted himself in his own eyes by pursuing his standard of greatness with all his might. He was mighty; he fought great beasts and won many battles. Around a table of his comrades, tales of valor were never short. Perhaps if everyone saw how great he was, he might even some day come to believe it himself. As his boisterous laugh filled the room, he looked at Edone with the pride he hoped he would see reflected in her eyes. She looked on quietly, somberly, and turned away—as if the only beasts she cared that he battled were those within himself.

"The journey is long, but as I said, so was my climb to the top of Mount Liombas. The length of the road and the hardships along the way should not keep us from making our final decision. Has Gorgenbrild ever backed down from difficulty? Never, and I least of all! With this mission in my capable hands, we shall retrieve the stone unhindered and faster than any Sumus might dream, returning it to bring safety and victory to our people. The Sumus shall be destroyed, and we will forever remain hailed conquerors on these mountains."

Bondeg set his mug down and tilted his head back. He took in a deep, slow breath and studied Canukke. "I do not question your ability or resolve, my friend. This enterprise has been explored at length and turned over and around in a hundred different ways. Surely such a mission requires strength, bravery, and intelligence to succeed. And yet, is it responsible of us to send our strongest away from the people when it is our homeland that stands in danger of invasion?"

"We've been over this. No one willing to embark on this wild undertaking has traveled as far or demonstrated as much resourcefulness as Canukke," Twedori put in. "If we are agreed that the Ecyah Stone is a myth worth pursuing—and apparently we have, or we have wasted a lot of time planning for no reason—then let him proceed as planned. It is too late in the process to make changes now, even last-minute ones. Provisions are already packed, and our window for decision may soon be drawing to a close."

Edone returned from delivering drinks and noticed Enouim peering around the corner into the hall. She cast a glance at Chayan, then back to Enouim. Chayan was intent on the conversation and looked very much like she had before Enouim's interruption, except that now her arm was in a sling. She likely had returned to the Mangonel at Bondeg's request, creating a splint for herself and a sling out of her mantle on the way. Her face oozed bitterness—or was that Enouim's imagination? Her facial expression was disagreeable even on a good day.

"What do you think you're doing?" Edone hissed, turning the corner to hide from view and setting the tray down on a counter. "Your little antics with Balat had the worst possible timing. This is not like any other night in Gorgenbrild. And now you're back." She scolded, but Enouim saw worry in her eyes.

"It was an accident. I came back to try to ... to talk to Chayan. Explain. Maybe she will give me the mercy of strength?" Now that she was here, face-to-face with the idea, it seemed weaker than it had in her home with Pleko and her mother.

Edone rolled her eyes. "Chayan was just told she couldn't go after the Ecyah Stone with the rest. She has been planning this for weeks. They don't want to send anyone with an injury through the mountain passes in case of attack, even though she insists she is just as deadly with one arm. Bondeg is grateful not to be losing another great warrior to this errand, but Chayan is not so grateful. Your timing is even worse now than it was this afternoon."

"What am I supposed to do? Run forever? It's just an arm, right?" A beat of hesitation from Edone. "Edone? It *is* just an arm, isn't it?"

"I don't know, Enouim. You have stripped her of more than a few weeks' recovery time. She may believe you owe her more than that."

Enouim's eyes went wide, and she chanced another furtive look into the hall.

Pryan was speaking. "So it is settled. Six will set out tonight instead of seven. Kalka'an will be ready to receive you, and eight will make haste from there. It is a great pity for the company to be losing Chayan, but there is nothing to be done about that now. I must admit, it gives me comfort to know Chayan will be remaining here at our sides and at Bondeg's right hand for whatever comes. Chayan, your strength and skill will be put to good use here."

Chayan looked like a small child that had just been slapped across the face. For a moment Enouim felt compassion tug at her heart for the fierce warrior cut off from a great quest. After all, she was one of the greatest advocates for going after the stone in the first place, and without her it may not have come about at all. All because of a stupid mistake. Guilt washed over Enouim.

Chayan looked up from the table and locked eyes with Enouim, and that surprising warmth toward Chayan vanished. The woman's gaze hardened like flint and her muscles tensed. Her lip curled into a snarl, and Enouim could only guess what pernicious, destructive thoughts dominated her mind. Hate seethed from Chayan's body like blistering steam, and Enouim thought she might faint from the sweltering pressure of it. She had to get out.

Was she really running for the second time today? Enouim whirled and sprinted for the back door. She was almost out of sight before she heard the dreaded sound of a door sharply opening and closing behind her. It seemed all terribly familiar, yet so foreign to anything Enouim would have dreamed of doing the day before. She flew down the hill and around the bend. She needed a plan. Yes, a plan would be good. Too bad all that consumed her thoughts was her need of a plan, rather than any semblance of what that plan might be.

For a few glorious moments, she felt the power in her legs driving her forward, lifting her spirits, and making her feel strong and capable, coursing with life. And then, just as quickly as it had come, it faded, replaced with the torrid sensation of slogging through mud. The flesh and muscle in her calves seemed to turn to lead against her will. She was exhausted.

Enouim approached another horse enclosure and spotted her family's pony lazily enjoying a graze. She entered the enclosure as softly as she could, crouched low, and risked a soft whistle. Several equine ears swiveled her direction.

"Pinky!" she called quietly. The dear animal faithfully trotted over.

Hoping not to be seen, Enouim awkwardly affixed herself to the pony's side, facing away from the direction she had come. She wrapped her arms around Pinky's neck and draped a leg over Pinky's bare back to keep her feet off the ground. Pinky reached her head around and nudged at her curiously. Surely the poor thing thought Enouim had gone mad. She clucked her tongue and whispered for Pinky to walk on, and the horse made her way to the other side of the pen.

Just before they reached the other side, a shout rang through the air. "I will *destroy* you!"

Well, Enouim was right. Chayan had been thinking pernicious, destructive thoughts. Enouim pulled herself up onto Pinky's back and urged her forward as hard as she could. Pinky happily obliged, grateful to see her rider's head squarely back on her shoulders, and leaped forward as they headed for the rock fence. Anxiety balled in Enouim's stomach. Pinky hadn't taken a jump in years. Enouim felt the old mare gather herself to prepare for the jump.

Pinky flew over the fence, landed safely on the other side, and ... came to an abrupt halt, breathing hard. Guilt mingled with panic in Enouim's chest. Poor, wonderful Pinky! At twenty-nine, she had pulled off her last big stunt. Easy riding and transport were her lot now, a far cry from athletic prowess. But Pinky was anxious to do all she could for her family. And "all she could" had ended precisely at the opposite side of the fence.

Enouim slid off and patted her neck. "Good girl, Pinky! Good girl."

Leaving her pony still heaving from exertion, Enouim ran forward on foot, already worn out. Regrettably, Chayan had endurance on her side. Enouim looked behind and saw the woman mounted on her own horse, right arm still secured in the makeshift sling. Unfortunately for Enouim, Chayan's ride was younger and far nimbler than Pinky. Just then Enouim spied another horse, all tacked and waiting outside some luckless soul's dwelling. She made for the horse and swung herself up, turning it round just in time to see Chayan bearing down on her.

Enouim turned the horse's head and dug in her heels. She heard the thud of galloping hooves in rhythmic motion like the beat of her uneasy heart. The familiar smell of fresh, open air with a slight metallic scent from the work of a nearby anvil reached her nostrils. She felt the horse's muscles roll beneath her and let her body flow with it as the horse brought one shoulder forward and then another in swift flight. Her hands gripped leather reins, smooth on one side, rougher on the other, desperate to cling to a filament of normalcy. This couldn't be happening.

But it was happening, and she took it all in with the blink of an eye against the wind. The unknown steed—a good one, it turned out—picked up on her urgency. They blew past house after house and approached a ledge with a drop-down of several feet to the next level. Enouim pushed her horse forward, making her intentions clear.

Chayan closed the distance between them. "I will *break* you! You *owe* it to me!" her voice rang out behind Enouim. "Your bones belong to me!"

The sound of steel sliding from its sheath sent a shiver down Enouim's spine as Chayan drew a sword from her back —of course she was ambidextrous! Enouim's mount took the challenge and left the ledge with confidence. Chayan's horse was equally fearless, accustomed to the unpredictable terrain and levels of Gorgenbrild, and Chayan made the leap bareback, gripping the horse only with her legs, one hand encumbered by the sling and the other grasping the sword. Enouim couldn't help but be impressed.

Swish. Enouim felt the rush of wind as metal cut through the air near her face. She ducked left and surged down a slope, regaining the advantage of space. Chayan grunted with frustration. Enouim turned up and around a sharp corner— out of Chayan's sight for a few precious moments—but her horse tripped from the tight maneuver on irregular footing and pitched her forward off the horse.

The ground raced toward her as if in slow motion, then

suddenly she was sucked back into real-time as she hit the ground. Floating lights flashed in her vision as she absorbed the jarring impact and tumbled down an incline. Her horse galloped on without her on the narrow path above while Enouim rolled under a covered horse cart and came to a stop in tall grass beneath it. A thundering of hooves swept past like a storm as Chayan barreled after the sound of Enouim's escaping horse.

Enouim's vision blurred. She had little time to hide herself before losing consciousness. Already a dark cloud edged in on her mind. Wearily she pulled herself up and managed to climb into the cart under the cover, nestling herself underneath bags of various supplies she didn't care to identify. Pain seared through her head so intensely that hot tears trailed down her face. She let out a soft moan, muffled against the sacks, before finally succumbing to the darkness.

4

Enouim gradually came awake and aware of her surroundings. At first she thought she was at home, under a cover, but in trying to reposition herself she recognized weights on top of her, hindering free motion. Bags. Sacks of some kind. And then it all flooded back to her. She must still be in the wagon. Had Chayan been back to find her yet? It wouldn't have taken her long to catch up with her runaway horse and realize Enouim was missing from it. How long had she been out?

Some time must have passed. Though evening had been fading when she lost consciousness, now it had fled entirely and given way to the fullness of night. But as she considered this, something more disturbing took precedence in her thoughts. She was moving. She felt the regular movement of a horse-drawn cart and heard the soft rumble of wagon wheels quieted by dirt or grassy paths.

With a jerk of realization, she became fully alert. Questions assaulted her mind. In the middle of the night? What on earth could this person be up to? Surely nothing good. Perhaps the bags had bodies in them. She shuddered. No, no, the bags weren't big enough and didn't feel like bodies. Regardless, someone driving in the middle of the night was unlikely to be fond of a stowaway. At the same time, she couldn't very well lie there indefinitely until she got to the destination, wherever that might be. If she could get a look at her surroundings, maybe she could find a discreet way off the wagon and find her way back home.

Or not home, if that's where Chayan would expect her to be. Her stomach turned. It seemed Edone was right—Chayan had no intention of being placated with breaking one of Enouim's arms. Her threats hinted at both arms, if not more. She'd been robbed of the chance to go on the mission for the Ecyah Stone and carry out her latest obsession—a once in a lifetime opportunity full of intrigue, adventure, and potential glory. Chayan *lived* for such occasions.

Nevertheless, Enouim needed to get off the wagon. She would figure out the next step later. Shifting as quietly as she could, she shimmied under the bags toward the end of the cart, pulled up the corner of the cover, and looked straight into the eyes of Pakel Hasolas, a proficient Gorgenbrild warrior in his late twenties. Equally surprised, they stared at each other for a moment in silence. Pakel rode on horseback at the rear of the wagon. In a forest, apparently. Definitely not at home. Tall, dark trees loomed above them and all around, pressing in on her. She guessed by the terrain that they were already descending through the mountains. Six armed warriors surrounded the wagon. The three in the rear rode single file behind, and all stared at her in disbelief.

"What the ..." Pakel cleared his throat, garnering the attention of the rest of the group, as Enouim scrambled to her knees. "Son of a zegrath."

"This is all a very terrible mistake," Enouim said.

"Keep your voice down, idiot," a commanding voice hissed from the front.

One of the riders had twisted back toward the spectacle. Just enough starlight filtered down through the trees for her to make out his face. *Canukke.*

He slowed his horse to draw next to the wagon. "Now what in the name of Glintenon do you think you're doing here?"

Enouim's stomach dropped like a stone. Canukke was supposed to have left on the Ecyah mission by now. Twedori had said they were already packed ... it seemed she had found the provisions.

"I ... I passed out ... in the wagon. I just woke up here." She wasn't sure how to explain it without sounding foolish. But then, what did she have to lose? They probably already thought she was a moron anyway. Pakel brought his horse to the other side of the wagon, and the other warriors closed in around her as much as the forest path allowed.

"Why were you in the supplies wagon to begin with?" whispered Oloren, a fierce and fiery woman with long dark hair and bronze skin. Though no taller than five foot three and quiet and soft-spoken at first meeting, her strength and skill more than made up for her short stature, and she was audacious and quick-witted among those with whom she felt most comfortable. Enouim considered her a friendly acquaintance, and she saw her mostly in passing at the Mangonel, or when she purchased goats' milk or vegetables from Qadra.

Enouim latched onto this sliver of safety. "I didn't know it was the supply wagon for the Ecyah mission. Chayan was chasing me. We had an insane misunderstanding, and she was too angry for me to explain what happened. I fell off my horse and ended up rolling under the wagon. I hit my head when I landed and just barely scrambled into the wagon after she rode through. That's the last thing I remember. Honestly, I had no idea whose wagon I was in!"

"Some mistake!" Canukke looked down at her, and she could taste his condescension. "You were the imbecile that broke Chayan's arm. No wonder you fled. She was ready to tear you to pieces by the look of her, and it would have served you right. You owed her that. Coward."

"What's done is done," Vadik, the warrior sitting on the wagon guiding the horse, said, "and anyway, this business with Chayan is none of ours."

Vadik was easy to pick out in Gorgenbrild not so much for his stature, though he stood at six-foot-two, but because he was always in the center of any theoretical discussion or debate. Quick on his feet, he thoroughly enjoyed a good verbal battering, no matter on which side of the argument. He was also dangerous with a sword and, his personal favorite, the spear. "What do we do with her now?" he asked.

"*Do* with me?" Enouim replied incredulously. "If my misunderstanding with Chayan is none of your business, then you turn around and drop me back off, right?"

"No, there's no stopping," Canukke said. "We left under cover of night by largely unused paths. The tribes are already beginning to choke off main routes, and we would tip our hand revealing ourselves now just to save you from your series of asinine choices."

"Fine, then I'll just head back on foot. What's the simplest way back?"

"We've been traveling on horseback for six hours already," Pakel informed her.

"*Six hours?*" She'd been out far longer than she thought.

"Keep your voice down or you might never make it anywhere," Vadik said. "either forward with us or back home. It would take you much longer to get back on foot and would make you easy pickings for any tribe scout or wild animal. And there are zegrath in these parts."

Enouim's mind reeled. The beasts were strong, cunning disasters on four legs. They had boxy heads with short snouts and razor-sharp teeth. Two sets of pointed ears, huge muscled shoulders, dark fur and thick legs ending in fearsome talons like those of a hawk defined the animal. The tail looked like that of a horse, but it was made up of sharp quills. Shorter quills ran up the ridge of its face above the eyes and along its hackles to the shoulder bone.

From the pot to the fire—things just kept getting better. Here she was, entirely by accident, the farthest from Gorgenbrild's borders she'd ever been. With no horse of her own, it would take her ages to get back on foot, even if she took the most direct course and encountered no life-threatening obstacles.

"How are your land navigation skills?" another of the warriors, silent until now, said. He was unknown to Enouim, but had a calm, stoic, confident presence. Was he making fun of her? No, he seemed to be asking the question in earnest. Did he actually think she might have some skill to keep her alive long enough to make it back?

Sadly, that was preposterous. Enouim was a strong rider, a quick learner, and a hard worker. Her father was a trader, before his passing when she was eight years old. As a whole, Enouim was good with people and perfectly adequate in other areas. Every Gorgenbrilder knew some basic fighting maneuvers, but Enouim hadn't expected to ever have to use them and didn't plan on becoming a warrior herself, so she hadn't thrown herself into it like many of her people. She could hunt small game, but nothing particularly savage.

"Um ...I get lost extremely easily. As in, I'm rather directionally challenged. But I'm not stupid or anything"—here

Canukke rolled his eyes—"but it's bad enough to be an impairment for any significant distances." The stranger looked disappointed, and Enouim supposed all his life-saving ideas for her predicament died in that moment. Hoping to restore it while remaining truthful, she added, "I could follow a compass though!"

An awkward silence filled the air as the troop plodded on. Canukke called the stranger to the front with him to discuss her fate and left her sitting in the supply wagon out of earshot. The two men conferred in low tones while the rest rode on without a sound.

The stranger, a broad-shouldered man, perhaps in his forties, with brown hair to his shoulders and green eyes, wore a long sword at his side, but Enouim guessed he had numerous other weapons hidden somewhere close at hand. Pakel rode to the left of the wagon and Oloren to the right. Vadik retained his seat at the front of the wagon, and the final member of the small band, who she also didn't recognize, rode in the rear. Pakel called him Gabor. Gabor had dark brown hair, and amber eyes that held a reserved mystery. He seemed to be taking it all in from a distance and mulling it over.

The longer they continued, the more nervous Enouim became. She couldn't wait forever, and the longer she waited, the more impossible it would be to return home. At the same time, Enouim couldn't shake the nagging feeling that perhaps going home was already impossible. All because Balat thought she would have a little fun and shove her in Chayan's direction. All because Chayan was enraged beyond measure at her broken arm and Enouim's unhappy flight. All because Enouim was a coward.

Canukke's words rang in her ears. Was she really a coward? But of course she was, part of her answered sharply. All she'd had to do was follow Pleko's advice and let Chayan break Enouim's arm. Simple enough. But it hadn't been simple, had it? Chayan had already decided that the injury was deeper than an arm for an arm. She'd threatened to break her. Both arms? An arm and a leg? A chill ran down her spine. How could anyone just hand themselves over to that? Yes, it was the Gorgenbrild way, but maybe Gorgenbrild's way was too extreme. It was an accident, after all. Shouldn't there be a concession written somewhere about accidents?

Soon the path narrowed off, forcing the party into single file once more. The stranger riding up ahead with Canukke fell in behind him. Enouim anxiously ran her thumb over a scar on her collarbone. After a while Pakel took out a karambit, a curved knife with a ring at the end of the handle, and spun it absentmindedly. Endlessly. Initially intrigued by his deftness with the blade, she eventually began imagining how she might knock it from his hands. But with nothing else to hold her attention, and his constant movement in her peripheral vision, she couldn't look away.

Finally breaking her gaze, Enouim moved to the front of the wagon and spoke quietly to Vadik. "What do you think they'll decide? Are they still thinking?"

She never heard the answer. A flurry of black-and-gray fur obstructed her vision, and chaos broke out around her. A huge beast, easily the size of a horse, jumped onto the wagon from above them, landing on supply bags and snapping its jaws inches from Enouim's face. The jolt rocked the wagon, and the startled cart horse tugged in vain for freedom under the extra weight. The zegrath dug enormous claws into the supply bags to keep its balance and took another swipe at Enouim. One long claw grazed her back as she twisted away to grasp at her dagger.

Vadik twirled his sword over his head and slashed at the animal, his priority divided between getting the zegrath off the wagon and passing the problem off to his companions so he could guide the horse, who stumbled and neighed in distress. Meanwhile, the stranger in front shot an arrow. The zegrath redirected it with its tail of tough quills, leaving its other side unprotected.

Pakel sliced at the zegrath with his sword, but was too far away to do any real damage. The zegrath threw itself off the wagon, took Pakel off his horse, and dragged him past Gabor to the ridge on the other side of the pass. Oloren sent a throwing knife surging into the beast's shoulder, and Gabor kicked his horse forward, commanding it to strike with its hooves.

"No!" Pakel screamed from underneath the zegrath. "You'll hit *me!*" He grunted. "Knife!"

Oloren shot off her horse with enough fury to fill a much larger frame. Two blades materialized in her hands as she launched herself onto the animal, securing her position by plunging the short swords deep into its flesh. It abandoned Pakel to roll over onto Oloren, who managed to free one of her swords in time to swing at its neck before its vicious teeth could find purchase. The zegrath crushed her other side beneath its weight, and Pakel took the opportunity to scramble out of the way and back to his feet. Gabor rushed to Oloren's aid, leaping directly onto the zegrath from his horse.

The wagon blocked Canukke and the stranger from the fight, but the stranger had an arrow notched and let fly, narrowly missing Oloren. The zegrath rolled off him to avoid the arrow, dumping Gabor to the ground and revealing frightening foresight and far more intelligence than other beasts. The creature lunged at the stranger, using the wagon as a launching pad. Enouim dove out of the wagon just in time, almost rolling to her feet before losing her footing and sliding down a steep forest drop-off, heart lurching into her throat.

She grabbed a small rotting stump to keep from falling the rest of the way and hung there, feet swinging in the air below her.

The stranger sidestepped and reared his horse, but with a guttural protest, the zegrath cut through his horse's leather saddle and girth. The horse let out a cry and shied away, the stranger leaping from its back before the tack on which he sat crashed to the ground. Vadik had gotten the wagon horse to strain forward again, but the beast's large furry body blocked the passage, stopping his further efforts cold. Oloren and Pakel took hold of Enouim's arms and swung her back to safety.

Canukke slung his broadsword along the beast's side yet again, and the stranger swung his sword, backing the creature against the wagon. Gabor, trapped on the wrong side of the wagon, climbed up the supplies to position himself over the zegrath. Vadik did his best to hold the horse steady, but fear overtook it. The horse pulled with all its might, but one of the wheels stuck in a rut behind a large root. Harness still partially attached, the horse broke from the wagon, skirted the two warriors, and galloped down the trail. Vadik abandoned the wagon and landed to his left, while Gabor pitched forward, fell on the zegrath, tumbled off, and rolled to his feet.

Dark, beady eyes gleamed in the night, and a flash of teeth created a stark contrast against the blackness of the forest. The short quills leading from the zegrath's head to the top of its shoulders—where Oloren's throwing knife still stood—stood on end. Its two large, pointed ears drew back away from its sinister face, while the two smaller ones just below them swiveled independently, ensuring the animal missed no audible signals from any direction. Its head hung low, and it crouched in a motionless standoff. For a long moment, nothing happened.

Then two snarls emitted into the night. It was difficult to say which came from Canukke and which from the beast as they flew toward one another. Dark fur and claws blended with Canukke's form. Canukke—sword in one hand, knife in the other—threatened the animal's throat with his knife, but the zegrath grabbed the blade with its teeth and tossed the knife aside in frenzied indignation, then it lunged for Canukke's throat. He tucked, rolled, and came to his feet, sword still somehow in hand. The stranger, Gabor, and Vadik joined him and cornered the beast between the forest wall and the broken-down wagon.

Pakel notched another arrow and waited for a good opportunity. Enouim stood with dagger extended, willing but rather unsure of herself. Oloren seemed frustrated to have been separated from the fight and appeared to be considering her options to rejoin it. Gabor lunged forward with his dagger, slashing at the beast as the zegrath pushed off the wagon and leaped in a high arc toward the other side. Seeing her chance, Oloren jumped onto the back of the wagon and, with a savage cry, reached up and sliced the vulnerable underbelly. Canukke climbed the wagon and several exposed tree roots in the forest wall, then crashed down on the creature from above to finish the job. Oloren had struck the fatal blow, but Canukke brought his sword plummeting down on the animal's neck for good measure.

"Get it off the path," the stranger commanded. "The tribes come this far, and this route is supposed to be abandoned. Gabor, get the provisions."

"We may already have drawn attention to ourselves," Vadik said.

While Canukke, the stranger, Pakel, and Oloren worked together to push the carcass off the ledge, Gabor directed Vadik and Enouim to assist him in salvaging as much of the provisions as they could. The zegrath's talons had ripped open several of the bags carrying weapons, food, or valuables brought as gifts to the cliff dwellers, and there was only so much room on the horses. Gabor called out instructions as they loaded the saddle bags with as much as they could carry, double-checking their work as they went.

A twig snapped from above. Enouim whipped her head up toward the ledge from which the zegrath had come and froze. A tribesman scout stood on the ledge, arrow on his bow string, aimed directly at Enouim's chest.

5

Enouim ducked and squealed just as an arrow and a knife embedded themselves in the tribesman's chest at the same time. Gabor and Oloren had each dispatched their weapon of choice at once, and Gabor's arrow and Oloren's knife hit the target a single inch apart from one another. The tribesman fell backward and out of sight without a sound. Shouts rang out from beyond the dead man.

"Go!" Canukke shouted, all hope for secrecy lost.

"The supplies!" Gabor exclaimed, unwilling to abandon his task.

"Leave the rest! We'll make do with what we have!"

All mounted their horses, Enouim jumping up behind Pakel. Vadik had been riding on the wagon, so he reached for Oloren's horse next to him. "Move back!" he called up to her, claiming the driver's seat.

"You move back! My horse, my rules. Let's go!"

Vadik reluctantly swung up behind her and they set off in haste. More calls and sounds of movement came from other tribesmen out of sight. The seven of them swept along the passage on horseback, relieved to find the trail open up as they continued down the mountain. Vadik shouted to Oloren when he saw that his cart horse had stopped in a grassy area. The rest of the group surrounded and herded the bay while Oloren brought her horse alongside, and Vadik transferred to his own horse without slowing the pace.

An arrow struck a tree a hair beyond Vadik's nose. They altered course, crashing through the brush, rode into a clearing on the other side, and bolted into cover on the far end. *Whizz, whizz.* More arrows. The ground leveled off, and Enouim glanced behind, arms squeezing tight around Pakel. "Horseback archer, rear left flank!" she called out.

A mounted tribesman bore down on them from behind. He wore loose, dark clothing under a leather breastplate and gauntlets, and directed his steed solely with his legs, leaving his hands free to work a bow and arrow.

Gabor reached for his own bow and arrow and twisted in the saddle to send one toward the unwelcome pursuer. The target maneuvered just shy of its reach and loosed his own arrow, which flew so close that Gabor may have lost a few strands of hair. The stranger shot back at the tribesman, and he banked further left and out of sight. Urging their horses ever faster, they gained space and the arrows began to drop away.

Canukke bore to the right and down a winding way to a stream where they slowed and entered at a shallow place, the water just above the horses' knees. They walked with the deepening stream until it reached halfway up the horses' bodies, then exited and picked up speed once more. They rode on, silent, alert, and in a constant state of tension.

After a time, the company grew confident that they'd shaken their tail, and Canukke allowed a more relaxed pace. Gentle rays of morning light sifted through the branches, dispelling shadows and reminding them that day waits to dawn after every somber night. The spirits of the company lifted like a shade taken up to let the shining hope of another day illuminate and refresh them. A docile breeze wafted over Enouim's face. Speckled pools of light played with the various tints of green in spongy moss, grass, and underbrush.

"By Glintenon, I either eat in the next ten minutes or starve," Pakel said, breaking the silence.

"Glintenon! And how far do you think his reach carries?" Vadik replied.

They spoke of the Malak, great shape shifters charged with guarding the realms of the world. Before the Great Rift five-hundred years prior, the Malak took their natural form more often than not and walked among men as they came and went performing their duties. Malak forms were humanoid, though larger and stronger than humankind, and had the ability to shift forms or hide themselves from the visible world. After the Great Rift, the Malak were given authority over various provinces, and their presence in the world diminished.

In Gorgenbrild, that powerful Malak was named Glintenon. In the First Morthed War, Glintenon appeared in his natural form to lead the charge against Morthed, but Morthed had its own Malak, Morales. In the heat of battle, Glintenon gained for Gorgenbrild tremendous advances, but Morales emerged in the pinnacle of combat to fight him herself, transitioning from a large raven in the sky and into her natural form. All seemed lost for a moment, until Glintenon seemed to tremble, then rose from the ground. With a flash of light from the Ecyah Stone in the hilt of his sword, Glintenon defeated Morales. Morthed retreated but inflicted great losses as they did so. As a people, Morthed drifted east to settle, and were now a formidable force in what was known as the City With No Walls.

"He is the protector of our people!" Pakel replied. "We are those people. He would be remiss not to watch over us as we go."

Vadik snorted. "Or would he be remiss to leave the rest of our homeland? We are but a few, and perhaps we will soon leave his jurisdiction behind."

"He would pass us off to an ally then, to watch over our progress," Oloren suggested.

"Have you ever wondered whether he is loyal?" Vadik spoke confidently, almost laissez-faire, but Enouim saw mischief subtly light his expression. Any fire worth having needed a little fuel.

"Loyal!" Oloren said, taking the bait. "Glintenon walked among us, knew us. After the Rift, we saw him little, yet he was there—he proved it in the First Morthed War! What else could he have done for us in that time, unbeknownst to you? And even since then!"

"There is plenty he didn't do during that time. By the hordes, where was he for the Second Morthed War? Gorgenbrild saw him practically as deity after the First, and yet the Second rolls around and what, nothing? I don't know. Perhaps he's not to be trusted."

"Vadik, you are loyal to your stomach and your ego," Oloren responded dismissively, signaling exit from the conversation. "You don't know what you're talking about."

Enouim saw Oloren's frustration with Vadik's stubbornness, but she thought she saw a hint of pleasure in Vadik's eyes.

"Who needs Glintenon when you have me?" Canukke broke in. "Where was Glintenon when we fought the Iyangas? Where was Glintenon when Malum Khoron-khelek was born? Who was it really that guarded Gorgenbrild, fought for you, bled for you? It was me, along with Bondeg and the rest of our leaders! Indeed, if Glintenon lives, he would choose none other than myself to lead this party to restore the Ecyah Stone to its rightful place with our people. Surely he recognizes his failure as of late." Canukke halted his horse, effectively ending the discussion. "We stop here. Pakel is right; we should eat and stretch our legs."

Oloren pursed her lips but said nothing, and the group dismounted. Vadik freed his horse from the remainder of the wagon harness, cut some rope, and fashioned a makeshift bridle while the others pulled fruit and dried meat from the saddlebags and let the horses graze. As everyone began to settle, the stranger nodded to Enouim and introduced himself. "Kilith Urul. Looks like you're going to be with us a while."

The comment brought Enouim's mind back to her troubles. Going home was now even more out of the question, and she seemed to have been grafted into the company. Unsure of herself in the new setting, she wondered what would become of her now. Would she be forced onto this mission? Had Canukke and this Kilith Urul come up with some plan to get her home eventually? He had said "a while," after all.

Remembering to introduce herself, she nodded back at him. "Enouim."

"I have convinced Canukke not to allow you any attempt at returning to Gorgenbrild on your own," Kilith said. "He sees you as a liability on the mission, but you would never make it back alive, and you're privy to our purpose.

"In roughly two weeks we will reach Kalka'an, and if they're still planning on trading with Gorgenbrild in light of the Sumus's encroaching position, you will likely be able to return with the traders. If not, you will have to decide where your desire lies. If you choose to continue with us on the mission from there, you may need to win over Canukke."

Kilith seemed serious, gruff, but not unkind. Enouim

found him both off-putting and comforting, a strange and confusing blend. "How do I do that?" she asked. "You know, if I decide to stay. Theoretically."

Kilith shrugged. "Prove yourself useful somehow. Right now he sees you as a problem if you were to attempt the trek home and be caught, and a problem if you stay and muck everything up."

Enouim nodded. "How do I decide?"

"That I cannot answer for you." Kilith dipped his head toward her once more, and promptly walked away toward the rest of the group. He allowed himself plenty of personal space while remaining close enough to be among them. Enouim moved also, seating herself next to Oloren. Vadik, Oloren, Gabor, and Pakel were in a semi-circle, and Enouim favored the familiarity of Oloren's friendly face. She wondered what advice Oloren or Pakel might have for her predicament and hoped she would soon get the chance to speak with one of them privately. Canukke and Kilith Urul sat together a little further off, strategizing best routes and other details in confidence, but close enough to engage in conversation with the group if they chose.

They ate quickly, making light conversation or none at all, and mounted again. Enouim, feeling as though she had been assigned to his horse since the tribesman incident, rode behind Pakel once more. As she listened to the people around her, Enouim took mental notes on her new companions, considering who she would feel safe to process with.

Gabor: detail-oriented, quiet, potentially condescending—of course, this could say more about her own insecurities than about Gabor. An excellent marksman, he loved the precision and accuracy necessary for shooting a bow and arrow. He'd said little during their brief respite, but Enouim got the feeling he was fond of most of the group—though perhaps not Vadik.

He seemed intelligent and willing to speak up when he disagreed with something, as long as he considered the effort worthwhile. Enouim thought Gabor harmless enough, but it might take some time to feel comfortable around him.

Vadik was a logical strategist, outgoing and outspoken. He enjoyed lively conversations, particularly those that allowed him to flex his mental acumen against an ideological opponent, and seemed dedicated to truth. He would certainly expose any areas she failed to take into account if she shared her dilemma with him. His rational mind was good with practical advice and problem-solving, which could be valuable to her. On the other hand, he might turn it into a debate of some kind, and she wasn't sure her thoughts were developed enough to handle that. Maybe further down the road.

Kilith Urul was a puzzle and rather unsettling. Mostly quiet, sometimes jumping in with a wry comment. Apparently prominent in his community, he lived so far on the other side of Gorgenbrild that Enouim had never seen him before. He struck her as preferring to keep to himself. Enouim imagined he would give wise counsel, but he didn't seem particularly inclined to part with it in her case. He'd said the decision was hers and left it at that. No, that wouldn't do.

Oloren was comforting, not only in her familiarity, but also her presence. A soft, confident air hung around her. She didn't seem to feel the need to speak, but when she did, people listened. In jovial discussion, she often joined in with the rest of them, apparently truly in her element here and comfortable in the group. Oloren had a level head and a kind heart. Enouim would appreciate her perspective.

Canukke was a definite no. She was fairly certain he was the only one of the company that would outright refuse to let her ride with him, and she was equally set against the idea. Canukke thought Enouim an idiot and inconvenience, and she thought him obnoxious and arrogant. Unfortunately, much of her fate was in his hands.

At the same time, Enouim saw what he had to offer. Physically imposing, mentally sharp, and an accomplished hunter and fighter, he was a natural leader, could delegate and make decisions quickly, and was skilled in survival tactics. Canukke had traveled greater distances than anyone else in the troop, except perhaps Kilith. Both he and Kilith Urul had personal contacts in Kalka'an. Though somewhat unconventional at times, Canukke was clearly an asset.

Pakel seemed to have an easy ear. Straightforward, good natured, willing to talk. He enjoyed conversation and people in general, was outgoing and enthusiastic, and didn't seem to hate her. Pakel would be a good candidate, and she was riding with him now. Perhaps today she could talk it out with Pakel, and tomorrow ride with Oloren.

"Do you mind if I ask you something?" Enouim said to Pakel quietly, keeping the conversation just to the two of them.

"You just did! Do you want to ask if you can ask me two things?" he replied jovially.

"Okay." Enouim fought a smile. "So Kilith said I may end up having a choice of staying with the group or going back to Gorgenbrild with the traders once we reach Kalka'an. It helps to talk it out when I have to decide something important. I'm not sure what I should choose."

"I'm not sure I understand. You didn't intend to be on this mission in the first place, and were appalled to discover you had ended up so far from home. What's to decide?"

"Well ... I'm not exactly sure what's waiting for me at home. Chayan wants her revenge, and I'm not sure what that would look like for her. She definitely wants to crush my bones, or at least break multiple important ones. She might even kill me. Everyone knows she tends to get carried away, and Deliberation lets her do it."

"In that case, stand up to her yourself."

"I'm not strong! She could kill me with one arm, blindfolded. I'm no match for her. And yet, what would I do if I stayed?"

"Hmm. I am surprised Kilith suggested you had an option. It seems you are making your decision based on fear, and you are not good enough to take on Chayan. Chayan was handpicked for this mission, and integral in the planning process, because this sort of journey requires skill and a tough skin. You think you're safer taking Chayan's place on the mission than you are facing Chayan herself? We are not on holiday. It isn't a choice of what best suits us, but of what best suits our people, for better or for worse."

Enouim felt her face flush with shame. It was true. She was afraid, and she was focused on herself. She had no larger purpose. But then, how could she? What did she have to offer? She'd run from Chayan, terrified and incapable of defending herself, because she had little to offer. Even now the idea of going back to Gorgenbrild was repugnant to her. By the same token, however, Pakel was right. If she wasn't ready to face Chayan, how could she ever hope to be ready to face the hazards Chayan had signed up for? This quest was not for the faint of heart, and there was no room for stowaways.

"I didn't mean..." Enouim trailed off. That's precisely what she had meant, wasn't it? All she wanted was a way out of her current predicament. Still, when she thought of returning to Gorgenbrild, the weight on her heart was undeniable. Perhaps there was more to her reluctance than fear of physical pain.

"I don't believe I belong anywhere," she said gloomily. "I dreamed of traveling with my father ever since I was small, to see the distant lands he saw. I've soaked up stories and traditions from many realms but never had a reason to go. And here I am, finally traveling, and I only got here by mistake. I know I don't deserve to be here."

Pakel allowed silence to engulf them, and Enouim's admission hung in the air. Finally, he spoke again. "Well, I suppose you are left with several possibilities. Either you do deserve to be here for some reason—and you need to find and fight for that purpose—or you need to prepare to face the tumult awaiting you in Gorgenbrild."

6

The rest of the day proceeded relatively uneventfully. They rode into the night until Canukke was satisfied they had enough distance between them and the tribes to go to sleep, and they made camp. The dawn brought with it fresh hope and a brisk wind, and Enouim hoped it would calm her mind as she continued to think long and hard about her dilemma. She rode with Oloren and asked for her perspective.

"Well, what do *you* want?" Oloren asked her.

"That's just it. I'm struggling to sort out what I want. Or even whether or not what I want matters. I was talking to Pakel yesterday and he seemed to be saying that it didn't make sense for me to continue on the mission because I hadn't intended to be here, and people were handpicked for this. If I'm not as good as Chayan, there's no reason for me to think I'm good enough to stay on the quest she was selected for. I either need to find out how I deserve to be here, and have a reason to stay, or go home."

"It sounds like going home is a hard decision for you."

"It is. I just ... there's nothing for me there. Chayan is

waiting to hurt me, or worse, so I would have that to look forward to. I don't seem to fit at home. I don't seem to fit anywhere. I've always wanted to travel, to see the world I've read so much about, but I am not a warrior."

"You are not a warrior *yet*," Oloren corrected softly. "No one is born a warrior."

"Not even Canukke and Chayan?"

Oloren laughed. "I admit, it seems some have an edge over others—but even then, a predisposition or hardened exterior does not make a warrior. It takes time to develop the skill and the mindset required. But this is not my decision to make."

"First instinct though, if you had to pick, what do you think would be the best option?"

"I would say that if there is nothing for you at home, stay on the mission with me. If there were something for you worth returning to, I would tell you to go back. As it is, if you are capable of learning as we go, I believe there is value in going forward with us. The tribes are closing in, so no option is without its dangers. But with us, you could have a part in helping Gorgenbrild. I know you a little and have watched you enough to be confident you will do whatever you have to when the time comes. You're a good student. Don't sell yourself short."

Enouim allowed herself to entertain the thought. The Ecyah Stone. It was a legend that had entranced her as a child and had a hold on her still. Was it a myth? Enouim wanted to believe it was real, as the others in the group clearly did, but what if it wasn't? The whole journey would be for nothing. Glintenon was most certainly real, or was in the First Morthed War, and Enouim wondered what had become of him. Had the Malak been recalled from the realms, abandoning them all? Why would the Arksar, the commanders of the Malak, order such a thing? Was Glintenon good, or disloyal as Vadik hinted? No, Enouim thought, he was good. She wasn't sure why, but she was convinced it was true. Maybe he had simply been defeated by Morales since his victory in the First War. Perhaps if she remained with the company she could find out.

The longer she allowed her mind to feast on it, the more the idea drew her in. Kilith had said she needed to decide where her desire lay. Pakel echoed this when he said that she needed to find and fight for her purpose. Finding a purpose sounded like a serious undertaking to Enouim, one that should take weeks or months rather than mere days. Her stomach twisted and turned sour.

When she thought of returning home, dread washed over her. Chayan was there, of course, ready to break her bones. But it was more than that. Enouim had wanted to be a trader, traveling the lands, but her mother had been dead set against the idea since before her father's passing. Working at the Mangonel wasn't what she wanted to do with her life, and her mother's other suggestions sounded to Enouim more like a dungeon than a purpose. What did she have to lose?

She could lose her life. She might not have a life in Gorgenbrild—that is, she might not *feel* alive—but her body allowed breath in and breath out. There was no chance of discovering something to live for if she was dead. Enouim sighed and tried to give herself a break from thinking through everything. Her brain never truly switched off, and distracting herself would end in her problem circling back to priority number one in her mind once again. Until then, though, she shoved it to the back of her mind like dirty laundry under a blanket. Stubbornly pretending it wasn't there, while entirely conscious of the fact that it was, Enouim brought herself to the present moment.

"Quarot will be waiting for us there," Gabor was saying.

"He has selected two men to join us in our mission and we will combine our knowledge as we move forward."

"Yes, we all know that part of the plan," Pakel put in, "but I mean after that. Were the Kalka'an men supposed to investigate whether or not the Levavin had the Stone? Or were they just trying to find out if Levav knew anything?"

"Both," Gabor replied. "Although they had precious little time to do so. Still, if the Levavin were in possession of the stone, we would likely have heard of it by now."

"Unless there's some rule they have that keeps them from actually using the Ecyah Stone," Vadik said. "So many rules! Perhaps they can use it as long as they have good motives. Which they have no way to prove." His sardonic tone was hard to miss.

"There is a difference between what they think is wrong and what is punishable," Enouim said. "My understanding is that the Levavin only punish what they *can* have evidence for, and though they have strict codes even for thought, they primarily judge actions, as an outpouring of the mind. So, if they have the Ecyah Stone and aren't using it, perhaps they don't believe it should be used or that no worthy motive has yet arisen to warrant its use. Because *using* the stone is an action that they could judge. It is observable."

"Your understanding?" Canukke prodded. Enouim pulled back in surprise. He had largely ignored her since the zegrath. "What is *your* understanding worth, Stowaway?"

Enouim lifted her chin. "I spent a lot of time reading the old scripts and journals from travelers and traders. I've always been interested in other lands and cultures, and have read first-hand accounts from Gorgenbrilders writing of their experiences over the past several hundred years. Though the Levavin moral standards are based on the motives driving a person, someone can do what is wrong inwardly without being punished for it outwardly. The Levavin do not claim to read minds."

Canukke looked annoyed but didn't come back at her with an argument. Enouim took pride in her small victory.

"With only motives to rule them, I should imagine less rules, not more," Vadik said. "Each person would do what they thought was right, and rationalize it how they saw fit. As long as the person was convincing that the motive was pure, they could get away with just about anything. Not so different from our own concepts of general self-rule."

"But even we have limits on what can be handled among the people on their own," Enouim said. "We have Deliberation and Justice Hall to intervene when necessary, you know? For Levav, their leadership decided what right and wrong was, and they believe some means are never justifiable ... toward any ends. Thus, they judge the people under these precepts. Following their rules seems exhausting to me, as they cannot lie, cheat, steal, kill, break marriages, or even act out of hate, and if there's enough evidence to show an action was born out of hate it is punishable. They believe emotions are aids rather than weaknesses, and they don't believe emotion poisons the mind. I find it intriguing, but I'm not sure if the writer I read had a good grasp of their perspective."

"That's true," Oloren said. "Levav values emotion perhaps *more* than the mind."

"It will make our time with them simple enough!" Kilith said. "One of you can cry, and we'll be on our way with all that they have."

Gabor shook his head. "Levav is a fortified city. Maybe we can get out once we're inside, but getting in may be more challenging. Our traders are never permitted entry past the first set of gates."

THAT NIGHT OLOREN checked the slash mark on Enouim's back from the zegrath and added more ointment to it. It could have been much worse and was healing well. Enouim had been lucky.

As the group continued across the mountains, still at a high altitude, the landscape began to change. The trees got thinner, with more pine, spruce, and aspen trees than the large, thick-trunked trees they had grown accustomed to in the past few days, and the rocks changed from shades of gray to lighter sandy colors. The terrain transitioned from steep slopes to flat ground for long stretches.

Days continued to pass, and Enouim settled into a routine. When it was time to rest, she ate with the others or took the small knife from her boot and threw it at a tree trunk repeatedly while she ruminated over her options. Oloren saw her doing this and praised her technique, as the knife hit the same mark each time. Though she'd always been pretty good at throwing knives, Enouim used the knife more for small game hunting or crude whittling than anything else. Oloren started spending more time with her, and they threw knives together on breaks.

In the late afternoon, sixteen days after their departure, they arrived on a plateau where the trees thinned out. Nothing could be seen in any direction save the sparse trees and increasingly rocky ground. On the far end of the scene, the landscape dropped away before blue sky—another cliff.

Canukke rode forward. "We're here."

"Here?" Vadik asked. "There's nothing here!"

Canukke ignored him and continued on. The rest followed with some confusion—except Kilith, who seemed to enjoy their befuddlement. Scanning the area, Canukke approached a slight dip in the ground difficult to see from a distance. As they neared it, Enouim saw that it was actually a steep ramp to a tunnel large enough for horse and rider to enter single file. Enemies would be unable to see it without close proximity or prior knowledge, and several of them scattered across the plateau. From the cliff side, it probably looked like the field was riddled with giant rabbit holes.

The company descended into the rocky tunnel one after the other. Someone coughed, and the sound echoed down the passage. Why hadn't they come across anyone yet? The horizontal strata of the rocky walls around them dissolved into black as they continued quietly at a walking pace for several minutes. Soon, light reached them again, revealing three men and a woman standing at the base of the tunnel armed with spears in their hands and bows and arrows at their backs. Their clothing colors reflected their rocky surroundings— mixtures of sand, taupe, or fawn—with leather armor laid over it.

Canukke reached them and dismounted, greeting one of the men with a good-natured punch and embrace. He passed the reins of his horse off to another of the men, who led the animal off to the left. The rest of the group followed his example, dismounting at the base of the tunnel and passing their horses off to be led to food and water.

The base of the tunnel was no more than twenty feet from a sheer drop-off above sparkling ocean that ran from the bottom of the bluff out to the horizon. Mountains gave way to beaches along the shore on one side, and nothing but water stood on the other. On the left another tunnel entrance sat ten feet from the first, and a narrow dirt path wrapped around the cliff face.

Enouim turned to the right and sucked in a breath of surprise. The community's dwellings were chiseled into the mesa's sandy stone, their walls made with bricks of the same substance. Homes had been built into clefts of the cliff, extending along giant lateral fissures for as far as she could see. The massive rock wall fell abruptly from the plateau above them, interrupted only by the deep recesses in which the buildings were hewn before continuing its descent to the sea far below.

The man Canukke was familiar with led them through a series of short tunnels and up ladders and steps to reach the main portion of Kalka'an. Houses, buildings, and passageways were all connected in some way, and a wall was never used just once, except for those on the edge of the cliff. Well hidden inside the mesa's cleft of the mesa, the entire civilization of Kalka'an was thriving under and in the side of the mountain.

Canukke gestured for them to leave their packs there with the four guards. "Quarot has left strict instructions for our provisions to be well looked after. It's best that they are not brought into the heart of Kalka'an."

"If we cannot trust them enough to bring our bags in, how can we trust them at all?" Gabor demanded in a low tone.

"Our nations have an established system," Kilith answered. "We are free to retaliate as we deem necessary should any of our supplies be missing upon our return. It is an exchange of trust and accountability that we not kill in their land, and they not steal in ours, even if provoked. There have been no major issues for many years."

Gorgenbrild valued honor, bravery, strength, and truth, and killing was generally acceptable. In contrast, Kalka'an valued wit, and a clever mind won out over strength. Practicality, balance, energy, and necessity ruled the land, with stealing and deception deemed perfectly agreeable. Kalka'an and Gorgenbrild were long-standing allies and often traded together, but Enouim had never thought of how they had dealt with their differences.

A guard led them to a place where no footpath jutted out from the cliff, and only a narrow bridge across a drop-off to nothingness connected them to the next landing and the main entrance. Next to the drop-off on either side of the bridge, three ropes were secured to the cliff at various heights.

"What are those for?" Enouim asked.

"We use them for faster travel across areas with little to no space to go on foot," the guard replied.

Enouim blinked.

"Not for the faint of heart, coward," Canukke said, brushing past her. "Don't worry, we can take the foot path."

Great. Enouim hoped that wasn't her new nickname. Oloren and Vadik looked longingly back at the ropes, but the company took the foot bridge in single file.

"Welcome!" said a friendly voice as the group approached the entrance. A slight man with a kind face stood beneath an archway with two carved eagles on either side. "We are pleased to see you again, Canukke Topothain and Kilith Urul. And a special welcome to the five of you who have the pleasure of surveying our great treasure for the first time. The mountain is our home, and the story of our people is written in its many layers." He swept his hand around him and toward the arch above their heads, beautifully engraved with ornate stonework. "The homeland is the masterpiece, its artwork like its people—strong but patient, clever and bold, and a work that can never be stolen."

The man showed them under the archway and along the path. "What more beautiful view could you ask for than this? How can you kill a man with this serenity at your doorstep?"

"Yes, serenity like this could turn the most vengeful man into a tranquil thief," Vadik replied.

"A man who believes he knows the world!" The guide laughed—genuinely, Enouim thought. "I recognize it well. But our peoples have always worked well together. Perhaps it is our shared tenacity and love of strategy that binds us as allies, though the same may cause us to part ways in smaller matters."

Vadik snorted. "Honor is sacrificed to greed in Kalka'an! Men of distinction do what is necessary to stand up for their beliefs without coloring outside the lines. They take what is owed in a manner befitting the crime, and are brave enough to own up to their actions! It takes true strategy and tenacity to obtain victory honestly."

"Vadik!" Oloren hissed, rebuking him with a word.

The man laughed again. "All is well, never fear. We are not so easily offended. The good in our community do not operate outside of bounds either, but our bounds are different. Taking the life of another is strictly forbidden outside of combat. Your survival of the fittest applies primarily to physical prowess, leaving the weak defenseless, but ours hones the intellect."

Vadik opened his mouth again, but Oloren shot him a glare and he closed it with a smirk. As they continued into Kalka'an and past various dwellings, a young man vaulted over a wall and sprinted round a corner, a satchel stowed under his arm. The guide sighed, shaking his head. "Take this young fool, for example. Strategy would say not to bring attention to yourself if you find what you want in a neighbor's house. According to our custom, if a valuable is hidden remarkably well, anyone whose cleverness gains him access will be rewarded by that which he sought. He deserves it, no? And anyone who leaves their valuables out for the taking is as foolish as this brash young fellow who has not yet learned the meaning of finesse."

"Zegrath's teeth, don't they just steal items back and forth in endless feuds all day long?" Gabor said.

The guide shrugged. "At times. But just because there is freedom does not mean that freedom is greatly abused. Kalka'an prospers as a people without grudges. We find it offers great personal freedom, whereas the person devoted to revenge gives the object of vengeance great power over themselves."

"Forever clinging to misguided ideas, but they are remarkable minds that cling to them!" Canukke noted, matching the casual enthusiasm of the guide. "It is a good thing that Gorgenbrild and Kalka'an have been blood brothers and sisters for so long. Was it not Kalka'an that assisted us in battle against Morthed? And it was Gorgenbrild, indeed I myself, who came in defense of Kalka'an when the Iyangas threatened it. But most importantly, both of our peoples appreciate a good brew!"

"True words, my friend! And Kalka'an has few strong drinks as worthy of a long draft as Gorgenbrilder brews. And a loyal ally is worth his weight in gold. Canukke Topothain gained our respect as we fought side by side, and Kilith Urul as well when ships from across the sea reached our mountain." The guide dipped his head toward Kilith and then waved off the topic with his hand. "But surely you are tired. Tonight we celebrate our bond, exchange news, and relax! Ours may not be a Gorgenbrilder brew, but I can attest that what the king offers tonight is an honest test of a man's constitution."

The group continued through rocky halls and passageways, most without ceilings and open to the air above, the natural ceiling of the cliff far over their heads. Particularly ornate engravings and carvings identified rooms for royal use. They ducked through an entryway into a large circular room where a gathering of perhaps thirty people sat around several circular tables arrayed with colorful vegetables, fruit, and roast fowl that made Enouim's mouth water. A series of ladders brought them to the floor which sat at a lower level than any others they'd seen.

Apart from the gold circlets around their heads and gold bands on their upper arms, the king and queen of the mesa were dressed nearly the same as everyone else, and in the same family of colors. The couple stood to greet their guests, and Enouim's eyes widened as she took in the beautiful pair. The queen, a dark-haired woman with tanned skin, wore loose fitting billowy pants that gathered at the ankle. Cloth crisscrossed over her torso in an X and tucked into the band of her pants. She wore jewelry on her feet, and a mantle hung from her shoulders to cover her bare arms. The king wore similar clothing, and both had tattoos, like red clay, wrapped around their hands and right forearms in meticulous designs. Next to them stood another man with many bands tattooed around his arm. It appeared that some of the tattoos denoted rank.

"Welcome to Kalka'an!" said the king. "Topothain, it is good to see you again."

Canukke bowed. "An honor, as always, to be with you both. And Quarot, my friend! It has been a long time," Canukke said to the man standing with the king and queen. The men clasped each other's forearms and dipped their heads toward each other in respect.

"It has! What a pity your stay cannot be extended. Kilith Urul, welcome back to Kalka'an. And I'm afraid I am not acquainted with the rest of your party."

Canukke introduced Pakel, Oloren, Gabor, and Vadik to Quarot and the king and queen. He paused at Enouim, tossing her a look of disdain, but Kilith jumped in. "And finally, this is Enouim Cokanda, daughter of Rotan Cokanda the trader."

Enouim looked at him in surprise. How did Kilith know her last name, much less her father's? Had they been acquainted? If so, how could she not have met him?

Canukke didn't look pleased, but he let it go.

Quarot nodded in her direction. "My condolences. Rotan was a good man." Enouim dipped her head, unsure of what to say. Quarot gestured to the tables. "Please, sit! You must all be hungry."

Surrounded by so many people of action, Enouim couldn't help but feel out of place. Everyone around her swapped stories of gallantry and mischief. Danger and intrigue dripped from every tale, though Enouim had a sneaking suspicion some of the stories were exaggerated if not entirely fabricated. The king and queen, along with the most distinguished guests, sat a table over, and Enouim could hear Canukke telling the story of the zegrath attack. He conveniently left out Oloren's fatal blow at the end, and the epic arcing motion he described to bring his sword to bear on the animal sounded as though he would've had to have sprouted wings.

And just like that, her mind returned to the dilemma she was supposed to have resolved by now. If she went on this mission—an undertaking without predictability or security— her life would never be the same. And an adventure never really goes according to plan, of course. If it did, it would simply be a venture, little more than a task or to-do list. Enouim wasn't fond of to-do lists.

Enouim set aside her thoughts and listened to the conversation around her.

"The Sumus have made it increasingly difficult to get through trade routes in the mountains," said the man seated across from her. "It has been challenging to determine how to proceed. It seems the tribes intend to isolate Gorgenbrild from the outside world, and they've been fairly effective thus far."

Gabor nodded. "That explains it. We expected traders two months ago."

"Yes," spoke up another. "I was one of them. Not all my companions were lucky enough to return home, and the last traders did not return at all. We were unable to make contact, but homing pigeons arrived just yesterday with notes saying that the heads of our men were catapulted into your village."

Enouim shuddered. The Ecyah Stone company had gotten out just in time. A moment of silence passed before anyone spoke again.

"But why the sudden change?" one of the Kalka'aner at the table asked. "Until now, the tribes have been satisfied to kill each other in their own little squabbles further north!"

"Come on, you know better," Oloren said. "The Liombas-Katan campaign was only thirty years ago. Urgil Khoron-khelek wanted to rule the whole mountain region, so he banded several tribes together, called them the Iyangas, and attempted to take Gorgenbrild, but we met them on the mountains in a final battle that left both sides mourning severe losses. Though in the end the Iyangas were diminished, it took years to obliterate them, and we have been in some manner of altercation with the tribes ever since."

"Well, there were a number of years of peace," Vadik corrected. "At least, peace on our end. Urgil's failure wasn't exactly met with understanding. The Iyangas split and the tribes fought one another again, sorting out their affairs in the fallout. Rumor has it his right-hand man killed him."

"That's not true." Pakel shook his head. "His right hand turned against him, but it was his own son, Malum Khoron-khelek, who murdered him before taking the splinters of

Iyangas and stitching them together into the Sumus he now calls his empire. And here we are today."

"Isn't his son only in his thirties?" asked the man to Enouim's left.

Another nodded. "If that. Thirty perhaps."

"But ... he had to have been a child when he killed his father!" Enouim exclaimed.

Pakel nodded. "Oh, he was. Young teenager maybe."

"Canukke made his first kill as a teenager," Oloren added. "It's not unheard of."

"Perhaps in Gorgenbrild," a Kalka'an man said. "We like our soldiers to have beards before sending them off to war."

"Ha! War? Gorgenbrild kills each other more than they kill their enemies," another Kalka'aner stated.

Oloren stiffened. "If it weren't for Canukke, far fewer of you would be alive to complain about him. Gorgenbrild was not the Iyangas's only target, nor, I imagine, the Sumus's. Canukke was the one who informed you of their fighting tactics and came down here himself to lead the charge against them."

"Why Gorgenbrild?" Enouim asked.

Gabor rolled his eyes. "Malum has already surpassed his father by bringing all the tribes under his power. He systematically targeted and defeated them one by one, enslaving and slaughtering as he saw fit. His reputation grew, and with each new victory the tribes became more pliable, even preemptively offering themselves to his service. In return, he rewarded prominent and skilled leaders with position and power. He is no idiot. His father's leadership was questioned, and Gorgenbrild was Urgil's greatest failure. I suspect Malum intends to establish himself once and for all by doing what his father could not."

Enouim nodded. She'd known about Malum bringing the

various tribes together, but not about his father and what role he might play in Malum's intentions. She swallowed.

"Not to mention our position on the cliffs," Oloren added.

Vadik cleared his throat, eager to regain the table's attention. "We have had quiet the last few years, as Khoron-khelek's priorities have been elsewhere, strengthening himself and expanding his reach. He is wiser than his father. But the quiet is only a ruse, and we have seen more and more tribal scouts in the last six months. Anyone attempting to leave Gorgenbrild has been attacked, and tensions are rising. The most recent incident was over the Carnat Route. The tribes covet its control, but Gorgenbrild refuses to stand down."

"Have all traders stopped going to Gorgenbrild then?" Enouim asked.

"No trade happens between the dead." The man across from her picked meat off the bone and dropped it onto his plate.

Enouim's heart hammered in her chest, her eyes fixed on the bone. No one was going back home.

7

"Not all of us are too young to remember the Iyangas," said the first Kalka'an man, carrying on as if Enouim's freedom to choose her future hadn't just imploded. "But how exactly a handful of you are going to fix all this mess is utterly beyond me. A fool's errand."

Vadik squared his shoulders. "Not with the Ecyah Stone."

"Vadik!" Oloren hissed.

He shrugged at her rebuke.

The man's eyes widened. "You've found it, have you?"

"Myth," spat another, shaking his head.

"No myth," Gabor said. "Oloren, calm down. Kalka'an sent people to Levav to investigate its location, so it's not like they're clueless about what we're doing. And to you, sir, your own fine men have reason to believe it is in Levav. We are going to claim it and bring it back."

Enouim turned back to her food, mind spinning. The table continued to discuss the stone, and debate swirled concerning what the Sumus might be planning. Perhaps they were going to simply wait out the inhabitants until supplies were low and they grew weaker and weaker until the Sumus could sweep through without much of a fight. Gorgenbrild would never wait that long to fight back, even if it was a suicide mission. A lump rose in Enouim's throat as she thought of her mother and brother, trapped back home.

Enouim tried to imagine being back in Gorgenbrild. She would be with her family, but only to powerlessly await whatever evil the Sumus unleashed. And with the new information about the Kalka'an traders, Enouim wouldn't be able to return with them as Kilith had suggested.

She glanced the next table over and saw Canukke and Kilith speaking softly with the king, queen, Quarot, and two other individuals. Canukke had probably already tried to pass her off somehow and would be disappointed the trade-route option was off the table. Resolve settled over her heart. Not just because returning was no longer an option, but the danger to Gorgenbrild was real to her now. She needed to do something. Anything. She didn't have to be the fastest or the strongest; she could get faster and stronger. She just couldn't sit back and do nothing.

Enouim got up from the table and made her way to the king's table. Kneeling by Canukke's chair, she quickly and quietly told him of her intention to continue, not wanting to disrupt the festivities. His agreeableness surprised her. He simply nodded and waved her off.

They indulged in a great feast and made plans for the next day. Though the troop had originally brought gifts for Kalka'an and provisions for the next leg of their journey, they'd abandoned much of it when the wagon broke. Their hosts graciously accepted what little remained of their gifts and offered provisions to fill their packs along with the two Kalka'an representatives that would be joining their quest.

At the end of the evening, the king and queen quieted the room. "Ours is a long-standing friendship that can only be strengthened by threats beyond our borders," the king declared. "May Gorgenbrild and Kalka'an continue united in purpose to accomplish victory together and bring peace to these mountains once again! We set aside our differences and revel in our strengths in strategy and sharp mindedness."

The queen, standing to his right, also spoke up. "Tonight we officially send out the members of the Ecyah Stone mission to find and bring back the weapon our shared Malak, the great Glintenon, once wielded himself. We thank our allies in Gorgenbrild for their continued openness with us and wisdom to include us in this matter."

Quarot rose to his feet to the left of the king. "Two of our own shall be joining the mission and representing our people. A special thanks to them for volunteering their skills and intellects to this journey. Better fighters or braver souls could not be asked for. To Baird and Silas!"

Baird and Silas, as it turned out, were the two other people sitting with Canukke, Kilith, Quarot, and the king and queen. Baird, six feet tall and strong but lean, had a beard, rather disheveled brown hair, and tattoos on his arms. *He dwells in a cliff but looks like the woods,* Enouim thought. Tonight he was high energy and smiling, talking comfortably with those around him. Silas was around the same height as Baird, clean shaven, and also tattooed but more reserved in nature.

Canukke introduced Baird and Silas to the group, and when the festivities ended, they lead the Gorgenbrilders back up the ladders. "It is a shame you will not see more of Kalka'an before we set out in the morning," Silas said. "It is a beautiful and unique place. So much history. Ours is the oldest civilization, you know."

"Oldest? The Rift happened at the same time for all people," Vadik countered.

"True, but we have never had to rebuild. Kalka'an is the longest standing."

Enouim wondered how she could be sure any of them told the truth if lying was supposedly so acceptable in Kalka'an.

"You might have old houses," Canukke said, "but Gorgenbrild holds the record for most proficient at war. Good soldiers, one and all, but none can compare to our demolition power. Nor mine for that matter! I can drink any one of you under the table and still shoot straight. As a lad I killed seventeen tribesmen at once while as hungover as a pelt on a rack!"

Enouim watched Canukke skeptically. She found it incredibly annoying that this arrogant nitwit was somehow so necessary. Something in her face must have given her away, because Baird dropped back next to her to comment on it.

"Not impressed?"

"Oh … um …" She sighed and took a breath. "He has frustrating moments."

"What was with that zegrath story? Scars, tell me you didn't really let him have all the fun."

"We all played a role," Pakel answered, overhearing. "I struck it first, and it had survived many blows by the time the end came. Oloren is the one who likely finished him off, slashing its belly from below as it leaped over her from the wagon. But Canukke did jump down on it and killed it once and for all … if Oloren's blow hadn't done the trick, that is."

"Interesting. Strange he didn't give credit where credit was due," Baird observed casually.

"What are those?" Eager to change the subject, Enouim pointed at strange goat-like animals on the cliff wall below them. They'd come to a break in the rocky floor, with a sheer fall opening at their feet. After about twenty feet, the cleft jutted out again and cliff dwellings continued, and the animals seemed to be standing upright on the vertical cliff between. "And what in Yatzar are they standing on?"

"Tsizas," Silas answered from the front of the group. "They like to lick the salt off the rocks and find water in small cracks as they go. We've trained some of them to transport heavier items across areas with no foot paths, like this one."

"Those little feet are something else." Baird shook his head. "They are masterful climbers and find footholds where there seem to be none! I have yet to see a better climber anywhere in Yatzar—indeed in all the broad world."

"What about us? How do we get across?" Gabor asked.

"Ropes!" Oloren grinned, eager to try out this mode of travel after all.

Baird laughed. "Yes, ropes!" He grasped one of the ropes dangling on their side of the drop, gave himself a running start and pushed off and away from the cliff face, then released the rope before his feet touched the ground on the other side, rolling once and springing to his feet. He looked back at them with bright eyes. Clearly experimenting with life and death tricks was one of the better parts of his day. Enouim shook her head. These people were crazy.

Silas handed a rope out to the group. Oloren stepped up and, imitating Baird, gave herself a running start and swung across, dropping to her feet next to Baird on the other side. Kilith went next and quietly whispered, "Don't be last," to Enouim as he passed by. Enouim thumbed the scar on her collarbone and paced, nervous. One by one the company swung over. She could do this. If she couldn't, she would die, and she wouldn't know the difference. No, no, it was a long way down. She would definitely have time to experience the full knowledge of her pathetic failure and death. Maybe she would take one of the tsizas out with her.

"You don't want to be last, do you?" Pakel offered, encouraging her.

Ugh.

"You coming, coward?" Canukke taunted from across the way.

Well, drat, maybe she really did have a new nickname. Enouim took a deep breath and gripped the rope tight in her hands.

"Just hold tight and push off with enough speed to carry you over. Baird can catch you on the other side," Silas told her.

Enouim nodded. Heart in her throat, she shoved off, and a sudden rush of wind hit her face. Far too terrified to see the draw of the thrill, she gasped as she left the safety of the rocky cleft and swung out over untold heights, her feet cycling into nothingness. As promised, Baird and Oloren waited for her on the other side and helped her steady herself before she released the rope. Enouim staggered and took in a ragged breath. Kilith winked at her, an amused grin tugging the corner of his mouth.

Pakel and Silas followed her over, completing the group again, then Baird and Silas showed them three small rooms where they would spend the night, three people in each room. Piles of blankets had been laid out for their arrival, and the only other things in the rooms were a two-person table and chairs chiseled out of the rock attached to the wall.

Oloren gestured at the table and chairs. "You really don't waste any part of the cliff, do you?"

"We like to be resourceful, yes," Silas replied. "Using the cliff itself is helpful, and these have been here for decades. Another reason is cultural. Whatever is chiseled into rock or tattooed onto the body cannot be stolen. It's strategic."

Oloren planned to get up early with Gabor to ready the horses, and the rest would gather the new supplies from

Kalka'an and then meet Oloren and Gabor. Enouim headed to bed with gratitude. Exhaustion took her, and she soon fell fast asleep.

She awoke the next morning to the sounds of morning bustle as people began their day. Enouim hopped up on the table, jumped to catch the top of the wall, and peered over it. Three women with small game tossed over their shoulders stood at a leatherworker stand, haggling over price and offering their catch. A man sat on stone steps, watching the comings and goings, while he cut up a piece of fruit with his knife and ate it off the blade. The sun was well up. Where were the Gorgenbrilders? Enouim hopped down and looked around. All the rooms were empty, their blankets folded and back in place against the wall. Had they left her behind?

Enouim thought for a moment. Only Canukke had known of her final decision. So much was going on last evening she hadn't wanted to disturb anyone or interrupt them. She had participated in discussions and been introduced to Silas and Baird like anyone else, stayed with the party. Surely they knew. But clearly they didn't know. And Canukke had never wanted her along anyway. Kilith had said she needed to prove herself to Canukke if she chose to stay, and she obviously hadn't. Perhaps they all saw her as a coward, unfit to be in their company. Perhaps they knew she was worthless to the mission. But why had no one awakened her to say goodbye? And Oloren and Kilith had both welcomed her along with them!

Canukke. He must have told them something to keep them away from her. She couldn't stay here. How could he think he could abandon her here in Kalka'an with no way home? Did he expect her to just live here forever instead? Outrageous!

Enouim stormed out of the dwelling and took off at a jog. When she reached the expanse without a footbridge, she took in a determined breath, grabbed the rope, and swung over to the other side. A few heads turned her direction, but she saw no one she recognized. She broke into a run, thanking Glintenon that Kalka'an was mostly long rather than deep, making it easier for her to remember from where they'd come. All she had to do was get to the horses and catch her comrades before they left. If they'd already left, she could ask the guards how long they had been gone.

Energized by her optimistic plan, Enouim ran past house after house, up ladders, through passageways, down ladders, until she finally saw the archway and stopped before the narrow footbridge. Steadying herself with several deep breaths, Enouim carefully crossed the bridge. Four new guards blinked at her.

"Have they left? When did they leave?" she demanded.

"It's you," said a voice behind the guards. "I thought you left with the others."

Their guide from last night stood inside the enclosure that had held the horses. Empty now. Enouim strode toward him. One of the goat-like creatures, a tsiza, stood beside him eating something from a bucket. Though its body and feet were much like a goat, it had a long neck and face, tapered nose, large eyes, and a tail that widened at the end into a flat almost fin-like shape nearly the length of its head—perhaps used for balance. The tsiza wore a harness around its neck and midsection, and it looked as though the man was about to load the tsiza with a bulky bag.

"Where are they?" Enouim said again.

"They already left. An hour ago. Why weren't you with them?"

"I need to catch up. What horse were they going to give me?"

"Blanket appaloosa stallion. Black, tall, can't miss him. We thought he might be too much horse for you, but the other woman said you could ride. He's far on the other side though. This area here is just a holding area, short-term. That second tunnel goes out to open land, and from there most horses are taken to the main pasture wrapping around the cliff. It takes some time to get there, but it's worth it for long-term care of the animals. We took them the long way round last night to the larger pen and some grass, you see. Down there." He pointed to a ledge jutting out from the cliff fifteen feet down and forty feet over. "If they left in a hurry I imagine Inferno may still be all tacked up, but by the time you make it over there, your friends will be long gone."

Enouim panicked. The Ecyah Stone quest was her quest now too. She needed it. She would fight for her people, doing something instead of nothing. She would learn as she went. She would traverse many lands and become someone along the way. Find her purpose. The only purpose she had now was wrapped up in the Ecyah Stone. How dare Canukke leave her behind? How dare he mislead the others? They wouldn't have willingly abandoned her. And she was not the coward he thought she was.

"How does it work?" Enouim asked the guide, gesturing toward the tsiza.

Surprised, the man glanced back at the animal, which stood perhaps four feet tall. "We use these weighted plates and match them to equal out the sack we're transporting so the weight is evenly distributed, and it doesn't throw off the tsiza's center of balance. The plates are on the side close to the cliff, so it can still hug the rock face as close as it sees fit, and the sack is on the other side."

"Great," she said, stepping forward. "I'll save time by getting across as the sack."

The guide's eyes widened. "No, I don't think that's a good idea. We do not transport *people* on a tsiza!"

"You do today! Now how heavy is that sack? Should we add another plate?"

The guide shook his head but looked her up and down. "The sack is pretty heavy. I can add one more plate to the vest. And how do you expect us to replace the trained tsiza should you both die in this reckless notion of yours?"

"Tell you what," Enouim answered, "If I die, I'll pay for it."

8

T he man added a plate to the tsiza's vest and led it to the edge of the precipice. He shook his head at her again. "You're going to die."

"Thanks for the confidence boost," Enouim snapped as she stepped up. She snatched an empty sack from a pile nearby and handed it to the man. "Put it on the tsiza."

"Look, it's not my fault if you die. I will tell everyone you did it without my knowledge."

"Don't worry, Gorgenbrilders are firm believers that stupid people have the right to be stupid and weed out the less intelligent. I am no one of consequence, and no one in Kalka'an who might possibly care knows I'm still here."

The man frowned but did as she asked. He slid the sack into restraints attached to the tsiza's vest. Enouim scooped up a few treats from the bucket and awkwardly climbed into the empty sack. She shifted uncomfortably as she pulled her knees up to her chest to fit in the sack, bundled into a ball except for her head sticking out the opening. Enouim slid her left arm out of the sack and around the tsiza's neck, grasping the harness, and nodded at the man. "Let's go."

He let out a resigned sigh and swatted the tsiza's hindquarters. Enouim's heart flew into her throat as the animal stood and moved to step dainty cloven hooves up onto the rocky face of the cliff wall. Enouim felt herself lifted up and the tsiza's weight shift as it made the transition to placing all four feet on the wall. Slowly it proceeded forward. When she glanced down, all Enouim could see was the animal's feet, the cliff, and lots of empty air. Air that would be no help whatsoever if the creature made a misstep. No trees grew on the cliff here, and no landings jutted out to slow a fall.

Something in her brain screamed at her now that this was a very, very terrible idea. The man was right, she would definitely die. No way could she cross the cliff here; no way could she climb anything quite so steep. But another part of her remembered that the tsiza had made this journey before, multiple times—probably practically a morning ritual for it. Enouim glanced ahead. Thirty-five feet to go.

She closed her eyes, trying to trust the tsiza's footing. Had it ever carried a load this heavy?

She felt a lurch. Another lurch. *Glintenon, I'm going to die.* A rock crumbled, and Enouim's eyes snapped open. The tsiza's back legs were several feet above its front legs, weight mainly supported by the front. One of the tsiza's front legs had struck unsteady rock, breaking it off, and the rock was still falling. Enouim hoped it didn't foreshadow her future. Fortunately the tsiza recovered and made steady progress to the other side, finally reaching the grassy landing forty feet over and fifteen feet down from where she started.

Letting out a sigh of relief, Enouim tumbled out of the sack and waved at the guide across the way. He shook his head at her in disbelief, shrugged, and turned away. She gave the tsiza one of the treats she'd taken from the bucket and looked around at the horses in the grassy pasture. The one she was meant to have, Inferno, was hard to miss. He was a beautiful black stallion with white markings scattered over his hindquarters and reaching up to the saddle area, almost as if a blanket had been tossed over him. He still wore a bridle, but the saddle blanket and saddle lay on the ground nearby.

Enouim took a few deep breaths to steady her nerves before approaching him confidently and gently. She offered a hand with the rest of the treats and was rewarded by Inferno touching her hand with his nose and taking her gift. She stepped in to pat him on the neck and shoulder, and worked quickly to saddle him. After mounting, she turned Inferno down the nearby trail that led to the bottom of the flat-topped mountain. Canukke had planned on going down the mountain and out along the sea.

They picked their way down the mountain side, descending past the treetops, a rocky wall rising on one side. Behind them, the mesa stretched up to meet a bright-blue sky, with the village chiseled in the rock beneath its high ceiling. When the path opened up and the slope eased, Enouim urged Inferno forward at a canter.

Now that her fear at the tsiza situation had passed, the anger of the morning returned. Canukke had left her behind, abandoned her in a strange place with no way to get home, and kicked her off the mission unceremoniously without the least courtesy. She'd told him she'd claimed the Ecyah mission as her own, and she would not be thrown aside.

The longer she stewed, the more she boiled. It took her several hours to get to the bottom of the mountain, but the time only served to feed her fury. At the end of the trees, she saw a group of eight traveling through the open land ahead. She'd caught up! She kicked Inferno into a gallop. Nothing filled her mind but the strength of her muscles against the horse, the wind on her face, the tension in her body. Hooves pounded into turf that turned to sand, and she took no notice of the glittering ocean to her right.

Silas and Gabor, riding side by side in the rear, heard her coming first. Gabor had an arrow notched when he turned in the saddle, but lowered it when he saw Enouim. She galloped past them, past Vadik, Baird, and Pakel riding three abreast, to Canukke, Oloren, and Kilith riding at the front of the group. By now everyone had seen her, and several paused to wait for her until they saw that Canukke wasn't slowing. They couldn't possibly have mistaken the intensity and anger on Enouim's face.

Enouim cut in front of Canukke's horse and pulled up short, horse and rider heaving. She pushed Inferno forward until Canukke's mount stopped, tossed his head, and stepped backward. "Where do you get off abandoning me in Kalka-'an?" she said. "I told you I was staying on the Ecyah mission. I told you, and you didn't even say no, you said yes and then left me there!"

Oloren's eyes widened. "Canukke, is this true?"

Canukke rolled his eyes. "You didn't earn your place here with us. You're nothing but a hindrance."

Enouim bore into him with eyes ablaze. "What honor is there in leaving one of your countrymen behind? What honor in breaking your word?"

"I promised you nothing. You told me you wanted to continue, and I acknowledged your desire. What you assumed from that is none of my concern."

"You told us she had chosen to stay behind!" Oloren exclaimed. "I was up early preparing the horses, and you said we had to leave quickly and that Enouim had chosen to stay in Kalka'an."

"She *did* choose to stay behind. She chose by her utter

worthlessness with the zegrath, her cowardice with Chayan, and her own self-doubt. She has no business here!"

"You lied to us. To me." Oloren's bitter accusation hung in the air.

Canukke looked at her, indignant but silent.

"Lying is lazy," Enouim said. "For all –"

"*Lazy!*" Canukke roared. "How dare you! Was I lazy when I scouted and killed ten Sumus in preparation for this mission? Was I lazy when I trained myself to be the best—in navigation, in war, in survival—that Gorgenbrild has seen? Was I—"

"For all your honor, all your courage, you lied to the company to serve your own purposes," Enouim retorted. "A responsible man, a real man, takes ownership of his decisions and states them plainly for others to judge as they will. You are a disgrace to Gorgenbrild. Hypocrite! Keep your fancy stories to yourself. Keep your accomplishments and all your self-awarded trophies. I am staying on this mission whether you like it or not."

Canukke curled his lip and stepped his horse forward, pushing into Inferno and leaning in, inches from Enouim's face. He spoke in a harsh whisper far more menacing than any yell could have been. "This is *my* mission, and I am its leader. You will not disparage me in front of my men, and I will dispose of whomever I see fit. *No one* stands in my way."

Enouim nearly choked on intimidation as a chill ran up her spine. This man was dangerous. She had woken a beast willing to do whatever necessary to continue his quest the way he desired. Her anger remained, and she glared back at him, but by the satisfaction in his eyes it was clear Canukke saw he'd rattled her.

"Enough," Kilith said firmly from behind Canukke as he moved forward.

Oloren also moved up. "I can't believe you did that to her," she said to Canukke quietly but angrily, clearly upset. "How dare you. As a team we need to be on the same page."

"I avoided sharing information that would interfere with our exiting on time and on course. I did my job." Raising his voice for the rest of them, Canukke added, "And what is most effective now is to move on from this needless delay and spend no more time out in the open than necessary. Never to turn. We go forward."

Oloren shook her head. "Canukke—"

"We're done here. If she slows us down, she's gone."

9

The tension was tangible. Canukke stepped his horse around Enouim and rode alone, leading the company on as if nothing had happened. Kilith joined him after a while. Oloren hung back with Enouim, and Pakel drew up on her other side, while Baird rode behind her. Silas and Gabor remained at the back, riding silently for the most part, with occasional soft exchanges back and forth.

"It's ridiculous that he thought he could get away with leaving you there and lying to us," Oloren said. "I'm sorry that happened. I would never have allowed it had I known what was going on."

"I knew you wouldn't have left me," Enouim answered quietly. "I assumed he must have lied. Do you think I'm safe now? On the mission, I mean."

"Probably. I mean, you didn't earn yourself any points with him today, but you did with us." Oloren smiled, but then bit her lip.

"So you just woke up to no one around? How did you find the horses?" Pakel asked.

Enouim briefly explained what had happened, from

waking up to find herself alone to running for the horses and finding the guide. She ended with her impromptu tsiza ride across the cliff, reaching the horses, and starting down the mountain.

Pakel whistled. "Well that doesn't sound like a coward to me," he said, eyes twinkling. "It sounds like you must have found a purpose for being here after all. Let me be the first to officially welcome you to the Ecyah mission!"

Oloren echoed his enthusiasm to have her along, and Enouim breathed out much of the tension she'd been carrying. She was grateful for their kind acceptance and company.

Pakel kept things light. "Well, like I said, welcome. And as for this morning, I suppose it wouldn't be the first time our fearless leader has stretched the truth! At Kalka'an Canukke essentially took credit for killing the zegrath."

Oloren's eyes widened. "He did what? ... Oh, he and I will definitely be having words later."

"Later is probably good—he may still need to cool off," Enouim noted.

Pakel laughed. "Don't worry, I set the story straight with Baird."

Baird spoke up for the first time. "A good thing too! It sounds like this Canukke fellow may have more Kalka'an in him than he'd like to admit. That's a surprise."

"He gets ahead of himself sometimes," Oloren returned, "but he knows what he's doing and is a good choice for a leader all things considered."

"Seems to me there are some serious trust issues to resolve though," Baird continued. "How *did* he end up being the head of this mission? Kilith seems like a competent man, and his name is known to us. And I have led a number of excursions myself, as I'm sure several of you have."

"Kilith only came on the condition that he be free to leave

at any time," Vadik explained. "That means no official leadership role. He doesn't like to be tied down."

"Practically it means that he follows along for as long as he wants to be here, but Canukke respects him, and they often confer together." Pakel pulled out his karambit and started twirling it in his hands again. "I imagine Canukke wouldn't try rebuking Kilith, knowing if he did it wouldn't go well. If there's something to discuss, they'll address it among the two of them and we probably won't even know about it. As for other leaders, aside from Kilith, Canukke is the natural choice despite all our experience."

"Canukke knows Gorgenbrild leaders well and is looked up to by many," Oloren said. "Like I said, he is highly skilled, and I've fought alongside him many times before."

Vadik grinned. "You sound pretty loyal for railing at him a few minutes ago."

"When it counts, I trust his ability and intelligence. He's strategic and he gets the job done, but I know him well enough to call him out when I see something I don't think is right. He can be arrogant, and I don't agree with everything he does, but we work it out in the end."

"I'll have to defer judgment then and see for myself if he is really as good as he says he is," Baird said. "Enouim, what do you think of him?"

"I don't know him as well as Oloren or the others."

"But you know enough to have an opinion. I mean, you charged up to him and weren't mincing words then. Obviously you have thoughts on the man."

"I think he's arrogant, like Oloren said. I think he fits Gorgenbrild stereotypes to a T, and I think he could treat people better, you know? I know warriors can be effective without caring about people, but I just feel like he could do better on that front. Maybe even ... well, anyway, I don't like him as a person, but apparently he knows what he's doing in military scenarios."

"You know something we don't?" Pakel pressed, a twinkle in his eye.

"Not really. It doesn't matter," Enouim replied, thinking of the little bit she had gathered about Canukke and Edone's relationship, and the way Canukke flirted back with the women that forever surrounded him. "So what about you, Baird? You talk about Canukke's trustworthiness, but you're from Kalka'an. Wouldn't he somehow earn points for deceit in your book?"

"Hey now! We can be trusted through our actions, and you'll learn that I'm here to further the mission. I was sent as a representative of Kalka'an, and if my people didn't trust I would be able to report back accurately, they would've sent someone else. Get to know me and see what you think."

"So they sent you, or you volunteered?" Oloren asked.

"Both!"

"What made you want to come?" Pakel inquired.

"Adventure! I love the rush of exploring something new. Unexpected turns of events. I am also here for the greater good, for Kalka'an, for our allies in Gorgenbrild. Finding the Ecyah Stone would be legendary to say the least. I wouldn't miss it for the world. And protecting our peoples at the same time? Nothing better! How can you say no to that?"

Enouim couldn't help but like Baird. He was easy going and animated, a free spirit with a genuine zest for life. Whether or not he was genuine in other areas, Enouim wasn't sure. She wanted to trust him, but she didn't want to be bitten for it later. He was from Kalka'an after all. But Baird certainly was friendly, and that put her at ease. He also seemed to have accepted her as part of the group back in Kalka'an, and Enouim hadn't forgotten that.

Enouim allowed herself to settle into traveling, enjoying a blissful breeze and marveling at the sparkling sea to their right. She learned that Kalka'an's investigation into whether or not Levav possessed the Ecyah Stone had returned murky at best. The stone had vanished without a trace after the Great Rift. Gorgenbrild believed they had a right to the stone, for they were the most skilled in war and followed a code of honor. Who better to remove every menace from the face of the earth? When The Ecyah Stone reappeared in the hand of Glintenon in the First Morthed War, Gorgenbrild held that their right to the stone was confirmed, as Glintenton himself must have intended it. But, to their dismay, the stone disappeared again, and three decades later rumors started that Levav had it.

Levav was a fortress, and though at one time they had an open-door policy to anyone desiring to enter, Levav soon discovered spies attempting to locate the stone and sabotage their control of the region. Levav shut its gates and, though they still traded with other peoples, became well-guarded and watchful. The Levavin often sent small groups out to the nomads in the desert and in boats across the sea on peaceful missions, but they were selective in who they permitted inside their own walls. One-hundred years after the First Morthed War, most in the surrounding areas were convinced the Ecyah Stone was with Levav. These suspicions were made stronger when Kalka'an, Morthed, and several other smaller groups each attempted to conquer it and claim the stone for themselves and were soundly defeated. Levav had lived in relative peace ever since.

The company continued along the coastline, but the space between the water and the cliffs opened up to about thirty yards, and they moved away from the beach to firmer ground. The waves lapped gently on the shore to her right, and as she looked up at her left she was astounded at how the cliff rose with hardly a rocky crag, as if it were cut glass. It would take them two months to get to Levav, and Enouim began to think about what lay ahead.

Now that she was on the mission, she realized that her only real fighting skill was with a knife, but a few knife tricks wouldn't be enough to get her through the mission in one piece. Even if the stone was in Levav and they somehow managed to seize it, getting it home again would be no easy task. The Sumus would know by now that they'd departed Gorgenbrild, and they may have hypothesized why.

For this reason Enouim resolved to learn to fight. With weeks of travel ahead, there was no better time to practice. She had the basics of course, like any Gorgenbrilder would pick up even without trying, but she had never applied herself to it and was far behind the skill of the warriors she rode alongside. Enouim brought it up with Pakel and Oloren, and they were more than happy to help.

The company stopped to rest the horses and eat, and Pakel and Enouim took the opportunity to practice combat. Pakel's eyes shone with excitement. Clearly, he thoroughly enjoyed taking on his new role as principal instructor.

"Close the distance—good," he said, moving toward her. He swung at her and she blocked, then he caught her off guard with a jab to the throat. "Aha! You have to be better with the fast attacks. Not every move is so easy to see coming."

"Sorry." It was a good thing Pakel had such a positive attitude. Any other teacher would dampen her motivation and discourage her efforts.

"No apologizing." He lunged toward her again. "Here's the thing. You don't have time to apologize in a real fight. You might not die from throwing techniques with imperfect form, but you will definitely die from stopping to berate yourself for doing it wrong. Again."

Enouim steeled herself and took a deep breath. Pakel came at her, and she moved into the motion, meeting him with force so that even a block was a counterattack. She picked up the pace to match him, and they quickly exchanged blows, deflections, and counterattacks in a rhythm that was almost poetic.

"Breathe," he reminded her.

Ugh. How could she possibly forget something her body usually did on its own? She *had* been holding her breath. Frustrated, she went into her next move but left her torso open, and Pakel made a slicing motion to signify that she would have been cut. He made several more slicing motions and then came after her again.

"I'm dead," she said flatly, backing away and breathing hard. "I would have died about five times by now."

"We'll probably all die soon anyway," Gabor said brightly from the sidelines. "Good to get used to the idea now!"

Silas laughed, but Pakel ignored them. "Every time you see a knife, you need to assume you're going to get cut. Getting cut isn't the end of the world if you can control where you get cut."

"Or you could avoid it altogether by disarming them before they get the chance," Vadik drawled.

"Even if some of those were just shallow cuts, I'm still dead," Enouim said to Pakel, ignoring Vadik.

"So what? You just quit? Come on, Enouim. Go again." This time Gabor's voice was less jovial.

Enouim felt like her energy had been drained just as quickly as her blood would have been if the scenario were real. She shook her head. She couldn't do this.

"Never stop moving," Oloren added softly but firmly. "I

know you're tired, but even if you're slower, hit harder and keep going."

"You're soft," Canukke commented casually. His condescending tone hit Enouim like a punch to the gut. Every look he gave her reeked of it. "You're thinking you aren't cut out for this. Glintenon, maybe there's a reason."

"Focus," Kilith said. Somehow Kilith watching her—quietly, intently—brought a sliver of determination back to her mind. Though he'd said little so far, he'd been watching with a keen eye from the start. Who was this mysterious man? How did he know her father? Kilith was older than her father had been and may have encountered him before she'd come along, she supposed. Why hadn't she heard of him? Why did he warn her about proving herself to Canukke?

Enouim wanted to impress Kilith, she knew that. And she wanted to prove Canukke wrong. But her body cried for reprieve. It would be counterproductive to try proving him wrong when failure was certain. At the same time, what other choice did she have? She couldn't very well train in private. Privacy was a thing of the past now anyway; the group was together every moment.

Enouim willed herself back to the present and faced Pakel. He came forward again, and she produced a side kick with enough force to send him backward a bit. She pulled out her own blade and closed the space between them, nearly getting the sharp edge to his neck before he deflected and spun behind her. Pakel put her in a choke hold from behind, and she tucked her chin as best as she could, but it was too late. She felt her airway constrict and tapped Pakel's arm. He released her.

"I survived my first fight to the death at fourteen," Canukke said. "Killed my first zegrath at sixteen. Here you are, unable to even stand on your own two feet."

Enouim's felt her shoulders fall forward, and a sour look settled on her face.

"I'm Canukke," Pakel said softly. "Perfectly cocky and obnoxious. Ignore him except to funnel all frustration with him at me."

"Breathe," Oloren reminded her again. "Relax."

Relaxing did *not* come naturally in fighting scenarios. How was she supposed to do that? Enouim drew her shoulders back and took a deep breath, and as she let it out, she felt her muscles release some of their tension. Another deep breath.

Silas whispered behind her, "She'll never make it."

With a guttural cry, she flew at Pakel, deflecting his front kick, throwing a jab and an uppercut to the chin, trapping one of his arms in an underhook and gripping the back of his shirt with the other. Enouim pulled his body down and struck him in the stomach with her knee. Cheers erupted from several of the onlookers. Feeding off their energy, Enouim dealt several more blows. Pakel went for a takedown around her waist, but she leaped backward in the nick of time.

Pakel regained his footing and smiled. "Good! We have a lot of work to do, but we're making progress."

Enouim glanced behind her and saw Gabor smile and nod. Kilith had a twinkle in his eye, but Canukke glowered at her.

They worked on hand to hand, knife, and sword. Enouim worked primarily with Pakel, but as they progressed, several others joined in on the fun. Vadik loomed eight inches taller than her own five foot-six height and gave her more aggression than Pakel. Baird was quick on his feet and used more feigning moves than her Gorgenbrilder companions, and Gabor was smooth as silk with his blade and footwork so that he seemed to glide across the ground.

Sometimes Enouim felt discouraged by the stark size and

strength differences between herself and the men, but Oloren showed her how to make the most of her size. At five foot three, Oloren held her own by manipulating torque rather than brute strength. She showed Enouim what weak points to target, such as bearing down on a fulcrum joint in a shoulder or elbow.

"It's not about size," she told Enouim as she doubled Baird over with one hand, twisting his wrist. "It's about strategy. You can appreciate that, can't you, Baird? And if he's too tall, a few strikes to vulnerable areas like the groin or knee will bring him down to your level."

The company continued on between the ocean and the cliff, and though night fell, still Canukke pressed onward. Enouim felt her eyelids drooping as she struggled to stay awake.

Gabor punched her in the arm. "If he sees you sleeping, you might never wake up," he hissed.

"Why haven't we stopped yet? We never go this long," Enouim whispered back.

"He doesn't like being surrounded by so many barriers with no natural cover or resources. No trees, no fresh water."

"Maybe he doesn't want more Kalka'an coming down the cliff," Vadik suggested.

Silas shook his head. "We don't live in the cliffs this far down. No one does. But we don't like to feel trapped in this funnel any more than he does, so I can't say I blame him for this one."

Up ahead, Canukke's horse stopped, and slowly the rest halted. Canukke's beady eyes glinted in the dim moonlight, and Enouim could just make out his gesture for silence before he walked his horse forward again.

"Who exactly does he think will hear us?" Vadik asked, looking to Silas.

"I think he's just in a mood. There's no one in this direction, not for miles."

"Is he ever *not* in a mood?" Baird grumbled. A small object whizzed through the air and hit Baird on the head. "Ouch!" he hissed, catching the seashell as it fell.

Canukke was staring back at him. Gabor snorted, and Canukke repeated his gesture for silence.

Another three hours passed before Canukke finally motioned for them to make camp. The air was brisk, and Enouim tugged the hood of her mantle up over her head.

"We may talk in low tones now," said Canukke.

"I don't want to talk," Vadik said. "I want to fall straight asleep!"

Baird grinned. "Well, *there's* a first!" The corner of his mouth twitched.

"Now if only we had a fire," Oloren said.

"No, it's a mercy there aren't any resources to tempt us here," Canukke said quietly. "Camrin ships target this strip, and many unfortunate travelers on this road go missing. Keep a weather eye out, and don't draw attention to yourselves."

"Camrin ships! Son of a zegrath, surely they don't have the gall to come this far?" Pakel looked concerned.

Kilith spoke for the first time. "Canukke has spent more time in this area than most, even more than many Kalka'an. I would take heed if I were you. Let's get some rest."

The suggestion couldn't have sounded sweeter to Enouim. She gladly unrolled her blanket and lay down, her comrades following suit. Wind blew the sand in her face, and she turned away, pulling the blanket tightly around herself. She woke during the night and saw only the sleeping forms of seven warriors.

Canukke sat alone twenty feet off, staring out over the sea. Following his gaze, she saw two twinkling lights in the distance, bobbing across the surface of the water. One disappeared for a moment, but reappeared a moment later. Anxious thoughts about Camrin ships came to mind, but Canukke was watching over them, alert, but unconcerned, unhurried, but prepared. He knew what he was doing. With this reassurance, she let herself drift away once more.

M orning came far too quickly, and being jostled awake before her body was ready to cooperate was among Enouim least favorite experiences.

"Time to go, Enouim! Wake up!" Vadik's voice was loud in her ear.

"You have way too much energy," Enouim mumbled, rolling over.

"Well, take some of mine then. Come on!" He shook her harder, and she groaned.

"Isn't she up yet?" Canukke called. "If she's not in the saddle in two minutes, I drag her behind my horse."

Enouim snapped her eyes open and pushed herself up, but the sudden motion made her head spin. She blinked and shook her head, trying to clear it. Canukke gave a sly grin, and Gabor and Pakel laughed good-naturedly.

Gabor took her under the arm and hoisted her to her feet. "That did it, eh?" He patted her on the arm, then released her.

Enouim took only a step toward Inferno before tripping over her own feet and falling right back on her rump. She rubbed her eyes and shook her head once more.

"And you people think *I'm* a liability," Silas muttered from somewhere behind her.

Oloren helped her to her feet, laughing. "Rough morning, En," she said with a wink.

Canukke put his left foot in the stirrup of his horse's saddle and swung himself up. "It would behoove you to learn some break falls, if you plan on falling often."

Enouim wrinkled her nose. "Break falls ..." Her fingers nimbly worked the girth beneath her horse and pulled the straps through to secure the saddle.

"It's a good idea, really," said Pakel, offering her a hand.

Enouim swatted it lightly. "I know how to mount a horse!"

"Honestly, it should have been one of the first things we focused on," Pakel continued, unconcerned.

"You're going to be doing a lot of falling," Gabor said. "If you're going to learn to do something well, falling is a good place to start."

"Not avoiding falling down?" Enouim asked.

"No, no, you should plan on falling down. You can hardly stand up straight *without* anyone fighting you. Add someone trying to lop your head off, and you're definitely going to fall. And then they're going to lop your head off."

Kilith smiled and nodded at Gabor. "If you're good at breaking your falls, you can fall off a horse without breaking a bone, or off a high wall and survive."

"You look like you've been in a scrap or two," Vadik said, turning from Kilith back to Enouim. "I mean, you don't look like you could have done very well, but you've got scars on the back of your neck."

"Just because she's a girl, she can't be a good fighter?" Oloren shot back.

Gabor laughed. "I think it's the physical mass, and that clueless look she gives when fighting."

"Your father was a trader, right? Did he teach you anything?" Pakel asked.

"Adopted father, as I recall," Canukke said, surprising Enouim that he'd interject in a conversation totally focused outside himself.

She'd always known she was adopted, but she'd been so welcomed into her adoptive family that the surname Cokanda had always been just as much hers as it was her brother's. Her father had found her abandoned on one of his trading trips, and he'd brought her home and raised her as his own. She'd been stung by some sort of water creature, and the wounds had never fully healed. "He was my father, and a great one," Enouim responded evenly. "He passed away. But somehow I think Vadik may have the best childhood story!"

Vadik laughed and launched into his tale.

Canukke had brought them nearly to the end of the cliffs the night before, and as the morning passed away into afternoon, the cliffs dropped away. Canukke left the shoreline and pushed further east, following the coast at a distance.

The group seemed eager to keep the lighthearted feel going, and Pakel started her break-fall training that very day. Of all her training so far, she hated break falls the most, mainly because she was terrible at them, but also, as a rule, she avoided doing things that inevitably led to significant amounts of pain.

Break falls regularly incurred physical pain, mostly by doing them incorrectly; they also incurred psychological pain because it was discouraging trying to do things she was bad at. Repeatedly, she practiced falling and smacking the ground with her arms to absorb her impact, and repeatedly Pakel told her she was more likely to break her arms than save her body. Enouim's imperfections and failures faced her every time she tried, and her failures only escalated with each unsuccessful attempt. Sometimes she simply told Pakel they needed to work on something else for a while.

The days passed, and uneventful travel allowed them to settle into a routine. Three weeks later, and Enouim was grateful for any prattle that would put off break-fall practice. Currently, there was a disagreement over how to approach Levav. They had over a month to decide, but Enouim was hardly about to offer reasons for them to stop talking about it when it kept her on her horse and off the ground.

"We should send several of us in as a diversion, then Silas and I will sneak in separately, scoping out the city," Baird said to Canukke. "You can use your reputation and position to gain access to Levavin leadership and information on the stone itself. Silas and I will steal the stone and meet you outside."

Canukke shook his head. "The two of you shouldn't be alone. We can negotiate first, get the information in a straight-forward manner, and come up with a sad story to tug on their pitiful heartstrings. If that doesn't gain us more information, we can get close enough to threaten the lives of the monarchy and take it by force. I do agree with having a few of us free to roam the city, however. Levavin are unlikely to have all nine of us inside, and you will need an excuse to slink in until we give some sort of signal so as not to raise alarm prematurely."

"Why shouldn't we be alone?" Silas inquired, an edge to his voice. "We are the ones with the most updated information on the fortifications and weaknesses of the Levav fortress."

"I am the leader of this mission. Kalka'an has been good to us, excellent allies, and good fighters, but Gorgenbrild is the head of this venture. Some Kalka'aners tend to think they are greater and more capable than they are. Quarot spoke highly of you, so I am sure you are skilled, but I don't know you well enough yet to let you have control over the purpose of our mission."

"Silas was trusted with many missions in the past," Gabor said, sticking up for his new friend. "He knows what he is doing."

"I am happy for him. But even so, I know better than he does. We're doing this my way."

"We need to talk about this," Baird spoke up. "If we aren't working together, no plan will be effective."

"He's right," Vadik agreed. "So how do we choose?"

"*We* don't do anything," Canukke responded.

"Missions are effective because there are leaders who are in charge of making decisions when there is a disagreement," Pakel said.

Canukke nodded at Pakel. "I haven't seen Baird and Silas' skills with my own eyes, and the plans of a Kalka'aner are different from the plans of a Gorgenbrilder. The Ecyah Stone is for Gorgenbrild, and it will be Gorgenbrild that takes the stone. I was appointed the leader of this venture for a reason. I am the best."

Silas spoke up several more times to revisit the topic, but Canukke had apparently said all he believed he needed to, and devolved into sharing his daring exploits and credentials when questioned further. The bitterness between Canukke and the Kalka'an members showed up only a little later as Enouim rode behind them and overheard Silas mentioning to Baird that Canukke was "messing with his bracelet again. Surely a bracelet branding him as the greatest gift to earth."

Enouim noticed that Canukke was, in fact, running his fingers over engravings on a leather band around his wrist. Now that she thought about it, she'd seen him do this many times.

Several days later the group started out in the morning and had gotten about an hour through the day when Canukke suddenly stopped his horse. "Where is my leather wristband?"

"What do you mean? You never take it off," Oloren responded.

"I know." His face darkened and he turned toward Silas and Baird. "One of you took it."

"Whoa! Just because we are from Kalka'an, we stole from you?" Baird returned. "We don't steal pointless things. I have no reason for it."

"You're the only two with motive. Perhaps you are bitter about my rightful leadership or simply wish to anger me out of spite—an idea no one has taken lightly in quite some time, except perhaps naive Enouim. And she obviously lacks the competence for a successful theft. So that leaves you."

"Maybe you're not as smart as you think you are, and you lost it," Silas suggested.

"Is this important?" Kilith asked.

"Yes!" Canukke snarled. "It's ... well, it doesn't matter why it's important, but it is."

"Seems to me if it was that important, you would have done a better job holding onto it," Baird observed.

"How dare you? I know it was one of you, maybe both of you. The venture we are on is for the lives of our people. The Sumus have closed in, Gorgenbrild is likely under siege, and matters are steadily growing worse. If I don't feel comfortable with you in my space or with my belongings, how can I trust you as a comrade in arms?"

"Son of a zegrath, come now," Pakel reasoned. "Perhaps it was a prank. Whoever it was, produce it now and let's get on with it."

After a pause, Oloren added, "Go on, he's not going to rest until it's settled. He's right, we need to be able to trust each other. This is ludicrous."

Silas looked intently at Canukke. "Look, what do I know?

Maybe it fell off and you didn't notice. If someone *did* take it, however, it was so easy to take that you deserved to have it lifted.If you are as good as you say you are, and if the bracelet is stolen as you say it is, it will be no trouble at all for you to find and take it back."

Canukke pushed his horse forward, drawing his sword. Silas drew his just in time as Canukke swung at him, but Canukke slipped the blade past the block and nicked Silas on the neck with ease. Glaring at Silas and daring him to retaliate, Canukke snatched one of the bags off the back of Silas's horse. "I'll find it if I have to search every bag and body. No one toys with me."

Baird leaned over to Gabor and whispered, "Apparently they do."

"There is no humor in this," Gabor answered curtly. "The games of children, stirring up trouble. I smell immaturity and insecurity." He abruptly turned his horse and followed Canukke.

"Did you really take it?" Vadik asked Silas, hanging back.

Silas's face was hard as flint. "You're welcome to search if you like. You won't find it. In Kalka'an a successful theft either reveals a fool or highlights someone who deserves respect. Perhaps, if the bracelet isn't lost after all, today accomplished both."

"This isn't over," Oloren said sourly. "If it continues, he will not be satisfied with a scratch on your neck."

Canukke rode with Silas's bag and rifled through it as he went. It wasn't long before he declared it was time for a break, during which he pored over every pack Silas and Baird possessed. The group rested the horses and ate, while Pakel took the opportunity to practice break falls with Enouim. They started small, kneeling and falling forward facedown on the ground. Enouim was supposed to stop herself with her forearms, but only an instant before the rest of her hit the ground, distributing her weight and lessening the impact. She couldn't help throwing her arms out in front of her as soon as she felt the falling sensation, and she ended up repeatedly striking the ground with her elbows.

"How am I supposed to be able to do this from standing or from a horse if I can't even do it from here? My elbows are already scraped raw," she said.

"It's the fear of falling," Pakel said. "You need to accept that you are falling and lean into it."

At that moment, Canukke threw down Silas's pack in frustration. He had thoroughly examined the bags on the horses, watched to see that Silas did not return to the horse, and gone through the pack yet again. Approaching Silas with a knife, he growled, "Hand it over, or I strip your wrist of skin and make *that* my 'bracelet.'"

"Aren't you the most cunning, intelligent man in Gorgenbrild? But you are thrown into a tizzy by such a small thing."

"I do not know what Quarot saw in you, but it will not earn you any points here. I owe you nothing. Respect is earned by honor, of which you have none."

"In the cliffs, skill is respected," Baird countered. "This looks remarkably like a child throwing a tantrum ... not a mighty warrior."

"We're not in the cliffs! Gorgenbrild leads this mission, and it is Gorgenbrild's standards that prevail!"

Baird shook his head. "This mission is not solely for Gorgenbrild, or your people would not have involved ours. You do not hope to locate the Ecyah Stone or fight off the Sumus alone, or Bondeg wouldn't have elicited our help months ago. We have much to offer you. You would do well to honor our codes."

"And you would do well," Canukke retorted, "Not to test me. You have until morning to return the wristband to me. If you do not, I will exact my revenge with force according to my people's ways, in equal measure with the value I attribute to my stolen item."

11

The day passed and still no one came forward. Silas got several more nasty looks throughout the day, and they weren't all from Canukke. Night fell and the company stopped, settling in to sleep. Enouim lay down and closed her eyes, but sleep refused to come. Her mind was busy with the events of the day, with what would happen in the morning if Silas didn't return the wristband, and with why on earth it was so important to Canukke. And what would happen when they reached Levav, as Baird and Canukke still held very different ideas of how to approach the situation. Would there be more conflict before reaching their destination? Would Levav have the Ecyah Stone? What if they couldn't retrieve it?

She lay still and quiet while her mind whirled with questions and unpleasant possibilities. Still unable to sleep, she snapped her eyes open in frustration and registered a dark figure bent over Silas. Six feet tall. A stranger? Canukke? Alarmed and frightened, she watched, unmoving. Should she wake the others? If it was Canukke after all, he would hate her even more for disrupting whatever shady business he was into. At the same time, attacking Silas before morning would be cowardly and dishonorable. Enouim wasn't sure it was in Canukke's blood to be cowardly. At the very least, he would betray himself if he did so.

Just then the figure turned, and in the dimness she saw the outline of a beard. Baird? As her eyes adjusted to the darkness, Enouim realized that Baird was not hunched over Silas, he was rifling through Silas's pack. He pulled something out and studied it. The moonlight revealed Canukke's leather wristband in his hands.

Canukke had looked through the very same pack multiple times. Curious, Enouim slowly brought herself to her elbow for a better view. Baird turned toward the sound. Seeing Enouim, he smiled and put a hand to his lips, gesturing her silence. Noiselessly he crossed over several of his sleeping companions to Canukke's sleeping form. Enouim's eyes grew wide, but she said nothing. Baird drew out several leaves from his pocket, crushed them in his hands and held them up to Canukke's nose, then he fastened the wristband around Canukke's wrist where it belonged. Grinning at Enouim, Baird motioned her to be quiet once again as if they had just shared the most amusing of secrets, then he returned to his place and lay down. Minutes later Enouim heard the deep, steady breaths of blissful sleep coming from his dark shape on the ground.

Morning came, and Canukke said nothing about the sudden reappearance of the leather wristband on his arm. Enouim imagined it would be rather embarrassing for him to admit someone had been able to get so close to him without his knowledge. Canukke was a warrior through and through, and unlikely to be a heavy sleeper. He was rather smug toward

Silas, believing he had intimidated him into returning the bracelet, but kept quiet rather than bringing up exactly how it was returned.

They ate breakfast and began loading up for the day, Silas scowling at Baird. Clearly, he didn't approve and surmised that Baird must have been the culprit. But Silas was in a similar bind as Canukke. He must now either admit that Baird had outwitted them both in their sleep, or accept the story that he had surreptitiously returned the wristband with flair.

Enouim sidled up to Baird as he saddled his horse. "How?"

"Scars, what could you mean?" he said with mock surprise. His eyes gleamed with mischief.

"Oh, come now. You know I know, so out with it."

"No one is better than a Kalka'aner at hiding valuable items. Silas's bag has false bottoms and hidden compartments that Canukke didn't know how to look for. I happen to be extremely good at it."

"And the leaf?"

"You saw that too, did you? Good eye. Ethanine. The seeds of the berry will kill you in the most relaxing of ways, but a whiff of its crushed leaves will render even the strongest of men unconscious."

Enouim raised her eyebrows. "Huh."

"I told you, judge me by my actions. I just saved us unnecessary bloodshed and united the group so we are ready for Levav. Infiltrating a city is less efficient when not everyone has their limbs." He winked.

"Infiltrate? I thought the plan was to arrive out in the open, gain entry, and negotiate, and use force as a last resort," Enouim responded, eyes narrowing slightly.

A subtle shadow fell over Baird's face. "Yes, well, that's the plan. I only said *infiltrate* because of the sob story bit—and we will be taking information from them as we go. Hardly a plan if you ask me. Even if they are so gullible, or we can so easily prey on their emotions, we may not be able to truthfully extract all the information we need. A waste of precious time. But if the greatest warrior to ever live says we go in directly and then raise their defenses under their watchful eyes, so be it."

The plans for entering Levav were hammered out over the next several weeks. Enouim continued to practice hand-to-hand combat, knife throwing, and fighting with her dagger. Break falls remained the bane of her existence, and though she had improved somewhat, the scrapes and bruises she constantly wore were reminders of how far she still had to go. She saw the landscape change yet again, this time to dry grasses, and only a day out from Levav it transitioned to patches of green grass and trees dotting the plain.

Finally, the fortress city of Levav came into view. White stone walls rose before them with four turrets along the circular outer wall, and entire buildings built on top, showing off its depth. A large moat ran around the walled city, spanning anywhere from thirty to seventy feet across at any given point. The moat was supplied by a river that had been diverted toward the city from its run west into the ocean. Several outposts sat along its edge, supervising its journey into Levav. The tops of the towers and turrets within the city up rose above the walls in a vibrant display of a variety of surprising colors—blue, orange, red, purple. Silas and Baird informed them some of the turrets rose from a smaller tier wall acting as a second line of defense beyond the first, and this wall was thick enough for several buildings to be built onto it.

The party would be seen long before reaching the gates, another reason Canukke advocated stealth from the outset as an unrealistic strategy. The group would enter as far as possible as one unit, though probably only several representatives would be permitted an audience with the governing authorities. For Levav, that meant Baron Javen and Baroness Jenulia. The rest of the group would wait outside the gates with the horses, keeping their eyes and ears sharp and positioning themselves strategically to takedown or sneak past guards should the signal come.

Kilith didn't like the plan, preferring negotiation to any resort of violence in Levav, but he said little once the plan was set. Canukke added several pitiable details to their dilemma to "pluck the heartstrings" of the weak, emotionally driven Levavin. He was also prepared to take hostages or slit the throat of every authoritative individual right down the line until they got the information they needed if the baron and baroness were not cooperative. Baird rolled his eyes at Enouim and shared knowing looks with Silas, but both agreed to the plan.

As the nine individuals approached a bridge across the moat, large gates standing fifteen feet tall opened. Two mounted guards rode across to meet them while guards on the wall observed them closely.

"Afternoon ladies and gentlemen. We have not received word of your arrival, and I see no supplies for trade; please state your purpose."

"Our deepest apologies, but our visit is a matter of life and death borne of such urgency that we were unable to provide notice," Canukke answered. "We seek audience with the lord and lady of Levav regarding the imminent danger of the peoples of Gorgenbrild, Kalka'an, and indeed the blight sweeping through the mountains that may reach you as well. As you may have heard, a conglomerate of tribes called the

Sumus have banded together and cut us off from the rest of the world. We seek counsel from our friends in Levav."

Enouim leaned over to Baird seated next to her and whispered, "Do you think he really believes the word 'indeed' makes him sound more troubled and serious, or he just likes the way it sounds?"

Baird smirked but said nothing. Gabor shot her a death glare and she shrugged back at him.

"We have heard news of your predicament," the guard said. "What manner of assistance do you require?"

"We prefer to keep the details discreet," Kilith replied.

"Surely a true crisis is afoot for men of Gorgenbrild and Kalka'an to come to *us* for help. Please bear with us as we relay the message and await further instruction."

After about an hour, the gates opened again and the guards reappeared to inform them that all nine of them could enter through the first gate, but only four would progress past the second. Canukke gestured to them that he, Kilith, Oloren, and Silas would go in to negotiate while Enouim, Vadik, Baird, Gabor, and Pakel stayed behind. The group followed the guards across the bridge and through the first gate. On the other side they dismounted their horses, and Canukke, Kilith, Oloren, and Silas parted ways with the rest of the company, going into the heart of Levav on foot.

A forty-foot gap stood between the outer and inner wall, the space that Enouim and the other four now occupied. Green grass swayed in the breeze, in stark contrast to the yellows and browns of the plain over which they had just traveled. Several guards stood by the outer gate, and more watched them from the top of the walls above them. Guards led the horses through the second gate after Canukke, Kilith, Oloren, and Silas went through.

Clouds covered the sky like patchwork. Mostly white, they

reflected nearly as much light as the sun would itself. Enouim wondered what she would see if she could be in those clouds looking down. She wanted to see more of the city and hoped the rest of them would be allowed inside soon. For now, they waited.

Vadik stood, pacing impatiently. Gabor, Enouim, and Pakel sat in the grass, engulfed by their own thoughts. Enouim thumbed the scar on her collarbone; Pakel twirled his karambit in his hands, and Gabor plucked at the grass with his fingers. Baird leaned nonchalantly against the stone wall, unperturbed. Enouim wondered how much of life was spent waiting, depending on other people to do things. It was maddening, having no inkling of whether the next five minutes were the last bit or if the three hours that had gone by already were only the beginning. After four hours, they were told they would be allowed past the inner wall and given a more comfortable place to wait. Two guards introduced themselves as Banor and Kenan and escorted them through the second set of gates into Levav itself.

Enouim's first impression was of color—color everywhere. The buildings and houses were all painted in vibrant colors, yet still somehow seemed beckoning and soft to the eye. Many dwellings shared walls, creating a row. Small waterways wound throughout the city dotted with short bridges and light boats not much larger than a canoe. Enouim's eyes drifted over the happy colors and glittering water roads, and she felt a warmth sweep through her that put her at ease.

Vadik whistled. "Hordes, that's a sight, isn't it?"

"The feeling you have soaking up the city sights is the feeling we hope to create for guests and for each other inside our borders," Kenan said. "For us, it is love, trust, mutual respect, compassion, openness, and vulnerability that we desire to come naturally. For these things to thrive, and for honest, raw exchanges between souls, there must be safety. Thus, physical safety is a precursor to any mental or emotional safety. We take it very seriously."

"That's beautiful," Enouim said, almost without realizing she'd spoken. She loved the view, the vivacious colors, the lazily running water. The idea of using the boats sounded lovely in theory, but Enouim thought she would rather watch than ride in one. Water made her nervous. She ran her thumb over the scar on her collarbone and wondered if the old scars on the back of her neck would still burn with the touch of water. Since childhood, whenever she bathed or found herself in the rain for very long, she'd carefully covered them with watertight bandages.

"It is a privilege for outsiders to set their eyes on Levav. Unfortunately some do not come with pure intentions, and we have had to put up barriers. We will keep close to you while you are here, though in your case it could be that the baron and baroness themselves will clear you. Trust breaks down all barriers with time. We hope you do not hold our protective procedures against us." Kenan smiled apologetically as they walked further into the city and down a gently sloping rocky path.

"It is said that the greatest protection Levav possesses is the Ecyah Stone," Baird prodded, as Banor and Kenan gestured toward two small boats.

Vadik and Gabor stepped lightly into the first, and Baird hopped into the back of the second. Enouim clung to Pakel, eyes wide as she stared at the water. Pakel looked at her curiously, and she steeled herself. Taking a deep breath, she allowed him to take her hand and gently help her into one.

Kenan stepped into the boat with Vadik and Gabor, and Banor took the second boat with Baird, Enouim, and Pakel. Both guards picked up long poles and shoved off from shore at an easy pace.

Banor arched an eyebrow. "The Eh'yeh Stone is much more than protection. It is life. It is the line in the sand between good and evil; it divides the soul and is not for the faint of heart. It is not for the greedy, either. I wonder at your interest in it."

Enouim, noting the difference in pronunciation, wondered if all Levav preferred this phonetic version of the name.

"It is a legend in Gorgenbrild that some do not even believe in," Baird responded easily. "We are divided as to the truth of the matter and placed bets. Is it real?"

"As real as you or I," Banor replied. "Perhaps more so."

"The legend of the stone has fascinated me since childhood," Enouim said. "I have heard of the power of the stone, like a great force moving in whoever holds it and granting victory. But what is this about dividing the soul? How can a soul be divided?"

"I wouldn't touch a thing that could split my soul in two!" Pakel exclaimed. "Surely you mean that the soul is tested by such power, and that by it one may see the real nature of a man."

"The genuine nature of a person is certainly illuminated by it, tested by it," Kenan answered. "The soul is divided against itself upon contact with the stone, as if the intentions of mind and heart were put on trial and waging war within one's chest. We are utterly exposed before it, ruled by it, and yet it is good to know oneself. Without it, we imitate its lessons as best we can and prioritize self-awareness. For out of the mind and heart come all manner of deceitfulness and darkness, and we protect ourselves and each other by recognizing when that happens."

"Zegrath's teeth, that's terrifying," Gabor said. "It sounds like you have personal experience with the Ecyah Stone. But now you say you are without it—did you have it and lose it?"

"Perhaps I speak too much for our guests," Kenan hedged, and transitioned into sharing information about the houses, the flowers, and the benefits of life in Levav within its carefully crafted structure of love and rules. Love *of* rules, it sounded to Enouim, after hearing that Levavin were not to kill, steal, lie, or even think about doing such things. They were expected to monitor motives behind every action, and often kept daily journals of mental wrongdoings to remember what to work on within themselves. Still, the Levavin seemed truly caring toward persons of any lifestyle. It was a strange mixture, and Kenan told stories of people receiving justice but also compassion, even after despicable deeds.

Approaching a small building with vertical slats for windows, Banor and Kenan apologized that this was where they would be staying for the next couple of hours but assured them of good food and comfortable bedding. Every effort would be made to bring them to the rest of their company as soon as possible. They passed under a low bridge, ducking their heads as they continued underneath it and around a bend. And that was when it all went wrong.

It took only a moment for the guards to realize that one of the party was missing.

"Hey! Where is the bearded one?" Banor demanded.

Enouim glanced about and saw Pakel in front of her—as he had been the whole time—and Vadik and Gabor with the guard Kenan. Baird, who had been sitting behind her, was nowhere to be seen. Banor and Kenan poled the boats to the water's edge and Kenan sent a loud, clear whistling signal to a nearby tower. A flurry of motion answered, and two guards ran from the tower.

Enouim's heart lurched into her throat as she spied Baird

making his getaway at full-tilt, clothes dripping wet. The kindly demeanor in Kenan and Banor's faces vanished. Leaping onto land, they ordered Enouim, Pakel, Vadik, and Gabor up onto the bank after them. The two guards grabbed onto the arms of their guests and began dragging them toward the small building to which they'd been headed.

"We know nothing about this!" Pakel yelled. "His actions have no part with us!"

"Oh, really?" Banor responded. "You all seemed pretty friendly a moment ago!"

Vadik sprinted after Baird, and Kenan let go of Enouim to tackle Vadik to the ground. "I can bring him back!" Vadik insisted, pulling his arm free. Pakel knocked Banor backward to go to Vadik's aid, calling out for Vadik to calm down and listen to reason.

Gabor and Enouim stood awkwardly to one side. Enouim couldn't imagine that getting further involved would help their case. Kenan was on top of Vadik, yelling, "Cooperate or be found guilty of espionage!" Five more guards from the tower ran toward them.

"Unhand me!" Vadik grunted. "You first!"

"Stop fighting," Gabor yelled. "We are on the same side!"

Pakel pulled Kenan off Vadik and stood between them. "We are here as friends!"

Just then the first of the guards reached them and swung a saber toward Vadik. Instincts kicked into high gear, Vadik burst in, pulling the guard toward him, stripping him of his weapon, and redirecting the man's momentum straight into the waterway. Kenan flew at him, but Vadik's hands and feet danced like lightning. Making quick work of him, Vadik thrust the saber into the man's side and pushed him away.

Alarmed, one of the tower guards ran to Kenan's side while Banor drew his blade and leaped for Vadik. Pakel jumped in front of his friend, throwing his left hand out to protect and move Vadik behind him. Pakel glanced back to check on Vadik, but a glance was all it took. Banor struck him at the base of the skull with the butt of his saber and Pakel crumpled. Enouim screamed.

12

Enouim ran to catch Pakel as he fell. She caught his head in her lap, and her fingers shook as she touched his face and watched his chest for movement. Nothing. Gabor restrained Banor in a single smooth motion, and the guard hovering over Kenan tore off the corner of his tunic to press into the wound, his hands covered in blood.

Vadik gaped at the scene as the reality of what had just happened sunk in. Several guards took hold of him, but he hardly seemed to notice. One of the newly arrived guards knelt by Pakel and began to examine his head and neck, but he wasn't moving. Everything had happened so fast. Enouim looked away, only to find Kenan's glazed eyes staring up at her. Accusing her for her people's brutal instincts. Dead.

They were going to take her. She was probably going to be thrown into some windowless pit and forgotten. Canukke never wanted her here anyway. No! She had to find Baird.

Enouim gently slipped out from under Pakel's head and stepped back. She was the lowest of priorities. The guards were consumed with tending to Kenan and Pakel, pulling

Gabor off Banor, and gaining control over Vadik. For a moment Vadik's eyes met Enouim's. Emotions swirled there: fear, desperation, sadness, pain. He looked ... lost. Enouim felt torn in that moment, but there was nothing she could do for him here. She turned and ran.

One of the guards noticed her escape and bore down on her from behind. Enouim's legs found a rhythm just as the guard lunged to take her down, and she dodged it. The guard regained his balance, grabbed her braid, and yanked her backward. He released her braid to hook his arm around her throat from behind and she instinctively gripped his arm with both hands. As she struggled, her right foot found itself on the outside of his. Enouim dropped her center and rolled him over her shoulder so that he crashed to the ground at her feet. She moved to flee but stumbled and landed her knee on his ankle, then she bolted.

Past rows of houses and waterways along the edge of Levav, she ran, until she thought her muscles would burst, then she pulled up behind a building at the edge of the fortress to catch her breath. She looked up at a stone building on top of the second wall. Maybe if she could get a better view of the city, she could see Baird. A six-foot locked gate blocked off winding steps leading up to the building, but Enouim found just enough footholds on the rock wall and gate to pull herself up and over.

She raced up the stairs as thoughts of Pakel assaulted her mind. Pakel blinking back at her from his horse when she first poked her head out as a stowaway in the supply wagon. Pakel listening to her troubles; Pakel patiently teaching her how to fight. Pakel helping her into the boat just that morning, confused by her fear but accepting. Pakel putting himself in the path of a knife to protect his friend. Enouim funneled all her energy into her legs. Her feet pounded the cold stone steps, hot tears trailing down her face, and she hardly noticed her surroundings until she ran straight into something solid. She rocked backward and something caught her from falling, then let her go.

Startled, she looked up to see dark, gentle eyes set in a kind face. The man was perhaps late thirties, bald with a well-kept goatee and warm, golden-brown skin. He wore a white tunic with grayish-beige robes and a quietly surprised expression.

"Whoa! I'm sorry, we seem to have collided. Are you okay?" The man looked her over and then peered down the stairs behind her. "What's happened?"

Met with gracious caring and oddly comforted by the man's peaceful presence, Enouim felt fresh tears escape. He searched her eyes, not alarmed, but attentive. She took a ragged breath. "I didn't do anything wrong; you have to believe me. It's all a big misunderstanding. My friend is hurt, maybe dead, another friend is missing, and I'm scared they're going to take me away from them ..."

The man swept his hand toward several small cushions arranged on the stone some ten feet further. The top of the wall where she found herself was twenty feet across and extended in both directions, but a solid locked gate to one side separated that side of the wall from this side. It felt isolated from the guards up here.

"Goodness, you've had quite a day," the man said. "Are you running *from* something or *to* something?"

"Um ..." Enouim paused to consider the question. "I guess both? There were guards that should be looking for me by now. And ... I was trying to find Baird."

"I see. Your missing friend. Well, here in Levav, sharing a fear with a stranger like you did with me is a sign of strength and character. I would say that starts you off on the right foot.

Let's slow down a second and maybe you can tell me what exactly is going on."

Though part of her still wondered if he was safe, her options were slim. She was desperate for the solace of a sympathetic ear. Besides, her gut said he meant well. "I'm not from here," Enouim began, the man nodding with her. Clearly this was no surprise. "I'm here with a group from Gorgenbrild, well mostly Gorgenbrild, and four of them went to meet with the baron and baroness to get help for our mission, and the rest of us were waiting and then Baird ran off, and the guards started to grab us, and Vadik lost it, and then the guards lost it, and then Pakel ..." In the span of a moment, her brain cycled through what felt like a hundred different priorities for what to do next. Suddenly she looked up and said, "We have to find Baird! He is in trouble, and caused more trouble than he knows. We have to find him before it gets worse."

"What might he be looking for?"

"He ... looking for?" Enouim paused. Of course. Kalka'an had investigated to see what the layout of Levav was and to find out whether they were in possession of the Ecyah Stone. They learned the lay of the land but not whether the stone was with Levav. "I'm not sure I'm supposed to say, but I think he is looking for ... a weapon. Not to hurt anyone here though. Just to save our people back in Gorgenbrild."

"Ah. The Eh'yeh Stone."

A clamoring noise came from below and the man nodded and motioned her to follow him into a nearly empty stone hall with tall windows on either side. There was a table with books laid out on it, and nothing else but a few floor cushions near the windows. They passed to the other side of the hall and out again through the doors, the man picking up a plain wooden staff on his way out.

As they stepped out again, high above the city, she couldn't help but notice the beautiful view. She must have climbed more steps than she thought. From here Enouim could see the outer wall on one side with the landscape sprawling out beyond it, and the colorful city and sparkling water on the other. She saw the building with vertical slat windows, but in the place she'd last seen her companions only matted blood-stained grass remained. They were gone.

Enouim followed the man's lead in ignoring the clamoring noise as it dwindled behind them, but a new sound came to their ears. This one was much more subtle, like a light tapping. The man put a finger to his lips and walked, almost floated, to the edge of the wall. He peered down and waved her over.

Curious, Enouim walked over and saw a small landing jutting out from the wall about fifteen feet away. On it stood Baird, dressed like a guard, with one foot on the landing and one foot placed in a foothold in the rocky wall. No stairs continued down to the ground from there, only ones leading from the top of the wall down to the door. Enouim noticed several landings like this along the wall, but Baird stood in front of an inconspicuous door also made of stone and cut into the rocky slab, practically imperceptible as it fit into the wall. He'd wedged himself into the wall as much as possible and was tapping lightly against the stone with the butt of a knife.

The man with Enouim walked down several steps , but Enouim stayed where she was and observed from above. The man spoke calmly. "Need a hand?"

Baird turned his head. "No, thank you. I'm almost there." He put his ear to the rock and tapped several more times.

"Are you sure? You've been working for a while, and that's not the only safety measure in place. You might hurt yourself."

Baird looked at the man quizzically. "I know. What, no guards? No raising the alarm?"

"I don't think that will be necessary, though I am sure they are all frantic by now. Why add fuel to the frenzy? I quite doubt you will find what you are looking for beyond that door."

"Is that so?" Baird made a last *tap* of finality and jumped as the door swung open. He grasped the top of it and swung his feet around, landing where the door itself had been an instant before. "If it were anywhere, I would say this is a pretty good bet."

"Definitely a good bet! Unfortunately, the Eh'yeh Stone has not resided in Levav for quite some time now."

"What do you know of it?" Baird asked, turning from his task and taking in the stranger more thoroughly.

"More than most, less than few, and regrettably not its location."

Enouim wasn't sure what to make of the cavalier exchange. She leaned forward over the wall, coming into his line of sight. "Baird! Glintenon, what are you doing? Pakel might be dead! A Levavin guard is dead! They have Gabor and Vadik!"

Enouim watched the blood drain from Baird's face and for a moment she was looking at Vadik's lost, childlike eyes. "Dead?"

A tug on her heart told her this news was enough to send Baird reeling, but she wasn't finished. Her chest tightened and her voice ticked up a notch. "You killed him. You killed them both. And for what? If you're so brilliant, show me the magnificent result of your genius scheme! Somehow it was all part of the plan, right? Did the plan involve bringing people back from the dead? Did it involve betraying us all?"

Baird looked at her blankly for a moment, then emotion seeped back into his face as if in slow motion. "No! This isn't my fault! How did this happen? How could they have been so stupid to let it go so far? At worst they would be held and questioned! Levavin do not kill lightly! This ... this is not my fault!"

In the space of a minute, the mischievous, quick-witted Baird was replaced by a terrified little boy desperately fighting off blame—for something he was knew belonged on his own shoulders. She saw his fear, his pain, his good intentions, and his guilt-stricken face pried compassion from her stiff, unforgiving hands. Enouim clutched at her anger to keep it alive a little longer. She wasn't ready to let it go. If she released her anger, she would be faced with the emotion underneath and melt into a puddle then and there.

She looked at Baird darkly, examining him for any hint of falsehood in his demeanor, but saw none. From under her glaring lashes, she felt the anger within her dim. Seeing him as that little boy, only trying to prove himself, only trying to be the hero, and the plan turning horribly awry ... she saw real regret, raw sorrow, ruthless finality. The remaining anger inside Enouim mingled with fear and anxiety and hung in the air before sadness and exhaustion overtook them, washing over her in a wave. The tightness in her weary muscles gave way and her shoulders sagged forward.

Sapped of all energy, Enouim herself was a lost little girl, looking at the lost boy. She wanted to cry, to crawl in a dark, isolated hole, to be comforted, to apologize, to scream. She wanted to say something cutting and evil, and she wanted to offer soft words of healing. All she could muster through the lump in her throat was a low whimper.

Guards poured into the scene below, and the mysterious man in robes calmly held up his hand. Baird still stood in the doorway of the vault halfway up the wall, frozen. Raising his voice to reach the guards, the man said, "I will accompany the gentleman and the lady to the main hall, and we will sort out this matter together. It seems a tragic misunderstanding may have taken place. I am sure Baird will be more than willing to come peacefully."

With that the mysterious man turned and walked back up the steps. The guards on the ground below hesitantly lowered their weapons. Enouim turned in a daze and ascended the steps ahead of him back to the top of the wall, noticing for the first time that several guards had appeared there as well. Seeing no practical escape, Baird made his way up to the landing and the staircase, following silently.

The robed man led the way, and Enouim and Baird trailed him closely, with only their own footsteps and the light tapping of the man's staff reaching their ears. The guards at the top of the wall closed in around them as they went. He led them back through the hall, out the other side, through the gate, and along the wall for quite some time. Eventually they went down a staircase to ground level and wound through the city, first on foot and then in boats. The guards produced ropes to bind their hands, but the robed man insisted it was not necessary, and the guards acquiesced.

After settling into a boat, the man turned to Baird and Enouim. "I'm afraid I haven't introduced myself. I prefer to know who I am dealing with and for you to know it too. Now seems as good a time as any to remedy the situation. My name is Ruakh, which means breath, spirit, wind. I am blessed to have received such a name. Most of my time is spent in meditation on the wall, welcoming the stunning views of nature and taking in everything around me. I serve as a protector of Levav, a teacher of The Way of the Stone, and a guardian of what we hold most dear—whether that be physical artifacts or, more importantly, the ideals on which Levav is founded."

"Enouim," she said, introducing herself in a word. Her

mind swirled with the events of the day and what unknowns lay ahead. A multitude of dark possibilities threatened to swallow her. She was grateful for Ruakh's soothing presence, though confused by what he shared about himself. What was The Way of the Stone? The Ecyah Stone was a weapon, wasn't it? Although, Levav clearly didn't see the stone the same way Gorgenbrild did. Kenan had said as much when they first arrived. She wondered how good a protector Ruakh could be if he spent most of his time meditating.

"Enouim. I like that," Ruakh said slowly, nodding. He seemed to sense her reticence and was easily accepting of it, allowing them to drift back into their own minds once again.

The group disembarked at a tall building near the center of the city. Enouim, Baird, Ruakh, and two guards approached beautiful, ornate ivory-like doors, rounded at the tops and gilded with gold that appeared nearly liquid. It swirled through the ivory grains in a way that begged to be explored by touch. Afraid to do anything wrong, Enouim clasped her hands behind her back, letting her gaze linger on the artistry for as long as she could.

Enouim had never seen anything like the long halls on sleek floors, or the fountains and lounges where people sat reading, quietly talking together, or shooting the newcomers questioning looks as they passed. Ruakh spoke softly to someone at the end of one of the halls, and they passed through another set of delicately carved double doors. Ruakh ushered them into a room with cushioned chairs situated in a circle. Oloren and Kilith sat in two, and Silas and Canukke stood in front of them. Five Levavin strangers were also seated, including a man and a woman clothed in colorful garments who sat beside one another, holding the attention of the circle, relaxed but intent.

Chaos broke out when Enouim and Baird entered. Yelling

filled the air, and Enouim could only pick out snatches of what was said.

Canukke let out a stream of curses before screaming at Baird, "You filthy wretch! What have you done!"

Oloren jumped to her feet. "Idiots! Quarot will have your heads for this! If a hair on their heads are harmed, I'll kill you myself! If Pakel ..."

Baird and Silas made eye contact, both men's faces lined with worry. Canukke pushed Baird as he let loose another stream of vulgarities.

Baird's eyes blazed with fire. "Mark me forever! *Me?* You're a fool! I was peaceful!"

"Friend of Kalka'an indeed! Here are your true colors!" Silas spat in Canukke's face, and Canukke decked him across the jaw.

Enouim felt like she was in a fog. Words and more words filled the air, but none of it mattered. Blame flew from one mouth to another. Anger, frustration, confusion, pain. She took in the tones and the facial expressions more than the words themselves. Half of what was said now would surely later need to be apologized for or silently regretted.

The man Enouim assumed was Baron Javen leaned forward and said in a loud, firm voice, "Enough! Eviscerate each other on your own time. Something terrible has happened, and blood has been shed. Our hearts bleed for our own man, and go out to you as well for the injury or death of yours, whatever the outcome may be. Rest assured we will get to the bottom of this, and none of you will leave until our questions are satisfied."

13

I t took three weeks for the Levavin to settle the matter and determine a course of action. Vadik and Gabor were returned, and they were all kept in comfortable quarters, though under guard and not permitted outside. Everyone was searched, weapons were removed, and they were given clean Levavin clothing to wear.

Pakel had lasted nearly an hour before succumbing to his injuries, and when they found out, a fog fell over the group, and time slowed. Vadik stared into space and sometimes did not respond to someone until they had tried two or three times to get his attention. Other times he seemed almost as though nothing had happened, and the two sides of him seemed to come and go. Pakel's death impacted everyone in the company, but it hit Oloren particularly hard, as she had known Pakel the longest.

Within two days of searching the group for weapons, guards had discovered several small devices near the gates of both outer and inner walls. Silas and Baird had placed one underneath each gate, and the devices could be triggered to expand from beneath the heavy door to jimmy it open without a key. In addition, several subtle footholds and possible anchors for ropes had been attached to the walls. Silas and Baird had clearly had their own ideas for an emergency exit.

The baron, baroness, and officials determined that Baird and Silas acted alone, without the knowledge or approval of anyone else in the group. Seeing Baird's broken spirit in the aftermath, Ruakh spoke on his behalf that, though his methods were wrong, his intentions were to protect a people, and it was acceptable practice in Baird's social context. This did not vindicate him of his deceptions, for he had still attempted robbery of the vault, and his actions had brought about the deaths of Kenan and Pakel. The baron and baroness would be directing a complaint to the king and queen of Kalka'an to address the breach. However, it was decided that Baird would be free to continue with the mission under Canukke's watch as a sign of good faith.

Silas, on the other hand, was not so lucky. The eight of them were scattered about in the quarters they had been allotted, absorbed in their own thoughts, when a door opened and six guards filed in. "Pardon for the intrusion," one began, "but we are here for Silas Detorum of Kalka'an." The guard nodded at Silas. "You need to come with us."

"For what purpose?" Baird demanded.

"An investigation has been opened into this man's conduct within Levav. He is summoned for questioning regarding what manner of darkness he has brought into our bright city." The other five guards surrounded Silas.

"You confiscated all the items he had with him, and the men of Kalka'an were returned to us in good faith," Canukke said firmly. "I will speak with the baron and baroness before allowing this man to be taken from our number." Canukke had been giving Baird and Silas the cold shoulder, but they were still under his care.

"It is not your right to demand audience about a Levavin concern," responded the lead guard. "However, we respect your interest in the fate of one of your own. Silas must be brought with us immediately, but you may accompany us, and we will see that you speak with the baroness."

Canukke left the group to follow Silas, and the seven remaining exchanged questioning. "What was that about?" Oloren asked.

"Silas was on the investigative mission a few months back to determine whether or not Levav had the stone, and to identify the fortress's weaknesses," Baird said. "I wonder if it has to do with that. If it were because he is a Kalka'aner, or because of what happened with Kenan and Pakel, I would have been taken too."

"It seems they trust you more than they trust Silas, and are tempered by your evident remorse," Kilith answered. "There is more here than we are privy to. We will know more when Canukke returns."

Canukke rejoined them shortly, and shared what he'd learned. Baird filled in any gaps of which he was aware, and together the group pieced together a general idea of what had happened. Silas and Baird had both entered Levav and left devices behind. Silas had gone ahead into the heart of Levav with Canukke, Kilith, and Oloren, and they had been watched so closely that his original plan to slip away and meet up with Baird was no longer possible. Silas had told the guards that as a sign of respect it was Kalka'an custom to wash hands with lavender before meeting royalty or heads of state, and that the practice removed blood and toil from the road so that a ruler might be greeted without symbolically getting their hands dirty—showing that Kalka'an do not expect anyone else to solve their own problems, and did not wish to bring troubles upon another people.

"But the story was a lie," Canukke explained. "Silas wanted an excuse for privacy, and set a colored cloth out the window to signal Baird. Did I miss anything?"

Baird shook his head solemnly. "No, you have it. The signal told me Silas was unable to get away and meet me as he had planned, and if either of us were to get to the vault in the wall to look for the stone, it would be me—going alone. When I saw the cloth I knew it was now or never, so I clung to the bridge as our boat passed under it and made a break for it. Silas was making me nervous. He was late."

"That's not all," Canukke said. "Silas was part of the mission to scout out Levav over the past six months to discover whether Levav was in possession of the stone and, if so, where it might be held. That is how you two knew about the vault, I guess."

"Yes. So they're holding that against him as well, as I feared. What will they do with him?"

"They wouldn't say. They questioned Silas and determined to deal with him their own way. I wasn't told what that way would be, but it was implied he will be held here at least until Kalka'an is contacted. Silas may be an assurance of Kalka'an's compliance, or they may keep him to make their point. Levavin are private people, and do not take it lightly when their privacy or security are trifled with."

The Levavin refused to speak further about Silas, but they were quite interested in the Ecyah mission itself. Canukke shared more details of their quest and their interest in the stone to save Gorgenbrild, and Baron Javen and Baroness Jenulia assured them Levav was not in possession of the stone. The Ecyah Stone had indeed been with Levav after the First Morthed War, and remained for two hundred and fifty years, but had departed from Levav roughly one-hundred-and-seventy years before the current day.

To Levav, the Ecyah Stone, or Eh'yeh Stone as they called it, was far more than a powerful weapon. It was somehow a standard for living, a lifestyle, perhaps even object of spiritual worship as best as Enouim could tell. The people held it in high regard, and kept its legacy alive in Levav by their regulations for how to live, by the love they had for each other, and by the historians and guardians of the stone. Ruakh was one of these guardians, a warrior monk of sorts.

As it turned out, the baron and baroness were invested in the search for the stone themselves, and they suggested a collaboration where they would replenish the company's supplies and share the information they had gathered on the stone's whereabouts in exchange for Canukke's taking Levavin representatives along. The baron and baroness were confident the Ecyah mission would fail without their help and suggested an alliance. Canukke would still lead the mission, and after some discussion, the group agreed to the terms. Ruakh volunteered to go, much to the baron and baroness' delight, and was officially added to the team.

Levavin leadership also wanted a historian along. The most highly respected historian of the Ecyah Stone was a man named Len Mandon, but unfortunately Len had fallen ill and was not well enough to travel. Baron suggested Len's daughter who could go in his stead, a young woman who had applied herself to her father's studies and was nearly as acquainted with the knowledge and legends of the stone as her father. Kilith suggested they promptly invite her to join them, but Baroness Jenulia insisted on going personally to Len's daughter, Mereámé Mandon, and requesting her participation one on one. Enouim got the feeling Mereámé might take some convincing.

The following day the members of the Ecyah mission assembled in a circle as before with Baron Javen, Baroness

Jenulia, and three other officials. They had received word that Malum Khoron-khelek had heard of the mission and sent tribesmen to enlist help in impeding their progress. Most of the nomads surrounding Levav were on good terms with the Levavin and would be of assistance if Levav requested it, but others would likely sell their services to the highest bidder.

Between the time spent in Kalka'an and the three weeks in Levav, the head start the group had begun with was ebbing away. In the meantime, Gorgenbrild had been totally choked off from the rest of the world by the Khoron-khelek's Sumus, and he had demanded enormous tribute be paid for the honor of being absorbed into his empire and protected from him. Resources were dwindling and their circumstances were becoming increasingly desperate.

The baroness had spoken with Mereámé the previous day and she had been considering the proposal, but upon receiving word of how time-sensitive the matter was, she was summoned posthaste and would be joining them any minute. Canukke was listing exploits to persuade Levav to keep the details of their mission as quiet as possible.

"Torture, ha! They didn't know the meaning of the word. Secrets in need of keeping are in no safer vault than with me," he said. "If I had dispelled the information I had too early, I never would have uncovered the betrayal in time. A weasel for Morthed was all he was. That might have been three years ago, but ears and eyes remain everywhere, and this time Morthed isn't the only threat. Khoron-khelek is a plague that must be wiped out, and we don't know who else we can trust."

The doors opened and a young woman entered. Close to Enouim's height, she had olive skin, long features, and beautiful dark eyes beneath thick lashes. She wore a flowing deep purple garment, fitted at the top and flowing seamlessly into wide trousers so that at first glance it looked like a long dress.

Sandals kicked up the hem as she walked, at once effortless and soft—out of place among the warriors. She gave a nervous smile and looked about uncomfortably.

"Welcome, Mereámé," Jenulia said warmly.

"Thank you!" Mereámé made eye contact with Jenulia, and her entire face and demeanor lit up. "Has something changed?" Enouim thought her voice was unhurried and pensive, emulating the experience one has hearing a flight of doves lift off from the earth.

"Yes and no." Javen sighed with a hand to his forehead. "The enterprise has not, but the timeline has. It seems we may not have the luxury of time we thought we had. Please, be seated, and meet your companions."

Canukke introduced himself quickly, then Kilith, Gabor, Oloren, Enouim, Vadik, and Baird. "From Kalka'an?" she asked, glancing at Jenulia.

"Yes," Jenulia answered for him, "But not that one."

Mereámé nodded and looked up at Ruakh. "I'm glad to see you here."

"Good to see you again, Mereámé," he responded with a smile. "We are grateful for your presence!"

"My father would be better fit for this mission than I," Mereámé said. "And there are more historians. Are we sure ..."

"No one is better suited for this than you," Javen said. "Len Mandon is the best of the best, and you are most certainly your father's daughter. We would not ask if it were not urgent."

Mereámé dipped her head and spoke slowly. "I fear leaving Levav at a time like this, with my father in his condition. If he had not insisted, I would have remained with him, but I admit it would fulfill a dream of both my father's and my own if we succeeded. Finding and restoring the Eh'yeh Stone would heal our lands and refresh our souls. It is for this reason that I put my comforts aside, turning instead to the yearning in my heart after the Eh'yeh Stone."

"Your strength is our strength," responded Ruakh, dipping his head in respect.

The other Levavin officials echoed, "Your strength is our strength."

"Thank you," Enouim said to Mereámé. "That must be hard."

"We should focus on the going, then," Canukke said, eager to return the subject to his own purposes. "As you have heard, I am more than competent to lead us beyond the river, and would hope to get a week behind us before the nomads of the region are alerted to our purpose. I have led perilous pursuits all over the mountains, and have traveled to the heart of Morthed. Neither man nor beast has yet hindered our progress, and it would be best to keep our intentions well concealed."

Enouim spoke up again. "If something must be said, perhaps a general approval of our mission, while omitting the nature of it, would do."

"That we can manage, I believe," Javen responded, nodding thoughtfully. "At least for a time. Know that we will have eyes and ears waiting and watching to hear word of you as you continue your work, but we will be discreet and certainly not pass along more than we deem necessary. Not all nomads are the same, and there are some more loyal than others."

"Excellent." Kilith slapped his hands on his knees. "Now, I imagine we should leave at once. Might our horses be readied and packed while we finish here?"

"Yes," Jenulia answered, "it is being done as we speak."

Mereámé blinked. "Today?"

"Within the hour, I should hope," Oloren said. "Without

knowing who has been commissioned to come after us, and with the length of our stay already, time is of the essence. Our presence will not have gone unnoticed."

Canukke nodded. "Indeed, it is."

Enouim and Baird made eye contact and tried not to smile. *Indeed,* Baird subtly mouthed.

Enouim had remained upset with Baird for some time, but after the incident, they grieved together, and Enouim had seen raw emotion she knew could not be faked. His intention had been to prove his mettle as a leader and strategist. The plan had gone horribly wrong, and the crushing consequences of his actions weighed heavily on Baird. He had been the picture of cooperation and respectfulness ever since, though certainly a downtrodden version. She knew what he did was wrong, but he was hurting as deeply as the rest of them. Enouim was grateful to see a bit of his spunk returning.

"It is decided, then," Jenulia said, rising. "We will see to it that your provisions are well stocked for the sparse lands you venture through next, and we will reach out to our nomadic friends with a general blessing. They are not always friendly with strangers. Your horses will be ready for you, and we will leave you to gather your things."

14

V adik was practically giddy as the guards returned their weapons. "I was dreaming of a beautiful companion last night," he said. "She was slender, perfectly formed, always at my side. And now she is again!" He hoisted his spear in the air triumphantly.

Oloren raised an eyebrow. "You dreamed of a companion constantly trying to leave you as quickly as possible? Sounds about right!"

"She always comes back to me one way or another." He winked. "They always do."

"I suppose we can't all have standards." Baird laughed.

Kilith rolled his eyes. "Careful with that thing. No need to cause any more trouble before we leave."

Ruakh traveled with only his staff, a small bag, and the clothes on his back. Mereámé changed into travel clothes, bid her father farewell, and apologized profusely for the time it took for her to get to the stables with her pack. Enouim breathed in the scent of leather and horses, and sighed as a soft breeze comforted her grieving soul.

Nine had entered, and nine now departed, but two had

been lost. An odd mix of emotions hung in the air like a dank mist. Relief to be back on the road mingled with the freshness that two new members brought to the team, almost as if the slate had been wiped clean to begin again. And yet the slate still retained memory of what had once been written there and could not shake the emptiness Pakel and Silas left behind.

The group crossed the bridge to the other side of the moat, and Oloren slid off her horse. She took Pakel's karambit off her belt, which she had demanded after his passing, and marked the ground with it. Along with her Gorgenbrilder companions, Enouim silently slipped off her horse, and each of them cut off a shaving off their belt and dropped it into the symbol Oloren had drawn into the earth.

"What are they doing?" Enouim heard Mereámé ask Ruakh from behind them.

"It is the tradition of Gorgenbrilders honoring their fallen far from home," he answered in a hushed tone. "The belt holds necessary items of protection, holding close to the warrior all that is dear, always bound to the body. A comrade in arms is the greatest form of protection a warrior can have, and no accessory can outweigh him. The brother whose blood was spilled in honor and sacrifice is dearer than any personal item, and the loss is to be bound to the mind forever."

Oloren was first to complete the gesture, and then Vadik, following suit with tears running unbidden down his face. He made valiant efforts to return his face to the stoic expressions of his friends, with only limited success. Kilith, Canukke, Enouim, and Gabor put their shavings in as well, and a heaviness fell on Enouim's shoulders as she realized this was the first shaving off her belt and may very well not be her last.

Baird observed closely, and after those from Pakel's own people had honored him, he dismounted, cut off a sliver of his own belt, placed it among the others, and touched his right arm to the tattoo of his Kalka'an rank and accomplishments. He moved his hand from his left arm to the shavings on the ground, denoting the elevation of rank to the deceased as was the custom of Kalka'an toward their fallen. Mereámé looked questioningly at Ruakh, who nodded at her as both reached to slice off a shaving from their belts in solidarity with their new cohorts.

A tangible change fell over the company as they rode out. Sacrifice and death for the cause had risen from a safe, theoretical bravery far from the fragile unknown of tomorrow to something that hovered over the future like an inevitable gray cloud just waiting to rain. A loud twig snapped under Inferno's hooves making Enouim jump as the real threat of danger began to manifest in the shadows.

Despite the emotional climate, the weather was fair and the sky a deep blue with clouds of different shapes stretched across the horizon. In one direction wispy cirrus clouds reached toward an uncertain future with blissful ignorance, and in the other, a strangely regular pattern of small white marks seemed to track their progress with mathematical footsteps. Greenery thinned into yellow grasses with occasional trees dotting the plain ahead.

Canukke's irritable, brooding mood ebbed when Oloren came to ride beside him at the head of the party. Vadik and Baird rode together in pensive, painful silence and seemed to have bonded through the tremendous guilt they each carried over Pakel. Kilith had called Gabor up with him and to speak about the events of Levav and the road ahead, taking Gabor under his wing. Enouim was left to ride with the newcomers, Ruakh and Mereámé.

Morning faded into afternoon, and as the day progressed, Enouim decided she could stay in her head no longer. "Beautiful horse," she said to Ruakh, who rode a deep bay mare with a shiny coat and a peaceful demeanor that seemed comparable to his own personality.

"Thank you," Ruakh responded, almost with surprise as she brought him from his thoughts. "Her name is Sky. When I first encountered her, she was terribly distrustful toward everyone. You wouldn't believe it now, but she has more scars hidden beyond those big brown eyes than she has on her body and legs. She is my reminder of resilience every day."

Enouim scanned Sky quickly and noticed some faded scarring. "What happened to her?"

Ruakh sighed and furrowed his brow. "She was found left for dead after a syndicate of perasors swooped down on the nomadic group that owned her then. Of course, perasors generally hunt fish and scavenge carcasses, but carrion was running low and fires had destroyed their favorite roosting areas. Sky was grazing in the open when a whole group descended en masse."

Enouim scrunched her forehead in confusion. "Wow. So um ... what exactly *are* perasors? Birds?"

"Oh! Apologies. You don't have perasors up your way I imagine," Ruakh replied. "Yes, they are birds, but ... also no. Their size would make 'beast' a rather apt description as well. They have large beaks, but no feathers, and they have wings, but more like a bat than anything else. Many are just a few inches shorter than you or me, with a wingspan of thirty feet from wingtip to wingtip. If a bird, a bat, and a reptile got together and then magnified its size, I would venture that this is what would result."

Enouim stared at him. They could run into reptile bird bats?

"Anyway," he continued as if he hadn't just dropped a bombshell on Enouim's brain, "my Sky was there, and the perasors attacked. The nomads, Pyren nomads to be exact, mixed some of their powders and lit them on fire, tossing them at the perasors. The spark is only a catalyst, but the combination creates a strong smell and a cloud of smoke which generally drives the beasts away. Perasors are venomous, and the Pyren requested my help to restore their steeds to health before it was too late. I was able to save most of them, and they are grateful to me. Sky here was in horrendous shape, and as it turns out, an abusive individual owned her prior to the incident. The Pyren take animal cruelty very seriously, and when they found out, dealt harshly with him, and once I stopped the venom I was permitted to keep her."

"You refused payment for your help, didn't you?" Mereámé asked. "Except for Sky."

"Yes, well, I took a liking to her. She had a tough time of it and was in no condition to leave with the rest of them, so I asked if I could keep her with me. Sky reminds me of myself, and in healing her wounds and working salve into her spirit, I found my own healing too. Perhaps if she can weather her experiences and learn to trust again, so can I."

A beat of silence.

Mereámé turned to Enouim. "What a beautiful horse you have, as well."

"Thank you. He is a Kalka'an stallion, one of their best. His name is Inferno." Inferno tossed his head, proud to have the topic shift to himself for a change.

And so the three of them spoke of horses and lands traveled. Enouim shared of her journey so far since Gorgenbrild, and Ruakh told of the desert, the flatlands, nomads, mysterious creatures, and life in Levav. Mereámé had traveled with her father as a child but had stayed in Levav for years since. She listened to Ruakh's tales with nearly as much rapture as Enouim did.

For the first several hours, they moved in a relatively

straight line, then they edged in close to the river, waiting for a place to cross. This river also fed the Levavin moat and was quite forceful in some areas. Enouim dreaded crossing it. She rubbed the scars on the back of her neck nervously, wishing she had brought watertight bandages to place over them. Once when she was small, she had forgotten the bandage before bathing. The cold water was a shock, but it was the sudden, stinging pain in her neck that held her memory.

The scars were strangely symmetrical, three small slash marks on either side of her neck, and then a single scar crossing over one of the slashes and draping slightly down her right collarbone. Enouim ran her thumb across this scar now, thinking about the river. Her parents told her she'd been stung by some sort of creature in the water where her father had found her, abandoned. She was only a baby at the time. Would the water hurt her now? Pakel had noticed her fear of water in Levav when he helped her into one of the little boats, and Enouim found herself wishing he were there now.

Ruakh and Mereámé assured the company they would reach a narrow section in the river the following day. Canukke and Kilith decided they would rather cross the river before stopping to sleep, so the troop stopped for a rest to prepare for a long night of riding. Baird and Vadik sat together with Gabor, and Enouim joined them, glad to see them in better spirits.

"Hordes, what an interesting mix we are now!" Vadik said. "Gorgenbrild, Kalka'an, and Levav, all riding together. Tell us, what is it like for you Levavin to be coming along with us?"

The corner of Enouim's mouth curled up at hearing Vadik's normal exuberance. Spending the day on the road with Baird seemed to have shaken some of the dust from his plagued mind.

"Well," Mereámé began, "My heart is torn, as I mentioned

back in Levav, because my father is not doing well. Knowing I may lose him while away is painful, though it would be harder still for him if the Eh'yeh Stone were within our grasp and I allowed it to remain in obscurity. It is the heartbeat of our people and would restore the brokenness within our walls."

"The stone is Gorgenbrild's," Canukke put in. "It is rightfully ours and will remain so."

"I believe the agreement was for Gorgenbrild to take hold of it, and once the darkness is lifted from your land, it would return to Levav," Ruakh said softly. "However, you may find it more difficult to wield than you imagine. The stone is not a weapon like any other. It cannot be bent to any will but its own."

"It has a mind of its own, you say?" Baird asked.

"It does. Better we conform to it, than attempt to conform it to us."

"What does it mean?" Enouim asked. "It seems you see it as a lifestyle almost. But it's a stone."

"A stone, and not a stone!" Ruakh chuckled. "Its power is not one-dimensional, and if we allow its desires to shape our own, that power is allocated to us."

Gabor arched an eyebrow. "An object is an object, nothing more. I look at this knife," he said, drawing his out, "and see only steel. The power and skill come from my mind and muscle memory, not the knife itself."

"At the same time, I suppose Pakel's karambit carries additional weight now," Enouim said. "Because of what it means to us. Not all power is visible."

"So this lifestyle," Vadik broke in, "the Ecyah Stone somehow shapes all the rules you have? What is it like for you traveling with us brutes?"

Ruakh smiled. "You have a code of conduct, and I respect

that. Gorgenbrild thrives from a sense of honor. We are different, and we are similar."

"And Kalka'an?" Gabor pressed dryly.

"What do *you* think of Kalka'an?" Ruakh asked him, returning the question.

Gabor grunted. "Personal experience so far has not been favorable. A society built on lies cannot rely on each other like comrades in arms must. And a company made up of a rat or two will be eaten alive from the inside."

"Strong words, Gabor!" Vadik spoke up, defending his friend.

"Where has our trust gotten us so far, Vadik? Silas stole the bracelet thing Canukke wears, only to give it back. And for what? To make a point? And then we go into Levav, and oh, the scouts that learned where everything is failed to mention a secret vault they knew all about, planning to sneak off to do their own thing. Silas is gone because Levav saw how treacherous he was. He *betrayed* us. I say good riddance, and we are fifty percent closer to being a trustworthy company once more! Baird and Silas got Pakel killed, and it is because of them that we are behind schedule."

"*Your* people murder each other over a squabble!" Baird's eyes flashed with indignation. "We value strategy and wit. We settle our disagreements peacefully, and Kalka'an flourishes without maiming or slaughtering those who slight us. And *we* are not to be trusted! Look in the mirror, friend. You will not like what you see."

"I am no friend of yours," Gabor spat. "I am here to protect my people from oppression and extinction. I am here to fight beside my countrymen, put myself in harm's way, lay myself down for the sake of the mission. And you! What are you here for? A fun story to tell your friends? A spy?"

"Spy! Silas taking the bracelet was a skill demonstration

that our own would have respected! Canukke threatened us with physical harm over the worthless thing. I am here as a representative of my people. Kalka'an and Gorgenbrild are allies. Who says you're right? What is your problem?"

Enouim sighed. Less than a day out from Levav, and already the friction had escalated. What was next? Listening to Baird, Enouim wondered why he'd lied about the vault. She wondered why he perpetuated the lie that Silas took the bracelet, and not himself, even now. She wondered a lot of things.

"It was such a useless, stupid lie!" Gabor continued. "Zegrath's teeth, it wasn't a show of intelligence, but a reckless display of selfishness and pride at our expense."

Enouim rolled her eyes and shook her head. "Hold on, stop. Gorgenbrilders don't even follow our own rules all the time. Canukke lied to me *and* to you about my part in the quest back in Kalka'an! That doesn't make what you did okay," she said to Baird. "It made me angry. You know it did. But I also know you care about the mission. You want us to succeed, but you and Silas disagreed with Canukke on how to go about it. So I tried to trust you again. And now you're lying again, about small things, things that don't even matter anymore. Why? And why don't we Gorgenbrilders even meet our own standards?"

"I did it for the mission!" Canukke and Baird said together. Both looked equally upset to have shared the same wavelength.

"No one would believe me if I explained," Baird added.

Enouim threw her hands up. "Why can't everyone just tell the truth? How hard would that be? If your intentions were good, share them; if your intentions were bad, own them. It is not your job to determine everyone else's response to you. It's your job to do the right thing on your end. And I know what you're going to say. What if they won't understand? What if they overreact? What if they don't believe me? What if this? What if that? *No!* If you don't want to tell someone something, don't tell them! Tell them they make you feel unsafe; tell them it's none of their business, or tell them nothing at all, but don't lie. *Oh, but they prefer the lie.* Maybe they do, but they would only prefer it if it were true. If everyone really preferred to be lied to, they would never be upset when the lie was found out. And yet here we are. Lying is lazy. Lying is cowardly. And I know it's what you're used to. I know there's a reason why you do it and that the reason seems good to you. But that's not good enough." Enouim broke off, breathing heavily.

Silence. Baird shifted his weight. Canukke curled his lip in a soundless snarl. Vadik grimaced.

"Break time is over," Kilith declared after a moment. "We had better get moving."

They rode on, each man immersed in his own bitter thoughts. The fresh start of the morning had soured, and as the light faded, so did optimism. The sunset was surprisingly lackluster, but it seemed to match their outlooks on the evening. A light wind ruffled Enouim's hair, the soft sound tempering the incessant cricket calls in the night. At last Mereámé and Ruakh directed them to the best place to cross the river. Enouim's heart beat loudly as she listened to the ripple of the water passing them by. She thumbed the scar on her collarbone and swallowed.

Canukke entered the river first, testing the water and urging his horse forward. Gabor followed close behind him, rather pointedly placing distance between himself and Baird. Oloren was next, with Mereámé and Enouim on the bank behind. Enouim stared at the moving water ... dark, mysterious, and unpredictable.

"Hey ... Enouim? Are you okay?" Mereámé's soft voice and

concerned expression brought Enouim back to the task at hand.

"What? Um ... yes, I'm fine." She took a deep breath. Canukke, Gabor, and Oloren were all in the river. They were fine. She was fine. They were all going to be fine. Another deep breath.

"Psst ... come on, En," Oloren whispered, turning in her saddle. "What's wrong?"

Enouim steeled herself and stepped Inferno's front hooves into the water. No hidden monsters of death came lunging at her from beneath its surface. She continued into the river, and they began to wade across. The bottom of the river dropped away and the horses were forced to swim. Enouim heard Vadik lean toward Baird behind her and ask him, "Hey, do you see anything dark in the water?"

"Just water," Baird returned. "It's night out; everything is dark."

Enouim searched her surroundings, but all she saw was black water moving past them. Vadik remained intent on the water. Canukke was wary but confident. Enouim caught Kilith's eye as she swept her gaze from side to side. He seemed focused on her, examining her. Self-conscious and wondering how paranoid she looked, Enouim straightened in the saddle and tried to turn her attention to her breathing as Inferno waded into the inky depths and began to swim.

A distinctive wave rolled past Ruakh, and the members near enough to hear it twisted back to look. "What was that?" Kilith asked.

Ruakh grasped his staff and stared into the blackness beside him, putting a finger to his lips for silence. Enouim strained her ears, but only heard the low ripple of the water and the horses' breathing as they swam. Her heart beat ominously like the pounding of a great drum. She imagined that the blackness of the water held unfathomable evil, and her breathing quickened. Looking about her, she saw the whites of her companions' eyes, their dim outlines, and little else. *Thud-thud, thud-thud, thud-thud.*

A subtle splashing sound led to chaos as a dark snake-like creature, two feet in diameter, broke the surface of the water, knocking Vadik off his horse and down into the depths. The horses uttered horrified cries and struck out for the shore in a panic. Kilith stayed his horse and plunged his arm into the murkiness. Gabor grabbed onto him from the other side to keep him in his seat, and it seemed Kilith grasped hold of something, but then lost it. With a grunt, Kilith dove into the water after Vadik.

"Kilith!" Oloren yelled, pulling out her short swords.

Slippery scales lashed out from the water again, and Oloren slashed at the beast with both arms while her horse carried its unwilling rider out of range. An arrow from Gabor hit the serpent a moment after Oloren made contact, and a throaty growl rumbled from what was unmistakably an enormous snake head emerging from the darkness, looming over them all. Large yellow eyes gleamed at them, slits for pupils piercing them like steel daggers. The mouth opened, and a forked tongue slithered out to taste the air. The snake's body coiled against itself, its scales producing an unearthly high pitched, hollow sound. Vadik and Kilith surfaced, kicking and sputtering. The beast seemed enraged to see them at the surface. It reached a short arm out of the water and plucked Enouim off her horse.

Enouim let out a scream that started in shock, then turned into rage. One arm free, she drew her knife and stabbed and sawed at the foot holding her fast. Oloren, seeing her predicament, leaped to her feet on her horse's back and thrust her short swords into the serpent. It took her several attempts, as the scales overlapped closely, and she finally shoved her swords up and into the softer underbelly. But the scales closed over the blades and held her to the animal. The great snake's head rose high over Oloren and thrashed Enouim about as it reacted. Using her daggers as handholds, Oloren climbed up the beast with her legs dangling in the air. Canukke called to Gabor to get Ruakh and Mereámé to the shore. Baird slung his broadsword and the beast dove back into the water, Enouim still in its clutches.

Her vision turned to blackness, and her world turned cold. The clammy grip of the snake was strong, and Enouim grew weary of her knife work. A sharp sting hit the back of her neck, and she cried out from under the water. The muffled sound gave her companions an idea of where she was, and Baird launched himself off his mount after her. Oloren had ridden the beast down into the water but the impact shook her off. Kilith got Vadik safely to the bank, but Vadik didn't allow himself to rest before pulling a spear off his horse and planting himself at the edge of the water, waiting for a clear shot. Enouim felt a lurch, and the vise around her loosened. A moment was all she needed to wriggle free.

Enouim's lungs burned as she reached the surface and felt strong arms take hold of her and drag her through the water. Vadik let his spear fly a moment later, but it glanced off. Canukke caught it in one swift motion as it fell, and tried again at close range. The snake's body rolled beneath his horse and it was briefly lifted out of the water by its force, whinnying in terror.

Kilith set Enouim down on the bank and returned for Canukke and Baird, just as Oloren made it to land. The beast rose up, towering over them, and they saw that it was indeed a snake of sorts, but had two short legs perhaps six feet down its body. The creature hissed at them and swayed for a moment, the end of its tail slapping the top of the water.

In a final dash, it rushed the company on the bank. Canukke had his sword at the ready, but Ruakh responded fastest and thrust his staff into the serpent's mouth. It writhed backward, gagging and hissing. Canukke struck its great neck with a deep blow, and, bleeding badly now, the beast melted back into the water. The travelers were left soaking wet and heaving on the shore next to a river that bubbled quietly as if nothing out of the ordinary had taken place.

15

T he river flowed by them, unhurried. Even the crickets, disturbed from their nightly song, resumed after a few minutes. A breeze tousled her wet hair, and Enouim realized how cold she was. It felt good on her neck, which still stung a little, but she hated being cold and would've rather taken the pain. Soaked to the bone, they remained scattered on the side of the river trying to absorb what had just happened.

"Away from the bank, quickly," Canukke commanded.

Kilith and Baird both appeared at Enouim's side to check on her and help her up, but Kilith sent Baird to help Vadik round up the horses. "You were under there a while. Feeling okay?"

"Yeah ... yes, I'm fine, just a little shaken up." Her heart ignored her mind's repeated directives to slow itself.

Kilith looked her up and down. "Nothing else?"

"No ..." She slowly moved her fingers to the back of her neck, but Kilith caught her hand and moved it away. He turned her so the moonlight shone on the back of her neck. "What? What is it?"

"Hmm."

"That's not helpful."

"I'm going to put a poultice on this. Don't touch it."

Enouim turned to look at him, bewildered. "Why?" She reached her hand up again, and Kilith swatted in away.

"Don't touch it."

"Fine."

Kilith gave her the look a parent gives a troublesome child, then walked away. Baird and Vadik caught the last of the horses, and the company headed toward a grove of trees a little way off. Canukke walked back to the bank and scanned it for some time before returning to the group. After a debate over the danger of lighting a fire, they agreed that drying off and staying warm was worth the risk. Gabor took charge of this, and Mereámé volunteered to assist. When Kilith wasn't looking, Enouim snaked her hand up to the edges of the scars on her neck. The edges were raised. Alarmed, she dropped her hand.

Canukke returned, looking troubled and feeling his wrist. The all-important leather wristband was gone. Enouim started toward him but paused as Ruakh headed toward Canukke ahead of her. She kept her ear in their direction, pretending to look for kindling instead.

"Pardon me, but I couldn't help but notice you seem to be missing something. And I found something floating in the water just starting to sink when we got to the bank. I fished it out. Is this yours?" Ruakh held out a wet leather band to Canukke.

Canukke's eyes widened, and he took it. "Thank you," he said in surprise. "Yes, I was looking for it. Must have come off in the struggle ... I searched the riverbank but thought it was lost."

Ruakh sat next to Canukke and they shared time in

silence, watching Gabor and Oloren start the fire. The two quietly squabbled about the best technique, until Oloren finally gave up and let Gabor do it his way. Canukke looked down at the leather band and ran his fingers over it. "It was my father's."

"Were you close?"

"Yes ... and no. He was a harsh man, my father, but the only one I got. Loved mead, like most in our country, but it made him violent. He wasn't always harsh though. My father taught me to hunt, to fight, to live, and ultimately to die. He wore this every day of my childhood."

"It's important to you to carry on his legacy," Ruakh observed.

"It is."

"If you don't mind my asking ... how did your father pass away?"

Silence engulfed them. Canukke stared into the fire from where he and Ruakh sat, removed from the others. Enouim remained still, paralyzed now as she'd been too long in this position to possibly still be gathering wood for the fire. To move now would bring attention to her placement and ruin this improbable vulnerability. Canukke could have bored a hole with his eyes into the logs of the fire, so focused was he on them. Ruakh remained silent, allowing the man beside him all the time he needed.

Finally, Canukke spoke. "Before Khoron-khelek formed the Sumus, his father had brought together another band of tribesmen called the Iyangas. My father went as part of a negotiation party to move them away from our borders. All but two of the seven-person party were murdered and brutally disfigured. The tribesmen killed him in cold blood in response to a peaceful entreaty. Savages!"

Canukke's eyes remained fixed on the fire, and Enouim

could see the blaze reflected in his eyes. His face twisted into a grimace of pain and hatred. "They know no mercy, and shall receive no mercy! The only language they know is in trails of blood, and I learned to speak their language that night. The two survivors returned in a panic, narrowly escaping. So I handled my anger the way my father always had. I drank. I drank to stop feeling, and when I could still feel, I drank some more. The more I consumed, the more my fury grew. In a rage I set out after my father's killers while they slept. I saw my father's mutilated body and could not contain the hatred that swept through me that night. My father and his companions were brutalized beyond recognition except for this." Canukke tapped the leather band on his wrist.

He continued. "I slaughtered seven of them before they even woke. I fought and killed five more and escaped on my horse, dragging the screaming body of one of them behind me. I cut out his entrails and disemboweled him. The next day I used a slingshot to send pieces of the tribesman into their camp ... intestine tied to a rock, an eyeball, one piece at a time, like the pieces of me they ripped apart when they killed my father and my people. I dumped the remains nearby for them to find. I learned that day that violence is the only thing they understand. They deserve it, because they destroy first. Like force and equal hatred are our only option. These wretches have nothing to lose, no shame, no honor. It is not by talk that we will defeat them, but by blood. Blood for blood, life for life, and hatred for hatred; yet my blood runs thicker in my veins, my life will be stronger than theirs, and my hatred greater than theirs. It makes me strong. They will see my face and quake with fear before the end."

A chill ran up Enouim's spine. Despite the graphic details, Ruakh's face remained serene. "You wanted them to feel the way they made you feel."

Canukke nodded.

"It seems to me," Ruakh said, "that you are part of a never-ending cycle of violence. Your path is lined with sorrow. What is it like for you to carry the responsibility for so many lives?"

Canukke shrugged. "I do not feel it. I feel nothing at all. They are evil itself."

"I cannot help but wonder what these Sumu tribesmen experience. Surely they, in turn, see Gorgenbrild as evil in some way. All behavior makes sense in context, even if we do not agree with it or excuse it. They marry, have families, mourn their losses ... they are human, after all."

"Humans without dignity do not deserve the title."

"It seems you place yourself in that category, then. You forfeit your own title when you lower yourself to animalistic impulses. There is a better way, one that doesn't come at the cost of your humanity." Ruakh let his words settle in before speaking again. "Violence begets violence. What happens when we continue this cycle? How does it end? I believe you are more than you give yourself credit for, and a part of you recognizes the crushing weight of life lost. That part of you deserves an outlet, deserves to be expressed rather than silenced. You have cut short lives with infinite possibility to grow, change, and mend their ways."

Canukke had been sitting with shoulders slouched forward and quietly absorbing Ruakh's words, but at this he straightened with a piercing glare. "There is no restitution. A better way? Where is justice for my father? Where is justice for my people? I am the arm of justice! I am the scales weighing the blood on either side and finding their deeds despicable. When I strike, all will know the power of Gorgenbrild, the fire of pure passion—and how deserving will their grotesque punishment be! Never to turn. I am the power of mercy with-held in accordance with the mercy withheld from their enemies. Never to turn. I am the essence of night terrors, the messenger of death brought to the door of those convicted. May they see my face and their hearts forever stop pumping blood into their icy veins. Never to turn." And with that he stood and stormed off toward the fire, leaving Ruakh behind.

Ruakh remained calm, but Enouim thought he looked sad. She was surprised Canukke opened up at all, and considered that perhaps he had surprised himself with his vulnerability and didn't like the feedback he heard. Maybe Ruakh was right, and that scared Canukke. Fear was not an emotion he deemed acceptable.

Enouim thought about all the people in the company, wondering what in their histories made them who they were today. For better or for worse, each had a right to their own story, and a past that shed light on but did not define their current identity. As Ruakh said, all behavior made sense in context, and all humanity retained the possibility of growth and change. Perhaps even Canukke was more than the arrogant, self-serving leader he appeared to be.

Enouim thought of her own father: kind, gentle, loving. She wondered whether the place she came from, where her father had adopted her from, defined her at all. It was a mystery to her. Kilith approached her with the poultice he had promised, and she spoke as he applied it to the back of her neck.

"Kilith? How did you know my father?"

"Who said I knew your father?"

"At Kalka'an ... you knew him. You introduced me as Rotan Cokanda's daughter, and said he was a trader. You also knew his name would be meaningful to Quarot."

"He was a good man."

"Were you close?" Enouim asked. "Were you a trader too?"

"I had the pleasure of traveling with Rotan several times. I was not a trader, but I went along for one leg of a journey here and there."

"Did he ... ever talk about me? My history?"

"I didn't come over here to tell you stories. He didn't spend every waking moment sharing his family secrets." Kilith paused, and sighed. "He cared about you a lot, but I'm sure you knew that already."

"But ... where I came from," Enouim pressed. "He told you?"

"You are a Gorgenbrilder."

"Well, yes, but I was adopted. I mean, they're my parents, but they didn't give birth to me."

A pause from Kilith. He finished with the poultice and stepped around to look her straight in the eye. "Rather liberal with your story, aren't you?"

"It's *my* story. Why shouldn't I be? I want to know if you know some of it. Maybe pieces I haven't had before."

"The important thing is not where you came from, but who you are now. You are a Gorgenbrilder, no matter where you were found. And you have come on this mission with a resolve and willingness to learn that honors Rotan. Be content." Kilith examined her for a moment and then walked away, leaving Enouim alone with a knot in her gut. She turned slowly and followed him to rejoin the others.

Kilith was strange. He seemed wise, reserved, strong, and quietly opinionated. Always thinking, that one. She wished she could know what was going on behind those dark eyes. He had tipped her off about Canukke when Enouim first landed on the quest, and stepped in to introduce her in Kalka'an when Canukke ignored her. Kilith had saved her from the water serpent and taken it upon himself to tend to her afterward. He was about the same age as her father would have been, and she wondered if they were closer than he let on.

Enouim also noted his use of the word "found." Why would he say it didn't matter where she was *found*, unless he knew she had been *lost*? If he did know something more than he shared, why was he being so secretive? And if not, why was she obsessing over it? Enouim sighed. There was just no winning with her brain. It wrapped itself up in complex possibilities, most of which would never actually happen. She sat down next to Gabor and Mereámé, running a thumb over the scar on her collarbone, and stared into the fire.

Mereámé leaned over and whispered, "Everything all right?"

Enouim started and glanced up. Dark doe eyes looked back at her with a concern that Enouim swore reached into her very soul. Enouim swallowed hard against the lump that lodged in her throat. "Um, yes, I'm okay. Well, actually, I'm confused and frustrated, but I will have to tell you about it later ... I will though." Enouim suddenly craved conversation with this gentle spirit. There was something about Mereámé that opened her up and made her want to share the depths of herself, to unravel her tangled thoughts.

"... they will know the final steps to the stone," Ruakh was saying to the group.

"I'm sorry, what are we talking about?" Enouim asked.

"There are invisible sky people that can help us find the stone," Vadik said casually, with a snarky grin.

"The Nazir," Ruakh clarified. "Not invisible. Just particularly hard to see." He smiled.

"How do we find people we can't see?" Enouim hoped she wasn't asking questions everyone else had already discussed. Sounding stupid was terrible, but not knowing things was worse.

"I have met them before," Mereámé said. "The exact location of the Nazir changes, but the nomads in the area will have seen signs of them even without knowing it. These we can use to seek audience with the Nazir and request their direction."

"We are doing a lot of going from place to place thinking the stone will be there," Gabor grumbled. "How do we know it will be near them?"

"You followed a rumor to Levav, because we were the last civilization known to be in possession of the Eh'yeh Stone, and you were correct about that." Ruakh took a breath. "Since its disappearance one-hundred-and-seventy years ago, Levavin have kept its history, its desires, its lifestyle alive as much as we could without the stone's actual presence. We have been actively searching for it ever since, and though our intel leans heavily on whispers, whispers are often more trust-worthy than shouts. We interact with some of the best whis-perers, as it were, quite frequently—they have proven effective in the past."

"Only recently we got wind that the Nazir now live quite close to our best approximation of where the stone resides," Mereámé continued. "They will know where to find it. As long as we can find them before they move again, we may get them to help us."

"If you have an estimate of where it has been all this time, why not pursue it before now?" Gabor asked.

"Our past estimates have not panned out exactly ... in history, the stone seems to find you, not you it. I'm not sure how it works. But we have never enlisted the Nazir quite like this before, and if we gain their help, it will be the closest we've ever been."

Enouim studied Gabor. Thinking of Canukke's earlier discussion with Ruakh, she wondered what was in Gabor's past that contributed to who he was today. Mulling it over now, she realized she didn't know Gabor well, despite the months they'd spent together. He was detailed, analytical, critical at times, and excellent at accomplishing tasks and giving specific instructions. Gabor wanted everything to run smoothly, and if he didn't like how something was being accomplished, he would state his displeasure while ultimately going along with the plan. Beyond that ... Enouim silently resolved to get to know him better in the coming weeks.

The group ate wildly unappetizing dried meat, which had gotten a little less dried in the river before re-drying over the fire. Vadik sharpened a new spearhead to replace the one he lost in the serpent, and Baird examined his work. Exhausted from the day, everyone found a place on the ground to settle in for what was left of the night. Enouim placed herself near Mereámé, who seemed grateful for the company.

Enouim spoke softly. "Thanks for checking in on me earlier."

"Of course! I just got the impression something was wrong. I mean, not that a giant sea creature trying to kill you shouldn't do that."

"No, there is. A lot of things are wrong, but not so wrong that I should make a big deal out of them. One is about Kilith." Enouim shared her mind's swirling quandaries about her past, and whether Kilith knew something he wasn't sharing, and whether it even mattered.

"Hmm. You're trying to make it less of a big deal, but it really bothers you."

"It does. I didn't grow up wondering who my other parents were or why they left me, because I figured I ended up with parents who loved me so it didn't really matter where I came from. I let it go. But my dad was on a trip when he found me, and now that I'm on a trip myself, and seeing how everyone's pasts influences them ... I wonder about mine."

"Sounds only natural. It's a journey of self-discovery, and it doesn't make sense why someone would stand in the way of that without reason. Especially someone like Kilith, who seems to care about you and be on your side."

Enouim thought for a moment. She wouldn't have said it that way, but she supposed it was true. The compliment he had given her earlier about her identity and determination was downright effusive for him. Enouim wanted his approval and was annoyed with herself for wanting it. She was also frustrated that his opinion of her was so difficult to decipher. One minute he seemed disappointed, and the next, telling her she should be happy where she is. What was that about?

"I think it *has* become a self-discovery journey. I had to find my own reason for being here, after tripping my way into it in the first place. I wanted to find out who I am, travel, explore—see what I'm worth."

"That's a lot."

It was, wasn't it? Lots of pressure she put on a life-threatening venture into shockingly vague tomorrows. They talked for quite some time together, physically tired but emotionally thirsty.

"So why is Canukke leading? How did that come about?" Mereámé asked.

"He is highly respected in Gorgenbrild, an accomplished warrior, etcetera, etcetera," Enouim said with a wave of her hand. "Nothing as important as this would be undertaken without him, and following doesn't seem to be his strong suit."

"He's just coming because it's some big fancy quest?" Mereámé said. "This is not a game. Not just a medal to be earned and worn, not bragging rights. I gave up a lot to come, and my father may be dying as we speak. This is personal to me. Why risk so much if it has little personal meaning to him?"

Enouim paused. Her heart went out to Mereámé for her sacrifice, and yet a piece of her rose to protect Canukke. *Protect him?* Heavens, what was happening to her? The look in his eyes as he sat with Ruakh resonated in her, and she saw him running his fingers over his father's leather wristband. She wondered what sacrifices he had made after all. "It's a brave, shiny quest for sure," she began. "It's also potentially the only chance our people have for freedom. Canukke is used to being free, to living life by his own rules. His father died by the hands of Sumus. Maybe it's more personal than we think." She hesitated. "He is a confusing, frustrating brand of human." Enouim felt a little bad for tacking this on, but couldn't quite bear to let the moment slide with so positive a spin on the man.

"Hmm. Yes. I suppose everyone is more complex than they appear at first glance. Still, I don't quite trust him. He doesn't seem safe to me."

"Oh, he won't hurt you. Not unless you do something terribly against the character I've judged you for. You'll be okay."

"No, I mean ..." Mereámé furrowed her brow. "I'm not worried about my physical safety. Although I believe he can be quite dangerous when he wants to be. I mean he doesn't seem *safe*. With my thoughts, my opinions, my story. Not safe."

"Oh ... no, I wouldn't say so," Enouim replied. "He's critical and condescending. His way is the only way."

Enouim told Mereámé about Baird, and how she had wanted to apologize for her harsh response to him before the river. Initially she felt self-righteous and fueled by her anger. As time had gone on, her anger ebbed, and she knew she needed to apologize for her approach but was not quite ready to give up enough of her pride to go through with it. Everything had gotten so crazy after that, she'd forgotten. Mereámé suggested clearing the air between them as soon as possible and relieving her guilt.

Mereámé shared some of her fears about leaving her father sick in Levav and her excitement about potentially being the first Levavin to set eyes on the stone in one-hundred-and-seventy years. As they talked into the night, Enouim found the understanding she'd been craving. Her eyelids began to feel heavy, and their whispers back and forth became slower and slower until they drifted off.

16

Enouim hardly felt she'd closed her eyes when Vadik shook her awake, a finger to his lips for silence. The sun was up, and the morning apparently well under way—although, by the expression on Vadik's face, it was not destined to be a good morning. Enouim furrowed her eyebrows and sat up slowly, following Vadik's gaze. A shot of adrenaline raced through her.

The Ecyah mission members were clustered beneath a small grove of spice trees. At the edge, only thirty feet from them, stood large bird-like creatures, roughly five feet tall. Their three-toed birds' feet carried a lot of their weight, and their wings forelimbs had another three toes to help bear the weight. Bat wings folded in, attaching at the end of the fore-limb and extending out backward to the same height as the head. Three had ruby-red crests on their heads, and the other two had smaller purple ones. Enouim remembered Ruakh's description of the perasors that had attacked his horse—no doubt these were the same.

Gabor nocked an arrow, Vadik poised both spear and sword, and Oloren gripped her throwing knives. Each held steady, tense, as the five beasts eyed them warily. Baird spoke softly. "We'll make a fire. Light our arrows and use that. Fire is a strong deterrent for many animals."

"Good." Vadik nodded. "We can use branches if they get too close."

"Get to it," Gabor said.

Canukke shook his head. "No good. Stay low. No sudden movements. The arrows would be effective on the wings, but not enough for their bodies. On the ground with us, wings tucked, there won't be many good shots. They're big enough to do damage without them. We would just piss them off."

"Pissing them off doesn't sound so bad," Oloren returned optimistically. "There are five of them and nine of us. Even given their strength, we can double up. I can take one myself and the other four can get two warriors each."

"Shhh." Kilith cast a look at Oloren.

The largest of the perasors cocked its head and clicked his beak.

"Ruakh?" Enouim ventured. "You know these creatures, right?"

"Spice trees," Mereámé whispered, glancing at the little canopy above them. "They're attracted to the smell."

"It seems we are trespassing on a favored spot," Ruakh observed. "They likely rove the skies for carcasses and return every morning to fish in the river and enjoy the scent and shade of the trees in the heat of the day."

"Zegrath's teeth, what do we *do*, then?" Enouim heard rather than saw Gabor's eye roll.

"Get out of their area?" Vadik suggested. It certainly seemed like the natural progression.

"Worth a shot," Ruakh said. "Not all at once though. Baird, Oloren, move backward slowly. Any motion toward them may be seen as threatening."

Slowly, slowly, they crept away from the perasors. The reptile birds kept their beady eyes fixed on their progress, cynically evaluating. Enouim's heart pounded.

One clicked its beak together several times and turned to the side. *Ugh, the horses.* One of the horses shied away back toward the trees as far as it could manage while tethered. Kilith crouched at the edge of the trees, waiting for the perasors' reactions to see if he could free the horse.

"Not good," Mereámé noted. "Smoke?"

"Yes, smoke!" Ruakh agreed. "We need something that makes a bad smell. Anyone have sugar?"

"I have some," Vadik offered.

"Good. Bring it here."

"What do you mix it with?" Baird asked.

"Hey, watch it!" Oloren hissed as Vadik moved a little too quickly toward his pack.

Several clicks came from the perasors' beaks. One moved toward the nearest horse. Another fluttered massive wings. Enouim hoped they would use them to fly far away.

"We're not in a hurry," Ruakh said. "Take your time."

"We sort of *are* in a hurry though," Gabor countered. "In a hurry to get out of their spot."

"If you move too fast, we will have to wait around anyway patching you up," Enouim pointed out. "And if we're not careful, we could be down a horse or two."

As if aware of the concern, Sky stamped and huffed nervously, tossing her head. Ruakh returned his focus to Baird. "Bring me the sulfur powder."

His jaw dropped. "I don't have any."

"There's no time," Mereámé responded. "We know you have it. Give it up."

Baird paused, then sighed and reached into his bag, producing a small pouch and passing it to Ruakh.

"Good." He nodded. "I have the salt. Baird, the fire idea is a good one, and I think we need to get one going. I'll measure out the ingredients and then we light it and toss. If all else fails, you can fall back on the flaming arrows idea. If they get closer than that ... be ready, friends."

A perasor stretched its wings out in an intimidating posture and strutted toward them. The wings at their full extension were thirty feet across, wingtip to wingtip. Enouim's eyes widened. They were truly enormous, but their bodies, already taller than Oloren, were quite small in comparison with the wings.

Oloren spun one of the knives in her hand. "Ready."

"Stay low until then," Canukke cautioned. "They are trying to give us a show that they are bigger and better than us. Let's not egg them on."

"*Aren't* they bigger and better than us?" Mereámé asked.

"Hopefully we won't have to find out," Baird answered, watching Ruakh mixing the various powders.

"But if we do have to, we can take them," Oloren added reassuringly.

"Okay, this is it," Ruakh said. "I am going to pass to Canukke to throw. When he makes the toss, nobody move. Let the smell and the smoke be the main deterrent, and if they back off, we'll take the horses and go." He made a final swirl to mix the ingredients together in the pouch, closed it tight, and chucked it at Canukke. *"Now!"*

Canukke caught it and in one swift motion wound his arm and threw the pouch in a straight line low to the ground. The pouch made contact near the feet of the first perasor, and with a hissing sound, gray smoke spewed from it, spilling out of the pouch and billowing up into the air. The first perasor screeched and hopped back as the heat gushed out and hit its feet. A putrid smell wafted over them, and Enouim gagged. The horses neighed and pulled at their ties.

The thick smoke rose high into the air, and the perasors screeched and drew back. They stretched their large bat-like wings and took to the air, alighting perhaps fifty yards from the spice grove. "Good," Gabor said, "grab the packs and the horses."

Enouim looked to Ruakh, and he nodded. "Be quick."

The group snatched blankets from the ground and slung packs on the horses, mounting within a minute. Enouim was grateful to have Inferno's strong legs beneath her again as they galloped away from the spice trees. The horses were only too willing to carry them off in the opposite direction from the huge reptile birds and foul smell.

Looking back, Enouim saw the smoke drifting gently with the wind. She guessed it was more than twenty feet high, and the chemical reaction had exhausted all its energy in the first few seconds after being thrown. The perasors waited anxiously at first, then circled the area twice before heading off to some other haunt. Enouim breathed deep, and let her body relax as it rolled with Inferno's motions. She leaned forward to pat his neck and looked ahead to the sparsely vegetated flatlands. They'd prepared to fight humans but had, so far, encountered a myriad of beasts instead. With nearly a month to go before reaching the Nazir, Enouim couldn't help but wonder if there were any use training to fight Sumus if they were to be overtaken by monsters.

Despite Enouim's fears, the days passed without incident. They continued west toward a forest Mereámé assured them was hiding the Nazir. When they got further west, they would talk to nomads in the flatlands for clues as to the Nazir's whereabouts, and the group would lean on Mereámé's experience with the Nazir.

The terrain was still flat, and spice trees remained an occasional oddity on the plain. The yellow grasses were new to Enouim's eyes, but she took solace in the familiar motions of the horse beneath her, the people around her, and the road beyond. She wasn't sure whether she should be thrilled by the excitement of limitless possibilities, like Baird seemed to be, or afraid of the many terrors lurking within each one. She looked at him now. Baird laughed at something he, Vadik, and Gabor were discussing together. How could he be so carefree? Enouim wished she were like that.

Her mind drifted back to her conversation with Mereámé the night before, about setting things right with Baird. It was hard to believe it had been no more than thirty-six hours since she chewed him out about deceitfulness in front of the group. Afterward they'd ridden in silence, reached the river, been attacked by a sea serpent, warmed themselves by the fire, slept briefly, and awoken to perasors. Not exactly the most conducive scenarios for heart to hearts. It felt so long ago. Should she really bring it up? Had he moved on? Maybe he didn't think it was that big of a deal, and her drudging it up again would add unnecessary drama. Or maybe he was still upset with her, and there had been so much going on that she hadn't taken notice.

She sighed. Ugh, how would she word it? *Just do it.* Fine. She rode up beside him and blurted out the words before she could reconsider. "Hey, um, could I talk to you for a minute?"

"Yeah, sure. Just step inside my secluded room built especially for secret discussions." Baird seemed to be in good spirits, but Enouim couldn't figure out if this comment was customary sarcasm or laced with bitterness.

Enouim waited for Vadik and Gabor to take stock of the situation and ride on a horse-length ahead. Not super discreet, but close enough. Even the illusion of privacy would do at this point. "I know this happened a while back ... I didn't really have a chance. I mean, I meant to mention this before. Not that it is a big deal, if it's not ... anyway, look." She took a breath. "I wanted to apologize."

"For?" His facial expression had become more serious and attentive.

"I ... sort of called you out earlier. It was harsher than I intended it to be, what I said about the lying. I meant it, and I still believe the things I said, but I don't think the approach I took was the best."

Baird let the horses' hooves fill the silence. It felt like an incredibly long stretch. "It's okay. We all come from different perspectives, different cultures. It's not easy."

"It's not. I know your background is different from mine, and you don't see things the way I see them all the time. I guess I lost sight of that, since we were getting on so well. Like I said, I know there is a reason for what you do. I know you don't lie without cause. To me, it just seems harmful and unnecessary." Enouim bit her lip. Was she making it worse?

"You're right. There *is* a reason for what I do. I'm not saying everything I've done has been the best, but the intention was good. I clearly haven't made great decisions this whole time. I know that. It's hard for me to admit it, but it seems important for you to know since we may very well have each other's lives in our hands at one point or another."

Enouim considered that. She remembered overhearing Gabor processing the sea snake scenario, and saying it had been Baird who dove after her when Enouim was first dragged beneath the surface. She shuddered, remembering. Baird watched her, catching every subtle cue. "I ... meant to thank you, by the way. The river. Thanks."

"You're welcome."

More horse hooves. Enouim became painfully, awkwardly aware of Vadik and Gabor's silence ahead of them. Great.

"You know," Baird added, "You are highly motivated by your standard of what is right. That's a good thing. You have great zeal for what you think the code should be, but how are you so confident that yours is right?"

Enouim paused. Baird believed in his standard as fully as she believed in hers, but she hadn't thought about how to defend her code of honor over his. Was there anything both trustworthy and objective enough to judge between the two?

Vadik couldn't help himself and tossed a comment back at them. "The same could be asked of you, friend!"

"True. But I asked first."

Until now, Enouim had been speaking in low tones. With Vadik's interjection, however, her illusion of privacy erupted. Feeling frustrated and somewhat trapped, she ventured on. "Honestly, I can see how cultures can be so steeped in their own mindsets that understanding others' views would be hard. This is as true for Gorgenbrild as it is for Kalka'an or Levav. For Kalka'an, specifically, it is hard for me to see how a society can stand together with so many lies and deceptions within it threatening to tear it apart. I get that deceit takes smarts, but I would prefer a mediocre-intelligence paired with honesty to a cunning snake any day. One will devour me, and the other has the courage to share what it really wants."

"It is not always prudent to share one's desires too quickly," Baird observed.

"Well, sure, that's true in Gorgenbrild," Enouim conceded. "But among one's comrades, disclosure begets disclosure and bonds people together. How are even the most elemental of friendships formed, or trust established, without the basics?"

"Nothing is as critical to the warrior as a trustworthy

friend," Oloren agreed, riding behind with Ruakh and Mereámé.

"Silas proved that true," Gabor jabbed. "As did Baird, in fact."

"If you have a problem with me, state it plainly, as your own code dictates," Baird spat. "Why boast about some ethical code if you have no intention of following it? Isn't it worse to have a code of honor and ignore it, than to have none at all? And yet Kalka'an both has and respects such a code."

"I do. I have a problem with circumventing our leader's specific instructions and doing whatever suits you. I have a problem with liars who boast about their lies, as if it were some admirable quality."

"And here we come to Kalka'an's greatest contention with Gorgenbrild," Baird said. "Allies we are, and allies stay. Yet it all boils down to this—you slaughter one another over petty disagreements, and take issue with us for what comes out of our mouths. No matter how we might despise our neighbor, we ensure that their blood remains in their body, while you seem to look for any excuse to spill it. If either of us were to be counted among the savages, it would certainly not be the cliff dwellers."

"I don't see the sense of all that myself," Enouim admitted. "That's why I kept my head down back home and tried to stay out of other people's business. I did okay until Chayan. Even if you avoid violence the best you can, chances are, sooner or later violence will find you."

"Shame on you and yours, Enouim," Gabor said. "You are of Gorgenbrild. What thin blood you must have. It is a simple principle for governing a people without needing excessive oversight. We aren't swinging our swords here and there for the sound of our own steel, but to show our mettle and become stronger as a people. The faithless are weeded out, and we are taught to step carefully. It is a refining process."

"Sounds like the rationalization of a hot-headed man," Baird commented.

"What do the Levavin think of this?" Vadik asked, eager to draw the peaceful Ruakh and Mereámé into the debate.

"It is interesting," Ruakh answered simply. "We seem a tightly-wound company."

Canukke signaled them to stop for a rest, and all dismounted.

"Interesting more so to hear such an observation from the lips of Levavin!" Vadik laughed. "In Gorgenbrild, Levav is considered sensitive and strict beyond measure."

"We recognize the deficiencies we all possess and strive toward continual betterment," Mereámé said. "Love should drive us, and when it does not, we are called upon to support one another and challenge one another to grow. Many things are less than ideal, yet this is common for man. We hope to work toward ideal a bit more every day."

"How are we to work together with such division among us?" Oloren asked, clear frustration in her voice.

"This is ridiculous," Enouim said quietly to Mereámé. "All this because I tried to apologize to Baird."

"They are oblivious to their vices," Mereámé responded sadly. "And worse ... apathetic."

Overhearing Mereámé's comment, Canukke spoke up loudly for all to hear. "You are more aware of yours, you say, as if that makes you better. Are you? Or does it just give you a self-righteous position and choke you with guilt when you fail your so-called ideals?"

Mereámé looked back at him, startled. She wiped the shock off her face at his boldness, but couldn't quite cloak the unease in her tone. "I did not say we were better."

"The intention is not to exalt ourselves," Ruakh said evenly, "but to aim for what we cannot yet reach so that as we stretch toward it, even falling short is progress from where we last were. I admit that it often produces guilt and a focus on that failure, which is forever a fear of my own. And these discussions of whose standard is right is stirring up fear in me that I have misplaced my trust. It keeps me from being able to be fully objective."

"Your strength is our strength," Mereámé said, nodding empathetically.

Enouim remembered Ruakh saying this to Mereámé back in Levav, and she saw now that it was a customary exchange. Sharing a fear was to them a symbol of strength and courage. It was seen as an example, and the leader's bravery gave others a portion of that bravery, to openly share their own insecurities and concerns. Enouim marveled at Ruakh's ability to share his in this heated moment.

As the argument continued, Kilith came over to Enouim to check on the scars at the back of her neck. "What do you make of all this?" she asked him.

"Fools, the lot of them," he said, unblinking. "This kind of talk is divisive and unnecessary. Each has been entrenched in his own mindset for years; a day's bickering will solve nothing." Kilith gingerly removed the bandage from the previous evening and pressed a couple fingers along the edges of her scar. Enouim thought his words wise and wished he voiced his views more often. She frequently wondered what he was thinking and had further confirmation now that his silence was rarely for lack of opinion.

"What if we're all wrong? What if there is no standard that is truly good?"

"We probably *are* all wrong. Every day we go about our business according to what seems best to us, and in my experi-

ence, humanity has rarely if ever made good collective decisions on what is best *for* us. At its finest, perhaps each code has
a sliver of something valuable within it. As long as each func-
tions, all is well, until they meet one another."

"I wonder where those slivers come from. As you said, I am
a Gorgenbrilder—yet, at times I don't really feel like I belong.
Some of our standards have never made sense to me, and I
understand parts of Kalka'an's, but could never follow it the
same way. Levav makes sense to me at times too. I wish we
could just all agree on something. It's sad to think we are so
stubborn that it is unlikely to happen."

"Perhaps," Kilith replied. "There, I think your neck has
healed up again. Now you can meddle with it even when you
know I'm watching." He smirked at her.

Oops. She must not have been as secretive as she thought
when she ignored his instructions last night. "Thanks," she
mumbled, half-embarrassed and half still focused on their
discussion. Was his attention span for serious things really so
short, or did he just not care to engage in it?

"If we're going to live and die together," Oloren said, "we
had better come up with an operational plan for dealing with
different cultural standards. We don't have to agree on everything, but maybe we can come up with some compromises we
can all live with that will keep us from tearing each other
apart."

"Sounds reasonable," Baird nodded. "What do you
suggest?"

"Your main complaint against Gorgenbrild is the concept
of physical vengeance to make right a grievance. The good
news is that Gorgenbrild generally stays all grievances during
military campaigns anyway, in favor of keeping able-bodied
warriors able-bodied. Gorgenbrilders will agree to suspend
physical retaliations of *any kind* within our company for the

duration of the mission." Gabor rolled his eyes, and Oloren broke in again before he could say anything. "If it helps, consider it the mercy of strength."

"And for our complaints against Kalka'an?" Gabor pressed.

"No stealing from within the company. If we can't exact revenge to even the scales, refrain from tipping them in the first place," Canukke stated gruffly.

"And lying?" Baird asked.

"No one can determine at any given moment exactly how truthful you are being," Mereámé noted. "It makes sense to keep this measurable. Being caught in a lie will be an issue, and to avoid problems, it is best simply to be truthful. Check your reason for wanting to lie, and act only on the most positive motives."

Ruakh nodded. "I agree. This is less of a command and more a focus on team-oriented actions, and keeping our common goal at the forefront of our minds can bind us together and increase our chances of success."

Vadik clapped his hands. "By Glintenon, all that motivation garbage has some use after all!"

17

With the focus back on what the group had in common, life on the road became routine once again. It only took a few days for Enouim to be bored silly. She picked clean the last of the fruit and rabbit they had enjoyed after the day's ride and wiped her hands on her pants.

"So who is going to train me now?"

"What now?" Kilith asked, pulling a chunk of cooked meat off the bone with his teeth.

"My training. Before Levav I was learning to be more useful in a fight."

"Wonderful! When did you practice?" Ruakh said.

"Anytime not on a horse ... and sometimes while riding too," Vadik chipped in, recalling the two months they'd spent doing little else.

"I'll help!" Oloren offered, jumping to her feet.

The suggestion fueled life into the group as everyone clung to the only source of entertainment available. Baird, Vadik, and Gabor were also eager to fill the void left painfully vacant after Pakel's passing. Even Canukke started throwing out pointers from the sidelines along with his snide comments. Kilith joined in on the fun regularly, though at other times he seemed equally pleased watching the rest of them fool about. Sometimes he corrected one of the others in their approach, so Enouim was no longer the focus of all lessons.

"You should try it," Ruakh said to Mereámé, smiling. "It could prove useful."

"I would hate to be totally helpless," Mereámé admitted, her eyes bright, but her expression hesitant.

Baird and Oloren excitedly beckoned her to stand. "Up you come," Oloren said. Her confidence was both encouraging and forgiving, and Enouim saw Mereámé relax a bit. "Okay, have you ever fought before? What do you know already?"

"Literally nothing," Mereámé replied. "Like, I would probably die fighting a pigeon."

"Hey, don't underestimate those little beaks!" Baird laughed. "Well, by the time we're done with you, you'll be able to fight off perasors."

They taught Mereámé some basic punches, hooks, and kicks. She needed some assistance with form, and when Vadik encouraged her and she hit him as hard as she could, he hardly blinked on impact.

"I've moved a few chairs in my time," she commented with a smile, breathing a little harder than usual.

Gabor laughed. "Here, like this." He turned her wrist so it aligned with her forearm and tapped the pointer and middle fingers of her fist. "Hit with these two." He held up his palms for her to hit. "Hooks—go!"

Mereámé bounced on the balls of her feet. "You ready for this? I was the arm-wrestling champion against a neighbor kid when I was five. I might blow you out of the water."

Kilith laughed aloud.

Gabor smirked and nodded. "Hit me!"

Mereámé hit his palm and shook her hand.

"Again."

She hit him again and began to fall into a rhythm. Right hand hooked across to strike Gabor's right palm, and left hand to left palm.

"There it is!" he encouraged. "Now cross punches. Try it."

They went at it, nearly every mistake being met by Mereámé's sarcastic self-deprecating humor. The effect was heightened coming from such an innocent sounding voice, and the members laughed along with her while also rallying to encourage and teach her. Enouim wondered if Mereámé really felt as lackadaisical about the endeavor as she seemed. Enouim knew for herself, she didn't like being less than perfect at just about anything. Too large a dose of mistakes and Enouim became exasperated and less motivated.

Enouim had plenty of time to practice avoiding this when Vadik was kind enough to remind everyone how much more work she had to do on her break falls. *Ugh. Break falls.* Couldn't she just learn to avoid falling? She thought about that for a moment and dismissed the idea. No, she was far too uncoordinated. The ground seemed to beckon for her company at the most inconvenient of times.

After rehearsing, Vadik noted the utter absence of "breaks" to her falls—and Oloren suggested that Enouim was too much in her head. They had been focusing on falls straight forward, facedown toward the earth from a kneeling position. "You're thinking way too much, En. If you over think it, you're going to catch yourself on your elbows and be no good to anyone. Remember, forearms, at the last second."

"Don't think too much," Enouim repeated. "Don't catch myself on my elbows like I do every single time. Fall on my forearms. Not too early. Not too late. Remember all of that, but, you know, without thinking. What do you want from me?!" She huffed and shook her head. "If I *don't* think, I automatically catch myself wrong. If I *do* think, I still end up messing it up. I can't seem to stop myself either way."

"Except with your elbows." Vadik grinned. "Maybe we just need to spice it up a little. Catch you off guard."

"I'm not sure I like the sound of that," Enouim said, eyes narrowing.

"Hear me out. Well, actually, everyone *else* hear me out. You can listen or not listen, but you don't really have a say in this. I propose an experiment where we let Enouim practice break falls at unexpected times throughout the day. Out of necessity she'll have to figure it out one way or another!"

"Or get black and blue before meeting my first real adversary," Enouim grumbled.

"It'll be good for you," Gabor said. "Worth a shot. If you take a tumble off a horse, you'll be grateful for the skill."

"You're going to throw me off a horse?" Enouim's eyes widened.

"No, no, of course not," Baird piped in. "Not until tomorrow, at least." He grinned.

She scowled. Still, she couldn't help the rush of adrenaline and excitement that coursed through her veins. Part of her was intrigued, but another part, the part Enouim was certain preferred her to stay alive, was very much against the whole idea. "Harumph."

"Think of it as on-the-go—" Oloren didn't finish speaking before Vadik walked up behind Enouim and shoved her off balance. She tumbled to the ground. "—Training," Oloren finished.

Enouim grunted. "Fine, but I'm not the only one who's going to practice." She hooked her foot around Vadik's ankle and, grinning, brought him down with a crash.

From then on, everyone was fair game. Even Canukke got in on the fun and seemed to enjoy getting to show off. He was hard to knock over, and Oloren was the first to be successful. While he gathered sticks for a fire, she swooped down on him like lightning and knocked him off his feet before he saw her coming. A collective intake of breath followed as everyone waited to see how he would react to a dose of his own fallibility. Canukke looked up at her from the ground in surprise, and then broke into a hearty laugh.

The company continued like this, coming across no one outside their own, for four weeks. Vadik gave Enouim Pakel's sword, and saw that she practiced with it daily, but little else of note occurred in those weeks. Once they saw a syndicate of perasors far off, and another day a solitary perasor flew overhead, but it paid them no mind. Mostly the only life they saw was each other and regular-sized birds. As Gabor said, "I prefer birds that fit on a spit over a fire." The group readily agreed with this sentiment.

Enouim gazed over the muted tones of dusty yellow grasses soaked in the sparkle of the sun's rays playing with the river's surface. It was a good day. Spirits were high, and soon they would reach green grasses and trees once again and be near, hypothetically, to the Nazir—for whom they still had no exact location.

The river wound in the distance to the left and behind them. After the sea-serpent attack, they'd been eager to put a healthy distance between them and it. Strange how something so beautiful could house something so sinister. Enouim closed her eyes and allowed the sun to warm her face, focusing on the pleasant feeling and Inferno's steady gait. She breathed in deeply, letting it out again in an unhurried sigh. The air was clear, the day bright, and Enouim had successfully tripped Kilith *and* evaded retaliation that morning. Her break falls were also improving at long last.

When she opened her eyes, she saw an odd-looking band of people on the horizon—perhaps twenty of them. The wore sandy-colored cloaks and sat astride buckskin horses, making it difficult to tell where horse ended and rider began. If it weren't for the blue sky beyond them, it would have been nearly impossible to distinguish them from the landscape. Startled, Enouim looked around at the others and saw that she'd been last to heed them. Everyone else was quietly riding, eyes fixed on the group ahead.

Mereámé spoke under her breath to Ruakh. "Pyren?"

"Could be. Hard to say from here."

"So, um ... what do we do?" Enouim asked.

"If they are Pyren, we are in good hands. Levav knows many of the nomads. These may be friends."

"And if they are not friends?" Gabor said.

"We will be unfriendly." Kilith smiled ruefully.

"They have already seen us, and are allowing us to take note of their position," Ruakh said. "Giving them a wide berth now would be a sign of disrespect."

"We will meet them," Canukke said. "Now would be the perfect time to come across allies in the grasslands and hear what they know. Be on guard."

"Nomads are the best chance we have at learning where to find the Nazir," Mereámé reminded them.

"A smile on your face and a weapon in your hand," Vadik said, nodding.

Enouim felt her stomach squirm. Nine on the mission versus twenty nomads left her with a mathematical responsibility to take down two of them if things got ugly. Could she do that? Maybe the others could kill more than their share. Glintenon, Canukke had bragged of killing far more than that in the blink of an eye. Mereámé wasn't ready to take on a real fight either, so she would need protecting as well. As if reading her thoughts, Ruakh spoke up.

"Mereámé, with me. Stay close."

The nomads remained nonchalant as Enouim and her companions drew near. Perhaps they would simply ignore each other. They could just turn aside now, leave the nomads to their nomadic ways, whatever those might be, and go on their merry way. Clearly the rest of the company didn't get her mental note, because the horses continued to carry the group straight toward the strangers.

Enouim's heart caught drift of her stomach's nervousness and beat faster. She wasn't sure she needed blood pumping through her veins that fast. If things went south it would all spill out that much sooner. On the other hand, thinking like that certainly wouldn't slow it down. She gulped.

"Breathe," she heard Vadik say beside her. "We've got you."

Enouim nodded and focused on bringing air in and out, in and out. She drew her shoulders back and straightened.

The first of the nomads glanced down at them, stoically taking them in from only fifty feet away. Canukke set an unconcerned, ambling pace, and the nomads remained stationary. Enouim glanced at Vadik beside her and wondered how he could be so calm in situations like these. This time, though, she saw a furrowed brow and an uneasy tension building within him. He caught her gaze and winked. Everything would be fine.

Forty feet. Thirty-five. The whole nomadic troop watched them. Silently. The wind blew, and the grasses waved. Thirty feet.

A tall nomad extended a hand toward them from his horse. "Hello there, friends!"

Friends. Enouim begged it to be true.

"We greet you," Canukke answered. "How do you know us as friends?"

"We see you have the administer of Akavah in your midst. We welcome you."

What was an administer? What was Akavah? Did the nomads offer friendship because they mistook them for others? If so, Enouim was fairly convinced they should play along.

"Have we met before?" Ruakh asked with a smile.

"Your reputation precedes you. We know who you are. Healer of Levav, friend to the wilderness. We are the wilderness." His voice was deep and strong. Dark eyes looked at them. Was that a sparkle? Enouim breathed a sigh of relief.

"Well then," Canukke began again, "we are pleased to make your acquaintance, friends."

"The administer rarely leaves the borders of Levav. What brings him so far from home? We see most of you are not Levavin. Come, sit with us and we will share the news." The tall one waved them over and clasped Canukke's forearm in a gesture of greeting and introduction. All were mounted, and they found themselves surrounded by the nomads.

"I'm afraid our task is time-sensitive," Canukke said, "but we may spare a few moments. It would be good to hear of the happenings in these lands."

"We make our way to Levav now, in fact, to trade materials and news." The man smiled. "I am Canus."

"Canukke Topothain of Gorgenbrild, and my companions. Ruakh you seem to know already."

"Gorgenbrild! My, you have traveled far! Why keep us in suspense? What is this task of yours?" Canus asked.

Enouim wondered what the rest of the nomads were thinking. They watched carefully but as of yet had said nothing.

"Alas, it is best we keep the nature of our mission discreet for the time being," Ruakh said. "But if you travel to Levav, inquire there, and they will share their blessing of our task."

Canus looked disappointed.

"We have quite some distance left to go," Oloren said. "And wonder who we may meet to assist us on the way. Have you seen any others in the area?"

"Not for miles," Canus answered. "Which direction are you headed?"

"We continue our trajectory for some time," Canukke responded, nodding at the change in terrain now visible from the crest of the hill.

Following his gesture, Enouim looked and saw green grass beginning again, and the beginning of a lush-green tree line.

There was an awkward silence for a moment.

"Well, we certainly wish you safety on your journey," Canus said at length.

Another pause.

"Tell us, has the weather been fair?" Mereámé's musical voice spoke up for the first time. "What has it been like?"

"Excellent," Canus answered her. "Blue skies and few clouds."

"What of rain? The land needs rain, does it not?"

"It did rain, two weeks ago," said a new voice. The speaker was young, and Canus glanced at him. "It was a strange rain, though. Uneven?"

"Uneven," Mereámé repeated to herself, thinking.

"What direction do you come from?" Ruakh asked.

"You ask many questions, yet have answered few," Canus said, eyes narrowing.

"The lady asked about the weather," Gabor said, a bite to his tone.

Something in the air changed. In that moment tension

rippled through the space surrounding them. Enouim wondered now if it was a spark she had seen in those dark eyes after all, or a glint. The glint in the eye of an evil man whose deception has been accepted.

Canukke and Oloren exchanged glances, and Canus observed it. Enouim doubted anything got past the man, however subtle. Suddenly with a subtle flick of wrist, metal met metal, and the resounding clang rang out in the empty air around them. It was hard to say who moved first. Canus and Canukke were blade on blade in the span of a breath, and Oloren likewise had brought her daggers to bear against a nearby nomad. Enouim drew her sword and swung.

Kilith slew his first opponent and closed in on two more. Ruakh sprung to action using only his staff—both graceful and effective. He knocked one of his opponents off his horse and maneuvered himself between Mereámé and the bulk of the nomads.

Enouim leaned back in the saddle, narrowly missing an oncoming blade, and Oloren used the opportunity to slash at the nomad's exposed torso. "You're welcome!" she called back to Enouim as she spun in the other direction to engage a new target. Enouim's attacker bent over the wound, and Enouim pierced him through, then pulled out her sword and twisted to face a new enemy, but a hit from behind flung her from the saddle and sent her sword flying. Inferno reared, striking with his hooves as she gathered herself off the ground. It hadn't been the smoothest of break falls, but effective enough, and now was not the time to analyze it.

Springing to her feet and taking stock of her new vantage point, Enouim found herself face-to-face with the fighter Ruakh had unseated. The nomad lifted his blade and launched toward her. Muscle memory shot her forward to meet her attacker, bursting in close to the man's body and drawing a knife as she moved. She sliced across his neck with her right hand, then hooked it around the back of his neck and yanked him down to her level.

Canukke or Kilith would have given a head butt, but she couldn't quite bring herself to do it, so she kneed him in the groin repeatedly instead. He buckled, and she brought her elbow down on his neck in one swift, powerful motion. Mere seconds had passed since Enouim had regained her footing after her fall. She struck him again before shoving him aside and looking for her next target.

But he didn't stay down. The man recovered and catapulted himself at Enouim's waist for a takedown. She leaped backward and, as he fell forward, used her body weight to fall on top of him, pushing him down and loosening his grip on her legs. She let her knife fall with her and made contact with his left shoulder blade from behind. This time he didn't move. Enouim stood again, and noticed that several bodies lay strewn in the grasses—all nomad. She hoped not to break their winning streak.

Another nomad came toward her. Enouim took a deep breath and ran to meet him, but an arrow pierced him through from behind, its point protruding from the nomad's torso only four feet from her. She glanced up in surprise and saw Gabor grinning from his horse as he lowered his bow. Baird wheeled his horse around and struck at a nomad to his left who had taken a swipe at Mereámé when Ruakh's back was turned.

Oloren stood, looking hungry for the next fight, but few nomads were left to engage. Baird and Ruakh each faced one, Kilith a third, Vadik a fourth, and Gabor a fifth on horseback. Canus was still locked in combat with Canukke, now hand to hand on the ground. Oloren leaped onto the back of Vadik's opponent and put him in a choke from the rear. Vadik stopped a final thrust with his spear, and let Oloren bring him to the ground.

Canukke had Canus' head in a vise tight to his chest and he snaked a hand down to Canus' chin to break his neck, but Canus tucked his chin tightly into Canukke's ribs and wouldn't let him find a hold. With a gutteral cry, Canukke twisted the man's head until he was forced to face outward in front of him, then he kneed him in the spine, kicked the back of Canus' knee so that he fell, and jumped so that Canukke's full body weight came down on the back of the nomad's heels. Canus let out a great cry, and Enouim winced.

"Look east!" yelled Gabor suddenly.

Enouim's head swiveled to follow his gaze. Another band of nomads. Enouim's heart sank to her stomach and her fatigued muscles groaned within her. This wasn't over yet.

This group was larger than the last—at least thirty thundered toward them. There could be no mistaking what had just happened. A bedraggled group of strangers to these lands had fought nomads and triumphed. The buckskin horses of the fallen were still scattered here and there, and several had galloped down the hill toward the plains. These distinguishing features would be impossible to miss.

Enouim called to Inferno and climbed onto his back, wondering if she did so just to be soon knocked off again. Baird and Kilith finished off their adversaries and turned to observe the coming danger.

"What are we doing waiting here?" Enouim yelled. "Let's go!"

"Ride for the tree line," Canukke ordered, indicating the forest now visible ahead and to the left. "We defend from there. Archers at the ready."

"Take some of their bows and quivers," Gabor added. "Even if you're not an archer, you are today."

Vadik and Oloren snatched a few bows and quivers and

mounted. Enouim dug her heels into Inferno's sides and away they went. Her messy braid flew behind her in the wind, strays caught in her mouth and across her face.

The green forest waited in the distance like a celestial hall drawing them into refuge. The swiftly approaching nomads came from the right, and the rhythmic pounding of horse hooves mixed with the thudding of her heartbeat. Her eyes watered as the wind rushed past her face. She leaned in close to Inferno and prayed to no one in particular that they make it to the trees. She begged it of the air, of Glintenon, if he was around this far from home, and of any other benevolent Malak that might hear her. Could Malak read thoughts? Just in case, she whispered against Inferno's mane, "Help us, if you're out there. Get us to the trees. Get us to the trees."

The nomads barreled down on them. The gap between the two groups began to close, then the company's horses got a second wind. Inferno started the push, tossing his head and driving forward with renewed strength. Sky saw Inferno and, indignant at being left behind, surged forward herself, carrying Ruakh along with her. The other horses followed suit, and they regained their distance. Ten of the thirty nomads branched off from the main body and headed for the battle site, presumably to examine what had happened and offer help to any survivors.

The safety of the forest approached, if only slightly faster than the danger behind. Finally they broke the tree line, and Gabor and Kilith let loose their arrows on the wing. Baird and Vadik picked up bows as well, taking a little more time to let their sights settle in on targets. The company turned to face their opponents from the shelter of the wood. At least two-thirds of the nomads now coming toward them carried bows and arrows, but they did not release a single volley. Canukke held up his hand. "What are they doing?"

Several of the nomads pulled out white cloth—or what was likely white at one point—and waved them high in the air. The group came closer, slowed, and stopped perhaps sixty feet away. One man and one woman rode forward, hands extended. Both were weathered by life in the wilderness and appeared permanently tanned by the sun.

Ruakh suddenly laughed. "Stay your weapons, friends! I know these fine people."

Enouim looked again at the two individuals riding toward them. The man sat tall in the saddle, long brown hair tied up, right arm extended with palm facing up. The woman, with dark wavy hair and an inviting air, held the same posture. Both seemed confident and relaxed, riding close beside one another. A striking pair.

Kilith lowered his bow, but kept an arrow on the string. Ruakh walked his horse forward, mirroring the body language of the couple, and the remaining nomads trotted forward in response. To Enouim's surprise, when the nomads came into clearer view, Mereámé exclaimed and rushed forward herself.

"Mayimesh!" she called in joy, and the woman's face broke into a smile that filled her face. The two women rode quickly to meet in the middle and embraced on horseback, speaking in animated tones.

Canukke exchanged glances with Oloren, then rode out to meet these apparently friendly wanderers. The rest followed.

Ruakh clasped the arm of the man, and introduced them to the group. "Brothers, this is Amun of the East lands, though he is bound by no geographical barrier. He is as loyal an ally as they come, and has come often to Levav. This is his wife Mayimesh, whose reputation precedes her as a generous host, faithful friend, and worthy adversary. And, apparently, previous acquaintance of our own Mereámé."

"We met a long time ago on one of my father's journeys.

She has visited Levav many times since then," Mereámé explained, smiling.

Introductions went on for several minutes, and then Canukke spoke up. "As lovely as this meet and greet has been so far, why don't we continue in the woods and out of sight?"

"Of course," Amun said. "Whatever makes you feel most comfortable. There are few that travel these areas, but I see you have met less than welcoming folk even so."

The two parties merged and entered the forest, only thirty paces or so in. "Forgive us, but we do not mistake the beauty of the trees for security," Amun said. "We rarely leave sight of its edges, as it is said the wood is beckoning and bright without, and dark and treacherous within."

"But the fringes are friendly enough, don't worry," Mayimesh added. "We've had a long day of riding, as it seems you have. What do you say we all rest a while and share news?"

The suggestion was a welcome one, and all dismounted. The ten Pyren that had gone to check on the skirmish aftermath returned and were introduced. They brought back some of the runaway buckskin horses and reported with disdain that they'd found Canus and his men. Clearly the two groups were known to one another, and there was no love lost between them.

"Canus seemed to be the only one allowed to speak," Baird said, as they recounted what had happened. "He asked where we were going and what we were up to."

"And seemed quite ill about our preference to keep our intentions to ourselves," Gabor added.

Amun nodded. "We heard news of you from Levav last week. The message said little, but enough to impart that your desires are noble and in the service of an afflicted homeland. Levav gave their blessing and requested we offer assistance if we encounter you. We now see they did not merely bless you by word, but also in deed—for here among you are Ruakh the administer of Akavah and Mereámé Mandon. It is hard not to wonder what venture would call for such an assembly."

"But we don't mean to pry," Mayimesh said, placing a hand over her husband's. "Unless of course you would satisfy our curiosity if we did."

Enouim saw a twinkle in her eye and wondered what kind of mischief Baird and Mayimesh would get into if they joined forces. They seemed cut from a similar cloth, fun loving and audacious.

Kilith couldn't help but smile at her pluck. "We seek restitution for Gorgenbrild. We fear our people are already under attack."

"Khoron-khelek's reputation has traveled this far," Mayimesh said with a nod of understanding. "So you are after the Stone of Eh'yeh."

Canukke arched an eyebrow.

"No need for concern. It's no leap to guess, seeing Gorgenbrilders this far from home, traveling from Levav with the historian's daughter and the man of peace, and keeper, as they say, of 'The Way of the Stone.'"

"We prefer as low a profile as possible," Canukke said. "But it seems impossible."

"Understandable. The stone carries great power, and were it to be rediscovered now, it would not go unnoticed. Many would seek it. But great power never comes without a catch. We Pyren wonder if it is not best that it remain hidden, but alas, we cannot avoid the evils of our time. At the same time, if the rumors are true, the stone benefits only those it sees fit to benefit. So maybe it would be of no help to unworthy. We will not hinder you."

"How can the stone have a way, anyhow?" Gabor asked

dubiously. "We keep hearing this thing about the way, or the stone having a will of its own."

"A divider of the soul," Enouim said, remembering Kenan's words back in Levav. Kenan. A wave of sadness washed over her at the memory.

"Yes, we have heard much of the same," Amun answered. "Mostly from Ruakh, who is among you. How is it that you do not know these things?"

"Only the open hearted ask the questions which are meant to be answered," Ruakh said softly.

"Mysterious as ever!" Amun laughed.

"What do you think of the stone having a will of its own?" Mayimesh inquired, directing her question toward Mereámé.

"My companions want to wield the stone as Glintenon once did at the close of the First Morthed War. I believe they will find that Glintenon did not enlist the stone's services against Morthed, but rather the stone enlisted Glintenon."

"Ah, yes, and it is my sword that kills," Vadik remarked dryly. "I merely do its bidding."

"The stone is no trifle, but a conduit for great power. It was infused with might before the dawn of time by Iamwë, even before he created the whole world. To craft the Eh'yeh Stone, Iamwë reached inside himself and tore his heart in two. One he keeps within him, for his heart is boundless and removal of half does not detract from it, and with the other half he wrought a stone to represent not only his power but also his desires. Iamwë allows much pain, but is unwilling for a part of himself to be used and abused in the foul purposes of humanity, which is why he paired the two. It is said he fashioned the stone and placed it in the world."

"Sounds like hogwash to me," Gabor declared.

"Any babe old enough to talk has heard of Iamwë," Vadik said. "But this part I have never heard. So you are saying that according to legend, Iamwë ripped out a piece of himself and placed it in the stone, and that is why its power is so tremendous. Why make the stone at all? Or has the story been convoluted from decades of oral tradition?"

"His involvement now is much debated," Ruakh answered. "I believe he fashioned the stone as a conduit through which to act, and that he has indeed been heavily, intensely at work. Why such time has passed since his motions have been clearly perceived is a question I have no answer for."

"Maybe he's not there at all. Maybe he never was," suggested Amun. "Or perhaps he is, and simply forgot about us. This is my personal opinion. If that is the case, perhaps the stone is now separated from the desires of Iamwë and can be bent to the will of any that possess it."

"We can only hope so," said Baird. "It sounds like a more intimidating thing than I had imagined. I do not think I should like to hold the heart of Iamwë in my hands, even if it is just a portion, and even if it were just for a moment."

"Glintenon is the known champion of Gorgenbrild," Canukke said. "If a stone can have a side, it seems to have chosen us. Whether the thing has a will or not, that will is still bound within an object and will be utilized with intelligence and lifted by brawn. We have both in spades. Once found, if we desire it, then we shall have it."

"Well, then, it seems debate is fruitless," Mayimesh commented. "Your priority is in locating it."

"It is."

"Before fighting broke out between Canus and ourselves, they said it had rained in this direction but was a strange rain," Mereámé said. "Did you experience this?"

"Why do you talk so much about the weather?" Canukke demanded.

"Let her say her piece," Ruakh cautioned. "We are entering

woods of which neither you nor Kilith have prior knowledge. You accepted a historian along for moments such as these."

Canukke rolled his eyes but looked expectantly at Mereámé. She turned back to Amun and Mayimesh.

"We traveled from the other direction, I'm afraid, although it did rain," Mayimesh replied. "Quite an ordinary rain. It was cold and wet and such." She grinned, wondering what Mereámé was after.

"And the stars?"

"Actually, there were a few out of place several nights ago. Northeast from here, hanging over the forest. We thought our eyes were playing tricks on us! What may have caused something like that?"

"Well ..." Mereámé at first seemed to be about to launch into an explanation, but harsh looks from Canukke and Baird stopped her. Mereámé swallowed, looking uncomfortable. "Just checking. Checking in about the weather."

Mayimesh gave her a look, but shrugged it off in respect for Mereámé's awkward position, sandwiched between friends of differing opinions. "Well, then, there you have it!" she said with a smile. "I'm exhausted. The sun is sinking low now, and we've spent far too long today in the saddle. I think we may 'turn in' right here. Or is it 'turn out'? We haven't seen the inside of a building in a long time. But then, I suppose in that case, leafy branches overhead is as 'in' a place as any." Chuckling a bit to herself, she excused herself and went to check in with her fellow Pyren riders and let them know they would be making camp for the night. Amun excused himself and followed, leaving Enouim and her companions a short distance away.

"So ..." Enouim said, edging closer to Mereámé and speaking softly. "The weather? What did you learn from that?"

"The Nazir are difficult to find because their network of

homes are an intricate blend of invisible and mirror, most of which is set high in the air. But although it is hard to see, the architecture is still made of matter and still inhabits space. I think Canus' men found the rain spotty because some of it was hitting the Nazir floor above their heads, and I think Mayimesh saw an inconsistency in the stars because the reflection of the night sky disrupted the usual pattern. There are subtle clues to finding the Nazir, and if you know what to look for, you can follow them."

Enouim wondered what kind of place this could be. She found it hard to imagine what Mereámé was describing. "So we're close?"

"Yes! I believe we are very close. I expect we might find it tomorrow."

"Thank Glintenon," grumbled Gabor, overhearing. "About time we find these mythical invisible-but-not-invisible types and get on with it."

"Are they nice?" Enouim asked.

"Very nice," Mereámé assured her. "A little odd. But very nice."

"Communicating with the Nazir is like speaking in a whole new language in a way," Ruakh added. "We are lucky to have Mereámé with us to navigate that hurdle. I do fairly well myself, but Mereámé is an artist."

Enouim wasn't sure what being an artist would have to do with communication, but decided to let it go in favor of more pressing concerns. "And they are willing to help us, you think?"

"Well, that's a whole different matter. They are firm believers that the stone is not just a stone, and I think that is why when I met them long ago with my father, they were so receptive toward us ... because we respected that. We will need to speak carefully. Actually, if we really are as close as I think, they may have heard us already."

Gabor glanced around him, apparently feeling a little self-conscious. The trees seemed suddenly to have transitioned from welcoming green boughs of safety to eerie, duplicitous eavesdroppers.

Oloren kicked at Canukke's foot as they sat on the forest floor. "You hear that? You need to shut up for once and let Mereámé and Ruakh do the talking." She said it good-naturedly, but Enouim knew there was real concern underlying her words.

"Yes, well, when other people do the talking they tend to muddle everything."

"The greatest risk of being a muddler with the Nazir is you. Keep quiet tomorrow."

19

Enouim woke from the deepest sleep she'd had in weeks. Amun, Mayimesh, and the rest of the Pyren were long gone by the time she awoke, though Mereámé relayed their best wishes and farewell. After a breakfast of roast rabbit courtesy of Gabor, the Ecyah mission members set out once more in search of the Nazir.

The Ecyah Stone ... or was it Eh'yeh? The Levavin called it one, and Gorgenbrild and Kalka'an called it the other. She wondered if they were both wrong and how the differences came about. Do other people's minds wander like this? She wondered. Oloren looked like she could be deep in thought. Mereámé and Ruakh were speaking together, presumably about the direction of travel. Kilith seemed dark and brooding, but he always seemed dark and brooding, and Enouim wasn't sure if how he came across to people reflected his inner experience.

Canukke was off-putting as always, but perhaps the prickly exterior was just his resting expression, and Enouim was projecting. She seriously doubted whether or not Gabor, Baird, or Vadik were thinking anything at all, so empty their faces looked. How did they do that? Could they actually turn their brains off? If so, could they do so at will, or did it just happen? What would that be like? Even in her most peaceful moments, her thoughts were ever rolling one into the next in a never-ending stream.

She thought of home. Visions of gray stone and green grass passed before her eyes, and she thought of her mother and brother far away. Were they okay? Had Gorgenbrild been long under siege? Or had tensions escalated beyond siege to invasion? Would her home ever again be the home she's known?

Unwilling to keep her thoughts contained any longer, Enouim turned to Gabor beside her. "What are you thinking about?"

"Nothing," he returned simply.

Hmm. She'd been right about that after all. *Weird.* "I was thinking about home."

"What about it?"

"Whether or not it will ever be the same. Whether or not there will be people left to save by the time we get back. Whether or not nine people can stop Khoron-khelek, powerful weapon or no."

"Sounds like you think too much." Gabor's face was unreadable. Enouim hated that.

"How am I supposed to keep from thinking?" Enouim said, exasperated. "Do you really not think about anything at all?"

A beat of silence. Two beats. Three beats. How did he stand it?

He spoke again. "I think worrying about things we can't control is a waste of time. We should think about the many problems we may encounter that are preventable or solvable."

"Okay, that makes sense. I know I sometimes exhaust myself thinking about things I can do nothing about."

Enouim felt a flush of embarrassment in her cheeks. "But still ... it's hard. Don't you have anyone you care about in Gorgenbrild to worry over? It's strange that we have been riding together now for over three months, and I still know so little about you."

He shrugged. "I don't make friends easily. My mother was a warrior, murdered by tribesmen. My father spoke only in heavy sarcasm and a heavy hand."

"He beat you?" Enouim asked, concern and compassion in her voice.

"Only whenever he was at home," Gabor answered dryly. "The sound of his boots crossing the threshold haunts me to this day. I used to beg Glintenon to strike him dead in his sleep. I imagined ways I might do it myself, but could never get up the nerve. He terrified me. He eventually drank himself into a stupor one night and never woke up. My relief the next morning cannot be overstated."

Enouim blanched, then took a moment to absorb this. She tried to imagine the horror of ongoing, paralyzing fear like that. "And your mother?"

Gabor shook his head. "She was strong physically, but as much a prisoner mentally as the rest of us. My older brother ran away when I was seven. He was an inspiration to the rest of us. We all wished we could follow, but weren't sure how to do it. I thought maybe my father would chase me down if I ever left. And ... well, he was my father. We only get one."

She wasn't sure what to say, so she decided to say nothing for a spell. They rode on for a few minutes like that, lost in their own thoughts.

"I want to apologize."

"For what?" Gabor asked.

"Well ... I misjudged you. When we first met. You're detail-oriented and a hard worker; that was obvious. But I thought you were judgmental and stiff, and I guess I forgot you have a story like everybody else."

The corner of his mouth twitched. "My sob story makes you like me more, huh?"

"I ..." Enouim tried to think of something to say, but luckily Gabor broke back in.

"Forget about it. We all have a story. To be equally forthcoming, your judgmental assessment probably wasn't far off. I didn't like you much either. I thought you were airheaded and clueless. I was right about the clueless, but wrong about the airheaded part. The way you think is dizzying, and a lot of it seems pretty irrelevant, but you have a strong work ethic and a desire to learn. And you're better with people than I am."

Enouim wasn't sure whether she felt complimented or insulted at first, but his last comment took her off guard. "Oh ... um ..."

"I haven't really needed people," he continued. "I've gotten by without them, anyway. But sometimes I wish I could say what's on my mind the way you do, or see more sunshine than clouds."

"You care a lot, I think. Maybe you just don't know how to show it. And don't think I haven't noticed you doing all of Vadik's work when he slacks off!"

Gabor laughed. "Yeah, that drives me nuts."

Enouim smiled, and rode on feeling she'd made a new friend.

They circled the same small area for three days but had no luck finding the Nazir, and Canukke became more and more frustrated. "Are we really waiting on a bookworm to navigate us toward the most powerful weapon in the world? You said you could find it."

"I have the best *chance* of finding it," Mereámé said, "and I have clues to help me. They're still difficult to find, and if we don't stumble upon it just right, we could miss it from ten feet away."

Three days turned into a week, then two. After two weeks of fair weather, finally clouds rolled in and the sky grew dark. Rain began to fall, and Mereámé clapped her hands in excitement. "Here we go! Yes! Okay, keep an eye out for inconsistent rainfall. The heavier the rain, the easier it will be."

The rain didn't disappoint them. It picked up quickly, and Enouim began to worry the extra bandages she'd put on her neck were going to soak through. She pulled her mantle tighter around her and shivered. They rode on, and soon a break in the trees opened up the view.

"There!" Vadik called out, pointing. "Do you see it?"

"Mark me forever, I think you've found it," Baird commented, taking in the strange sight. Above the trees in one place they could see rain falling and then disappearing from view, so that it looked as though rain simply ceased to fall the rest of the way down, while on either side it continued to descend to the forest floor.

Mereámé nodded. "That's it. We need to make our way there."

With renewed hope they struck out for the place without rain. Dense thicket replaced the spacious trees and soon slowed their passage as they hacked through coarse underbrush. The cold and mundane work of plodding forward dampened their spirits, which had lifted for a time. Hours passed, but they took no rests.

Eventually the ground became softer and turned into a river bank, and the company came to a halt. The river pooled in the area before them, taking respite from its journey through the wood. On the other side, the bank, completely overgrown with bristles and thorns, dropped suddenly to a bubbly river where water gushed into the pool from some unseen tunnel or crevice. The river ran across the exact place through which they desired to pass, and going around would take time Oloren was not willing to waste.

"We can swim across it," she said. "There may be some underwater channel feeding from the river upstream, and if it's wide enough, we should take it. It will be the most direct path by miles. We should check."

"I'll go," Canukke said, dismounting. "This is as protected a place as any to leave the horses and continue on foot if need be. If there is an opening here, we'll pick them up on our way out. Based on the last rain, if Mereámé is right, we should be very close now."

Enouim's heart started to pound. She couldn't swim underwater! What might be lurking underneath? What about her neck? She stroked the scar over her collarbone, thinking of her parents' many insistences to stay away from large bodies of water. But no, she went off and got herself on a dangerous mission. And what did they do on dangerous missions? Go to cities with water for roads, and cross rivers with giant sea serpents, and *then* decide that wasn't enough water for one lifetime, so they found yet another river, deep in a forest the locals warned them against entering, and their first suggestion upon setting eyes on it? Yes, let's cross it.

Canukke took off his cloak and dove into the water.

Glintenon, that's just fantastic, Enouim thought. *Not only is it a river running against the direction we plan to go, but even the pool on this side is deep enough to dive into.*

It wasn't terribly far across. Canukke swam perhaps forty feet and examined the place that fed the river, then he ducked underwater and vanished from view. Well, if he died under there, she would *not* be leading the group, that's for sure. But if she were, the first thing she would do is send them all on the longer but far more sensible land route around the river.

As it turned out, Canukke wasn't drowned or swallowed by sea monsters. He came back up and called to them to join him, saying there was an underwater tunnel wide enough to fit through. Everyone started to dismount and prepare to cross, but Enouim sat frozen in the saddle. Her stomach turned in knots and did somersaults. Something lodged in her throat out of thin air, and she felt she couldn't speak. She could not get into that water.

"Enouim?"

She started and glanced down at Oloren and Baird, both standing at Inferno's head and looking up at her in concern.

"What's wrong?" Baird asked.

"I'm not getting in there," she managed with effort.

"It's not that bad. You'll only have to hold your breath for a minute."

Enouim shook her head. "I'm not doing it. I'm not."

Oloren walked up to the horse and gently laid her hand on Enouim's hand, over the reins. "You can do this. I know how brave you are. The water is clearer here, and Canukke says he hasn't even seen any little fish."

"They were all eaten by the bigger fish!" Vadik called back from the river, laughing. Oloren shot him a glare that could kill, and he rolled his eyes.

Gabor reached Canukke and turned back to see what was going on. Kilith was only halfway and returned to the bank. He got out of the water, walked up to her, took Inferno's bridle and lead him to the water's edge, then looked up at her, his gaze intense. "You're okay. Still on the horse, see? And look, Inferno doesn't mind it. Let's just give it a try, shall we?"

Enouim looked into his deep-green eyes and tried to soak up his confidence. She slowly swung a leg over and allowed herself to slide off the horse with Kilith guiding her descent. Her thumb tapped feverishly on her collarbone, and her breathing was ragged. All eyes were on her now, and her face flushed hot. What was happening to her? Why did no one else have this reaction?

"You can do it," Kilith said. "It's not going to hurt you. We're all here. Breathe."

"I c-c-can't."

"What is it?" Vadik asked, treading water halfway across.

What was it indeed. Enouim wished she knew. She must be going crazy. That didn't help her situation though, and it didn't slow her breathing. She took a step into the water and froze. No, no, no! She had to get out. Had to get out. This was wrong; she wasn't safe, not safe. It was going to kill her. Pakel had known, he'd known her fear in Levav. If only he were here now. Now everyone knew, and they all thought she was crazy, but there was nothing she could do about it. She watched the water swirling around her feet. Dark it seemed, full of malicious intent and a thousand opportunities for failure. Able to suck her down, down, down until she didn't know which way was up. Able to snuff her out.

Enouim grew dizzy, and her body felt tingly all over. Her heart lurched into her throat, and she was certain it could do little good there. The world seemed to close in on her, and her vision narrowed so that all her focus fixated on that dark, churning water plotting her demise. Yes, it was churning, wasn't it? Rolling, churning, surging. Enouim wavered and then stumbled back, vomiting the morning's roast rabbit onto the bank.

She was only vaguely aware of Kilith and Ruakh's presence by her side, saying something to her. "Enouim? Listen to me. Listen to my voice. Breathe."

Ruakh spoke this time, his voice even and soothing. "You're safe. Breathe deep, deep breaths. Slowly. In through your nose

... out through your mouth. In through your nose ... out through your mouth ..."

Enouim struggled to focus on his words, and took in jagged shallow breaths at his bidding. It wasn't working, not working.

"That's it. Slow, deep breaths. In through your nose, out through your mouth ..."

Several minutes passed this way, and slowly Enouim felt control of her body return to her. Her peripheral vision returned, and her breathing steadied. She looked up. Apparently she'd curled into a ball on the ground at some point after throwing up.

The next voice she heard was Oloren's. "Canukke, no. She's not coming. We'll go around."

An agitated response floated back across the water. Enouim couldn't make it out.

"I said we're going around. It's just a few more hours. If you don't get back here now, it will be *you* that is wasting time!"

Canukke, Gabor, and Vadik returned to the bank, soaking wet. No one bothered mounting again, as turning to the left to start their alternate route on land required hacking their way through unyielding brush. Enouim walked in silence, confused and ashamed. Mereámé looped her reins over her horse's head, trusting the animal to follow Sky in front of her, and came to Enouim's side.

"Want to talk about it?" she asked tenderly.

"I lost it."

"That really scared you."

"I don't know why I reacted that way. I just couldn't do it."

"Well, that's okay. Now that we know where we're going, we'll get there sooner or later. What's a few hours' difference?"

20

The sound of metal cutting at thorns and stubborn shrubs filled the silence for the next several hours. Mereámé remained by Enouim's side, except twice to check on her horse, who was plodding faithfully after Sky. They spoke quietly to one another on occasion about this and that, and finally arrived in the place they'd seen without rain. A glade opened up before them as they cut through the brush, and Canukke called Mereámé up to the front to confer with him and Ruakh. The group fanned out to painstakingly search the area, and Enouim thought they must look like tremendous fools, stumbling about. Gabor and Baird had their arms out, afraid they would run straight into some invisible wall and look even sillier.

Kilith angled his way toward her, and Enouim racked her brain for what to say. Surely he thought her ridiculous for her antics earlier. She still wasn't exactly sure what had come over her.

"So that was interesting," he said..

"Sure was," she answered flatly, feeling her defenses rising.

"Hey now. I didn't mean any harm. Just making an observation."

"Nobody just 'makes an observation' like that."

Kilith shrugged. "Maybe not." A pause. "It seems your relationship with water goes deeper than the surface."

"I see what you did there," Enouim said, evading the prompt.

Kilith rolled his eyes and gave her a pointed look.

"What?"

"You know what."

"Okay, tell me this. How is it that before you were all about me keeping my story to myself and being dark and secretive like you, but now all of a sudden you want me to spill?"

"Dark and secretive, eh?" Kilith arched an eyebrow, humor in his eye. But he didn't let the moment last long enough to derail the conversation. "Before, you were divulging personal history with hardly a thought. Now your life may be on the line. I was hoping our route would take us around large bodies of water, and it mostly has, but now I see that it is likely even one or two more such instances could mean the difference between your safe return to Gorgenbrild and endangering not only your life but the rest of your companions."

"It's not like I was shelling out information left and right. I share things with people I trust. As for the route ... you've been trying to avoid water? For me?"

"Don't change the subject," Kilith answered, tone clipped.

"I don't like water. And no, the incident with the world's largest sea snake was not my first fear of water." Something in Kilith's face made her heart skip a beat. "It's *not* the world's largest sea snake? Are you kidding me?"

"A story for another time," he said with a laugh. "Back to the water itself."

The water itself. Was he really that intuitive or did he know something? Well, he clearly wasn't going to own up to anything if she went fishing about what he knew. So she decided to answer honestly. She did trust him, after all. And Kilith's relationship with her father made her feel secure. Maybe if he knew something, he'd let it slip once she told him more.

"My scars ..." Enouim tapped her collarbone it, bringing his attention to the mark on her skin. For some reason the scar draping over her collarbone didn't burn like the ones on the back of her neck, so she hadn't put any bandages over it. "They're from some kind of sea creature. My father told me it made me sensitive to water somehow and that it wasn't safe. Apparently that's where I was found as a baby —in a body of water, bleeding. That's how my father—my adopted father, but my only father, you know—that's how he came to have and raise me. Both my parents warned me about lakes, rivers, and the sea. They said it was a place of beautiful majesty and power, and darkness and despair. It was better to admire it from a distance than to get too close and get stung."

"So there we have it," Kilith said after he'd taken a moment to absorb what she'd said. "You learned your fear from your parents."

"Well, and I was hasty once or twice with my bath and didn't put the watertight bandage over my neck like mother told me. That taught me pretty quick! It burned."

"You were taught it was dangerous. And here you are, not running from peril but toward it. Danger is inherent to our mission."

"You don't understand. It's not just that it was dangerous. Other kinds of danger are scary, but doable. This I could not do. I physically, mentally ... could not do it."

"Enouim. You didn't *believe* you could do it."

"And what exactly would that have gotten me? I'm not an

incredible swimmer. I know how to swim, but I hardly spent any time in water. My brother taught me in secret and only with bandages firmly taped down. I wasn't even supposed to learn—it was sort of a rebellious thing. And I am particularly horrendous at holding my breath. Maybe my lungs are worse than everyone else's."

"It seems you're convinced of your inability."

"Yes, well, I'm right, so believing it is the only way to avoid drowning."

"Maybe if you believed in yourself more, you would discover that it isn't as true as you think."

Enouim stopped short and turned to him, looking him in the eyes. "Believe in yourself? That's your big secret? Just believe in yourself? If all it took was believing I could do something, I could have become the first human to fly. When I was three. Just because you believe something hard enough, doesn't make it so. If I declared with gumption that the sky was purple, and believed it to my very core, it wouldn't change the fact that the sky is in fact blue. Not one iota."

"Yes, but do you believe in the mind-body connection?" Kilith responded evenly. "How was your psychological state impacting your breathing, your heart rate? Once your anxiety began to build, it played off itself. I can see it. You overanalyze everything."

"Thanks."

"Self-awareness is important. Lack of it can be lethal in circumstances like ours."

Enouim lifted her chin, glaring into the trees up ahead. She knew she overanalyzed everything. It just sounded so nasty in his mouth. What must he think of her? What did it meant about her that she overanalyzed? Maybe she was stupid, or crazy, or just incredibly insecure. *Ugh.* Now she was overanalyzing her over-analytical nature. *Fantastic.*

Kilith spoke again, softer this time. "I want you to know what you're capable of. Nothing more, nothing less. Sort out the logical from the illogical."

"I *have* been, for the last four hours! I don't know what happened to me. I don't know what's wrong with me. I panicked. I was terrified. Everything was dark; the water was evil, and I *knew* it wasn't evil—it was just water—but I felt so strongly that it was the depths of hell that I couldn't shake it. My breathing escalated and my brain went a thousand miles per hour. I just felt so anxious, and then I was anxious about being anxious, and I was angry with myself for being anxious, and for being anxious about being anxious, and there was nothing I could do but exhaust myself with my failure."

Enouim blinked. It all stumbled out so fast. She hadn't even been aware of exactly what the bottom of this sinkhole was. And there it lay, on a silver platter. *Failure.*

Kilith looked back at her with concern, but said nothing. What could he say? For a moment they locked gazes, still silent, each waiting for the other to speak. Or was he processing what she'd said? Maybe he already had, and found her hopeless. Enouim's eyes pricked with tears, and she turned away, shoulders slumped in defeat. She tried to distract herself, watching the rest of the company as they searched the glade for some invisible entryway.

"I think I've got something!" Vadik's excited voice rang out. "Mereámé? What do you think?"

"Well, if it feels like a wall, and you can't see it that great, my guess is yes," Oloren put in.

Mereámé picked her way carefully toward Vadik and put her hand timidly into the air in front of her. It flattened against a surface, and she knocked on it. "This is it." She moved her hand along the wall for several feet until she found open air, then, leaning down, she took two handfuls of earth and sprinkled them over the area in front of her. The dirt seemed to float in midair, its resting place revealing steps that had been quite invisible before. Baird stood on the other side of the stairs, eyes widening. He walked forward, hit his head on something, and reeled backward.

"Ow! Didn't you say this wasn't really invisible? How can I see through it?"

"Okay, so the entrances generally are essentially invisible. In just the right light you may see a shimmer, but the Malak have gifted the Nazir with cloaking ... well, I'm not sure with what, but with something able to hide the entrances."

"Wouldn't that be called magic?" Vadik asked.

"I don't think the Nazir would call it magic, but I suppose the rest of us might, lacking the knowledge to know better," Mereámé answered thoughtfully. "Once beyond the cloaking barrier, we'll be able to see more clearly. The Nazir have their own power, and their constructions are generally a mix of mirroring and semi-translucence."

"I've heard it's rather difficult to describe, and it sounds so," Ruakh said. "Why don't we see for ourselves?"

"Are there any cultural considerations for us to be aware of when we talk to them?" Enouim asked.

"The Nazir are the keepers of the sky. I met them once, as a child, with my father. They speak in beautiful and sometimes complex imagery, and are less versed in the common, casual language we use. Be gentle, be genuine, and pick it up as you go. Do your best, and when in doubt, say nothing. They are forgiving, but observant."

Canukke, now standing at the edge of the stair, watched Mereámé intensely. Searching, Enouim thought. She wondered for what. Canukke seemed somewhat satisfied by the explanation, and much to Oloren's relief, held out his hand in a gesture toward the stair for Mereámé to lead the way.

"Shouldn't we tie the horses?" Gabor asked.

Oloren shook her head. "They're exhausted. Let them rest. Besides, this brush is so thick we couldn't ask for better fencing. There are only a couple spots thin enough for them to get through, and the only tempting grass is here in the glade."

Baird nodded. "We shouldn't be gone longer than they would normally be turned out to pasture anyway."

"Okay, then," Mereámé said. "Here we go."

Mereámé started up the stair and Canukke followed close behind. Enouim wondered if he was letting a guinea pig go first to make sure the stairs were where he thought they should be.

"Watch your step," Mereámé warned. "It's slippery."

"Zegrath's teeth!" Gabor exclaimed. "How can I watch my step when I can't see it?"

Enouim stepped gingerly onto what looked like floating dirt particles, and carefully transferred her weight onto something solid. She wondered if unwelcome guests had toppled off it before and doubted the floating staircase had invisible handrails. Baird soon proved her right. His footing slipped and his arm struck out into nothingness in a vain effort to catch himself. Kilith and Ruakh each threw a hand out to grab hold of him, and they tugged him back to safety.

Mereámé led them slowly and steadily up the stair. Gabor took up the rear and carefully wiped the dirt off the first few steps as he crossed them. Enouim knew it wasn't good for her mind to watch the mindboggling reality of stepping onto what looked very much like air, but she could hardly take her eyes away. She looked down constantly, watching her feet in a sort of anxious fascination, and then looked up to make sure she was continuing in the right direction. She placed a hand on Oloren's shoulder ahead of her for comfort.

About twenty feet in the air, with trees rising on either side of them, Enouim startled when those ahead of her vanished one after another as if they'd passed through a film or membrane of some kind. When Oloren disappeared, Enouim could still feel her shoulder. The next second she herself passed through it as if she'd walked through a bubble without it popping. What she saw next took her breath away.

Networks of footpaths and bridges connected larger, circular meeting grounds like a multi-layered web. She'd never seen artistry like this, strong, yet delicate. Semi-translucent material enclosed some of the circular spaces and formed columns and archways, like sculptures of ice—smooth, clear, and beautiful. Another mysterious substance made the stairs and flooring, its texture sleek and flawless, like the archways, but the look of it mirrored the sky.

Still, it wasn't quite a mirror either. It seemed to mirror the sky but nothing else, and they left shadows on the floor but not reflections. She could see the sky, now clearing from the earlier rain, and several stubborn dark clouds returned to her in its surface. Enouim was grateful to be able to make out her footing again, as there was contrast between the forest falling below them and the azure steps.

Her gaze meandered from one transfixion to another. Figures with silhouettes like people walked as ethereally as their environment and seemed to be made of the same substance as that on which Enouim tread, their skin also reflecting the firmament—no wonder Enouim hadn't seen them initially. Adding to the illusion, they wore ice-colored silky robes that looked like they should be sheer and yet revealed nothing but a general lightness or darkness beneath.

At the top of the stair, Enouim reached out to touch the

side of the archway under which she passed and found it cool to the touch, like the marble in Levav. The network of platforms and pathways spanned numerous levels and frightening heights until the clouds covered them. At the higher levels, shapes moved to and fro, apparently taking off and landing. Were they flying, or was there some other structure she couldn't see?

Two female figures approached them, suddenly startlingly close. Both dipped their heads in respect, their blue skin dotted with the remaining storm clouds in the sky.

"May the sun's rays warm our introduction," said one, in a low and lilting voice. "We see fog rolling into a private harbor, bringing news of a troubled sea."

Mereámé dipped her head. "Let the fog lift. Humbly do beggars enter the house of the heavens. The sea may be troubled, but the guests ask only for directions to a seaworthy ship. Let the harbor remain in obscurity, forever to continue its admirable purpose."

"The sun shines ever warmer," said the first, smiling. "To whom do we owe the honor?"

"Mereámé Mandon is blessed to return, with Ruakh of Levav and companions from Kalka'an and Gorgenbrild."

"Strange dealings down below. I am Poleia, and this is my sister, Yadara. The daughters of the sky greet you."

Yadara nodded toward them, taking them in with interest, but remained silent.

Poleia spoke again. "Please, follow us."

Poleia and Yadara led them across the circular platform, up a softly inclined path, and to another landing. The group crossed the landing and proceeded from platform to platform for several minutes. Enouim glanced around at her companions. Gabor looked more and more nervous as the group increased its altitude, and Kilith's even-keel nature seemed to have a chink in it for the first time, but Vadik and Baird seemed charged up by the thrill. Ruakh and Mereámé appeared both comfortable and excited, and Canukke remained surprisingly mute. He seemed out of place for once, and Oloren's eyes were wide as she took in everything around her.

They came to a partially enclosed circular structure, which they could see was empty through the semi-transparent walls. Intricate archways, like fragile glass trees, danced up and over the entry to make a door. The beauty of it all enthralled Enouim, a welcome distraction from just how far she was from the ground, and just how flimsy her footing appeared to be now that it blended into its surroundings more completely. When she did remember, she could feel icy fingers of fear clawing to take hold of her, but she took deep breaths and steeled her mind to focus on the next step forward. After walking so long without railings, she was grateful this room had walls.

Poleia invited them to sit on seats, that looked to be carved of ice, set around a small circular table in the middle of the room. Canukke, Kilith, Vadik, Oloren, and Ruakh remained standing as there were not enough seats for all of them, and Baird, Enouim, Mereámé, and Gabor took their seats at Poleia's request. She excused herself and bid them wait there, leaving Yadara standing quietly at the doorway.

Yadara shifted her weight restlessly as nine earth dwellers sat about, some openly staring, others awkwardly trying to avoid such rudeness. Enouim warred with herself between the two, not wanting to embarrass the girl. But her curiosity got the best of her and she snuck glances the girl's way. Yadara's smooth and soft-draping garments were like a filmy, partially opaque mirror of the sky set on cloth.

The clouds had scattered over the past ten minutes or so,

and Yadara's reflective countenance lightened with it. Long, wide sleeves fell at her sides, and silver hair flowed freely down her back. She was a young woman, appearing perhaps Enouim's age, and Enouim wondered if time effected the Nazir the same as it did humans. When Yadara lifted her hand to brush her hair behind her shoulder, Enouim noticed silver marks on her wrists, like pools of molten silver. The marks were about an inch long and half-an-inch wide, apparent on both sides of the wrist as if piercing her flesh all the way through. Yadara's blue-gray eyes met hers in an accidental moment that surprised them both—Yadara smiled uncomfortably and both averted their gaze. Enouim wasn't the only curious one.

"So ... daughter of the sky, huh?" Vadik ventured clumsily.

Yadara glanced up at him with surprise. "I am a daughter of the sky. You are a son of the earth. This is as crystal, is it not?"

Vadik stared back at her dumbly, mouth parted.

Just then, three Nazir entered, tall and slender, with long limbs, and fair features. A man and a woman came in side by side, with Poleia following several paces behind. Enouim thought they seemed to glide rather than walk, so smooth were their gaits. Young they looked, yet ancient in the eyes and soul. Wonder filled Enouim at the sight of them.

The pair stepped into the middle of the room, standing before their worldly guests, and Poleia rejoined Yadara at the doorway, one positioned on each side. An air of confidence and authority hung over them, and Enouim felt quite small in their presence.

"The sun shines," said the man, opening his hands before him in a welcoming gesture.

The woman stood with her her hands folded neatly in front of her. "Let it bless our meeting."

"Let it bless our meeting," Mereámé agreed softly.

"I am Nyeur," the man said, "the Supreme Golden Guardian of the First Layer. This is Laskallel, Supreme Golden Keeper of the same. Tell us of yourselves."

"My name is Mereámé Mandon of Levav, and with me I have the administer of Akavah, Ruakh of Levav, and friends from Kalka'an and Gorgenbrild. We greet you as the birds greet the morning. Knowing your generosity, we seek only counsel from your expansive knowledge and wisdom."

Laskallel nodded. "We received a vision of an eagle in the sky roaming over the earth, seeing many creatures moving to and fro upon it. From its height, the eagle sees a mystery. One creature has the head of a lion, the body of a wyvern, and the wings of a molting swan. This cryptic beast circled in the wilderness, searching, searching, and spied the eagle's haunt upon the cliff. Seeing it, the beast wound its way toward the cliff, defying the laws of nature by ascending to a place it did not belong and had not been invited. The eagle sees its home is threatened and swoops down to protect it. What should be done to the invading creature?"

Mereámé's mouth opened, but no sound came out. She looked to Ruakh.

"If the creature is truly a threat," Ruakh began calmly, "then by all means, the eagle should protect its home however it sees fit. It is the eagle's nest after all, and it is the responsibility of the eagle to fight for its dwelling as well as any young fledglings in its charge. If, however, it only *appears* a great beast, and is in fact a mouse escaping a great cat, the mouse is at the mercy of the eagle, requesting the covering of its wing, if only for a moment."

"You speak well," Nyeur said. "And tell me, what are you called?"

"I am Ruakh."

"Ruakh. I am not familiar with you, nor the title your associate ascribed to you. What does it mean?"

All heads spun to Ruakh. Enouim had wondered what "administer of Akavah" meant for ages, and had kept meaning to ask him, but somehow never had.

"Akavah simply means 'brotherhood.' I provide and nurture it, and promote peace and healing among men."

"Your presence is peace, your modesty refreshing, and your companions clearly hold you in high regard. And how do we know your brothers hold to your values?"

"Well, I can speak only for myself, and as there are nine of us, we certainly are not all the same. But I have faith in each of them, and believe in the cause we serve. Our common goal has brought us together, as odd a group as it may be."

"I see you are a swan. And what of the lion?" asked Laskallel.

Canukke spoke, and Laskallel turned to him. "My purposes are pure, and my desire to protect a people defenseless and weak, losing hope and abandoned by Glintenon."

Oloren held her breath.

"A man who presumes to be the lion, naming himself the strongest while in the company of his friends. Bold, to be sure." Her voice was silk, but every thread disapproving. "A poisonous darkness billows from the earth, and the sky does not receive it. Tell me, when the eagle discerns a snake in its nest, does it not crush it with its talons and consume it?"

21

Canukke glared at Laskallel; his lip curled, but for once he sat silent. Enouim's heart beat wildly, and she twirled the end of her braid with shaking fingers. A moment passed and the indignation vanished from their leader's face.

"No leader can care for his men without traits of a lion." Mereámé glanced between Canukke and Laskallel. "It is fitting, no? But a lion in his territory can be a cub in the eagle's nest, and a snake may learn it is little more than a worm in the eagle's home. We have much to learn from you."

Canukke crossed his arms. Enouim knew he would feel Mereámé's words painted him as weak. He would want to be seen as an equal. And yet, could he really feel equal to these beings?

"You and your friend"—Nyeur nodded at Ruakh—"are morning doves to us. Ruakh answered the test well when it was posed, and we are inclined to accept and hear you. But *now* you tell us ... this man with the hate in his eyes is your leader."

"We do not yet know one another," Canukke said. "In dealings with men, even an enemy is given a chance to speak."

"In dealings with *men*," Nyeur said, "we have learned that words are often empty."

"Hasty to make judgments, from up here in the clouds!" Canukke exclaimed. "What dealings with men have you had? So removed are you, you do not know with whom you speak. Indeed, if you had bothered with reality beneath you, perhaps you would have heard of Canukke Topothain of Gorgenbrild!"

Laskallel arched an eyebrow. "And who is this Canukke Topothain of Gorgenbrild?"

Enouim gulped and looked at Oloren. Oloren caught her eye and widened hers to silently share her concern. Letting others lead and speak on his behalf was beyond Canukke's comfort zone.

"I am the greatest warrior to be found in the mountains, the most formidable foe to be faced in the east. My sword has hewn more enemies than could fit in your little sky pads here. Perhaps as we become better acquainted, your opinion will rise to match my reputation."

Oloren spoke up: "He is well known in his circles, and his name travels from land to land in the surrounding areas, speaking of his accomplishments. He comes across harshly, but only because loved ones at home hang in the balance."

Laskallel narrowed her eyes slightly. "A man whose temper is so easily triggered has reflected little on himself. He looks in a mirror and goes away, instantly forgetting what he looks like. What good is it to tell such a man anything? Who would advise a friend to disclose sensitive information to him?"

"I knew this was a bad idea," Canukke scoffed. "How could these pretentious people expect to understand? Every person east of here, and even further in all directions, knows who I am and my litany of accomplishments. We are here on a humanitarian mission and were led to believe you were knowledgeable and wise. I see neither knowledge nor wisdom."

Enouim had no idea how they would recover from this. Canukke was generally arrogant, sure, but more controlled than this. Still, Canukke was for the first time in a totally foreign environment and any semblance of control had been disrupted. Another authority had insulted him in front of his friends and subordinates.

On the one hand, any attempt to salvage the relationship with the Nazir would best be accomplished in Canukke's absence. On the other hand, any move to cut Canukke out of the loop would agitate him even further, as he already felt his leadership was being undermined.

"Please," Mereámé said. "I have had the pleasure of your hospitality once before, and I think you will find we have common loves and interests. Consider us with grace."

Nyeur and Laskallel observed Mereámé carefully and scanned the group. It was deathly quiet, as if no one even breathed. Canukke held a self-righteous posture, arms crossed, chin jutting upward. Everyone else was tense, the atmosphere taut between them. Enouim imagined time passing them by, as even a minute in that silence felt like a lifetime.

Nyeur broke the silence.

"Those who allow themselves to be alone with their thoughts often get to know themselves, but those who do not, do so on purpose, afraid of what they might find. We will confer privately with Mereámé and Ruakh and hear your proposal from them."

With that, Nyeur and Laskallel turned and exited the room. Mereámé and Ruakh looked questioningly at Poleia, who motioned for them to follow. They glanced at one another, cast looks back at the rest of the group, then quietly got up and left without a word. Poleia left also, trailing their Nazir superiors and Levavin guests.

As soon as they were out of earshot, Oloren hissed, "I can't believe you did that. This is *exactly* what we talked about! Your grand achievements mean nothing up here. The Nazir culture is not impressed by what impresses down below. And the moment they assess you as anything less than amazing, you insult them!"

"I never did that! I simply pointed out what may have been amiss. They jumped down my throat and called me hateful when I hadn't even said anything. If they were as blameless as you think, they would have taken my words to heart and apologized for their mistake."

Oloren shook her head. "This is ridiculous. You always do this. You get caught up with yourself, and here we are strung out in limbo while these people decide our fate."

"Caught up with myself? I am the one who earned this position. I am the one who saved your life countless times, on the mountains and in the plain. I am the one who carried you half dead for five miles that time. And what thanks do I get? I think this has more to do with you than with me. Why is it that you feel the need to undermine me? Does it make your own insecurity less intense?"

"*My* insecurity? No, don't make this about me. And for the life-saving bit, I have done the same for you. We are in one another's debts. But what comes of Gorgenbrild if they stop us here? All our work will be for naught. The trail ends here. The journey a waste."

"I don't think this is productive," Enouim said.

"I didn't bring this up," Canukke answered casually. "They started it, and Oloren kept it going. I clarified what needed to be clarified. Move on."

Kilith spoke for the first time, voice low and graveled. "The only thing to save us now is silence."

The group caught the look in his eye, and a blanket of unnerving quiet settled over them. At length Poleia returned to summon Kilith, saying nothing except to call for him. He dipped his head graciously and followed her. Enouim thought he was relieved to be rid of their presence. Neither he, nor Ruakh, nor Mereámé returned, but periodically Poleia would come again and call someone else. Oloren was next, leaving five of them remaining.

"Scars, this is a sticky situation," said Baird finally.

"They're probably killing them off one by one," Gabor grumbled.

Vadik shook his head. "It's more likely they are interrogating us individually to see if our stories match. We didn't even say what we came for as a group. So they heard it first from Mereámé and Ruakh, then Kilith, and now Oloren. The Levavin they trust, but the rest of us have said little. They get the most, least edited or rehearsed information by hearing from each person alone. It's smart."

"Do you think we will sound that different?" Baird asked. "We're all here for the same reason."

"Well," Enouim said, "Mereámé and Ruakh see it more as a personal, spiritual journey I think." She thought about what she'd heard from her Levavin friends, and what Kenan had shared about the stone as a way of life. "Almost like a historical artifact, maybe, but one that represents far more than power. A lifestyle, as they have said. While our cause from Gorgenbrild is to save our people from oppression and annihilation."

"And Kalka'an is an ally to Gorgenbrild and has interest in the whereabouts of the stone as well. It's natural to have some variation in our reasoning," Baird noted. "Surely they will see that. They seem intuitive."

"Too much, maybe," Gabor said. "And if our stories come across as incongruent rather than differing perspectives, they may think we are all lying. What might the Nazir do if they think we have tried to deceive them?"

"Birds have no business with beavers, until the beaver gnaws through the tree the bird calls home." Yadara's voice startled the group. She'd been so still and quiet they'd all but forgotten she was there.

Baird frowned. "Um ... wait, what?"

"Speak plainly," Gabor said. "What is this about birds and beavers?"

Enouim stared at him. "It's a metaphor."

"Sons and daughters of the sky do not meddle overmuch with the dealings of earth dwellers." Yadara's manner was frank and innocent, her vocal register on the lower end for women, soothing and unhurried.

Baird nodded. "So she doesn't think they'll do much to us, since sky people don't generally bother with us insignificant earth folk."

"Or they normally wouldn't, but since we gnawed the tree and invaded their home, they are now forced to deal with us," Vadik suggested.

Enouim examined Yadara for a reaction. She gave none outwardly, and Enouim wondered what Yadara made of them and their strange interactions. Gabor plucked at his edge of his tunic and sunk lower into his seat. Vadik paced back and forth for several minutes before finally settling into one of the ice-marble chairs, and Baird simply leaned his head back and closed his eyes. Canukke still sulked self-righteously against the wall behind them, saying nothing.

Through one of the archways on the other side of the room, Enouim saw Nazir people going to and fro, each of them unhurried but purposeful. Three stood together one level up at the base of a flight of stairs, and two walked together over a seamless bridge, their shimmering cloaks and sky-painted skin only slightly contrasting against the horizon they reflected. Through the archway on the right, several more could be seen, walking in ones and twos. Enouim wondered what it was like to live here, and what business they could be busy carrying out.

Poleia returned, feet making no sound on the smooth floor. Gabor swatted Vadik, and he straightened, opening his eyes. Poleia surveyed them for a moment and then looked at Enouim expectantly. "If you would," she said.

Enouim nodded and stood, her racing thoughts and restless spirit grateful to escape the apprehension of that room. Poleia led Enouim away, leaving Canukke, Vadik, Baird, and Gabor behind her, with Yadara still standing by the archway.

They crossed to another platform, seemingly floating in the air but for the branches of bridges it had to everything else. Enouim dutifully followed behind Poleia as they went up, up, across, and then down. She was thankful for her leather footwear and the little traction it provided, but even so she slipped several times on the smooth surface.

The sun began to set, and Enouim noticed Poleia's hair slowly exchanging the silver of an overcast day for a gentle ombre of blue, pink, orange, red, and yellow. Her shimmering garment reflected the same, and her skin blended so well with it, that were it not for the silky contrast of the folds, it would be challenging to decipher where one ended and the other began. Enouim marveled at the change, and the beauty of the world from this height. Up here, with the green of the forest far below, it seemed ludicrous that any threat could encroach upon their freedom to soak in a sunset sky or bask in the light of the coming moon. The two women came to yet another platform, as if webs of lily pads made of ice were floating in different layers of sky. This time, the platform had descending stairs into a large orb with a flat bottom that created another nearly enclosed room. Poleia led her down the steps into the room, stepped to the side, and gestured she seat herself. Nyeur and Laskallel sat opposite a single chair with a soft light-blue cushion placed upon its seat. Nyeur and Laskallel's complexions had shifted also, colors of the horizon gradually intermingling upon their skin and robes. Their hands lay folded in their laps, and their faces turned toward her in a sort of tranquil expectancy.

Enouim's nerves called out to her, telling her what a bad idea this was and how likely she was to mess it all up. No pressure, but the lives of a nation hung on this moment. She took her seat, working her hands anxiously. Never to turn. This was the moment she would share her story, her purpose, and leave her life and the lives of those she loved in these gilded hands to decide their fate.

"And what are you called?"

22

"Enouim Cokanda," she replied. The two tall, beautiful figures before her looked unmoved, so she added slowly, "of Gorgenbrild." She wondered if any of this information was meaningful to Nyeur and Laskallel.

"Enouim Cokanda," Laskallel said thoughtfully, as if savoring the name. "Tell us, Enouim. What brings you so far from home?"

She wasn't sure why, but Enouim felt a wave of emotion wash over her. *Home.* So, so far from home. Pleko teasing her, her friend Balat joking along with her in the Mangonel, that blessed old bag of bones Pinky, and mother pretending she hated the pig. Would she ever see them again? Were they alive? If they were, did they wish they weren't?

What answer could she give? Enouim was not one of the six valiant warriors handpicked to carry the hope of a people. And she was quite sure she would crumble with the weight of her deception if she lied about it. She'd always been a terrible liar. Enouim sensed these two beautiful, timeless beings carried enough wisdom to decipher the truth of anyone, even a practiced fibber like Baird.

Pakel's words floated back to her from three, nearly four months ago. *Either you do deserve to be here for some reason, and you need to find and fight for that purpose, or you need to prepare to face the tumult awaiting you in Gorgenbrild.* And she had done that, hadn't she? Enouim remembered the terror that had come over her when Canukke abandoned her in Kalka'an. She hadn't been in fear of her life and was physically far safer there than in her own home. That fear, the fear of being useless, stagnant, purposeless, a roving soul in a world cut off in both locality and philosophy, had moved her to go to lengths that had surprised herself. She had found and fought for her purpose.

"I am here quite by accident," she said. "Or, at least, I was at first. I am not renowned in my land or an experienced fighter. I was afraid and stumbled onto this mission through a series of unfortunate events. Yet, now, I wonder if it were not fortunate after all. My family and friends are in fear of death, or worse. I am here to do something instead of nothing. To *become* something. To travel like my father and perhaps draw closer to his memory through it."

"You seek to learn about yourself."

"I suppose, if I am being honest with myself, my purposes are rather selfish. I do want to save my people, to restore the stone—erm, I suppose the others already talked about that— to whomever it belongs to, if indeed it belongs to anyone ... and let the light of a civilization shine a little longer. I have both altruistic and selfish motives, but they blend together, and I wonder if they aren't inescapably intertwined." Enouim furrowed her brow, pondering the matter.

"Self-awareness is a critical skill," Nyeur noted. "Two other things I notice about what you said: one, that your purpose is restoration of the stone, and two, that you question its rightful ownership."

"I assume everyone else has already told you about the stone? The object of our nation's hope?" Enouim asked.

"Speak to us as if we knew nothing," Laskallel instructed.

"Okay." Enouim swallowed. "Do you know what it is?"

"What is it that *you* know?" Laskallel returned, gently but firmly.

"Right. Well ... it's a weapon. That's what Gorgenbrild says. A stone imbued with great power, wielded only by the mightiest, and last seen set in the hilt of the sword of Glintenon in the First Morthed War. It is mysterious, and there is much I do not know. Gorgenbrild and Kalka'an call it the 'Ecyah Stone,' and Levav calls it the 'Eh'yeh Stone.' Who knows which is right? The Pyren say that the stone's power originates from Iamwë himself, who rent his heart in two and placed it among men in the object of the stone. To protect men from abuse of its power, Iamwë placed heart and might into the stone at once, irreversibly. As a result, from what I gather, the stone has a will of its own and allows its strength to be allocated only to those with whom the stone's desires align.

"As I understand it," Enouim continued, "the Levavin hold that the stone represents a way of life, an inner purity of sorts or ideal standard of living they hope to emulate. The stone divides a man at his core, able to discern good from evil intentions. I wonder what would happen if someone with mixed motivations attempted to wield it, like mine have been on this mission? I suppose that is a question for another time. Hmm, that is an interesting thought though. What of it? If you know the answer, or have a guess, I would surely love to hear it."

Nyeur smiled. "You are an investigator."

Enouim warmed at the word. He seemed to *see* her, beyond what came out of her mouth. "I like to know the truth of things. I'm not sure how to tell though, with so much variance in information. So far it has been piecemeal at best."

"And whose is this stone? What would you do with it were you to reach it?"

"I don't know, exactly," Enouim responded, fidgeting in her seat. "I suppose I would aid in its return to Gorgenbrild and lean on the mightier of my companions to lead the charge to redeem my homeland. After saving my people, if they are able to be saved, I would endeavor to return it to its rightful owner. Gorgenbrild and Levav both lay claim to it, and Glintenon is Malak over both Gorgenbrild and Kalka'an, so I would want to observe the stone and its effects to determine whose information was closest to the truth once the facts are in front of me. Personally, I don't care too much whether it stays with Gorgenbrild after we are set free, if we are not meant to have it. But in honesty, I am no one of significance at home, and would probably have nothing to do with the decision."

Nyeur nodded. "Wisdom begs to be set free, unhindered by folly of any kind. She does not listen to Folly when he speaks, lets him not into the recesses of her mind. She looks to the counsel of sensible and weathered friends. When a wrong is revealed, Wisdom and Justice work together as allies, setting forth what is right and setting aside what was misguided from the beginning."

Enouim looked at him, waiting for further explanation. She agreed with it, as far as she understood it, but what was he talking about exactly? To her disappointment, no clarification came, and she found herself blinking back at them. "I see," she answered dumbly, if only to fill the space in the room. Because she didn't see. She wasn't sure what he was hinting at, and she wished he would just be out with it.

"Chains wrought by our own minds are not loosed easily,

but they are those we need rid of the most," Nyeur said, looking at her intently.

Enouim felt herself caught up in his eyes, deep pools of knowing that she wished could be transferred with the directness of his gaze.

"An inquisitive mind and open heart are great assets you have. Nurture them," Laskallel told her. Enouim nodded, and Laskallel continued. "Tell us, what do you make of your companions?"

"We meant no disrespect," Enouim stammered hurriedly, as if speed would convey more convincingly the truth of her words. "Canukke is ... well, he is good in his way, and he's used to being in control and in command. His negotiations with other leaders are generally favorable, and most know his name and welcome him."

"You defend him," Nyeur said, leaning back in his chair.

"No! Yes, well, yes, and no." Enouim thumbed her scar. "That is ... I defend him as a person, but not in action. I'm not sure he always realizes what he does—knows how he comes across."

"Or perhaps he does, and does so on purpose," Nyeur returned. "But, as you say, perhaps we do not yet have all the facts in front of us. We will suspend judgment on this matter until we are through. As for you" —he shared a meaningful look with Laskallel—"We see no malice or danger, but rather a dry land thirsty for streams of knowledge and a rough-cut rock not yet hewn to reveal its crystal."

Nyeur's words felt like a soothing salve for a wound she didn't know she had. Enouim found herself choked up, feeling herself quite like a desert desperate for rain and resonating with that imagery. She wasn't sure about the rough-cut rock bit. What did he see in her? Would she see it in herself eventually? Or was Nyeur misled?

Laskallel observed Enouim keenly for a moment as she absorbed Nyeur's words, and then she spoke, "And what of the others? What do you think of them, and what do you see as their purpose?"

"Oh, I am honored to be in their company," Enouim said easily. "They are a good group. Ruakh and Mereámé are precisely as they seem to be, and every bit as lovely as you interpreted. Both perceive the Ecyah Stone as something more than an artifact or a weapon, something to return Levavin life to what it once was, I think. The city longs for it, but none long for it more than Ruakh and Mereámé. Ruakh is a teacher, I believe, of the 'Way' developed from the values Iamwë placed on the stone. Something like that. Mereámé comes in the service of her father's work, as her father is a well-known historian who has been taken ill. Mereámé did not want to leave him, but sees this as a personal and family mission preserving and extending the legacy of her father. She sacrifices much in coming with us and is outside her comfort zone but eager and willing.

"Vadik is a thinker, from every side of things, and I think he sometimes prefers whichever side has not yet been defended. But he is a loyal friend and a strong fighter with a strong heart. Baird is funny. He is adventurous, and I'm not sure I've seen anyone quite so full of life. Baird delights in the unexpected, in well-meaning mischief, and in dreaming. He strikes me as a dreamer, anyway ... and, though he may be from Kalka'an, I do believe that inside he may belong somewhere up here with you rather than down on the earth. But then, he would probably install insane ropes to swing off, introduce everyone to pranks, and generally change the whole operation you have going." Enouim smiled thinking about Baird gallivanting about up in the clouds, making trouble. Maybe they could use a little loosening up around here anyway. "As he told me when I met him, he should be judged by his actions rather than the reputation of his people or the culture within which he was raised."

Enouim took a breath and continued. "Oloren ... what a gracious friend. She welcomed me, she and another friend that was lost to us in Levav ... they took me in when no one else did. Before anyone else was ready to accept me as a member of the team, they did. Oloren is encouraging, kind, quiet in large groups, comfortable and fiery in small ones, and a force to be reckoned with among enemies and friends alike. She seeks to mediate between friends, and whatever she does, she does with passion.

"Gabor has been a puzzle, or at least he was to me. When I think of Gabor, I think of precision. He picks up the slack when others don't do their part, because it drives him insane to see a job half-done. He is a hard worker with a shrewd mind, an able fighter, and loyal. I believe his mind, once made up, is not easily shaken ... for better or for worse."

"And the eldest of your collective?"

"Kilith Urul is a wise man. He is well traveled, well versed in culture, and shrouded in the mystery that accompanies rangers. Kilith is rarely without opinions, but is slow to speak. Rough around the edges, dangerous to foes, kind to friends. I trust him with all that I have."

"You speak fondly of your friends," Nyeur said, his eyes soft and kind. "We thank you for your time."

"That's all? Will you help us? Do you know where the stone is?"

Laskallel shared a look with Nyeur. "We are well acquainted with that which you seek. We have yet to speak with four of your company, and will deliberate together after having done so. One does not plan a journey without considering what will be necessary for it—the supplies, the cost, guidance of the stars, the weather foretold by the sky."

"Thank you for your consideration," Enouim said. "Much hangs upon your decision."

"Indeed it does. It is a decision of weight in either direction, and were it placed on a scale, it is difficult to say which side would be heavier. The more information the better. Haste is not the friend of good judgment."

Laskallel gestured toward Poleia, and Enouim's eyes followed her hand and noticed that Laskallel also had marks on her wrists, similar to those that Poleia and Yadara had, but hers looked like liquid gold rather than silver. Enouim glanced back at Nyeur and saw that he, too, had gold marks on his wrists. She found them intriguing and beautiful, and wondered if it was a family or blood bond of some kind, a birth mark, or something more significant.

"Poleia will see you to your friends, and you will stay with us tonight," Laskallel said.

"We will give you news of our verdict in the morning," Nyeur added. "May the stars shimmer upon you."

"Thank you," Enouim said, unsure of what else to do. She gave an awkward half-bow, half-nod to her hosts, and followed Poleia up the stairs.

Once again Poleia led her through various windings, up, down, and around, until arriving in a large, wide-open rectangular platform with rounded edges. Enouim was surprised at its shape, as most landings had been circular. One-half had cubbies, perhaps eight feet by four, cut out from its surface and dropping below the landing itself by approximately six feet, so that from the side one could see the cubbies from a distance. Enouim thought they would look like graves in any other setting.

Upon closer examination, Enouim now saw that although

there were perhaps forty holes set up in four rows of ten. Each cubby had a hammock made of mirror material strung inside it. Each cubby had a floor and two sides, but lengthwise the hammocks were open to the air. The other half of the landing, to her joy, contained her friends—Ruakh, Mereámé, Oloren, and Kilith—sitting in a circle and talking together.

"Enouim!" Mereámé waved her over.

Poleia waved her on and disappeared without a sound, leaving her alone with her companions. Enouim hurried forward and seated herself in the circle between Oloren and Mereámé, who made room and patted the space between them.

"How did it go?" Oloren asked.

"Okay, I guess," she replied, somewhat unsure herself. "They were nice enough."

"Lovely, aren't they?" Mereámé smiled. "Such grace. I'm sure you did great, and they saw you the way we do."

"They asked me what I'm here for, what we want, and what I thought of all of you."

"They asked the same of us," Ruakh said. "It seems after the incident with Canukke, they thought it more effective to speak to us individually."

"Best way to find the truth, and see whose story doesn't match up," Kilith said. "Like separating witnesses. They are systematically screening us for holes in our story, and any red flags that might give them pause in handing us the keys to the most powerful weapon in the world."

"Wow. When you put it like that," Enouim said, "I'm surprised they're still speaking to us at all after Canukke went off on them."

"Gracious, I told you." Mereámé seemed delighted and downright dreamy after her interview.

"Really, what happened in yours?" Oloren asked. "You never rightly said."

"Oh ... the same as the rest of you" Enouim thought Mereámé pulled back a little as she spoke. "You went together with Ruakh, didn't you?" she asked her.

"Yes, we were together," Ruakh replied. "They asked us first what our business was about, and questioned us about our interest in the Eh'yeh Stone and our knowledge of it. Then they wanted to know our thoughts of you all, as it seems they did with each of you. They kept Mereámé longer though, saying they wanted to talk to her about her previous visit."

Mereámé flushed. "We shared history, news ... information."

"Secretive," Kilith observed, casting a sideways glance her way.

"No, it's nothing. Nothing you won't find out soon yourselves, anyway."

"And we should wait because ...?" Kilith arched his eyebrows.

"We talked about my father, and how he and I have been. We spoke a little of the stone, but they asked me not to share everything until the timing was right."

"When exactly is the timing right?" Oloren put in.

"When it is apparent to all of us, I suppose," Mereámé answered, clearly feeling self-conscious under the scrutiny. "I want to tell you, I do. But I can't break my word. Let's talk about something else."

Kilith raised an eyebrow. "Your loyalty is closer to the Nazir than to us?"

"Now, now," Ruakh said evenly. "What is your impression of these Nazir, Kilith?"

Kilith narrowed his eyes, disapproving of the topic change, but he let it go. "Enouim, I think you're right. It says something that they are still speaking to us at all. They don't strike me as brash types, and will do nothing without adequate consideration. It could be they hold us here until they can consult with allies on the ground. Perhaps they are friendly with some of the local tribes or have representatives in Levav or other places. That would take time we do not have."

"They are acquainted with Len Mandon, but from his expedition some fourteen years ago and not from Levav," Ruakh returned. "I think any consulting they do will be in-house."

"Glintenon, if only Canukke had kept his trap shut like he was told," Oloren grumbled. "He had only one thing to do. One thing to focus on not doing. But no! That is precisely what he did. Couldn't help himself."

Mereámé shrugged. "It can't be helped now. Maybe one reason they are asking us all what we think of each other is to find out if we are like him, or if he stands alone in his folly."

"Which means they are at least mulling over the possibility of giving us information on the stone, in spite of him," Enouim added.

"I certainly hope so," Oloren said. "Or they are determining whether to dispatch with all of us or only a few. They've expended quite some effort into hiding themselves up here, only to be invaded by dirty, bumbling loudmouths."

As Enouim pondered their potential fates, she breathed in the restful dynamic of the five of them. These were the gentle spirits of the group, and even in tension, they remained unified, respectfully batting ideas and worries back and forth. Kilith might be harboring hidden judgments, of course, but it didn't show.

As minutes turned into an hour, and then two, the rest of their band was returned to them. Baird came first, making a few jokes, which Oloren easily jumped in to embellish. Vadik was next, followed by Gabor, and finally Canukke.

Canukke appeared to have pulled himself together enough to be diplomatic, and Enouim hoped to Glintenon it wasn't an act, and that he had behaved himself. He was clearly still on edge, and Gabor didn't help things. His eyes glared daggers when he saw Canukke, and they both bristled upon eye contact. *Please no,* Enouim begged them from the safe confines of her mind. Luckily, they shook off the moment and avoided each other.

Enouim wondered how his interview had gone, but their fearless leader didn't have opportunity to share. Poleia had escorted him to rejoin them, as she had each of the others, and now she called for their attention.

"Thank you for your patience," she said. "The Supreme Golden Guardian and Keeper of the First Layer request that you remain here tonight. Blankets and pillows you will find already prepared, laid out in each of the fall-ins." Poleia indicated the cutouts in the surface of the other side of the landing, leading to the sleeping units Enouim had seen on her arrival.

"Our horses are down below," Vadik said.

Gabor nodded. "Yes. And I am not too keen on closing my eyes up here. Perhaps we should go down tonight and return in the morning for the verdict."

"The request was only a courtesy," Poleia said simply.

Gabor and Vadik exchanged glances, but said nothing as the truth of her words settled in.

Willing or unwilling, they would be staying the night.

23

"**B**ut no sparrow flies to nest without sustenance, and since your stay here interferes with hunting and gathering, food will be brought shortly. Thank you." With that, Poleia dipped her head and left them.

"Pious wretches, all high and mighty with their heads in the clouds," Canukke said as soon as she'd gone. "And actually in the clouds! Can't get more on the nose than that."

"What happened?" Oloren asked.

"They asked my purpose, and about the stone, and what I would hope to do with it. They said I was a liar, and that I didn't know what I was doing. The gall on these people."

"Somehow I doubt they said that," Ruakh commented.

The company cast glances between one another in a shared understanding.

"Well, what do you know? You weren't there. That's what they said. Trying to subvert my position, I'm sure. Let them. They're the ones causing problems. And you blame me."

Enouim and the rest of them gave Canukke plenty of space for the rest of the evening. None seemed too eager to engage him, and they were all too happy to give him a wide berth in favor of more pleasant company. Enouim thought a whipped dog wearing a crown would look much the same as he did. He would probably bite the same too, snarling at the hand that feeds him, afraid of betrayal at every turn.

As promised, a late supper was delivered within the hour. Enouim had very nearly expected to be served a plate of something that also mirrored the sky, as nearly everything else seemed to, or perhaps cut into a large ice cube. But one-third was made up of something in small, flat, white circles; the second third was, to her relief, familiar enough as roast bird of some kind; and finally the last third was some gray substance she was disinclined to touch much less eat. The circles she found harmless enough; they tasted like honey wafers. The bird was as delicious as she hoped. The gray stuff she tried at Oloren's insistence and found it nearly as unfortunate as she'd imagined, though everyone else seemed utterly enchanted by it. Enouim traded some of her gray substance to Baird for more honey wafers, after looking around to make sure no Nazir hosts would see.

Darkness descended and the stars came out, but neither Nyeur nor Laskallel came to them again that evening—nor any other Nazir, for that matter. The company stayed up together talking quietly, before eventually accepting that no word of a decision would come that night and began choosing cubbyholes in which to sleep. Enouim squinted to examine the hammocks in the dim light. The floor still reflected the sky, but the blankets and pillows were solid blue and the surface strong beneath her feet. She chose the cubicle next to Mereámé—one row down so that Mereámé was at her head—and gingerly descended using cut-out footholds. Happily, Enouim was also sandwiched between Oloren and Baird in hammocks beside her.

She curled into her hammock on her side, wrapping

herself securely within the warm blankets and listening to the comforting sounds of her friends' murmuring voices. To her left, a grinning Baird and Vadik tossed something back and forth to one another from their hammocks. To her right, Oloren smiled and waved at her. Enouim bade her good night, twisted around, and said the same to Mereámé.

Flopping onto her back, she gazed at the stars and let the sight soothe her mind. It had much to be soothed from, as just this morning she'd had a panic attack by the riverbank, and since then had marched hours through a forest, attempted to analyze the meaning of said panic attack, and had been exposed to entirely novel and remarkable people and places. Of course, then Canukke had gone and muddled things just as Oloren had feared, and here they were, awaiting assistance or death. The usual. Enouim sighed and sank deeper into her blankets. Nothing could be done about it now. She imagined it was just as helpful to be well rested for bad news as for good, if not more so.

The morning came in soft, the moon loath to relinquish the night. Yet soon the sun overpowered the moon, and made a glorious entrance in vibrant reds and oranges. Red and pink trimmed three small clouds, and the light advanced until fire enveloped the clouds. Enouim found it at once aggressive and soothing. In the opposite direction, a blended purple and blue washed the horizon. Life was like that. Looking in one direction, one might be convinced that a situation was one way, and based on the opposite direction, another could be equally persuaded of his perspective, only to discover that something connected both. Complexity was precisely what enhanced the beauty of life. Enouim wondered which sort of morning it would be today.

She couldn't help staring at the brilliant color all around her, and at this height, she was in the best place for appreci-

ating such magnificence. Enouim got up slowly, entranced by
the sky and wrapped up in her own wistful thoughts. Breakfast was brought to them, and all ate, saying little. At the close
of the meal, the moment came that they'd all been waiting for.
Nyeur and Laskallel glided onto their landing and made their
approach.

Nyeur appeared to represent the eastern sky, while
Laskallel presented the west; the same was true of Poleia and
Yadara, respectively. They followed dutifully behind their
superiors, and when Nyeur and Laskallel came to a stop, they
fanned out one on either side, two steps behind.

"May the morning mist rise with us," Laskallel greeted
them.

The company, all seated, stood abruptly in response.

"May it rise," Mereámé and Ruakh answered in unison.

"Long have we bent our thought upon your troubles,"
Nyeur said, jumping straight into the matter at hand. "I will
not delay in allaying the fear I see in your eyes. We are"—he
looked at Laskallel—"willing to offer you our support, in our
way, to the extent that our role permits."

Silence. A grateful smile and nod from Mereámé. But what
did it mean? Enouim was certainly grateful they were not all
going to be "dispatched" as Oloren had postulated, but this
brought up more questions than answers. After another
stretch that made Enouim wonder if time passed differently
for everyone else up here, she could take it no longer. "Thank
you," she heard herself stammer. "Tell us, what do you mean?"

"Ah, yes. There are varying goals among you. This is delicate. We are in no position to wage war, as birds and fish do
not judge between foxes and wolves. But in one matter we
may be able to benefit you. Despite your differences, all of you
agreed on a primary objective: the Eh'yeh Stone."

Laskallel picked up where her partner left off. "This stone

is not to be sought lightly, and you would do well to count the cost. There is no going back."

Nyeur nodded. "Some of you may wonder at our decision, after the events of yesterday, and our concerns are not altogether eliminated. We have determined, however, that none go to the stone unbidden. In our efforts to protect it, perhaps we forget that the stone does not need to be protected. Let our judgment of you be suspended, and may it be picked up again by Eh'yeh. We have been persuaded to grant you access to the information you desire."

A tremor of excitement rumbled through the company. Their mission lived on. Their hope was secure!

Laskallel held up a hand. "We desire to ensure your safe passage there and go with you on your journey, as a scroll of answers, a shepherd in uncertain places, and a light to lead you when the floor beneath our feet confounds the map in the sky from down below. Unfortunately, our duties require our full attention, and we cannot be drawn away."

"It is for this reason that we send one of our own in our stead." Nyeur turned to his right. "Yadara, daughter of the sky, we commission you to accompany the nine you see here to the stone. A redwood lacking even a single root is less secure for its loss."

"The redwood thrives in community," Yadara responded, eyes wide, glance darting from the speaker to her new associates. She refocused on Nyeur and Laskallel and dropped slowly to one knee. "And the sparrow always finds its way home."

Nyeur and Laskallel each took one of Yadara's hands, raising her to her feet. Turning back to the mission members, Laskallel spoke again. "You are pressed for time, and we waste none here. Yadara has within her all that you will need to reach your destination, and you may confer with her en route.

May the stars shimmer upon our parting, and the sun's rays find you again after every storm."

Simple and strange, the meeting adjourned as swiftly as it had begun. Brief goodbyes were exchanged, nearly all questions deferred, and Poleia and Yadara walked them back through the network of platforms and pathways until they arrived at the same one by which they'd entered the Nazir domain. No one said a word as they walked. At the top of the stair, Poleia and Yadara turned as one to face them.

"I take my leave." Poleia turned to Yadara and bowed. "May the stars shimmer on your departure."

Yadara bowed back. "May the winds be favorable should you meet them before I return."

Poleia smiled, and turned to the rest of the group. "Few are the miles, but long are the days. Feel within yourselves the strength of the redwood. Eyes of the hawk and grace of the swan are my invocation for you. May the stars shimmer on you all."

The company bowed, and Mereámé said, "Be blessed, even as the sky from whence you came is blessed. Thank you."

Poleia nodded and left them alone on the platform, nine earth dwellers and a single daughter of the sky, blinking at each other in the morning light. Yadara's eyes were wide, innocent and curious, unsure of herself. Enouim wondered if she had volunteered for this enterprise or been volunteered.

Yadara shook herself out of her reverie and drew herself up tall. "The sun rises," she said, and began to descend the long stair.

The mission members looked at each other, shrugged their shoulders, and followed. Enouim let her gaze linger on the beautiful architecture, like floating panes of mirror beset with immaculate ice-sculpture columns and archways. She doubted she would ever come again to this place and wished for a happier occasion by which to come again. Gabor tapped her lightly on the shoulder, nodding his head toward the road before them. Time to go.

Enouim reluctantly acquiesced, wanting to soak up every extraordinary sight from far above the tree line. She couldn't help her thoughts wandering to what other spectacles she might come across by the end. The end of what? The end of the mission? Or would her end perhaps find her sooner? There was no way to tell, and nothing she could do about it one way or the other. Inhaling deeply, she breathed in the tranquility of a gentle morning surrounded by tender views of celestial splendor and breathed out the stress of unknown tomorrows.

A pensive stillness fell upon the travelers as they continued down, down, down. As they went, the world transitioned from gradients of blue to variants of green and brown, and nearly as soon as they broke the bubble-like barrier, they broke also the hold of the world in the sky. Enouim's mind moved from the beauty of her surroundings and the mystery of the Nazir to the task ahead and the troubles that followed her.

Exactly how "few" miles were "few" according to Poleia? And what might the road ahead hold? What would Canukke be like now that they'd returned to the forest floor. She remembered regrettably how she'd left things with Kilith just the day before, and again that word rose up like a ghost refusing to give up and die—*failure.* How many rivers were in the miles ahead? Once the stone was reached, would it divide her soul also? Questions swirled in her head like a whirlpool, gnawing at her consciousness and pulling her further into herself. Until Vadik's sharp cry broke through her awareness with an urgency she could not ignore.

"The horses! They're gone!"

24

Gabor bounded down the remaining stairs past Enouim and landed lightly on his feet, despite a complete inability to see his footing. "What happened?"

"It's the woods. Anything could have happened. They weren't tied," Baird said dolefully.

Oloren sighed. "They weren't tied because there were barely any places they could even fit through!"

"*Barely any* was clearly just enough," Gabor bit back. "How could we have been so stupid?"

"They could still be nearby," Vadik suggested.

"Unless something spooked them," Ruakh noted.

The company spent the next forty-five minutes whistling, calling, and roaming out further into the wood. Kilith shook his head, disapproving. The minutes ticked by, but without horses, minutes would turn to hours more on the road. Yet if the horses really were out of reach, they were wasting already precious moments.

"Useless," Canukke growled, kicking at a stone. It skittered across the ground and took a tumble through the brush. "We go on foot. You there" —he turned to Yadara— "you know the way?"

"Yes," she answered, eyes wide at his harsh tone. "I know the way."

"On, then. Show us."

Yadara nodded, turned on her heel, and stepped forward out of the glade and into the thicket. Canukke strode after her, and the rest followed. Enouim placed herself near the front to hear any critical conversation she could.

"How far?" Canukke asked.

"Not far. Less than a week."

"Where is it hidden?"

"Where few look. But it is always accessible to those who seek it," Yadara replied.

"I have no patience for riddles," Canukke shot back.

"The servant can do only what the master bids."

Canukke grabbed her arm and yanked her back to him. "Listen here. Who is higher than I on this mission? Up there you have your own rules, but down here, I am in charge. Answer me straight, sky wench."

Yadara drew back in surprise, looking at him with consternation, and examining his grip on her arm. They were nearly nose to nose.

"She's not allowed to say!" Oloren protested. "Leave her be."

"She certainly won't be permitted *not* to say," Canukke retorted, never removing his gaze from Yadara.

"They mean us no harm," Gabor said from the sidelines. "She takes us to the stone. Does it matter how she does it?"

"I have encountered too many liars in my life. If something seems too good to be true, it's because it is," Canukke replied.

"Where is your evidence?" Baird asked.

Vadik and Kilith slowly edged forward to Yadara's side.
"This is not the way to get what you want," Vadik cautioned.

"Put away your ego, boy," Canukke responded. "Which among us was best fit for this mission? Did you choose me, or the other way around? Do tell. Tell me of your remarkable accomplishments. Line them up end to end, and see if they reach a tenth as far as my own."

"Enough!" Kilith's tone, though quiet, was venomous.

"And you, Kilith Urul," Canukke spat. "What are you to me?"

Enouim looked between them. Canukke was unraveling before her eyes. The man so cool and arrogantly collected in the company of kings and so comfortable in the wild, now a great wolf turned into a cornered dog.

"A friend worth having. An enemy worth avoiding," Kilith replied. "I volunteered my sword in the service of Gorgenbrild, as did you. I was sought out for leadership on this venture, as were you. I offer now my consult, if you would have it. If she wants to tell us, she will; if she wants to lie, she will. Words from the mouth of a threatened captive are worth little, but the same from a devoted ally are priceless. The last thing we need right now is the full weight of the guardians of the heavens bearing down on us, the revenge of those who see the Malak themselves pass through their gates."

Canukke and Kilith stared one another down for an insufferably long moment. Canukke's lip curled, then his face smoothed as if nothing at all had been amiss. Loosening his grasp without letting go, Canukke slowly leaned into Yadara, almost gently, and spoke so that only she could hear. Enouim watched Yadara's blue face flush white, as for a moment a wisp of cloud colored her cheeks before it faded away. Clearly it wasn't a tender declaration of love.

"Southeast," Yadara said. "The lion shakes his mane and

leads the pride as he demands. The day shows him to be who he desires to be in the mirror, but I see a black panther leading from the shadows. Yet as daylight reigns, so also will the lion." She twisted back to Canukke with a renewed strength and strong sense of self. This time it was Canukke that reeled back from the invasion of personal space he himself had created. The fire in her eyes when she turned grew soft before she spoke. "Lead on, young lion. Southeast."

Canukke stared at her in wonder, but released her. Sweeping his gaze over the company once more, he turned on his heel and forged ahead in the direction Yadara had instructed. Kilith waited a moment for Canukke to get a head start and then followed, as did Vadik, Gabor, and the rest. Enouim caught up to Yadara and walked with her.

"How are you doing?" Enouim asked earnestly.

"I am trapped on a dais," she said, "cornered by a man with a sword. The walls are thick and opaque, and fog engulfs me. It swirls around me, with many different colors, taking me aback." Yadara looked pensive, as if seeing quite a different environment than the one surrounding Enouim.

"What does that mean? Is the man Canukke? What do you mean, you see fog?"

"I ... I think so. I do not always know what it means. But my not knowing does not diminish the meaning it holds." Yadara pulled her brows together in thought.

"Are you okay?" The voice came from Mereámé, who held back waiting for the pair of women to catch up to her. When they did, she drew alongside them.

"It is a strange new place with strange people of many sorts," Yadara replied.

"It is," Mereámé agreed. After a pause, she spoke again. "If you don't mind ... what was it that Canukke said to you?"

"He is afraid. He trusts sparingly, if at all. He threatens me to speak truth, yet I have said little, and nothing I have said has been false."

"He wants you to tell him everything you know," Enouim said, " and sees it as a mark of deception that you do not. Maybe even insubordination, though you are not actually sent as we are from Gorgenbrild. I think Canukke was shaken by his time with the Nazir. He's been off since yesterday. But it's like it all caught up to him at once. I don't know what has gotten into him." She hoped things would fade back to normal with time, as he reacquainted himself with the familiarities of the forest. Maybe he just couldn't handle feeling so out of control.

Curious as to what had happened and what their new companion was like, Baird, Vadik, and Gabor drew around the trio.

"I was told to share only what is needed at any given moment, and to allow each of those seeking Eh'yeh to make of it what they would," Yadara explained. "I can do nothing more and nothing less. I may not say everything, but everything I say is as true as the sky is blue."

"No, no." Baird shook his head. "A lie of omission is a lie all the same in Gorgenbrild. Mighty picky, aren't they? You might not think so, just to look at them. But they're terribly harsh about it. Do things their way, or they toss you right out. That's what happened to my colleague, Silas. Their main complaint with him wasn't a brazen lie—nothing nearly so fun—but an absence of telling. And he was thrown to the wayside, just like that."

Yadara's eyes opened wide. "Did no one even help him up?"

The group exchanged bemused glances before Vadik answered her. "Well, no. Helping him up would have defeated the purpose of throwing him out."

Yadara's face turned somber, absorbing this troubling news.

Presently Enouim broke the silence. "So ... what exactly do you do up there?"

At the mention of her home, Yadara brightened up and snapped back to the present moment with enthusiasm. "A great profession," she assured them. "As the river daughter returns the waters to the path it was meant before man broke the dam, so the sky daughter seeks the correction of atmospheric tragedies. All nature desires order, and was made to order. The guardians of the elements have charge of returning the peace to these that have been stolen, to whatever extent can be achieved. The work is long and ever incomplete."

"River daughter?" Enouim asked. "There are more like you?"

"She is talking about the Madzi," Mereámé explained. "Like the Nazir, they are not human, though living in similar forms, and were commissioned by Iamwë himself at the dawning of time to protect the waterways of the earth—just as the Nazir were commissioned to protect the heavens."

"Yes, yes!" Yadara nodded. "The Madzi are our brothers and sisters, along with the Gudira, guardians of plant life."

Gabor's eyes widened. "Glintenon, what is all this? I have never heard of such things."

"Glintenon?" Yadara asked. "Is that where you get your information? No use asking him out here. His northern territory line runs from the Canobi Islands beyond the western coast, through your own mountains, and down to Morthed. Glintenon's responsibilities are focused within those boundaries. Unless something special has called him away, he will be found there."

Gabor blinked at her.

Yadara continued, earnestly trying to solve Gabor's problem. "If you would like to contact him, I'm sure the stone could pass along your message. The stone is a link to Iamwë himself, who of course rules over all the Malak. Out here, the sentinel Malak of the land is Fetrye."

"So they are bound by geographical constraints, each appointed to an area of the world?" Baird asked.

"I knew it!" Vadik beamed with pride.

"You did not," Oloren said, blending into their cluster as they walked together. The brush had grown more accommodating, and the group had begun to close the gaps, all ten walking within reasonable earshot.

"Prove it," he challenged with a grin.

Oloren rolled her eyes.

"Yes, each Malak is assigned territory and kept within it even as the ocean is kept within its bounds," Yadara explained. "Iamwë determines how far the waves on the shore are permitted to wash and how tall each wave can become."

"What's on your wrists?" Vadik asked.

"Oh ... it is my ensign," she answered.

"For what?"

"Phases. Phases of training and development. They determine one's role. The first is as black onyx, the second silver, the third grandidierite green, the fourth jeremejevite blue, the fifth amethyst purple, the sixth gold, and seventh red beryl. It is only diamond and the fire opal that remain beyond this." She paused, enraptured by some dazzlingly magnificent vision of greatness. When she spoke again, it was with reverence. "I have never met such a one."

"Nine ranks, then. And they sent along one of their lowest?" Gabor seemed disappointed.

"We do not glory in rank for rank's sake, for no one comes by it easily. Power is not to be feared, but to be respected. Suffering is the herald of new growth and understanding, a great horn crying, 'Behold! From the ashes arises a new and more beautiful thing with the wisdom of the ash intact.' We view higher ranks with solemn regard, honoring what it reveals of the bearer: a past of pain. The higher the ensign, the greater the history of pain."

"It is sacred," Ruakh said. "A hallowed process that no one who has experienced or even seen up close can laugh off or make light of. A child only laughs at a lion because he knows no better, and because the lion is in the dell while the child clamors from a mountaintop window."

"Just so," said Yadara, pleased.

"What suffering might you experience up above the world?" Baird asked.

"The vale is deep as it is wide, unsearchable and indefinite to all who enter it. There is no knowing what may be found there, even if one might venture to guess, and no knowing how long a sojourn it might turn out to be. The plain may show clearly to expect a dip in altitude, or a mountain may turn quickly down into an unexpected valley. There is no knowing—no knowing at all. It is perhaps the first and most common suffering, light though it may seem, to sit with a lack of knowing like you might sit with a friend in need, who desires your presence rather than your many careless words."

The earnestness in her expression gave them pause as they listened and soaked in her words. Enouim wondered what it must be like, to have rank determined by pain, wisdom from suffering, a physical representation of one's emotional afflic- tion that is so often hidden away with shame. Somehow in this, the misery borne by a Nazir was honored, accepted, and seen as an opportunity.

Baird broke the silence, a playful edge to his tone. "So if Ruakh smacks you over the head with his staff, could we expe- dite the process?"

Yadara looked questioningly at Ruakh, suddenly concerned.

Ruakh shook his head in dismissal.

"A canyon can be made over time, or in an hour, depending on the amount of force with which the water overtakes it," Yadara said. "Both are organic, and self-inflicted pain is a symptom of something deeper, not the thing itself. Only that which is deep and true, encountered honestly and processed with bravery, will be put toward advancement of phases. Many go through suffering, many change from suffering, but not all grow. Suffering is a fork in the wood, one path leading to wisdom and healing, the other folding in on itself to a torment of bitterness. One becomes wisdom and one a prison of the soul."

Gabor frowned. "So ... if Baird hits you over the head when you're not looking, multiple times—either all in an hour, or spread out over the next week—*then* you'll get your next phase."

"You're welcome!" Baird said with a grin.

"Mockery is folly," Yadara said with finality, indicating they should drop the matter.

"They mean no harm," Oloren said. "It sounds like a difficult process."

Yadara examined Oloren, and then nodded. "It is a bird carried along by the wind, or fish in a riptide."

Mereámé nodded. "I think I know what you mean. One must lean into suffering to move through it."

Yadara softened, seeing that Mereámé understood.

For a while they traveled quietly or with light conversation, and Enouim listened to the crunch of leaves underfoot and occasional *wack* as her friends cut away stubborn underbrush. The further they got from the Nazir, the more the wood opened up so that it became more ordinary forest than the impenetrable wall of thorns they had first encountered. The travelers continued in a south-easterly direction for some time before Yadara adjusted their course. Kilith spoke to Yadara quietly for several minutes and then walked back toward Enouim.

"The last time we walked together in the woods, I felt our conversation went unresolved," he said quietly in his usual husky voice.

Enouim thought about the moments before finding the stair, when Kilith had tried to talk to her about her panic attack and she'd snapped at him. "I'm sorry I lashed out at you."

"It seems I came off as less than understanding. I know I ... do that sometimes."

"I know you were trying to be encouraging, but it just felt like you wanted me to be able to tap into a mental space that was supposed to be obvious and easy, and it wasn't. It makes me feel worse, not better, to know you think I should be able to just will things to be different. I wish I could have handled it differently too, but I don't know how. It's embarrassing. And then I just went and dug myself deeper by telling you about what a failure I felt I was, and you had nothing to say to that."

Kilith looked her sternly in the eye. "I wasn't silent because I agreed with you. I was silent because ... I'm not good at this sort of thing. I didn't know what to say. I don't think you appreciate how hard it is for me to say what I did say to you."

Enouim looked up. "You mean give complements? I'm sure it's tough to find something," she said dryly.

Frustration built in his tone. "Stop being so focused on yourself. I'm talking about *me*."

She searched his face. He looked uncomfortable ... vulnerable, even. "Oh." She kept walking, not sure how to salvage this.

"I don't talk things out much ... things like this," Kilith said. "It doesn't come naturally to me."

"I don't know. You've initiated twice now."

"I felt it was important."

Another stretch of silence.

Enouim thought back to their conversation about her panic attack. She talked about being a mediocre swimmer, being bad at holding her breath, being terrified of water, totally breaking down and being incapable of holding it together at the river, and generally being a failure. He told her thinking too much about how bad it was getting had likely made the situation worse.

"So ..." Enouim cleared her throat. "The fact that I started to lose it could have snowballed into my losing it completely. I think that's what you said last time."

Believe in yourself, he'd said.

"Yes. Your mind and beliefs are going to impact what your body is willing to attempt."

"What about starting to lose it in the first place?"

"Well, now that it's happened, I imagine it will be difficult to shake the memory. The fear is not only of the water now, but of the fear itself and what it does to you."

Enouim thought about that. It was true. She had even dreamed last night of crossing another river and having a panic attack worse than the last, with everyone laughing at her, and Canukke condescendingly sneering at her. *Pitiful,* he seemed to be saying. And it hurt her because in the dream, in that moment, she was convinced she was exactly that.

"How much of your father's travels did he tell you about?" Kilith asked.

Surprised at his mention of her father, Enouim considered this. "He told me about a zegrath attack once. About the gates of Levav, the colors, and being kept between the two walls, permitted no further. He had also been to Kalka'an, and talked to me of the cliff dwellings, though it was hard for me to picture in my mind. My father told me of rivers running to the foot of the mountains, and dangerous creatures in the rivers. He told me tales about strange people he met, about hot sands, and the wide-open ocean. I was a child. They were adventure stories to me, and I am sure some were embellished for my benefit."

"Like what?" he pressed.

"If you're after something in particular, why don't you just tell me what it is and maybe that will help me narrow down the search."

"I was with him long ago on a new trade route. It passed below Morthed to some of the hill people, and back up through the mountains. Giving Morthed a berth required him to travel further down and through lush forest divided by rivers and lakes. His own distaste for water began on that trip."

"I don't remember a story like that," Enouim said. "He did talk about something in the water that scared him though, on one of his trips. It had a small body, tentacles, and a poisonous touch. They were beautiful but deadly. His descriptions changed every time he told it, though—the creature some-times had fifty tentacles, sometimes hundreds. In one telling there were hordes of small tentacled creatures, and in another, several massive ones larger than himself."

"He did not get a good look up close. They are nicknamed 'fire fern' by rangers in that area, because upon contact a shock runs through the body. If it's large enough, the fire fern can knock out a full-grown man underwater, leaving him inca-pacitated. They generally lie on the river bottom, but can loose themselves to float along with the current and attach somewhere else if needed."

"What? I thought you were supposed to be making me feel *better* about water, not worse!"

"That wasn't helpful?" Kilith smiled. "There are many dangers in the world, Enouim, and many more on land than beneath the surface. If we know how to combat them, we are safe. If we know we successfully lived through them before, we are confident."

"I don't know either of those things," Enouim said.

"But you can. For example, the fire fern are not fast or particularly mobile. They are languid and largely left to the mercy of the current."

"Are we expecting to come across this fire fern?"

Kilith shrugged. "Never can be too prepared."

"I feel like that means yes."

He smiled again—not comforting to Enouim in the least.

She tried again. "Are we going to come across fire fern?"

"Yadara says there are many rivers and lakes where we are going. It seems plausible that they are connected to the rivers upstream to Morthed, and may indeed contain the same creatures. That's not the point though. The point is that you can get through it."

"I think I missed that one."

"You will be fine. Take deep breaths like Ruakh taught you. You've been through worse."

Enouim dearly hoped he was right, and that the sea serpent was the worst she would encounter.

25

They continued to travel for six days. The forest, once composed of bright, leafy emerald ceilings, began to choke off again into thick brush and dark thorns. The colors seemed no longer hopeful but gloomy and full of dark shadows. The overgrowth became so great that she yearned for a sunbeam to find its way to the wooded floor, and the rabbits and squirrels they'd caught to eat before were nowhere to be seen. Surely the horses couldn't have come this way. Perhaps it was better they were free. She missed Inferno and hoped he'd found a grassy plain somewhere.

Everyone felt the difference and everyone was on edge, but Vadik became truly uneasy, looking this way and that, skittish toward the empty air. Canukke remained in his brooding state for hours, saying little, except to complain that in the shade of the wood Yadara shone like a beacon of bright blue and white. Enouim had wondered if her skin would eventually start reflecting the forest, like a chameleon, but she continued to reflect the sky even when dense trees overhead obscured the sky. Kilith offered Yadara his cloak after Canukke's remark. She wrapped it around herself and lifted the hood to cover her hair, so that from behind she looked like any one of them and from the front only her face stood out. Everything out here seemed so hidden away and abandoned, who could Canukke think of coming across? It didn't look as if anyone had been here in many years, if at all.

With Ruakh's help, Yadara climbed a tree in an effort to see the stars, but the branches were too weak to carry her to its full height, so she was cut off from her map of the world. "I can make estimations as best as I know how, but without seeing the stars, we are lost," she said apologetically.

"Don't you have the stars on you already?" Vadik asked. "You know, look at your arm, and then we're good to go."

Yadara looked at him incredulously."Does a single leaf reveal the entire tree? Does a feather reveal the whole bird?"

"We need to get to higher ground, then," Kilith said.

Gabor spat to one side. "It's been flat for ages, and we can't see far enough to know what direction might lead us upward."

"There should be hills near here," Yadara stated. "Perhaps more to the west?"

"Our supplies are thin. We can't afford to wander in circles," Baird pointed out. "Even the animals seem to have forsaken this dark place. I can't say I blame them." He shivered.

As if on cue, a bright flash in Enouim's peripheral vision caught her attention. The whole company saw it, and all hushed and turned toward the sight. A white stag! Majestic and graceful, he bounded through the wood and came to a sudden stop within their line of sight. Gabor raised his bow.

"No," Ruakh whispered, "Such a creature does not deserve death. And I sense something more to this animal than meets the eye ... see, it is looking right at us!"

"No creature is worth dying of starvation for, however

beautiful," Gabor hissed back. "That could last us quite some time, and I'm sick of dried stuff."

The stag slowly and deliberately walked toward them several paces. For two long minutes the stag and the band of warriors stared back at one another. Unconcerned, the animal walked away in a new direction, but then paused and looked back at them. It took another few steps, then turned to look at them again.

"Is it doing what I think it's doing?" Oloren asked.

She didn't need to explain. They all felt the stag beckoning them to follow.

"What do we do?" Enouim asked.

"Perhaps it is a messenger. A stag is a protector of the forest, a peaceful animal," Mereámé suggested. "Fetrye is in this area. Do you think she could be doing this?"

"I've not heard of anything like this, but then, we are out of my depth here," Ruakh said. "It could be as you say. Still, something in me hesitates."

Vadik shifted uneasily, staring after the animal.

"We are already lost," Canukke said. "If deer do live in these parts, they would know the area, and at least wouldn't run in circles. Perhaps it is rabid, and that is why it isn't afraid of us, or perhaps it simply has never learned to fear humans. Either way, I say it can lead us to more navigable ground and maybe water, and then we can let Gabor kill it."

Kilith nodded. "Bow low, arrow on the string." He pulled out his own bow.

Cautiously, they crept after the luminous stag, impossible to mistake in the dimness around them. A fog fell, and eerie light suffused the forest. Enouim was aware of her pounding heart and the faint sounds of her companions padding along the forest floor beside her.

At first the stag paused often, checking to see if they were still following, but soon the animal picked up its pace and halted only briefly before taking off again. What began as almost a quiet stalking of the stag transitioned into low running, and finally, a full-tilt pursuit. Panicked at losing not only their spontaneous guide but also their only chance at food, Canukke called out, "Gabor, now!"

Gabor and Kilith raised their bows and let loose arrows at the last glimpse of the animal as it passed out of sight. Running forward, they went to see if dinner was to be served or skipped, but when they reached the point they'd last seen the stag, it suddenly reappeared and reared on hind legs to strike at them. As it did, a burst of white light appeared where the stag had been, and from it came a dark willowy figure, arms as frail and thin as bone, skin stretched, and only a dark abyss where a face should have been. All hint of the stag was gone, save three short horns protruding from the figure's head. The shadowy shape, which stood nearly eight feet high, reached up and snapped off one of its horns like a twig, and as he held it out toward Gabor and Kilith, it grew like a weed, fashioning itself into a mace club with large spikes.

Kilith raised his sword just in time to meet the mace in the air. The two held firm for a moment, but then the shadowy figure shoved him aside with ease. Gabor and Canukke reached it at the same time, Canukke closing the gap in mighty leaps. With a sweep of his hand, the faceless shadow struck Gabor to the ground, and Canukke sliced off its foot with a great blow. The foot, previously shaped like a human's, instantly grew back as a great claw, like a zegrath or a great bird of prey.

Oloren swung herself into the branches and launched herself up into the air, daggers in hand. Canukke joined her in an attack from below as she met the thing from above. With a horrendous screech from deep in its throat, it deflected the first of Oloren's daggers and tossed Canukke aside like garbage. Oloren wrapped her legs around its shoulders, and as her second dagger came down, the figure collapsed in on itself, depositing Oloren on the ground, then it expanded again, towering over her.

"What is this devilry?" Gabor yelled.

Baird, Gabor, Vadik, and Kilith all leaped forward. Enouim had frozen for a moment, but now grabbed Kilith's fallen bow and arrow and scurried up a tree, Mereámé close behind. Ruakh ushered Yadara up a neighboring tree and brandished his staff.

Enouim felt the rough bark under her hands, the cool air at her face. Adrenaline pumped through her veins, and she felt both alive and very nearly dead. Perched in a fork of the tree, she allowed herself several deep breaths as the shadow raged against her friends below her. Enouim would be worthless without her aim, and her aim would be worthless without her head on straight. Taking one last deep breath, she crawled out onto the long limb hanging over the fight and readied her bow and arrows.

Ruakh was moving fast as lightning, smooth as water, and Enouim had never seen anything like it. Mesmerized for a moment, she watched as he used the staff in fluid motions to redirect his opponent's energy and recapture its attention when the shadow threatened a final fatal blow to a comrade. Even so, Ruakh was no match for the shadow. It drew back from the staff, and then from the faceless shroud, two eyes like fire suddenly blazed and drove toward him with roiling fury.

Enouim nocked an arrow and drew the string back to her cheek. Hold, hold. Vadik spun across the creature's back. Release. Her arrow flew true and burrowed into the shaded figure just as she'd hoped. Another screech permeated the air, and those eyes of fire turned upward, like funeral pyres lit on the darkest of nights. From the void of its face, a mouth formed and opened to release a torrent of flames.

Enouim roiled back and stood on the limb, reaching for another arrow.

Vadik cut off the shadow's hand, and this time it grew back as the forearm and claw of a wolf.

"What's the point if it just grows back as something else?" Baird yelled.

"What else are we supposed to do?" Vadik shouted back, indignant.

The figure leered over Ruakh now, sending short huffs of fire into his face.

"He's toying with us," Ruakh called.

Enouim shot another arrow, and Ruakh rolled to one side. Oloren and Canukke prepared another assault, but the figure turned, whirling a blaze of fire, mace flying, wolf claw swiping until, in the span of a few seconds, it had cast each of Enouim's companions beneath her upon the ground. Enouim reached for a third arrow in vain—none were left. The shadow pulled up to its full height and looked up at Enouim. Suddenly, relentless and strong, it leaped up to the first limb and released another fiery breath at the branch upon which she stood.

Dry wood crackled and caved under her, and as Enouim fell straight into the mouth of the shadow, she drew her dagger and plunged it into the demon's face. Shrieks shook the air, and Enouim fell, rolling through her momentum as she hit the ground, then stood. "I did it! The break fall!" she said, unable to help herself.

"That's great, En," Oloren said. "More fighting!"

The shadow twisted, writhed, and produced a wretched head with a long snout, rows of teeth, flames for eyes, and a haphazard way about it that could put a person into a frenzy by sight alone.

"We're all going to die," Gabor moaned.

"Oh, come on!" Enouim said. "Stay positive."

"All right. *You're* all going to die. More food for me!"

"That's the spirit ..."

The miserable thing roared at them with renewed hatred, and Enouim's braid flew behind her at the blast of air that came from its malodorous mouth. Dagger still in hand, she drew the throwing knife from her boot and steadied herself for another go. Gabor might be right after all.

The wretched creature hovered over all its prey with relish, snapping its jaws. From the tree above, Mereámé threw a knife at the shadow. Canukke, Oloren, and Vadik attacked from behind it, while Kilith, Baird, Gabor, and Enouim attacked from the front and sides. Ruakh raised his staff. Hope was fading fast, their strength sapped.

Mereámé dropped to the ground and took hold of a fallen sword, forging ahead with questionable form and indisputable courage. Yadara also slid to earth, shaking off Kilith's cloak and raising her wrist toward the creature. Afternoon light emanated from her, filling the wood and shining in stark contrast against the dark figure and the receding blackness of her surroundings. From her wrist the molten silver ensign seemed to boil, moving, and glowing with a soft light. The creature recoiled, snarling and thrashing, eyes of furious fire meeting the soft and determined eyes of Yadara, one blue and one light gray. Gathering itself, the shadow abandoned the mission members and bore down on Yadara, snatching Ruakh's staff as it did so and flinging it aside.

Mereámé drove between the demon and Yadara. Her blade sunk into the shadow's side before it lifted her high above its head and slung her with all its terrible might into a tall tree.

With a horrifying crack and a thud, she fell fifteen feet to the ground. Enouim and Ruakh cried out together, agonized cries mingling with the mist.

Just then a golden eagle swooped down through the trees and latched itself onto the shadow's villainous form. To the surprise of the company, the demon was unable to shake the eagle. The two locked in combat with flashes of fire, claws searching, mace hurling. The mace dug itself into the eagle's back, and the eagle transitioned before their eyes into a much larger creature, with tremendous wings, a dragon's head, and a body like a great cat. Shrieks and roars filled the air, and a tremble rocked the earth.

26

Then two creatures fought on, changing forms or partial forms as fit their need. Enouim and her companions stood transfixed by the sight, frozen in uncertainty. Should they run? But Enouim's feet seemed glued to the ground. Yadara, too, stared like a statue at Mereámé's motionless form as the creatures flashed from this to that all around her.

Ruakh shook off the trance and rushed to Mereámé's side. His movement seemed to wake Gabor, who followed. Canukke, Vadik, and Oloren remained in combat-ready stances looking for chances to join the fight or defend. Kilith and Baird placed themselves between the fight and Mereámé and ushered Enouim and Yadara behind them.

Enouim looked back and forth between Mereámé and the ever-transitioning creatures before them, unwilling to linger too long on either. All color had fled from Mereámé's face, and she wasn't moving. The shadow, now slinging what looked like chains, became a looming two-legged creature with a head like a huge wolf. Where had the chains come from? And where had the mace gone? The other became a lion and roared as the chains entangled it.

In a flash, the lion, their saving grace, vanished into thin air. Enouim's heart lurched,. The shadow, however, realized the lion had become a hummingbird whizzing haphazardly overhead. The bird flew above the wolf's head, transitioned into a massive boulder taller than Enouim, and then thudded to the ground with such weight that it rocked the earth and crushed the wolf-headed shadow beneath it. For a moment, its body lay conquered on the ground, then it melted away into nothing.

The boulder rolled toward Enouim. Terrified to suffer the same fate as the demon, she dove out of the way, taking Yadara with her and covering her with her own body, calling out to her friends as she did.

Enouim looked up in time to see the boulder shrink as it rolled and twist into what looked like a human form stepping out of the stone. At first the figure looked like a statue, until skin climbed up like vines to wrap itself around the shape. A woman now stood before them, dressed in an off-white tunic, raven black hair falling freely to her waist. She held her hands out, opened toward the travelers, and stepped toward Mereámé's still body and her band of protectors. Gabor listened for a heartbeat, Ruakh cradled her head in his lap, and Kilith held one of her wrists, observing her carefully.

Canukke held up his sword. "What new calamity is this?" he demanded.

"Peace," she said, with a voice like song.

"The stag seemed peaceful enough," Canukke replied. "Shrouding yourself in white provides little comfort after the deception we just endured."

"Perhaps another color would suit." The woman tugged lightly on her tunic with her index finger and thumb. If clothing could wink, hers did, blinking black twice before settling into a grayish blue.

"Your power is more disconcerting than soothing," Vadik remarked.

"There is no need for fear. And yet, the decision of belief is yours alone to make. Choose carefully, but do not delay. The master waits, and Mereámé is in need."

Enouim's gut pinched. How did the shapeshifting woman know Mereámé's name?

"She's dead," Gabor said flatly, rocking back on his heels.

Enouim rushed to Mereámé's side. Her friend's face carried the bleak pallor of death. Mereámé, the gentlest and sweetest of them all, her excitement mounting as the legacy of her father came ever closer, meeting her demise at the doorstep of the stone. It couldn't be. It couldn't. A lump lodged in Enouim's throat. Hot tears ran down her face.

"She sleeps. Bring her and follow me."

"I am acquainted with death," Kilith said. "Let's not raise naive hopes. She has passed. She was gone the moment she hit the tree."

The woman looked at him with compassion, but her voice was firm and commanding. "Bring her, and follow me. It is not far, but we must leave this place at once. It isn't safe."

"She could have killed us by now," Oloren said when no one moved. "We all know it." To the woman, she said, "Tell us, what does this master intend to do with us?"

"Surely nothing worse than you do to yourselves," she answered. "No, he is tenderhearted and gracious, welcoming to all."

"We'll see about that." Baird sighed but sheathed his sword.

"Who are you?" Ruakh asked.

"I am called Fetrye, and it is my duty to protect these lands.

Conand, whom you met, is a dark Malak. Had his supporters not delayed me, I would have come to you sooner."

The travelers shared astonished glances. Fetrye was the Malak governing the territory neighboring Glintenon's.

"Yes!" Yadara exclaimed with excitement. "I believe I saw you passing through our gates once, at a distance. You were in this form briefly. I ... I sometimes watch the great gates, though its levels are above my ensign."

"I have passed many times through your people's well-preserved airways," Fetrye said with a smile. "But come. It is time."

Warily, the rest straightened and acquiesced to the woman's direction. Kilith bent to lift Mereámé from the ground, but Gabor stopped him and gingerly pulled her into his own arms. Enouim walked as though in a daze, unwilling to accept what had just happened. Mereámé was a dear friend, and Enouim needed her to help her organize her thoughts and emotions, and to be gentle with her in mistakes. Enouim needed her bright eyes and salve spirit.

Now again they found themselves trudging on foot through the wood, as light began to dwindle into evening. Hungry, fatigued, and psychologically wearied, the band of warriors struggled on. Enouim wondered if this was Fetrye's true form, or if she had chosen it because it was more likely to put them at ease.

Details of the changing forest edged vaguely into the periphery of Enouim's consciousness, and some part of her was aware that the leaves were becoming greener and bright-green grass had sprung up lightly underfoot to pad their way. Enouim mildly resented the grass for its hopefulness, but was too exhausted to complain outright, and her aching feet were grateful for soft reprieve. Grieved as she was, she began to feel that their current circumstances would never change, that they had always been walking in dead-tired dread, and they would forever go on in that attitude. Time slowed down, but even so, Enouim was surprised by how quickly they arrived.

The trees, previously scattered throughout the forest without rhyme or reason, had become tall columns on either side, perfectly in line with one another so that they walked through a natural hallway extending perhaps thirty yards. Fetrye led them into the hall, the trees so close together it was impossible to guess what was beyond them on either side. Branches from both sides reached toward each other above their heads, forming an elegant arch. Green boughs spilled over and around them, with spongy moss and thick new grass carpeting the way ahead. At the end of the hallway an expansive meadow spread out before them, flowers laughing and whispering to the wind as it played lightly with their colorful petals.

In the center of the meadow sat a round stone table, perhaps six feet across, with small foreign lettering wrapping around the thick edge of the table in rows. At the end of the tree-lined hall, the entirety of the glade became visible, but not a soul could they see. Yet as they approached the table, two men materialized out of the air and stood, holding torches, on either side of the table. The men wore light-colored robes, in stark contrast to their metallic-bronze skin and eyes of fire. Enouim found their expressionless faces utterly terrifying.

At closer inspection, Enouim saw that the writing on the table was of many different scripts, most of which she couldn't make out. But one she recognized; it read, *Eh'yeh asher Eh'yeh.* Her heart pounded within her. Eh'yeh! It was here! So the Levavin were the closest to the right pronunciation after all. Perhaps the table itself was the stone. If so, how on earth would they manage to take it back with them to Gorgenbrild?

Fetrye walked up to the table and flipped her hand in a swift gesture, palm out. The circular tabletop began to spin, then swiveled upright so that it rested on the ground, nestled vertically between its front two legs like a door. "He has been waiting a long time for you," she said.

Enouim knew she was speaking to the group, but she felt Fetrye's words as if they came directly to her own heart, for her alone. She wasn't sure what to make of it.

Fetrye ushered them toward the tabletop.

"What are we supposed to do?" Kilith asked.

"Walk through it," she replied.

Kilith looked between her and the tabletop. Vadik's eyes grew wide, staring at the large stone slab. Canukke took Yadara's arm as if for insurance of his own safety, but Baird and Kilith gave him a hard look and each stationed themselves on either side of her. No body shield for him today.

"Do it," Gabor said, still cradling Mereámé's cold body in his arms.

Do what? Get knocked out? Enouim walked up to the tabletop and placed her hand on the stone. It was solid. To be expected, she supposed. It was made of rock, after all. She looked questioningly back at Fetrye, and saw nothing but patient expectation in her expression. Enouim lifted her hand and rapped on it lightly. Nothing.

"Walk through it," Fetrye said again, eyes on her.

Enouim felt her chest tighten, and butterflies fought in her stomach. *You can't do this. No one can. Even if someone could, it wouldn't be you.* Enouim shut her eyes and shook her head. Fetrye had saved them, and she said to walk through stone.

What if? That one thought took hold and sunk in deep. *What if the stone is real, and everything you've done for the past months will be worth it? What if there is hope left? What if there is something to be found out that you will never know unless you try this now?* Enouim hated not knowing things. If there was a chance she could find out what was beyond, if anything was beyond, well, she would ruminate on it forever if she gave it up now.

But how could she walk through a table? *You're being ridiculous. There is nothing for you here. Pakel is dead. Mereámé is dead. Your family is probably dead by now too.* No, no, it couldn't be. *What if?*

"Won't you lead us?" Enouim asked, looking pleadingly at Fetrye.

Fetrye shook her head. "No."

Seeing the calm finality in Fetrye's face, Enouim swallowed and turned back to the tabletop. She placed her hands behind her back, determined to keep herself from testing the waters by reaching out. Surely it was a test. Reaching out had returned only hard rock, and if she was to discover what there was to find, she couldn't test it. There was only stepping or not stepping, moving or staying still, and if her hands were free, she would definitely protect her face like any sane person would before walking into a wall.

Her many doubts still swirled in her mind, but the ounce of "what if" belief embedded in Enouim's core and took control of her feet. Hands clasped securely behind her, she walked straight into the slab of stone. Through it. Yes, *through* it! She found herself stumbling into open air. She caught herself on the grass and looked behind her, but she was alone. The table was gone, her friends were gone. She spun around.

The glade looked the same size and shape as it had been in a moment ago, though this one was filled with flowers and the other was simply grass. Beyond the glade, fruit trees and bright colored petals interrupted flowing green. There, not ten feet from her, stood a man. He wasn't nearly so impressive as the bronze men had been, and in fact was average on all counts —brown hair, brown eyes, mid-tone skin, neither attractive nor unattractive. Nevertheless, something about this man drew her in. He looked at her, and when she met his gaze, it cut to the core of her soul, at once alarming, vulnerable, frightening, and refreshing.

Enouim shared a wordless moment with the man as the two of them looked at each other. Though she was sizing him up as a stranger, he looked at her as though he'd known her all his life—his face tender, his eyes unyielding and affectionate. Though disconcerting and certainly bizarre, somehow Enouim felt no fear.

Oloren came through the stone table next, bumping into Enouim and jostling her out of her reverie. Baird followed, then Yadara, Kilith, and Ruakh. Brief pauses passed between each entrance—or exit. Enouim really wasn't sure which it was. Finally Vadik joined them, and after a pause, Gabor pushed through the table with Mereámé in his arms. Canukke didn't come for a moment, and when he did, he arrived with Fetrye's hand on his shoulder. She removed her hand once he was through.

Enouim returned her focus to the man, whose face was twisted in an anguish of grief, his eyes fixed on Mereámé's lifeless body.

"What happened?" he asked.

"She's dead," Gabor said, voice cracking.

A tear ran down the stranger's cheek, and Enouim felt the lump returning to her throat. An eerie silence stretched between them, strange for having just walked through the impossible. No one had slowed down enough to really process what had happened until this moment, and with this mysterious man's welcoming tear, the floodgates opened. Gabor slowly began to sob, sinking to his knees, tears dropping onto Mereámé's ghostly face as he held her.

Enouim's eyes stung and watered. Here, in front of this weeping man who joined their sorrow before they had even joined with it themselves, each of them felt the gravity of their own burdens. Enouim saw the terror of Chayan's murderous face, the fear of waking up in a rumbling wagon under a pile of blankets, and of finding herself on this mission. She saw herself comforted by Oloren and Pakel, offering a sense of belonging for the first time since leaving home—all stripped away with Canukke's abandonment in Kalka'an. Enouim saw Pakel crumbling with Banor's fatal blow. When Pakel died, a part of Enouim had been lost as well. She relived the simple ceremony shaving off a sliver of leather belt to honor their fallen friend.

A botched apology to Baird by the river, the horror of water and the sea serpent dragging her down to the depths, the perasors on the other side. So much fear and running, so little time for mourning. The nomad attack. More dead bodies. Their faces had filled her dreams that night. She had told no one but Mereámé. *Mereámé.* The ache inside of her grew with such a sudden strength that she could no longer fight it, and the lump in her throat turned into sobs that racked her body.

There they were, all weeping, some silent, some wailing, for a long and unhurried time in space. Some stood, some sat, some curled into balls in the grass. Enouim wasn't sure how long it was that they spent there. Her weeping eventually ebbed and her breathing steadied. Fetrye remained solemnly at the back of the group, where Canukke still stood ... gruff, but shaken. And the strange man, the ordinary man who was not ordinary, knelt over Mereámé, his eyes still glistening with tears.

He took her hand lovingly in his, and looking her in the

face, he spoke to the dead woman in Gabor's arms. "Wake up, little one."

Immediately, color flooded Mereámé's body and breath returned to her. She opened her eyes, smiling with wonder at the man who had called to her, and sat up. Gabor drew back in shock. She'd been dead for over an hour.

"Mereámé!" Enouim rushed to embrace her friend.

Mereámé held her close for a moment, but her focus remained on the man. The average man who was not average.

He raised Mereámé to her feet and addressed her friends. "Welcome. You have traveled long and are weary of body and spirit. Come, and I will refresh you. Mereámé must eat, and a meal is prepared for you all."

"Who are you?" Vadik stammered.

"I am Eh'yeh."

27

E *h'yeh?* Enouim's head spun. Surely he meant that he was the guardian of the Eh'yeh Stone, its protector, or maybe even its keeper. How could a man be a stone? But then ... how could a man make the dead come alive?

Enouim walked in a daze, following the man through beautiful natural enclaves and doorways of tree and vine. Moments ago, Mereámé had been *dead*. No breath, no color, no nothing. And now she was excitedly bouncing along after this magic man. The man who called himself Eh'yeh—though Eh'yeh was supposed to be the powerful object of legend that could save her homeland. If the stone didn't exist, where did that leave Gorgenbrild?

In a green glade bursting with life sat a long wooden table filled with an extravagant feast overflowing from golden dishes and accented with sparkling goblets. Eh'yeh bade the befuddled travelers take their seats, and Enouim sank into the most comfortable chair she'd ever known. Long after this day, Enouim would struggle to recall what they talked about at this meal. She remembered sitting down, vague discussion and food passed around the table, but could hardly catch one of her thoughts long enough to understand it. Her world whirled around her, confused. Though a happy occasion, and the food revived her spirit, none of it quite made sense.

During the meal no one spoke of Gorgenbrild or their mission. Eh'yeh told them Fetrye would care for them while they stayed and encouraged them all to get some rest. He assured them he was available whenever they needed anything, and Fetrye led them through a door of hanging vines into a warm meadow covered with even more colorful flowered bushes and plants than before.

The open sky above allowed soft evening light to play in the petals and leaves. A number of the flowers and bushes Enouim had never seen before, but one plant seemed particularly strange. Like a hydrangea at the top, but only perhaps a foot-and-a-half across, it sat atop a thick, curving base of bark. From the sides sprouted long fingers, thick like branches but fluid like roots or vines flowing down into the ground in different directions. Baird stepped forward to examine it, then yelped as the plant turned around to look at him.

Enouim realized that the hydrangea was the creature's bright-blue hair, the bark its body, and the flowing branches or vines its arms. She had no nose, but large eyes with what looked like a hundred tiny circles of petals all in a cluster for pupils—almost like a dragonfly's eyes. The plant woman dipped her head at Baird and turned back to her work. The vines of her arms went down into the ground, and where they met the earth, lush beds of spongy moss sprang up tall in just the right shape and size as a sleeping cot. To her left, her other arm's many roots embedded in the ground again, and a second sleeping cot sprang from the earth. Retracting her arms from the ground and letting them flow long and languid about her legs, she stood and bowed to them. She was only perhaps five feet tall.

Fetrye spoke briefly to her in a language Enouim didn't understand, then said to the company, "This is Linyanet, one of the Gudira, guardians of plant life throughout the whole world of Yatzar Hei. She is making your beds."

Linyanet move down the row creating more beds until there were ten laid out in the meadow. A man appeared, his hair branches accented with new buds waiting to bloom, arms more human shaped than Linyanet's, though still wrapped in bark. He reached up and removed a bud from his hair, and as he touched it, it bloomed into a large, thick-petaled purple flower. He laid it on one of Linyanet's beds, whereupon the flower sprouted stems, more buds, more flowers, and wove itself into a blanket of petals before their eyes.

The Gudira said nothing as they went pleasantly about their work, but they dipped their heads at the company before exiting. Fetrye smiled at them as they passed and turned back to the group. "You are safe here. Please, stay as long as you like. You will need your strength for the journey home."

"How do you know where we're from?" Vadik asked.

"I know many things," she said. "Get some rest."

With that they were left alone in the meadow, staring at one another in awe.

Canukke shook his head. "I can't rest now. And I'm not entirely sure I want to sleep on these." He nudged a petal-blanket with his foot. "Who's to say it doesn't strangle me in my sleep? I need to find this Eh'yeh character again and figure out what is going on and where the stone is."

Oloren sighed. "It's getting dark. Fetrye saved us, Mereámé is alive, and I just had the best supper of my entire life. There's no hurry. Let it be. I've never known hospitality like this before."

Canukke shook his head and took off through the hanging vines through which they'd entered, Vadik on his heels.

"I don't believe there is a stone," Kilith said slowly. "At least, not like we thought."

"Of course," Mereámé said. "Isn't it obvious? Eh'yeh is Iamwë's heart. Iamwë's power is in the stone, and Eh'yeh is the stone."

"Obvious?" Baird looked dubious.

She raised an eyebrow. "Pardon, but how many people have you brought back to life?"

Enouim smiled. Mereámé seemed happy and confident. Pluckier than she had been.

More than an hour passed before Canukke and Vadik returned. Canukke was scowling.

"No luck?" Kilith asked.

"He likely abandoned us. Left us in this ... whatever this is. Are we even in the same wood we were in this morning? How do we get out? This whole thing was a mistake. I will find him or Fetrye at first light."

"Perhaps he is a sorcerer," Vadik said. "This place is amazing."

Enouim hoped for her own encounter with Eh'yeh. She had so many questions, about the table that was really a door, and about how dead people could come alive, but more than that, she wanted to figure out who *he* was. Was Eh'yeh really a sorcerer, or was he Iamwë's heart, as Mereámé had said? If he was the stone, would he return with them to Gorgenbrild?

Enouim woke sometime in the middle of the night. Her companions still slept, but her mind was wide awake, so she slipped off on her own. While wandering through the meadows not far from camp, she came across Eh'yeh himself. He sat, watching her patiently, on a large rock half sunken into the earth and partially covered with soft moss. Was he waiting for her?

"Um, hello," she said awkwardly as she neared him.

He smiled in a warm way that reached all the way to her toes. "Hello, friend." Eh'yeh gestured at the rock and Enouim took her seat beside him. After a pause, he spoke again. "How did you sleep?"

"Fine. Great. I mean, until I woke up." Enouim scratched her head.

"You want to know who I am."

"I ... I want to know a great many things," Enouim admitted.

"Tell me."

She paused, and then questions spilled out at once. "How are you a stone? Was there ever a stone? How is Mereámé alive? What do you do here?"

"I give rest to weary, peace to the burdened, life to the dead. And all are dead, in one way or another. I am the same essence as Iamwë, we are one; his heart is mine and mine is his. Mereámé is alive because everything that has been made answers to him who made it."

Enouim took a deep breath as she tried to grasp what he had just said. "All are dead? I am dead?"

"No one can be brought to life without dying first. It's much easier to accept life when you know you are dead."

Not sure what to make of this, Enouim changed the subject. "How did Fetrye know Mereámé's name? How did you know we were coming?"

"I know many things. I knew you before you ended up on the supply wagon and joined this mission. I knew you before you met Rotan and Qadra."

How could he know these things? There was no reason for such an extraordinary man—if indeed he was a man—to apply himself so thoroughly to the details of her life. If he were essentially Iamwë, as he seemed to be saying he was, then he would be the great divine power of the universe. Why care about her? If he did care, why was Gorgenbrild under attack? He claimed to give peace to the burdened. Did he have to wait for her family to be enslaved before he set them free? Enouim furrowed her eyebrows in thought. When she looked up, he was examining her face with pain etched into his own.

Ashamed to ask her questions, she decided to respond to his statement directly. "I found myself on this mission entirely by accident," she said.

"And have you?" Eh'yeh questioned her.

"Have I what?"

"Found yourself."

The question took her off guard. *Had she?* Well, she had found a purpose in finding her purpose. She had struck out from Kalka'an knowing she couldn't go back to Gorgenbrild and that she couldn't sit back and do nothing. She had run from danger in Chayan, and now was running back into danger with the Sumus. *Had she found herself?*

"I don't know," she answered honestly.

"When you find something worth chasing, you chase it with all that you have. But you chase yourself, and you tire."

Enouim *was* tired. She was utterly sapped of energy. She leaned forward and put her head in her hands. In that moment, lost to herself, Enouim found comfort in the man who was and was not a man. Eh'yeh sat with her, quietly, patiently, speaking on occasion. They spoke of her childhood, her journey thus far, and of home in recent years with her mother and brother. He laughed and cried with her, held her, and spoke tenderly to her. When she returned to her companions she had utterly forsaken time, and felt immediately a longing to return to the side of Eh'yeh—to him who knew everything there was to know and felt everything with her that there was to feel.

The stars were out, and when she returned, Yadara met her with pitch black hair, dark eyes, and twinkling skin. "You *see*," she said with delighted relief, searching Enouim's face.

"I might," Enouim said, amazed by the experience of Eh'yeh, while still raging with questions. Enouim sat in the grass and Yadara readily joined her. "He is ... like nothing I've ever encountered. It's like being stripped bare with your full mind and thoughts on display, and I expected him to be disappointed by me, to meet me in my unpleasant appraisal of myself. But he didn't praise or condemn. He just ... was."

"I knew you would understand once you met him!"

"You knew? Eh'yeh ... he's not a stone."

"Well, he is called the stone. At first I didn't realize you didn't know he was a man, but once I did, I knew the mouse does not tell of the lion's affairs."

"So it's true. He really is the stone. We've been searching for months for this powerful weapon to take back with us and ... it's not an 'it' at all. And he knows about the mission but has said nothing about his intentions concerning it. If he's the creator of everything and knows everything, why wouldn't he have done something about Gorgenbrild by now? Why did we even have to make the journey?"

Nearby, Kilith stretched and rose from his bed, coming to sit with them as they spoke.

"Well," Yadara began slowly, "there was a lion watching over his kingdom when all the mice started to squabble. They fought each other and hurt each other over and over, forgetting that a great lion was watching them, and they should have been more concerned about the lion than the other mice. One little mouse left the fighting mice and made friends with the lion, and he lived in the lion's den.

"One day the little mouse watched down below as all the other mice were fighting, and asked the lion why he didn't just put a stop to it. He couldn't stand to watch it anymore. 'Wipe them out! Make it stop!' he said. The lion answered, 'Another little creature asked me to stop all the fighting a day before you came to the den. Had I wiped out all the mice then, you would be dead. What if other mice come to the den and join us, if only they are given enough time? I am helping the mice in more ways than you know. But if I make it all stop now, I also end lives of mice that may yet come to the den.'"

Enouim cocked her head, unsure of what to make of the story. "But ... that's not ..." her voice trailed off.

Kilith shook his head. "The way I see it, there are many types of answers to difficult questions. Some answers make you feel good, some make you feel rotten, some answers you give up on finding, and some answers you avoid because they would demand you do something you don't want to do.

"Sometimes we want the answer we get at face value, sometimes we hate the answer until we get to know it. Sometimes we expend our lives searching for answers we are disappointed by, and will do anything to fill the void ... not with a real answer, but just fluff to make us feel less empty. We can mistake the fluff for substance, ignoring the issue, or replace the fluff with something more convincing. And then there's the truth."

"What of the truth?" Enouim asked.

"I can't know exactly what the truth is yet," Kilith replied, "but if we ever hope to find it, we must resolve ahead of time to accept whatever the truth is. If it is not our intention to deal with truth, then we can come up with whatever flimsy substitute we find most comforting. But if something has compelling evidence to be real ... well, follow it to the end, whatever the end may be. We cannot ignore Mereámé's experience. There is something here. Something genuine and absolute. Death to life; perhaps life itself."

Enouim nodded. "Truth is all I care about. Even if it is uncomfortable, even if it requires much of me. But how do I find out? This doesn't make sense!"

"Would you rather have something that makes sense, but doesn't work, or something that works, but doesn't make sense?"

Enouim considered this. She so desperately hated not knowing things. "I think," she answered slowly, "I would want something that works. And if I work backward from that, maybe what doesn't make sense will start to. Like how I saw Mereámé die. She had no breath, no heartbeat. Eh'yeh spoke to her and she ... woke up. It didn't make sense, but it worked, and she's alive now. I don't understand it, but I can't refute that truth."

28

The next day the company explored the area. All was outdoor and green, with the earth itself providing surprisingly perfect but natural gazebos, seating areas, and soft mossy beds. As they walked, Enouim asked Mereámé about the moment she came back to life.

"It was like I had known him all my life," she said, a dreamy look in her eyes. "He *saw* me, you know. Really saw me. There wasn't anything I could do about it—and for a moment I was terrified—but after I saw how he looked at me, I knew I didn't want to stop him looking. Energy flowed through me at his touch, calling me home, but home wasn't Levav, it was here. With him. I'm not sure how to describe it, but spend some time with him and you'll see for yourself what I mean."

Enouim pondered her words all morning.

As they continued looking around, they came across a clearing with stone steps leading up to a large dais. It was strange to see stone after so much greenery. The stone was weathered and worn, and plants sneaked through its cracks as though it were ruins that had stood in this spot for millennia.

On the dais set atop another short flight of stairs stood a gilded armchair, sparkling in the sun. A circular platform three feet in diameter sat opposite the chair. Two guards stood on either side of the stair.

"What is this?" Canukke directed his query to the guard on the left.

"This is Deliberation. It is here that Iamwë himself will weigh the lives of every soul under the sun. All matter is subject to him, and Iamwë gifted mankind with free will unlike any other living thing. With this freedom mankind was brought to a fork in the road to choose to lift up others or to destroy others and abuse their gift. So the observed shall stand on the dais there" —the guard nodded to the circular platform— "when the time is right. The Deliberation of how their gift was utilized will be made here."

"What makes him fit to decide?" Gabor asked.

"He is Iamwë," the guard replied, as if surprised by the question.

"He who brings forth life is able to judge that life," Mereámé explained. "It's only natural."

The guard spoke again. "At his right hand are two scepters: one for mercy, one for justice. He may touch either upon the entrance of one unbidden, and again either after hearing one's plea. Mercy and justice are equally his right to pass out, and neither is primary in goodness or importance. One is not better than the other save for the one on whom judgment is passed. Thus, the mercy and judgment scepters are both on his right, rather than one on his right and one on his left."

There was a long silence.

Canukke spoke first, sarcasm dripping from every word. "Excellent! Finally someone willing to do the dirty work that needs doing. Let him judge the realms this very moment, and let me see the destruction of the Sumus and the justice of my father carried out before my eyes. Let them discern the strong from the weak, the good from the evil, and decimate those who do not make the cut."

"Before being quick to demand justice for the wicked, make sure *you* are not the wicked." The guard drilled him with a cool stare, striking Canukke speechless.

In stark contrast with Canukke, Kilith spoke pensively and respectfully, "You speak as if justice is always a thing of dread for the observed. What happens if a person is rightfully deemed just?"

The guard frowned. "That has never happened."

Another stretch of uncomfortable silence engulfed them, and Enouim felt anxiety grip her stomach. Would she one day stand on the platform, as the guard said she would? How would she fare?

"How are the people judged?" Baird demanded. "Surely it is harsh and unreasonable that no one has been considered just!"

"Stringent, yes. Unreasonable, no. The standard is total perfection."

"By the hordes, he is a villain!" Vadik exclaimed. "The judgment is a game. There are many good and decent people!"

"*Perfection* is the standard," the guard repeated.

Vadik shook his head. "It isn't right. You've got it wrong."

"Right?" Oloren asked. "If he is who he says he is, I'm not sure we get to decide what is right. We only have the right to be insulted by this if we hold the high ground, but I see now that we may not."

"Should murderers determine whether another person is a murderer?" asked the guard pointedly. "You ask which actions are worse, to feel better about yourselves, but you need not ask whether or not you have broken the standard. The answer is clear. No matter how the ants build their hills, they never reach the sky."

"What happens to ... to people who are not perfect?" Enouim asked.

"Death, and more death," the guard replied. "The first is like passing through the shade, and the second is a terror no one who has seen it could wish on their worst enemy."

Enouim's eyes widened.

"What is the point of it all?" Canukke demanded. "This Eh'yeh, he is a deceiver and betrayer. His silver tongue tricks all into trusting him, and then he ushers them in to be judged and tortured! Only a monster relishes the pain of others."

Ruakh gave him a knowing look, and a flicker of shame crossed Canukke's face but then he masked it with practiced skill.

"Eh'yeh cannot break the code," the guard said. "Iamwë set the standard himself. Eh'yeh and Iamwë were deeply grieved by man's abuse of their gift, but even more so were they grieved by what justice demands of man for recompense."

"He can't be good. He can't be, if he sends so many good people to 'death and more death,' whatever that means," Vadik declared.

The second guard spoke for the first time, voice deep and commanding. "The marvel is not that the people you consider good need saving, but that he cares at all to save bad people."

"So that's it then," Oloren said in resignation. "We deserve torture, live miserable lives until the end comes and we die, and then we are handed over to our fate."

"How long would a man have to pore over old documents to find an acceptable way out within the law?" the second guard said. "But there is a way out, and that is why Iamwë tore his heart in two and wrapped it in flesh, naming it Eh'yeh and sending it among you."

"I'm not sure I see the point," Gabor said. "So he ripped his heart out. Melodramatic, sure. Helpful? I think not. It doesn't change the content of our lives."

"Under the law," the sentry said, "someone whom Iamwë deems flawless can choose to offer themselves as a substitute for a guilty party. That person volunteers for torment in exchange for the freedom of another."

"No one would volunteer for that, perfect or not," Kilith noted.

Canukke shook his head. "Glintenon, I am the strongest and bravest of my people. I have saved lives upon lives. I have nothing to be ashamed of, and I am not to be disregarded." He looked at the dais with determination. "Judge me now, and I dare you to find me any less worthy than this sniveling impersonation of a weapon! Who is greater than I?"

Canukke leaped up the steps onto the dais, and on his final step up onto the circular platform, an invisible force blasted him backward, flinging him from the dais. He landed on his back on the ground, wind knocked out of him for a moment.

"The time is not yet come," the guard said, irritation seeping into his tone. "And though Eh'yeh would not say it, may I say on his behalf, you're welcome."

Canukke stood. "I do not need your charity. I can do whatever needs doing on my own, making up for any misdeeds that tip the scale. But there is nothing to make up for in my case. I have had good reasons for all that I have done."

"You misunderstand," Ruakh said. "It is not a scale to weigh good and evil, but a test to determine whether any evil has ever existed in any measure within your soul."

"And the guard says no one passes that test," Baird said.

"No one but Eh'yeh," the guard added. "That is why Eh'yeh is here."

"If he knew me better, he would rescind his offer," Oloren said quietly.

"He knows you better than you know yourself," Yadara stated in the simplest sentence she had perhaps ever spoken.

Canukke swore under his breath. "Waste of time. We leave in the morning."

"To what end?" Kilith asked.

Canukke refused to answer and stalked away. The group exchanged glances, but pulled into their own thoughts, a hushed solemnity had fallen over them. One by one they drifted away, enveloped in torrid streams of thought.

ENOUIM SPENT MORE time with Eh'yeh that evening, but she kept the conversation to herself. The whole matter seemed muddled at best. How could Eh'yeh offer himself as her substitute? Yet he had assured her both that justice required more of her than he could bear to watch, *and* that his offer would last for as long as breath remained in her body. She had told him that she couldn't ask him to do that, that there must be something she could do herself, or accept the responsibility of her actions if truly she was as heinous as the standard said.

He told her he'd already been tortured on her behalf, as it was his right to offer himself for her, and that now it was her choice to either accept the offer and live, or refuse the offer and be handed over to torment when the time came. He just wanted her safe, and to be able to stay with him in the meadow when Deliberation came and went. It didn't make *sense*, but somehow ... somewhere in her soul ... it *worked*.

That night Enouim slept even more restlessly than before. But this time, she dreamed, and she dreamed so vividly that she would remember it in detail for years to come. In her dream, Enouim stood watching her troubles sweeping toward her in a great unstoppable tidal wave. She saw Pakel, Mereámé, her family, and the mystery of her abandonment as a baby. She saw the faces of the dead she'd seen since leaving Gorgenbrild. She saw Gorgenbrild set to flame and her mother and brother screaming, fleeing the streets in panic. She saw herself, helpless, hopeless, a worthless failure powerless to stop any of it.

As she observed her life, it seemed that suddenly she came to a fork in the road. To her left, the fork sloped gently and she stepped forward. All of a sudden the terrain beneath her feet dropped away, and with a lurch she was pitched forward and felt herself slipping down, down, down. She fell about six feet and landed with a crash. Bars appeared above her, closing her in, and darkness overshadowed the sun. Her breathing quickened, her heart pounded as though it might explode, and her nails dug into the earthen sides of her prison.

She shook, and her thoughts raced. She had to get out, had to get out, had to get out! *It won't work. I'm not strong enough. It's not working!* Kicking, slashing, ferociously throwing herself against the bars, she quickly earned herself bruises and lacerations she hardly felt in the face of crushing hopelessness and powerlessness. Frantic, her antics exhausted her, pulling her deeper into that powerlessness. The tidal wave kept coming, overwhelming, unstoppable.

Just before she was overtaken, in the blink of an eye she found herself standing above the pit at the fork. Down and to her left she saw herself, and yet not herself—she was in her own body, standing at the fork, alive and in control. And yet she could not deny that it was also herself she saw in that pit, the same self that had slid there only moments ago. Standing at her vantage point at the fork, she saw what looked like a deranged woman with unkempt red hair and dark beady eyes darting back and forth, searching, ever searching, and seeing nothing. Dirt began to pile in on top of her through the bars, and she filled the air with a blood-curdling scream, her face distorted into a hideous grimace. Her nails were like daggers, her body slathered in filth, grime, and her own blood, and she reminded herself of an animal gone mad.

Enouim shuddered and looked away, desperate to get her mind off the horrific sight she saw of herself in that grave. Turning from the nightmare of herself, she glanced to her right. Here the road climbed upward, steeply—too steep to climb, she thought. Thick clouds engulfed the road briefly and then she saw herself on a platform. Except this time the Enouim she saw stood tall and serene, unconcerned by the impending tsunami. She stood in a meadow looking with compassion on standing-at-the-fork Enouim. Something behind her caught her attention. Her face lit up with glee, and she turned away from Enouim and she threw herself into the arms of the man who had called to her. Eh'yeh.

Above her, tranquility, acceptance, joy. Below her, blood-curdling screams that made her skin crawl. For a few horrifically confusing moments, Enouim couldn't focus on either scenario, but both sights and sounds intertwined in an utterly chaotic discombobulation that left her feeling overwhelmed and anxious. Her palms started to sweat; her hands shook; her eyes darted this way and that. An onslaught of stimulus overtook her mind, and she began to scream. The world turned black, and she lurched awake, the echo of her shriek still ringing in her ears.

29

A river of blood poured from Eh'yeh's body, tortured and torn to shreds. Canukke didn't understand it. He'd told Eh'yeh not to bother, had told him he wouldn't accept the exchange. He'd rejected the offer of Eh'yeh's life for Canukke's life, yet here he was, that enigma wrapped in flesh, beaten and bleeding. It was so needless. *How dare he?* How dare Eh'yeh try to die for him when Canukke had so vehemently opposed it! He would stand before judgment head on, look his accusers in the eyes and spit in their faces. Canukke Topothain would take whatever was coming—if indeed it *was* coming—and die a heroic death. An honorable death. The death of a man willing to accept his own fate, with dignity and strength. It was Canukke's *right* to refuse such a ludicrous offer!

And it was Eh'yeh's right to die.

The blood ran down toward Canukke and pooled at his feet. So much blood. More blood than any man contained in his earthly vessel, surely. More blood than a hundred men. Eh'yeh's veins were a fountain of crimson that never seemed to end. A wave of nausea rocked Canukke at the sight of so much blood, the first time he had ever experienced such a reaction to gore. As he watched the river of blood, he saw the heads of all the men he had ever murdered flowing toward him, their faces frozen permanently in their final expressions: fear, horror, anger, hate. He saw a vision of himself, always thirsty, never satisfied, exacting revenge on those he had deemed in the wrong, destroying those who had dared cross him. Canukke heaped the bodies on Eh'yeh's slumped form, and as Canukke's eyes watched the vision of himself, he saw Eh'yeh looking back at him with piercing eyes that saw the depths of his soul.

Canukke wanted to run, wanted to hide. He did not want Eh'yeh to see his soul. But it was too late. He felt the retching of his heart as it seemed to vomit up every evil thought he had ever had, every depraved thing he had ever done or considered doing. The hate was black, deep black, as never ending as the blood in Eh'yeh's veins. The jealousy, lust, selfishness, and greed was thick like coagulated blood trying to keep from emptying a body of its life. No clot could stop his soul's outpouring. No bandage was strong enough to restrain the force that had broken down a dam somewhere inside him where all wickedness had been hidden away from prying eyes.

He saw Edone with pain in her eyes as he gave attention to other women. She unhooked the sleeves from her thumbs and pushed them up to reveal bruises all over her arms, bruises he had put there. Canukke was not honorable after all. He had allowed himself to express his anger physically toward another person, someone he said he loved, someone he should have loved. Edone, beautiful, smart, incredible Edone! Remorse seeped into his mind, unbidden.

A flurry of images passed before his eyes: pairs of people, couples, filing by at lightning speed until finally it slowed and he recognized his grandparents, his parents, himself as a child.

Canukke hit his brother on the head to take a toy that he wanted, and Canukke saw that he had hurt others to get what he desired for many years. He had even stolen, in years past. Emotions came out of him like colored smoke as events in is life beginning at his earliest memory cycled through before him, and he saw darkness in it. Green jealousy, black hatred, purple lust, red selfishness. Canukke's soul was laid bare. Its deepest cravings, desires, regrets, maliciousness. It was seen by Eh'yeh and known fully.

Blood rose to his neck, and he gasped as he was stripped from his visions. Canukke's arms and legs tried to tread water but the sticky blood was like mud, slowing his progress and impeding his effectiveness. The familiar, metallic smell of blood filled his nose but brought with it a panic like Canukke had never known. He was stained by this blood. Condemned by this blood. The blood knew everything he had ever done, ever thought. The blood was choking him. He had to get out. He had to be free. How many dungeons he would prefer over this blood!

Suddenly he saw. He was drowning in this blood that Eh'yeh claimed was his salvation. It was Eh'yeh's right to die for Canukke, and Canukke's right to refuse that gift. Yet Eh'yeh's torment was complete, the exchange approved by all relevant governing authorities. Canukke's refusal didn't keep Eh'yeh from sacrificing himself on Canukke's behalf, but only kept Canukke apart from the benefits of that promised salvation. Canukke was choosing to drown in Eh'yeh's blood, because his pride was too great.

Only Eh'yeh could satisfy the requirements of the charge against Canukke, only Eh'yeh could pay the price for Canukke's head with his own and yet live. The choice to accept was still Canukke's. This kind of sacrifice demanded something from him. If Canukke gave in to Eh'yeh, if he accepted the gift of life from Eh'yeh's hands and the blood from his veins, Canukke would owe him more than he had to offer.

Canukke locked eyes with Eh'yeh. Soft brown eyes looked back at him knowingly. Loved him. No other love could be compared to this love, and Canukke felt drawn to it while simultaneously squirming under the pressure of it, the vulnerability of that love. Eh'yeh's love demanded something from him. Eh'yeh wanted nothing from Canukke but Canukke himself, yet Canukke knew that to give himself over would be complete and total realignment of his loyalties. Receiving Eh'yeh's gift would be to acknowledge that Canukke could not pay the price for his own head, and to be forever indebted to Eh'yeh. Canukke would owe his sword, his allegiance to a king not of his own making. Canukke would either surrender his life to Eh'yeh or die in his stubbornness and pride.

The blood rose up and engulfed him completely. Hemmed in all around, limbs exhausted from fighting, mind drained from the mental battle, Canukke knew he didn't have long. His energies were spent, all resources depleted. The time was now. He had to choose. Canukke woke with a weary, desperate cry.

EH'YEH WAS A GREAT CATALYST, like a lit fuse left to each person to bury, to smother, or to allow to burst into a great and unquenchable flame. For Enouim's part, she was ready to let the flame burn. As for Canukke ... well, Enouim assumed he leaned heavily toward the first or second option. Still, something had happened to Canukke in the night, and he was less anxious to leave when morning came. He was also even moodier than before.

The company stayed with Eh'yeh for days, and days

turned into weeks. Eh'yeh himself came and went, but Enouim found that whenever she really wished to see him, it wasn't long before he would appear.

Canukke was in a bind. He did still want to return to Gorgenbrild, and had begun trying to convince his companions to leave the meadow and head back home on their own. Although the company knew they would have to return home eventually, no one was quite ready to go.

One afternoon, Enouim came across Canukke, Kilith, and Ruakh speaking with Eh'yeh and overheard part of their conversation. Canukke was having a heated conversation with Eh'yeh. She concluded without much difficulty that the point of contention was Eh'yeh's being a man with the power, divinity, and code of Iamwë rather than a mythical weapon that could be bent to the will of anyone in possession of it.

Canukke's face was hard as flint. "This is not what I was looking for."

"I am exactly what you have been looking for," Eh'yeh said. "You have simply decided, now that you have found me, that you do not like the truth of what it is you have found. Many look for what they do not want, and many do not recognize what they need though it slaps them in the face, and they go on looking until they exhaust themselves."

Canukke closed the distance between them, face full of rage, eyes blazing, and stood nose to nose with Eh'yeh—who, for his part, remained soft and calm. "I need a weapon to destroy my enemies. If you cannot produce this for me, you are worth nothing."

"Careful, Canukke," Ruakh cautioned. "There are ways to seek weapons that do not come at the cost of your humanity. Remember who you are."

"Humanity!" Canukke spat. "What is humanity, anyway? Are you better than I am? Is anyone? Humanity is rotten to the core. The cost of my humanity ... what is that worth? Can a being sink any lower?" Canukke had no weapon to protect him from this, no experience to prepare him for such an encounter. He'd been undone and was unraveling from within. He stomped away to sulk.

Enouim wasn't sure how long they stayed in Eh'yeh's glade. Time felt as though it passed differently there, but she thought perhaps it was a couple of weeks. At varying points during their stay, almost all of those in the company came to accept Eh'yeh's offer to be their substitute and subsequently spent their time sitting with him, talking, learning, and soaking up like sponges every word he spoke.

The fact that Eh'yeh had accepted her was mindboggling, and she considered it often. Sometimes she diverted herself because her mind simply couldn't fathom what that might mean, but at other times when she sunk into its truth she was able to marvel in it all. She felt not special and elevated by Eh'yeh's affections, but low. Humbled. And she rested in the glory of being safe before the face of perfect purity.

As Enouim was pondering this one morning, surrounded by her friends, Canukke came storming through, considerably hot and bothered.

"Practically begged me to join him, he did," Canukke said, with the air of a king too high and mighty to hear the plea of a peasant. "*Begged*," he muttered again under his breath, passing beyond them into the brush.

Kilith's eyes followed him as he went. "Eh'yeh? He did nothing of the sort," he said softly—but danger coiled in his tone. "He's not the begging type. No, Canukke was unwilling to accept what Eh'yeh offered, and refused to give his allegiance to any but himself. It will be his downfall. No greater offer will come. In Canukke now stands a man tormented, in sight of what he wants most, but separated from it by a great chasm of his own making."

The others knew this to be true, and they respected Kilith's wisdom in putting it to words. Eh'yeh was kind, compassionate, and soft … but these were not his only attributes. He carried an ease of authority and power that could not be ignored. Eh'yeh was no beggar. He simply was what he was, offering himself as a gift, humble but never sniveling.

Eventually the topic of home came up again with Eh'yeh. Enouim had nearly forgotten this beautiful place wasn't home, and that she hadn't always lived here. Eh'yeh told them that he was sending them out from this place, and Enouim's heart grew somber. She didn't want to go.

"Tell of what you have seen, and indeed the Eh'yeh Stone will be with you on whatever paths you take," he said.

"How will you be with us if you are staying here? Come with us!" Baird said.

"It is in your best interest that I remain to prepare for when we are reunited once again. It will not be long. But I will always be with you, and I am sending you the Pneuma to guide you and remind you of everything."

Enouim wasn't sure what a Pneuma was, but she was pretty sure it sounded miserable. She wanted Eh'yeh himself to come with them.

Gabor clearly agreed."Best interest? I beg to differ. *Best* is you returning with us."

Oloren looked at him with the shocked frustration of a mother when her child has spoken too bluntly. Gabor ignored her, and Oloren said nothing, but her disapproval was clear. Who was he to question Eh'yeh?

"There is much to say, too much to convey to you now. But the Pneuma will give you all you need. You came here looking for the stone, to be equipped to save your people. You will not leave empty handed, for I am with you always."

"When will we see you again?" Mereámé asked. Enouim was glad she did, because it was the very question she wanted answered most, but she found she was unable to speak.

"Soon," he said.

Cryptic. Enouim's time with Eh'yeh had not diminished her hatred of not knowing things. It had been tempered for a while, but returned with full force every time it ebbed. And yet somehow, she knew that vague answer was all she would get at this time. She would have to accept it.

Eh'yeh stepped up to them all and breathed on them, and from his mouth flew a white heron. The heron was bright and shimmering, and became translucent as it flew. It seemed to enter them as they stood there, flying through them and vanishing from sight. Enouim didn't feel any physical difference, but a peaceful sensation came over her. She was going to be all right.

Yadara took several paces toward them and stopped. "This is where my journey with you ends," she said. "My heart is a great weight. I wish neither to leave Eh'yeh in this glade nor you as my ... friends." Her voice cracked and a tear ran down her cheek. It traveled down her face, and as she reached up to wipe it away, the tear landed on the ensign on her wrist. She cried out in pain, extending her arms. The silver was bubbling, boiling, and steam rose up from it. Alarmed, Enouim watched with eyes wide. After a moment, the pain dissipated, and where once was silver, grandidierite green swirled within her ensign. "I will miss you dearly." She wiped her tears at last and then marveled at her wrists.

"Your strength is our strength," said Ruakh quietly, "and our hearts go out to you in your pain."

Yadara nodded and stepped back beside Eh'yeh. She would remain briefly, soon to return to her people in the sky.

"It is time," Eh'yeh said. "I am sending you now, just as I was sent. Your horses are safe and completed an errand for me; I sent them ahead of you to the Rehi where they will be waiting. It is not far. I have told Kilith the way."

Enouim looked at Kilith, who was focused solely on Eh'yeh. Was he now their leader, then?

The travelers said their goodbyes and turned again to the road. And so it was that there were nine again setting out to complete their mission, faced at last toward Gorgenbrild. Now, for perhaps the first time, it was the Eh'yeh Mission in earnest. Unsure of the road ahead, unsure what they would do upon return to Gorgenbrild, but trusting somehow in the mysterious plan of Eh'yeh, they left the glade behind and stepped out into the wild.

30

Kilith said it was several days' march to the other side of the forest where the Rehi would be willing to receive them. Eh'yeh had not said what errand he'd used the horses for, only that he'd called them away and they would be waiting at Rehim. Now that they were on their way again, Enouim was anxious to reach Inferno and be back in the saddle.

Vadik, walking next to her, seemed preoccupied by something over their heads.

"What do you see?" Enouim asked.

"What do you mean?" Vadik asked, confused. "How can you *not* be distracted by a heron flying over your head? I can't help it."

Enouim looked up, but only saw the green of the trees. "Vadik ... there's nothing there."

Vadik's eyes flared with indignation. "No, he breathed on us back there, and a white heron came from him. Everyone saw it!"

"Yes, it did. But it disappeared after it flew at ... flew through us, or whatever."

"No, it didn't. It's still there, and flying right over us. How do you not see this?" Vadik started to look uncomfortable but couldn't keep his eyes off the invisible heron.

"How often do you see things above us? You look around yourself more often than the rest. At first I thought it was just a nervous tic or something."

Vadik swallowed. "Um ... sometimes. Look, don't tell the others. But the heron is real, everyone saw it at first. The Pneuma that Eh'yeh talked to us about. So I can't be crazy. Not totally crazy, anyway."

"Well, I'm with you on that," Enouim agreed. "Okay, so what else have you seen?"

"Something dark ... swooping overhead and then down low, stirring up the water. Right before the sea serpent. It was already pitch black around us, and I thought it was a trick of my eyes—especially when no one else said anything. I saw dark and light figures fighting in the air when we met Canus. And in the forest ... a couple other times too. Ugh, maybe I really *have* lost it." Vadik rubbed his eyes.

"You know ... I think you're on to something," Enouim said thoughtfully. Seeing the look in his eyes, she corrected herself. "No, no, not that you've gone crazy! I mean, you seem to see flashes of things before they happen. Well, not exactly. But some kind of warning. Or something else we don't see. I don't know; I'm not saying I get it, but the Nazir were invisible too until they weren't."

"I have a confession about that too. The Nazir staircase I could see a little bit. Not totally, I mean it still took me some time to find, but I could see shimmers and reflections off it, and that's how I came to locate it."

Enouim's eyes widened. "I think you're seeing real things that the rest of us can't see. If what you were seeing wasn't linked to events, and there wasn't a consistent pattern, I'd say you ate something fishy, or something fermented had gotten to your head. But that doesn't line up."

Vadik furrowed his brow. "No, its real."

"Do you still see the heron?"

Vadik nodded. "He has been with us since we left Eh'yeh."

The forest became dense again, like it was when they left the Nazir. A sense of foreboding filled her as the looming trees oversaw their progress. Enouim wondered what unsavory things might be hiding in the forest, remembering how even birds had forsaken the place where they saw the stag—the stag that was really a murderous, shapeshifting Malak.

A flutter above her head made her flinch, but when she glanced up, she saw nothing. *It's all in your head, Enouim. Calm down.*

Again a flapping sound, and this time the dark shape of a large bat, body a foot long, swooped by and clung to a tree up ahead. A chill ran through her, and goosebumps materialized on Enouim's arms. She nudged Vadik next to her and nodded toward it. His eyes widened, and he looked around him warily. Another bat flew up ahead and took to a tree further up. The light was unnaturally dark for the middle of the day, and Enouim felt more than a little uneasy.

The rest of the company noticed the bats, no fewer than five surrounding them in nearby branches. More came. Six, eight, ten. The bats flew through and lighted on trees up ahead, then those in the back did the same. Moving forward in stages, they followed the traveler's progress through the wood. Anxious anticipation gripped Enouim like a vise. What were they doing? Surely no good would come of this. Unless the "good" was for the bats—in the form of free meals. The bats were so dark brown that they were almost black, their eyes gleaming, their fangs like polished daggers.

Tension grew thick, and the dark anticipation among them

became tangible. Not a sound was heard but leaves underfoot, wings up above, and the pounding of Enouim's own heart. In a flash the waiting was over, as the first bat took a dive straight down at Ruakh. He beat it off with his staff as more began to pour down on them from the sky. *"Run!"*

They ran. Bats plummeted down on them from above, and Enouim ran with a dagger in one hand and a knife in the other, slashing as she went. One sunk its teeth in her upper arm as she crossed her arms over her face, and she let out a yell as she careened by a tree and the bat was ripped from her flesh. The din of the screams and curses of her friends nearly drowned her voice as they fought off the beasts and crashed through the forest.

Oloren caught one on her dagger and slung it into the body of another. Both shrieked and as they fell, entangled, to the ground. "Glintenon, where are they coming from?"

"Does it matter?" Gabor yelled back, tucking his chin to protect his neck and ducking as a bat flew at his face.

"They're going for the eyes!" Baird cried as Enouim felt something sharp rake across the side of her face.

Great. At least without eyes, she wouldn't have to look at the grotesque creatures. Few beastly faces were as repugnant as the scrunched up wrinkled snarl of these bloodthirsty over-bite bats.

Enouim called out to Vadik. "The heron! Is he there?"

"Yes, he's there!" he called back through the fray.

They hadn't been abandoned. Eh'yeh was with them still, through the heron. But if Eh'yeh was with them, why were the bats still there? Enouim propelled herself forward on fumes of adrenaline, her skin a battlefield of biting and clawing. She was constantly in motion, a blur of arcs and stabs, ducks and weaves. More bats poured in, and still more. She cried out again, "And now? Is he still there?"

Vadik swung his sword at an incoming bat, letting out a feral cry of rage and exasperation. He didn't bother to glance at the sky as he surged forward to rejoin his companions. "Stop asking me that! I have better things to do than check if the sky is falling every three seconds, when we all know it's up there. Has he ever *not* been there when you've asked?"

Enouim felt slapped in the face, adding to the battering she was already receiving in that area. She set her jaw, grabbed a bat's head out of the air with her hand and smashed it into a tree trunk. Stooping to retrieve her fallen blade, she sliced up as she straightened, felling another dark creature.

"The river! It's up ahead!" Canukke called.

The river. Relief and panic mingled in her belly.

"Go, go, go!" someone screamed.

Kilith appeared by Enouim's side, though she hardly noticed until he spoke. "This is the time," he said to her, as they both hurtled themselves toward the water.

Enouim focused on her breathing as she covered her face once more, and inadvertently made contact with another bat as her knee raced forward in full flight. *Breath in, breath out.* She could do this. She had no other choice. *Breath in, breath out.* A vision of the riverbank before Eh'yeh filled her mind, of the dark and swirling, plotting water, of her panic attack, and of the sea serpent.

But that was before Eh'yeh. And Vadik said the white heron still flew. *Breath in, breath out.* If Eh'yeh wanted her to die, so be it. She would see him again that much sooner.

The river rushed toward them, as a horde of bloodthirsty bats chased them down. Thirty paces, twenty. Ten, nine, eigh t...

Kilith urged her on with one last pronouncement: "You were born for this!"

Her feet left the bank.

Enouim was airborne for a moment, frozen in time. She saw the water coming for her, reflecting a thousand evil creatures filling the air around them. She saw Mereámé had been practicing with a blade, and gave a smooth final thrust before being immersed. She saw the rest of her companions, some already leaving wakes in the water and others arched in the air as she was, seeking the safety of the river like a chick flying from the fox to its mother's underwing.

Ploosh. Enouim hit the water, arms extended above her head. She was surprised to discover that the river was cool, but not cold, and quite comfortable. Immediately the swarming bats lifted, hovering over the surface but not touching the water. And this time, the moment Enouim hit the water, she loved it.

Plant life waved at her in greeting, and a colorful school of fish scattered at the disturbance. Blues, greens, and grays alternated and mingled, bringing a sense of novelty and amazement, but also reminding her of the greens and grays of home. It was like her world had been turned on its end and slowed to a leisurely pace. Enouim felt like she had entered a time warp, isolated in space so that all she could hear was her own breathing.

And she was breathing, though it wasn't the normal kind. The scars on the back of her neck opened up and welcomed in the river like a desert desperate for heavy rain. They acted as gills, allowing life in and keeping death out. The scar draped over her collarbone was apparently still an ordinary scar, but the symmetrical slashing scars on the back of her neck had always been more. Enouim reveled in her newfound freedom, and felt a surge of energy like nothing else. It hummed with life, and she felt alive, more than she had in all her days. She found that as she opened and closed her hands, they seemed to direct the current around her so she could propel herself through the water without exhausting herself kicking or paddling. Enouim plunged deeper and deeper into the river, twisting, twirling, and playing with the current as they traveled upstream.

She felt the pleasure of Eh'yeh, his love coursing over her as his powerful creation surged around her, his delight filled to overflowing. Enouim was in awe as she experienced an encounter with Eh'yeh for the first time outside of his meadow. She gaped at the ethereal beauty of the underwater world. *How did you make all of this?* She breathed, soaking up the shafts of celestial light as they drifted to the river bottom. *For you,* he seemed to say, with an enchanting bubble of laughter encircling her. Enouim allowed herself to hang in blissful suspension and be captivated by Eh'yeh and his many fascinating worlds. She wondered even at her wonder, for it was a marvelous thing to marvel.

Something was pulling at her, trying to get her attention. She didn't want to turn around, didn't want to be ripped away from the glories of that heavenly serenity. Enouim shut her eyes. No, she was still being tugged on. So bothersome! Whatever could they want?

Twisting around, Enouim saw that the nuisance was Gabor, urging her forward toward a dark underwater tunnel much like the one she had staunchly refused to enter previously. Gabor gestured above, where the bats still swarmed, and made gagging motions to show that they would all run out of air soon and needed to get some distance between them and the vampiric wretches behind.

Enouim had entirely forgotten about the importance of oxygen, and wondered how much of Gabor's own air he had sacrificed to get her attention to save her. He wouldn't have known she didn't need saving, of course, and probably thought she'd been drowning. Enouim nodded and twirled through the water. She felt powerful in the river, and shot forward with ease, quickly closing the gap between her and the rest of the troop.

Enouim glanced back for Gabor, and discovered with alarm that he had snagged his pants leg on the rocky bottom. He struggled to free himself, but his efforts were slower now. She saw the last of his air abandon him in a bubble, escaping his lips and moving to the surface. Enouim dashed back to him, tugging at his leg in a futile attempt to free him. Finally she grabbed a stone on the bottom of the river and crushed the rocky crag with it so that it broke off, releasing Gabor at last. Enouim gathered his limp form in her arms, and pushed off through the tunnel at an unprecedented speed.

The tunnel closed in around them briefly, and Enouim was dimly aware of her companions moving at a glacial pace as she passed. They were traveling upstream, and midway through the tunnel the water level dropped below the ceiling, with space to come up for air while still protected by the natural shelter of the rock. Enouim brought Gabor to the surface and began to pound on his chest. Canukke was nearest to her, and swam over to take charge of the situation. Treading water, he angled Gabor so that he was facedown over the water, and Enouim assisted in holding him in position. Canukke delivered several blows to his back, and Gabor began to cough and sputter, spewing water from his lungs and gasping for breath.

"You all right?" Canukke asked, examining him.

Gabor looked from Enouim to Canukke, and reached a hand out for the solid rock wall. "Yes," he stammered. "I'm fine."

The others caught up and found that at the edges of the

tunnel the rock had ledges to stand on to rest. At most, there was about two feet of air between the surface of the water and the tunnel's roof.

Canukke turned his attention toward Enouim. "Now," he said. "What in the blazes was that?"

31

"What was what?" Enouim hedged, unsure how to answer Canukke's real question.

"Oh, I don't know, the crazy fast water-demon magic you just pulled? Glintenon, thick skull!"

How delightful. She may have just been endowed with a new nickname. Although, Enouim did consider "thick skull" an improvement over "coward." "I don't know," she said, thumbing her collarbone nervously. "It just happened. Good swimmer?"

"Please. Up until now you've been like a fish out of water even *in* water, and in fact anytime we are within a hundred leagues of water. I don't know how you get up the courage to drink enough to survive."

Enouim raised her eyebrows. "Okay, that sounds a bit harsh. Can we all agree that's just a little exaggerated?"

"A smidgeon," Mereámé agreed, a smile flickering across her face.

"This isn't the time." Kilith nodded toward the mouth of the tunnel. It extended another twenty feet, and bats had begun to crowd the opening, waiting for them to emerge.

"They may grow impatient if we don't come up with a plan soon."

"The river certainly seems to have been friendly to us thus far," Vadik said.

"Friendly to you, maybe," Gabor murmured darkly.

"Fine, sure, so the river hates you and loves Enouim," Vadik conceded. "And we were all shocked that Gabor wasn't the most likable fellow in it. He's just such a ray of sunshine. But once we picked our jaws up off the floor, we still recognized the river as our best bet for safe passage."

Gabor rolled his eyes but said nothing.

Baird snickered.

"I think you're right on this," Oloren said. "Where else are we to go? I don't know about you, but I am nowhere near ready to get eaten by bats. There are so many better ways to die."

"We don't want to get eaten, and we like the river, got it," Kilith said with annoyance. "What we need is a plan. Air supply, for example. Until we shake the bats, we will need a steady source. We could always come up for air on occasion, but I can only hold my breath for a couple minutes. If they come at us when we come up, that will still be pretty miserable."

"A couple minutes! I'm lucky to go a minute," Mereámé remarked.

"Wait, bats can swim," Ruakh said. "Why haven't they just followed us in here, if they're so intent on having human for lunch?"

"Maybe these can't swim," Gabor said.

Canukke shook his head. "I think something in the water repels them. They seem to avoid it."

Oloren looked at the water in fright, then relaxed. "It's just regular river water. Nothing unusual that I can see."

"That you can *see,*" Vadik noted.

Enouim cast him a questioning glance, but he shook his head. No invisible evil seemed to be in the tunnel with them now. Then again, Enouim thought, his visual field was constricted by the cloud of bats before the tunnel, so he may have missed something. She shuddered.

"Why can't we just swim from here out, then, if they hate the water?" Ruakh asked.

"We don't know for sure they hate the water," Gabor said, "and even if they do hate it, they might hate us enough to overcome their fears."

"Or love us enough for snack," Oloren said.

"But not Gabor. Even the bats don't need that kind of negativity in their lives," Baird chirped. Oloren gave him a look. Baird gave her a lighthearted shrug.

"Reeds!" Enouim said.

Canukke frowned at her. "What?"

Kilith followed Enouim's gaze to the riverbank outside the tunnel, and sure enough, reeds grew further upstream. He grinned. "Reeds are hollow. Nice catch!"

Kilith and Enouim dove beneath the surface, sped to the bank and, while remaining underwater, plucked the longest and sturdiest reeds from the bottom, then returned to pass them out. Enouim awkwardly spun one in her hands, though she didn't need it. No need to stand out even more than she already did.

They moved out from the tunnel slowly, dipping into the water one by one, and breathing through the reeds to remain underwater and away from the bats. At first Enouim felt rather than saw the bats following them along the river. Their shadows fell like a black cloud hovering above them, unrelenting, thirsty for blood. She dangled her reed behind her and twisted around to look. Hundreds of enormous dark bats flew after then as one seething evil entity.

The company traveled upstream for several minutes in peace before one of the bats swooped down and snatched the reed sticking out of the water from Oloren. After a minute had passed, she had to come up for air, and then several more swept low, careful to avoid the water itself, and made off with the rest of the hollow reeds.

Left with no alternative, the company had to breach the surface, and when they did, the bats flew at their heads with ear-splitting screeches. Oloren plunged her knife into one and thrust it underwater, and four more dove at her for revenge, pulling up at the last moment when she ducked back into the river. Canukke came up next, shielding his face with his arm, dagger in hand, and the others followed his lead.

"We can't go on like this!" Baird spluttered.

Enouim spun and rose to cover Mereámé as she took a breath. As Enouim shot upward, it was as if the river itself moved her, rather than Enouim propelling herself through the water. She met the surface with great force, covering Mereámé's emergence and showering the bats with water as she did so. The bats drew back, shrieking their displeasure.

Again she ascended, this time with a rush of water greater than before, and the bats flapped their wings madly. One seemed to have gotten water in its face, and bobbled around in the air as if drunk, then smacked into a tree and dropped to the ground. Still, this couldn't carry on forever. Enouim drew herself down into the river again, and grasped Mereámé's arm to pull her along upstream. Pausing, she let go of her friend and saw that, for a moment, the water driving Enouim upstream continued to carry Mereámé along.

Enouim took a moment to play with the water between her hands. It swirled as she bade it, and passing it back and forth between her palms created a small current. She held out her hand and a gush of water, halting at first, fled from her fingertips. When she pulled her fist in toward her chest, the river came to her, washing her hair out in a wave behind her.

Enouim returned to her companions and gestured them to cluster together. "This is going to be a trial run," she said, "so keep your arms and legs in and take a deep breath. And try not to hit any rocks or anything."

"What?" Vadik asked.

"What do you think you're ..." but Ruakh never got out the rest of his sentence.

Enouim plunged into the river, down, down to the bottom, breathing in the water around her and gearing up mentally and physically. With a deep inhale to settle herself, she bent her mind on her friends, heads still bobbing at the surface, and then, drawing the river's currents around her, she flew like an arrow from the string. Enouim shot past them, drawing the water around them to her with all her might, and she was half surprised to glance back and discover that they followed her, carried along by the river like fish in a net.

Canukke looked entirely unsettled, disheveled and cranky; Gabor's mouth was still gaping open and Enouim grew concerned that he really hadn't taken that deep breath she'd instructed. Vadik was stunned but practically smiling, and Oloren was positively thrilled by the novelty of the experience. Baird also seemed fascinated, reaching out and pulling his hands back in again, exploring the ride. Enouim would never understand adrenaline junkies. But then, the river was more than adrenaline to her now. It was life.

Ruakh looked surprised but went with it—not that he had a choice—and Kilith was challenging to read as always. Mereámé looked as if she might be seasick. Enouim drew them further upriver, and further, until suddenly she noticed her tagalongs were beginning to grow pale. Startled, she released them, and they careened off into eight different directions. Enouim's stomach dropped. She jerked Canukke away from the rocky wall of the river and pushed him toward the surface, grabbing onto Gabor's leg as she did and redirecting him also. One by one she caught her friends and let them catch their breath, but then they were off again, Enouim pulling them along and stopping to let them breathe in short sprints. She continued for ten minutes before she saw no sign of the bats and was satisfied. She slowed her friends, this time being careful to deposit them more gracefully near the surface.

The bedraggled company looked terrible as they clambered out of the river sputtering and worn. What had begun as a fascinating new means of transportation resulted in hacking, coughing, heaving, and generally feeling as though their insides wanted suddenly to be turned inside-out.

"What in Glintenon's name was that?" Canukke demanded angrily, still spitting up water.

"Well, the bats aren't around anymore, are they?" Enouim countered, acknowledging with relief the emptiness of the surrounding trees.

"But ... what *was* it?" Vadik asked, color returning to his face and changing into wonder.

"It just happened."

"It didn't '*just*' anything," Ruakh said, leaning on his staff as he found the riverbank.

"No indeed." Canukke eyed her warily.

"Whatever it was, we can be grateful for it," Baird broke in. "I for one was not too fond of the blood suckers." Here he took a moment to examine himself, still bleeding up and down his arms. "Say, how could you be so scared of rope swings with that little trick up your sleeve?"

"It's not a trick, and I didn't know I had it," Enouim said. "Anyway, it's not the same. Water feels ... safer."

"Didn't feel that safe to me," Gabor commented, still coughing.

Enouim winced.

"We're safe now, though, right?" Mereámé asked.

"We'll certainly follow the river just in case, but yes, I should think so." Kilith glanced about. "Luckily, this is the direction we were headed. We should still reach Rehim on time—perhaps even ahead of schedule."

"Well, that's a mercy!" Oloren piped up. "I'm ready for some dry clothes and traveling by horse again. My feet are dead tired."

"We should move off the bank a bit, but we'll rest again soon." Kilith stretched his legs from where he had seated himself on the bank. "I'm anxious to get the bats behind us, but I feel about drained myself. We'll rest another few minutes, and then get going."

Thankfully, no one engaged Enouim for the first couple minutes, though she got many questioning looks which she tried to ignore. Enouim drew her knees into her chest. She had far too many questions of her own to deal with others' inquiries. What was she supposed to say? Reaching up to the back of her neck, she found that the old scars—or rather, gills —had sealed back up once dry. They were more raised than usual, but closed.

Vadik approached her, more tentatively than was his wont. "Just because you feel alone doesn't mean you are."

"I'm not alone," she mumbled, staring off into the river. It passed by them lazily, its recent excitement already washed away.

"Sure, sure. That's why you're sitting over here, by yourself, looking miserable."

Enouim looked up at him, soothed by his compassion, yet unmoved in her disorganized thoughts. She turned her gaze to the ground and picked at pine needles she found there.

Vadik took a seat beside her. "How are you doing?"

"What do *you* think?" Enouim shot him a sarcastic glare. In the wake of her shocking discovery, she felt herself growing irritable. She had been fascinated by it in the moment, absorbing the energy of the river, falling in love with the feel of the water. It had been beautiful, lovely, serene … and then it had been twisted around to nearly kill her friends. On top of all of that, she had no idea what had happened to her, and had no answers to give her friends—much less herself.

"Okay, so not great." He sighed and leaned forward over crossed legs. "What is it about the situation that you're finding particularly irksome?"

"You aren't at all concerned by finding out I'm some kind of freak?"

Vadik grinned. "You're saying you didn't know you were a freak? We've all talked about it for months."

"I'm being serious."

"Okay, then so am I. *Your* weird thing is totally awesome. *My* weird thing is seeing stuff no one else should believe is there. So what is it about yours that has you so upset?"

"I don't know."

"I bet you could guess."

"No, that's the part that is frustrating me. *I don't know.* I don't know what happened. I clearly didn't know how to control what happened, and I nearly dashed everyone to pieces. I don't know what's wrong with me."

"Wrong with you?"

Enouim glowered at him. "Yes. Wrong with me. I have a

weird, uncouth ability. With water. Of all things! Water, which I was taught to hate. Water, which my father wanted me to avoid, and I didn't even bathe without a watertight bandage over my neck. Water ... with all it's terrifying mystery. And yet it wasn't mysterious in the river. It was beautiful. But it betrayed me just the same when I almost killed you all."

"Why were you told you had to avoid water? That seems awfully suspicious."

"Well ..." Enouim paused. It was such a normal part of her upbringing that she hadn't spent much time considering how strange it was. "Um. I'm adopted. And nobody knows from where. My father found me on one of his trading trips, traveling. Somewhere out in this direction, actually, though he never told me specifics. And he said that when I was found, I was half drowned in water and that the scars on my neck were given to me by some tentacled sea creature. Or, I guess it could have been freshwater. There isn't any ocean in this direction, anyway. Water used to sting when it came in contact with the scars, but not the one on my collarbone. Just the ones on my neck."

"But it doesn't anymore?"

"No ... this time, no sting. And I can breathe underwater with them. Like the sting was more because they *need* water than because they are averse to it."

"So all your life, you have avoided water as much as possible. It's possible you've had this ability the whole time and just didn't know it."

"Possible," Enouim agreed thoughtfully. "But why would my father lie?"

Vadik shook his head. "I don't know. You do still have that one scar though, that is actually a scar. Maybe it was a half-truth."

"I don't understand. Why would he keep this from me? No one else ..." Enouim trailed off. "Kilith!" she hissed.

"What about him?" Vadik asked, startled by her intensity.

"He knows something. I *knew* it! He kept checking on me after water, talked to me about my 'relationship with water' after the panic episode. And this time ... this time, right before we got to the river, he said I was born for this. Born for what? Well, I don't know, but he definitely knows something. And he knew my father!" Muttering to herself, Enouim abandoned Vadik on the bank and headed for Kilith.

Kilith saw her coming and stood. "All right," he called to the group, "rest time is over. Time to get a move on."

He wasn't getting off that easily. Everyone else stood, and as Kilith struck out first to lead the group, Enouim let him get a few paces ahead of the rest before dashing up to his side.

"You know something. You know something, and you've known it a long time, and you kept it from me on purpose."

Kilith looked down at her. His face was drawn, like a man who had lived a thousand lifetimes. He turned back toward Rehim, but his shoulders were slumped forward and the lines on his face seemed to deepen. He drew in a great, unhurried sigh, and let it out. "Yes."

Impatient, Enouim waited a full two seconds before demanding, "Well?"

Another sigh. "It was never Rotan's wish that you discover who you are. He was content that you would find it out for yourself, developing a full identity and personhood outside of your origin. With him."

Enouim looked up at him eagerly, waiting for more. Kilith glanced down at her and laughed. "You never could stop asking questions," he said softly.

"But I never knew you before this mission."

"You did ... long ago. I saw you often when you were very

young, but I thought you deserved to know where you came from, and Rotan did not. I kept my distance after our final disagreement, but I never stopped watching. He was afraid. You need to know that it came from a place of love. All of it."

Enouim took a moment to absorb this new information. Still, there was more pressing news she had yet to hear. "Tell me my story."

32

Kilith took a deep breath. "I told you that I traveled with your father on occasion. Well, that's true. What I didn't tell you is that ... well, I was the one that found you. I wasn't on the trip with Rotan, but on another mission at the time. I happened upon Rotan with a group of traders shortly after, and I was able to hand you over to his care.

"I no longer think it was luck that drew us together—first you to me, and then me to Rotan. Rotan and Qadra had not been able to have another child after your older brother Pleko, and Rotan had confided in me their struggle. I knew Rotan to be a good man, intelligent and kind, with a stout heart, and it was with these traits in mind that I, in good conscience, entrusted you to him on that day. But I'm getting ahead of myself.

"The first and most important thing you need to know about where you came from is directly related to the scars on your neck that are not scars, and the abilities you were so baffled to have stumbled upon just now in the river. I wasn't sure whether anything unusual would manifest, and that's one reason I didn't say anything until now; another is to preserve the desires of Rotan, a dear friend of mine, who shortly before his passing secured my promise to carry out his wishes regarding you. He didn't want you to know.

"I don't know all the ins and outs of your history, but I do know that you are the product of what was considered an undesirable relationship that caused your biological parents to be cast out of their respective societies. Your father was a man, and your mother, one of the Madzi."

"Madzi!" Enouim exclaimed. "You mean I'm not even fully human?"

"No."

"I'm sorry ... *what?*"

"The Madzi are not to become romantically engaged with humans, just as the Gudira or Nazir are not to become romantic with humans. Your mother's love affair with a man brought a lot of heat. From what I gather, your biological father had traveled from the eastern hills and he and his compatriots had a disagreement with the Madzi after building a dam for their own convenience. The Madzi are charged with protecting the rivers, and they became angry. They traveled upstream to punish them, but your father fell in love with your mother and eventually abandoned his own people to run after her. After finding out you were on the way, she panicked and tried to return to her people. She was terrified to lose her place with the Madzi. But it was too late, and while her mother, your grandmother, hid her until you were born, it was too great a secret to keep under wraps forever.

"I tried to find out more about you after I pulled you from the river. I was there tracking a great beast known as one of the tannin, which had come curiously far from the hill country where its kind are more prevalent. This one loves oceans and streams, and I was afraid because of the rivers that run up into the mountains of Gorgenbrild, as well as the one that runs into Levav. I tried and failed, first to find the beast after it slipped away from me, and then to find your biological father, when I turned my attention there. I feared the worst, and wondered if his unhealthy proclivities got the best of him ... I have not heard particularly glowing reviews of his character. He wasn't a tremendously terrible person, but he was self-absorbed until he became obsessed with his Madzi muse."

"What about me?"

"Like I said, all trace of your father disappeared, but your mother hid you for several months. After that, some of the Madzi decided to cover up the scandal before any higher ensign Madzi could pay them a visit. Your mother fled with you, but they caught up with her. When I found you, you were gliding along in an artificial current I can only assume was made by your mother, but you were surrounded by fire fern. You escaped with only one souvenir," he said, touching her collarbone lightly. "It's a wonder you lived."

Enouim reached up to thumb the scar on her collarbone. "So it's true. The tentacled creature you told me about is like the star creature my father—Rotan, that is—told me about. You talked to me about it after my panic episode, and the scar really does come from that. He just decided to say the gills on my neck were caused by the same."

Kilith nodded. "Just so. The star creature he described is the fire fern. I found you there and got you out, but not before I was stung myself. I hung onto consciousness long enough to get us out of the water. You were only a couple months old. When I came to, you smiled at me, and it was the most beautiful thing I had seen in years." Kilith's expression softened as he gazed off into distant memory. "At the time I knew only rumors of the scandal beneath the surface, as the Madzi rarely dispense internal matters to outsiders. But I'd had dealings with several of them previously, and I knew enough to guess who you were.

"I stumbled my way out with you tucked in close to me and came across Rotan and the rest of the traders. They were already on the return journey, loaded with supplies and wares and on their way back to Gorgenbrild. He was overjoyed at having a second child and a daughter, and he knew Qadra would weep with delight to welcome you into their family. After you were safe, I returned to the river to learn more about the events leading up to your discovery, and that is when I uncovered most of what I've told you. Your grandmother— your mother's mother— urged me to keep you safe and far away, unsure of what would happen to you if you were ever to find your way back to their river."

Enouim walked side by side with Kilith in silence. This man had saved her life, investigated her origin story, and upheld the desires of her beloved adopted father. Her anger melted away, replaced by a solemn gratitude.

"What was her name?"

"Who?"

"My mother."

It was now Kilith's turn to be quiet. On they walked. When he spoke, his voice was low. "I'm not sure I feel comfortable sharing that information."

"Does that mean she's alive? Whether you feel comfortable is quite beside the point. She was or is *my* mother." Enouim glanced at him and saw only concern on his face. She softened, placing a hand gingerly on his arm. "I appreciate all that you've done for me, even if I wasn't aware of it until now. You have carried the burden of secrets for many years, but today that ends. I have a right to my history."

"I'm afraid I have been protective and distant for far too long, and now that I can be protective and close, it is slipping away from me entirely." Something in Kilith's eyes spoke of a deep emotional turmoil threatening to escape.

Enouim felt her own stomach tighten and a lump rise in her throat.

"I was terrified when I saw you in the supply wagon," he said. "On the one hand, excited; on the other, absolutely terrified. I wanted you to branch out and be who you were, to be as brave as I believed you could be. I wanted you to be strong but without ever having to encounter anything that might develop that strength. Your mother ... your Madzi mother's name is Nymrenil. I'm afraid I don't know what became of her for certain, but I believe she was killed."

Enouim took a moment to digest this information. "Thank you," she said.

Kilith nodded and fell again into thoughtful quiet. The leaves crunched softly under their feet, and the indistinct voices of their friends wafted up from behind.

"Kilith?" Enouim asked.

"Yes?"

"Why didn't Eh'yeh tell me? He didn't say anything of this, or of special abilities I might have. But he must have known. He knew everything else about me, childhood memories, everything. He knows me better than I know myself. How could he keep this from me?"

"Hmm. Maybe he doesn't always tell us everything all at once, but rather he tells us what we need for the moment we're in."

"I wish I knew why. I wish he could tell us right away."

"Well ... he *could* have. And I think that the fact he chose not to means he had a good reason, even if we can't see what it is. Maybe he knew you needed to focus on other crises back then, and this one would come up when the time was right."

"So what am I supposed to do with this? I'm some half-human mutant rejected by both sides who also happens to have abilities controlling river currents. Great, you're welcome; here you go. Best of luck! Now we're throwing you to the wolves. Blind."

Kilith smiled. "I think sometimes we do so much damage with our eyes open that we need to close them. That way our other senses are heightened, and we aren't as threatened by the sight of the wolves but instead can listen for the whisper of the white heron, telling us to turn this way or that."

Enouim was startled. "You've seen the white heron?"

Kilith's eye's widened in surprise. "Only when Eh'yeh first gave him to us. Why? Have you?"

"Well, no, not exactly," she replied awkwardly. She hadn't meant to give up Vadik's secret, but at the same time she needed a confidant to process it with. "Um ... don't tell anybody, okay? But Vadik can see it. All the time. Flying with us."

Kilith paused, then laughed. "Of course! Well, I knew it—or is it a him? —was there. I wonder why Vadik can see it though."

"So you don't think he's crazy?"

"Vadik? No, of course not. Do you?"

"Well, no. But if I didn't know Eh'yeh and I didn't know Vadik, I would definitely think he'd had a few too many ales. But wait ... you knew the heron was with us without seeing it?"

Kilith looked at her questioningly. "Of course. Eh'yeh said the Pneuma would be sent with us to guide us. And he has been."

"Huh. When the Pneuma first came to me, a deep sense of peace, and sometimes a thought comes into my head that I'm not sure I put there, like before I went into the river. But I wasn't sure whether that was really the Pneuma or something else."

"No, I think it was the Pneuma," Kilith said. "He tells me when to speak and when to be silent, and so far I have tried to just keep my mouth shut to keep from getting myself into trouble. Eh'yeh wants me to love people the way he loves them, but my thoughts about others aren't always kind, so the most loving thing I can say at times is nothing."

Enouim laughed. "That sounds about right." She glanced behind her. "So what do we do about Canukke?"

As if on cue, Canukke joined them up front. "Far too much whispering up here," he grumbled. "How much further to the horses?"

"We have a ways yet."

"We need to strategize about our return. I say we go to Kalka'an first to gain the support of their horsemen, resupply, and scope out the land. We will need a way to see what we're getting into, and the status of our people. They have already suffered siege. The cliffs to the west are too steep to scale, which leaves mountain and river options on three sides only."

Kilith nodded. "Yes, we will need to evaluate. I don't think we need to decide everything right away though. First, we get to Rehim. Second, we listen for the leading of Eh'yeh."

Canukke snorted. "He's not here. All we have now is you and me. No one else is leading this mission, and I didn't see Eh'yeh jumping at the chance to lend his sword. And what we really needed was a stone! Useless."

"Useless!" Gabor yelled, overhearing Canukke and closing the distance. "Yes, and I suppose you see Mereámé's life as useless also. You never wanted her here in the first place. And no one who disagrees with you is allowed to be along—isn't that right?"

"You don't know what you're talking about," Canukke retorted. "If you read into situations this heavily, you've hit your head a few too many times! What would you be without me? Nothing! Where would you be without me? Dead!"

Gabor shook his head in disgust. "I followed a man I thought I could learn from, a man I wanted to be like. Turns out that man was all brawn and steel with a heart as unflinching and cold as the sword he carried. What good is skill misused? The stronger a dark-hearted man, the more dangerous he is. And the light is winking out."

"Don't test me, boy." Canukke's voice lowered. "I used to think you were worth something. That there was potential. Now I see you're only a frightened, oversensitive puppet, tugging at your strings when it rains a little. You don't have what it takes!"

"Oh, I think you've proven your mettle," Gabor said. "Yes, you've made your abilities quite clear. I believed in you. Zegrath's teeth, I've fought with you. But do you know what I've found? I have defended your honor more doggedly than you have. It is tiresome, carrying the character of another man on your shoulders, brushing the grime off his name when it is dragged through the mud, only to discover the man to whom it belongs tramples it himself!"

Canukke's expression darkened even more. "Wretch! Everyone else can see me for who I am, and if you fools are blind, it is to your own undoing! Mine are the only hands that can save us now. Yet still, I would have us bind together. We need each other as comrades in arms. I know why you're doing this. You say I am dark hearted? You only wished you had had the strength to kill your father years before he kicked the bucket with liquor. You saw I had, what it took to get things done that needed doing. I took you under my wing because I pitied you. Pitied you! Because your mother was a spineless pariah who didn't love you enough to stop the fighting when she saw you weren't worth saving. Indeed, she was right, because you are as baneful and toxic as your father, but you inherited cowardice from your mother, with no way to let your destructive tendencies—"

Gabor let out an enraged snarl, balling his hands into tight fists. He swung at Canukke's head.

33

G abor's first strike was a feint. Canukke reached up to block his face, and Gabor slugged him in the gut.

"Canukke!" Oloren yelled, rushing forward, her tone full of angry reproach. It was unclear if she meant to save him or destroy him herself.

Kilith threw out a hand and stopped her. "This is between them."

Gabor tore into Canukke like a lion, and Canukke was up for the challenge. They were locked onto one another, duck, weave, strike, dancing in and out to make their moves.

Enouim threw her hands up. "They'll kill each other!"

Vadik watched closely. "Better now than in battle."

Canukke was a magnificent fighter, but Gabor had channeled his anger into an unparalleled rage and aggression. Still, he made the first mistake. Canukke pinned him to the ground, and Gabor parried, bucked, and rolled so that Canukke was now underneath him.

"This can't go on!" Baird yelled.

Ruakh stepped forward, at the ready should the encounter grow too dangerous. They looked to be fighting to the death.

Canukke nearly placed the knife to Gabor's throat, but in a swift move Gabor trapped Canukke's arm and stripped the knife from his grip, deftly turning the tables and returning the favor—with Canukke's own blade pressing into his carotid. Ruakh, Baird, and Enouim stepped forward as one, weapons drawn, and closed in.

Oloren broke free from Kilith and was nearly upon them when Gabor yelled, "Wait!" and swept his free arm, tripping her and effectively stopping her approach.

The rest watched breathlessly. Enouim felt her heart pounding in her throat.

Gabor seemed to be regaining use of his faculties. Blade still at Canukke's throat, he commanded the man's full attention. "You are nothing but a hypocrite and a coward—a coward of character and a coward of heart. I let you live now, not in weakness but in strength. Let it be known that I held your life in my hands, and my debts to you are canceled." Gabor flicked the knife, deliberately drawing a trickle of blood. Canukke winced, and Gabor continued, "My soul is dark indeed, very dark. My thoughts are more abase than you can imagine. As for me, I would exact my pain on you physically as is the custom of our people, and my pain is such that there would be nothing left of you. But let it be known—I release myself from the cycle of bitterness, and I release you to your misery, in the name of Eh'yeh."

Gabor shoved off Canukke in a swift tactical retreat and wiped the sweat from his brow. He glared at Canukke and took several deep breaths to steady himself before stalking away in the direction in which they'd been traveling. Canukke lay for a moment as if stunned, and Ruakh slowly stepped forward and offered him a hand. Canukke swatted it away and got up independently. Saying nothing, he followed on Gabor's trail. The rest quickly filled in the gaps between the two men.

As Enouim hurried to catch up, still processing what had happened, Oloren shot past her to catch up to Canukke. She gave him a rough shove, and her confidence paired with their striking height differences might have been comical if it weren't for the look in Oloren's eyes. Enouim was pretty sure not even a giant would want to cross her now.

"Listen to me, and you listen well," Oloren demanded, getting up in his face so that he backed against a tree. "If you so much as lay a finger on Gabor, I will have you out of the mission. I don't care if you were handpicked; I don't care about your accomplishments, or the ones you attribute to yourself whether or not you should. You would never survive without us. But we? We are already together. And we would do just fine without you. Don't think for a second that we would shrivel up and die without you ... we've done well without your leadership since Eh'yeh."

"He is the one that—"

"Shame on you! I am ashamed for you, to see you sink so low, belitting those you would call brothers. We all have weaknesses, and I know somewhere deep inside, you recognize yours. You're not as tough as you seem. We need to be prepared to defend and protect any of our own, from the greatest to the smallest. That is our duty. I will not stand by and watch while you destroy others. Whether or not you choose to destroy yourself is on your own head, though I would rather not see that either. Wake up!" Oloren turned on her heel and walked after the others, muttering, "I can't look at you right now."

Clearly Canukke wasn't getting any more words in today. Enouim was grateful for that, because he'd already said plenty, and she wasn't sure she could stomach any more. She cast a sidelong glance in his direction and gave him a wide berth as she passed, trying to pretend she hadn't just witnessed the stern rebuke.

Enouim speed walked past Ruakh, who seemed to be waiting for Canukke, and past Vadik, Baird, and Mereámé to Gabor. They were spread out now, walking through the woods at a measured pace in twos and threes. Gabor was alone, and Enouim placed herself at his side. She watched his chest rise and fall quickly, and he pressed on with vigor, pouring his focus into every step. Finally Enouim saw his tension begin to ease, and she lasted only about two minutes before bursting in to say something. It had felt like an eternity.

"Hey."

Silence. No eye contact.

She tried again. "Hey. You okay?"

"No. But then I haven't been for a long time."

"You haven't been okay?"

"No."

Enouim racked her brain. What was she supposed to say now? She thought about Canukke's below-the-belt digs at Gabor's family constellation, and Gabor's confirmation that he had a "dark soul." She saw pain, deep and heart-wrenching pain, and her own heart ached for him.

What should she say? What *could* she say? In the absence of any brilliant thirty-second cures, Enouim remembered Kilith's assertion that silence is often the most loving gift. With effort, Enouim selected this option. The wind played softly with her hair, and she tried to focus on the feeling of the breeze. Presently, he rewarded her with his reflections.

"I think it has been years since I've been okay," he said in a small voice, like a child's. "He's right, and I hate that he's right." Gabor sighed.

"What is he right about?"

"My parents. Me. He's wrong in so many ways about so many things, but this? He pegged me."

"That you are worthless?"

A tear slipped down Gabor's cheek. He wiped it away with annoyance. "I know it's not true. I know I have some value."

"I'm confused," Enouim said. "You're saying Canukke is right about you, that you are worthless, and also that it's not true."

"I ..." Gabor stammered, then trailed off.

Their pace slowed, and Mereámé drew closer behind them. Overhearing the tone, she said tenderly, "I'm sorry, I don't mean to intrude. I can drop back and leave you alone."

Gabor shook his head as another tear escaped down his face and off the end of his nose. "No, stay." He glanced behind him to observe the distance between him and Canukke and picked up his pace a bit. After a moment, he continued. "I think ... I think there are two sides of me. One thinks I am not worth anything, and the other rises up and calls the first a liar. But the first says the defense is weak, and it's afraid to see the truth. The truth that I am nothing."

"Nothing," Mereámé repeated, empathy warming the word. "What does that word mean to you?"

Enouim felt tears well up in her eyes.

"It means," Gabor replied, "I wasn't good enough for my parents. My father was garbage, sure, but Canukke is right. I wanted him dead, and didn't grieve his passing. I berated myself for not having the guts to kill him long before, and I did admire Canukke's strength. I think he's right, I wished I had been able to do what Canukke would have done in my place."

"Hmm," Mereámé said, then let the moment marinate. "You think you deserve every bad thing that has happened to you."

"Why else would my life have turned out this way? Why wouldn't my mother stop my father? Why wouldn't my father love me? Why can't I stop the barrage of evil thoughts from assaulting my mind? And yet Eh'yeh ... he is changing all that. I don't know how, but things are starting to shift."

"What do you mean?" Enouim asked.

"Well ... I felt a peace deep in my soul. I thought it was a trick at first. I wanted it to go away; pain made more sense than peace. More trustworthy. After all, it's what I deserve. Nothing else felt ... right. When people have cared about me before, I can remind myself it is only because they don't know who I really am. If they knew, they wouldn't stay. So I hid myself from them, afraid to share, afraid they would see me for me and desert me like my parents did. But with Eh'yeh ... he knew. He knew all of it, and he stayed.

"I had a dream one night when we were in the meadows with him. I dreamed ... I dreamed of a love I had never imagined. An intimate trust, a deepness, a vulnerability. It terrified me. There was a house, and I was the house. Eh'yeh stood at the door and knocked. I went to the door and opened it, and he wanted to come in. I saw how he looked at me, and I didn't want to refuse him. But all my memories, and every thought I'd ever had, hung on the walls of the house. Everything I'd ever done or considered doing. It was humiliating, and I was terrified for him to see it. So I left him at the door and went to rearranging everything in the house. I ripped the memories from the walls and tried to burn them, but they wouldn't burn. I tried to shred them, but they wouldn't shred. I could only move where they were in the house.

"So I organized all my happy memories in the sitting room, and my decent deeds in the hall. The further into the house I got, the darker my thoughts and memories, until finally the worst of the worst I shoved into a closet and locked the door, throwing away the key. I went back to the front of the house and let Eh'yeh in, and he went with me to the sitting room. But soon he told me he wanted to see the whole house. I couldn't, I wouldn't let him see it.

"After some time passed I decided to let him see the hallway, and the loving look in his eyes toward me did not subside when he saw the hallway. I risked showing him the kitchen, and if possible, the love I saw in him deepened. *Deepened!* I was now desperate to show him more of me, so that he could accept more of me—but still, I was afraid. Finally, I had shown him the whole house except for the closet.

"He looked at me, and he did not ask, but I knew he wanted to see the closet. I wept at his feet. I threw a tantrum. I screamed in his face. I threw whatever was in reach at him, but still he stayed with me; still he wanted me, and still he wanted the closet. Wouldn't he ever leave me alone? But he didn't leave me alone, and at long last I handed him a great hammer to break through the closet, but Eh'yeh withdrew a key. He'd had the key to the closet the whole time. I don't know how he got it, but he could have looked whenever he wanted but chose not to without my consent. We opened it together.

"It was then that I learned something I may never understand. He never wanted me just for the living room; he wanted the whole house and would have nothing less. When he knocked on the door, he already knew about my closet and everything in it. He knew all my dark secrets; he knew my fears, my fantasies, all my deepest desires. And still he loved me. Loved me!

"This is how I know that I am worth something. The look in Eh'yeh's eyes, and his pronouncement of my value is enough. Mentally I know this, and in that moment I felt it as deeply as I knew it in my mind. My emotions will tell me I am nothing, but even remembering the dream now in this moment, I remember that somehow ... somehow I have a worth in spite of myself. And maybe it wasn't all about me to begin with."

His dream struck Enouim. She hadn't known others had had dreams in the meadow, and she thought how poignantly the house related to her own pain and fears. It was a beautiful tangle, and Eh'yeh showered all of it in grace.

Suddenly, grateful she hadn't said anything at the beginning of the conversation, she almost laughed aloud. A great weight had lifted off Gabor's shoulders, and she hadn't done a thing. The Pneuma had reminded her to be silent, and she breathed thanks to Eh'yeh for not letting her say anything stupid.

To Enouim, the dream was hope. Hope that it was possible to be completely understood and completely loved. Hope that she could overcome her own fears. Gabor's courage inspired her. He'd spoken about things he'd never have dreamed of sharing before. He'd found his voice, and safe people to use it with.

"I think you are incredible," she said at length.

Gabor looked up, surprised. "What?"

"You heard me. I think you are incredible! You have amazing insight and learned from Eh'yeh that you have worth. You were strong enough to face Canukke and call him out, without sinking to his level or even the totally acceptable 'normal' physical response of our people. What is acceptable at home, you have risen above, in favor of Eh'yeh's standard. You found mercy where there had been none before, and you followed through even while your heart still needed time to catch up to what your mind knew you needed to do. I wish I was as dauntless. Thank you. I know it's not easy for you, and I am honored that you allowed me to hear it."

Mereámé smiled and nodded, eyes bright. "Your strength is our strength!"

Gabor looked uncomfortable, but a grin snuck across his face.

Yes, things had begun to shift. Many things were changing, and Enouim couldn't help but think this was only the beginning.

34

T he rest of the trek to Rehim was uneventful. Ruakh spoke to Canukke in hopes of learning what had caused him to snap, and shared his concerns with Enouim and Mereámé. Canukke's actions upset him, but he was also distressed by whatever internal struggle could have pushed the warrior so far. Ruakh believed unflinchingly in a goodness within people that, though spoiled, could never be fully snuffed out.

"Only the truly distressed cause such distress," he said. "There is a raw humanity within each of us, something Canukke buried years ago. He has bitterness in his heart, fear, sadness. I think he sees himself as forfeit ... that he believes somehow he gave up that humanity."

Enouim spent much of the journey to Rehim turning these thoughts over in her mind. On the one hand, she admired Ruakh for his determination to see people beneath the surface. She respected his belief in human dignity and the light within each person. He couldn't fathom a world where people could be evil for the sake of evil. Enouim both believed and disbelieved this premise. She didn't necessarily think people considered "bad" were evil simply to be evil; the world was far too complex for that. Many evil people, she presumed, were acceptable in their own minds, or hated themselves so much that they lived up to their own expectations. The latter was likely truer of Canukke, though he masqueraded as the first.

On the other hand, she didn't agree that people had a tendency toward good. As far as Enouim could tell, the natural course of the world was discord and affliction. The world had much to love and much to fight for; however, if the bend was toward good, would there be a fight at all? What would it be like to see the world the way that Ruakh did? She saw how he treated everyone, and his sincerity was refreshing. Still, she couldn't quite adopt it for herself.

Eh'yeh had shown her the evil in her own heart, that at her core she was the caged woman in the pit trying in vain to claw herself out. She was also the serene woman on the ledge dressed in white, and this she was unsure how to take in. Somehow both were true, but she was pretty sure the woman above the fork in her dream got there only by Eh'yeh, and not because her humanity drove her toward it innately. No, the easy, automatic slope would take her to the pit.

Evening began to fall, and as it did Enouim noticed the trees getting taller and thicker than any she had seen before. Kilith instructed them to look for abnormalities in the trees, and Enouim wondered what exactly that was supposed to mean. They all seemed pretty unusual to her. Still, she looked. The boughs were dense and green, and the river no more than a bubbling brook in the distance. The trees grew close together, interlocking leaves creating a network of greenery blocking out the sky.

Vadik tapped Enouim on the shoulder and pointed. Following the direction of his finger, she saw that he indicated a particular tree. Its trunk was even more enormous than those already surrounding them, its girth easily ten feet in diameter. Certainly a sight worth taking in.

"It's huge," she acknowledged in a whisper. "Crazy."

"Not that," he replied in a low tone. "It's the white heron. As soon as we got close, it went and stood at the base of that tree. It pecked at the tree, looked at me, pecked again, and seems to be waiting."

"What? Go over then. Check it out."

"I ... don't want everyone to know. They'll think I'm insane."

"I don't think so." She thought guiltily of when she'd shared Vadik's secret with Kilith. "Besides, they won't know *why* you found whatever it is you'll find."

Vadik considered this. "What if it's nothing?"

Enouim examined him for a moment. It wasn't like Vadik to be so hesitant. He was a go-getter in every sense. "Come on," she said. "I'll go with you, but you will have to tell me what on earth I'm supposed to be doing."

Together they walked forward, and Enouim placed her hand on the trunk. Regular tree bark.

"Higher. And to the left."

Enouim glanced around, but no one was paying close attention. Kilith caught her eye, and casually kept tabs on the pair. Enouim ran her hand over the lines and knots in the tree. She traced one of the knots with her fingers. Nothing.

"That's it," Vadik said.

"It's a bumpy tree, I guess." As she said it, Enouim knew the Pneuma had always meant something significant so far. She sighed and pressed on it.

"The heron pecks at it."

Enouim looked at Vadik, frustrated. "Why don't you do this?"

He gave her a look, but after checking behind him, lifted his index finger and tapped lightly on the knot several times. A light creaking could be heard inside the tree, and three portions of the tree unhinged and swung inward. One portion pulled to the right, one to the left, and one lay down like a ramp inside the tree. Before them stood a doorway into the tree, five feet tall, revealing a hollowed out inside and a wooden stairway.

"So, um, by your expression I'm guessing you see that too, right?" Vadik asked.

Enouim just nodded. She heard Kilith call to the others behind them, and soon the rest of the company was circled around the opening.

"Well, what are we waiting for?" Canukke said. "Let's go."

Kilith stuck out a hand and stopped his progress. "Baird and Oloren. You start."

Both nodded, clearly excited about getting to be first in line to check out the secret hideaway. Kilith nodded at Vadik, then passed into the tree. Canukke followed, Vadik next, and Enouim was close behind. Gabor, Mereámé, and Ruakh brought up the rear.

The outside of the tree was rough and irregular, but inside it was smooth as butter. A winding stair ascended further than Enouim could see, which she found unnerving. A column ran up the center of the tree, and the stairs were part of the tree connecting the core of the trunk to its sides. The stair was beautiful and novel at first, but Enouim soon wondered how many more tight turns she could stomach. Did it really have to be a spiral? But then, it was a tree after all.

The stair continued upward, but after five minutes they came to a landing. Baird pushed lightly on the inside of the trunk and was rewarded with a creak and an opening. The troop spilled out onto a circular landing around the trunk of the great tree. Enouim didn't remember seeing it from the ground.

Her eyes widened at what she saw. Ropes stretched from landing to landing around tree upon tree, some with sturdy wooden bridges and some with bridges made only of rope. Only rope bridges led from their tree, and a pulley system ran between each network of trees. No harnesses in sight. Enouim gulped. The most secure bridges were little more than rope webbing and less than confidence-inspiring rope rails hanging over empty nothingness. Baird and Oloren grinned ear to ear.

People of all ages bustled about, going in and out of the trees. The trees supported entire homes that wrapped around trunks at multiple levels. Some included slides from one level to another. As the group took in the scene before them, a blur dropped from a level above. It turned out to be a young boy about thirteen years old. He hung upside down at eye level, holding onto ropes from above. As he flipped right-side up and landed on one of the posts at the edge of the landing, Enouim realized he had no legs. Instead, he hung onto the post by strong, wiry arms, his body ending at the base of his torso.

"Good evening, Kilith Urul, and friends of Eh'yeh!" the boy said, eyes bright, face split into a wide grin. "My name is Rindyl. We've been waiting for you. Welcome to Rehim! Please, follow me."

Enouim exchanged glances with Kilith, who shrugged and smiled. Rindyl dropped to the ground and swung himself along the rope bridge like a monkey. Enouim's eyes widened. The kid was clearly incredibly strong, and paused halfway across the first bridge to urge them after him. "What are you waiting for? This way!"

"Are you kidding me?" Mereámé said.

"I'm with you." Enouim grimaced. "How am I supposed to do that?"

"Oh, come on!" Oloren appeared unable to contain her excitement.

"I think I preferred the bats," Enouim muttered.

Mereámé laughed. "I didn't care for the bats, but I'm not loving this either. I'm not cut out to be a squirrel."

Kilith marveled at Rindyl as he sped across the rope bridge, whistling. "How is he doing that?"

"What happened to him?" Vadik wondered aloud. No one answered.

Baird balanced on the bridge, swaying back and forth, his feet balancing on taut rope, one hand holding a rope railing. Vertical ropes ran from the foot bridge up to the railing at intervals. He extended his other hand to Enouim. "You can do this. It's like Kalka'an! You conquered the ropes there. These are just new kinds of ropes."

Enouim gulped. Some of the paths were wooden swing bridges. Why couldn't they have taken a route with more of those? They were dizzyingly high in the air. A fall from this height would certainly kill.

"We're a hundred feet up!" Rindyl called, apparently very proud of himself. "Can you believe it? The trees are two hundred feet tall!"

"Don't look down," Oloren warned. "Move cautiously, but the longer you let your feet stay in one place, the shakier you will be." She positioned herself by Mereámé and held out a hand.

Enouim took Baird's hand and, with his encouragement, slowly made the crossing, Mereámé and Oloren not far behind. Mereámé wavered and Oloren caught her, but the whole swing rocked, and Enouim pitched forward. Baird grasped her by the arm, and Rindyl spidered his way back in time to take hold of her other arm. His torso balanced on the rope, one hand reaching above him to the rail, and the other on Enouim's upper arm.

Rindyl grinned again. "Maybe you need the pulleys next," he said with a laugh.

They pulled her up and continued across the bridge to the next landing.

Rindyl produced a strong metal ring two inches across and examined Enouim's belt. "This'll do. I think."

"You *think?* How often are your rough estimations life or death?"

Rindyl laughed. "Don't worry, we do it all the time!"

Enouim harrumphed. Did he mean they used the pulleys all the time, or gambled with life all the time? Was there a difference? Suddenly Vadik's question about how exactly Rindyl had lost his legs sprang to mind. While she mentally debated this, Rindyl looped the metal ring around her belt and hooked her to a similar one on the pulley system. "There, you're ready. Off you go!"

"Wait, whaaaaaaaaaaaaaaaaaaaaaaaaaa!" Enouim felt herself shoved off the platform, her feet suddenly swinging in the open air. Baird helped Rindyl with the pulleys, and she lurched along on her way to yet another landing. She held tight to the rope above the rings, terrified that if she touched them they would somehow detach. "Worst nightmare," she grumbled under her breath.

"You're doing great!" Vadik yelled from the landing.

Enouim felt sure her face was whiter than the clouds.

Rindyl fell over laughing, and Baird and Kilith took over the pulleys. "It's better if you don't think about it! You just got to jump off, you know?"

The group watched, enraptured. Ruakh looked stunned, somehow both empathetic and amused. Vadik seemed to be sharing a moment with Rindyl at her expense, and Enouim did not care for it. She couldn't think of a witty response, and her mind was so focused on the dangerous height that she wasn't sure she would've been able to get words out anyway.

Oloren elbowed Vadik hard in the side, and he jumped. "You're almost there!" she called.

Enouim hung helplessly from the ropes as they transported her across to the other platform. Once there, she reluctantly disconnected herself from the pulley and sent it back. While the others made their way across, Enouim stood close to the tree trunk and looked around her. An entranceway led into the tree and a stair ascending several levels, and a slide wrapped around the outside of the tree in a spiral descending several levels below. An adult with a disfigured face holding a child passed her going down the slide with squeals of laughter, waving at her as they went.

She couldn't help but smile and turned in wonder to look at the structures among the trees. What must it be like to grow up in a place like this, with treehouses and rope bridges? Thoroughly exciting, certainly. Also wildly unsafe, she thought, though she doubted the children here would say so. Ruakh landed, laughing, eyes wide from the adrenaline rush, and then he turned to help Mereámé off the pulleys. Once all were across, Rindyl led them inside the tree, up two levels, and out onto a larger platform with a significantly sized structure on it. He bade them wait there and bounded off inside.

A child perhaps four years old ran up to Canukke. Her eyes were more widely set than most, with upward slanting eyes and a smile that took up half her little face. Looking up at Canukke's tall frame, she extended her chubby fingers to him, holding out a leaf. Canukke looked down at her, and though he looked somewhat uncomfortable, his face softened.

"Very nice," he told her gruffly.

She held it out again, this time with the slightest pout.

Canukke knelt beside her and tentatively took the leaf.

The girl giggled and threw her arms around his neck. Enouim wasn't sure she'd ever seen anyone quite so adorable as this girl and was positive she hadn't seen someone as gleeful.

Canukke held her awkwardly, smiling in spite of himself, and let the girl tuck the leaf behind his ear.

She ran away laughing, looking back at him intermittently, then disappeared down a slide followed closely by an older child. Enouim's heart warmed to see him like this. Maybe Ruakh was right. Something untainted remained in Canukke, and it was as pure as the child that revealed it.

Canukke grunted and stood, crossing his arms as if to ward off any lingering vulnerable energy. He seemed to have shaken off the encounter and pulled back into himself when a tall, dark man emerged from the building before them, Rindyl close on his heels, both smiling.

Reaching out with his right hand, the man grasped Canukke's wrist, and Canukke instinctively did the same, creating a gesture of greeting the man seemed to expect. The man stood several inches taller than Canukke, who was not a short man himself.

"I am Koko," said he with a smile that flashed polished ivory. Koko continued with the wrist-clasping gesture until each of them had been formally greeted and introduced. "Welcome to Rehim! We hear you must soon be on your way, but hope you will not be in too much of a hurry to enjoy your stay. We love to share what we know with outsiders and hear the stories of those walking different paths than our own."

"Thank you," Canukke said, taking point on the conversation. "We are grateful for your hospitality and do not wish to take advantage. I'm afraid our errand is pressing, and we are anxious to be reunited with our horses."

"Yes, your horses are with us. And you will be with them again soon. But even so, you will not ride off tonight. Much urgent travel, whether the errand be pleasant or painful, wears out the body. Let us restore you. And as for our hospitality, it seems you've already been adopted into the family."

Koko nodded good-naturedly to the leaf still tucked behind Canukke's ear, raised an eyebrow and smiled. "She does not choose lightly, little Urou. She has a sense of people, and she was saving that leaf for someone truly special. Marched it all around for over an hour, showing everyone but not letting a soul touch it. Consider yourself lucky."

Canukke's face turned beet red and he reached up and snatched the leaf from his ear, suddenly self-conscious. For a moment Enouim feared he might toss aside the little girl's precious gift, but he twirled it between his thumb and index finger instead.

"You will stay with us tonight. Never fear, your horses are well cared for and waiting for you. Meanwhile, refreshments. This way."

"I would still like to see the horses tonight," Baird said.

Koko waved them after him as he headed for the spiral staircase wrapping around the tree next to them. He turned to speak over his shoulder as he went. "A good horseman always does! As soon as you've had something to eat, I will show you to them myself. How were your travels?"

"Started off a little rough," Baird said.

"Today, or overall?" Enouim asked.

"Both!" Gabor said.

"Yes, well, the journey as a whole started with Enouim stumbling her way into a wagon unannounced!" Vadik noted.

"How do you think it was for me waking up surrounded by you crazies?"

"I don't know, I thought somebody would mention the zegraths, but sure, go with Enouim as a terrifying encounter," Oloren joked.

"Chayan had it pretty rough from the start," Canukke said.

Enouim's heart sank. Still? A stubborn resentment.

Oloren shook her head. "Oh, come on. Chayan gets herself into enough trouble for all of us, and would have brought it with her if she'd made it on the mission. Things are as they were meant to be."

"And then you were all stuck with me," Mereámé said. "By then Enouim was the least of your problems. And I sincerely doubt she was ever a source of major stress."

"You'd be surprised," Gabor said, but his expression was affable.

"Quite a time you have had!" Koko brought them out on another landing and lead them across a rope bridge.

Rindyl swung himself past Enouim, laughing. "Perhaps she belongs here after all!"

Enouim frowned. "What do you mean?"

A man walked by, grinning from ear to ear, and gave everyone a high five. Vadik tried to avoid it, shuffling behind everyone else, but the man made a beeline for him and gave him a big hug. Vadik froze, then detached himself from the man, eyes wide and shifting his feet as the strange man ambled away.

"Rehim is not like other places, if you haven't noticed," Rindyl said. "Not everybody has arms, not everybody has legs, not everyone can move the limbs they've got, and not everyone is happy in the fully functional skin they were born in. People who don't belong will belong with us. People who have always fit in sometimes feel a little uncomfortable."

Koko reached the other side of the bridge and swept his arm to many people among the trees. "The Rehi are a community thriving off the strengths of each individual, creating a living and ever-changing organism that grows as we grow. No one is without strengths, and every physical weakness is an opportunity for mental and spiritual strength building. But most who come here have afflictions that do not reach the surface. After all, our pain and suffering rarely lie evident to all, and no visible condition impacts the soul visibly. No, it is the mind and heart that take the hardest hits.

"Societies at large—for there are many societies, and yet they are all the same—do a horrendous job when it comes to accepting that which it does not understand. A lack of knowledge leads to fear, disconnection, and a desire to put out of sight the things we wish not to consider. Our own mortality or selfishness are prime examples, as are our utter loss as to what to say or do in situations foreign to us. And so society runs away.

"Rehi do not run away. The hill people toss aside children with visible disabilities, and we regularly look for these children and take them in. Similarly, those who see and hear what others do not see and hear are often cast out, no matter the origin of their perceptions. Preventatively, Rehi Waymakers are sent out to work with villages to learn the culture of each place and share information back and forth. Each village must feel understood before it accepts anything from us, and then we too hope to instill understanding and acceptance of children and adults as they are, celebrating their strengths. But this is not always possible. Therefore, some we save from the fringes of the hills, some we take in when they have nowhere to go, and some are inspired by what they see us doing and choose to join in the effort."

Oloren smiled. "That's incredible."

"Why not let nature take its course?" Canukke said. "Is it not kinder to save future generations the pain of disfigurement? Let society be purged of the pain of these conditions. Would they not prefer to be let alone? I would surely count my life forfeit and rather die than live the life of an invalid."

"Do I look like an invalid?" Rindyl laughed as he shuffled toward Canukke, doing his own version of a cartwheel with his arms and torso.

Canukke doubled down on his position. "Surely this has been hard for you, and you would rather not have gone through it."

For the first time since entering Rehim, Rindyl's smile vanished, replaced with a profound sadness. "It is not easy to be different," the boy said. "But here I have a home. Here, your normal is our abnormal. Here, seeing people like me enjoying life and doing more with two limbs than you could do with your whole body, your excuses are burned up. And here ..." Rindyl swung himself up and perched on a post to bring himself closer to Canukke's height. "Here you learn that what is even harder than going through hard things yourself, is coming out the other side having learned you can do anything, but that others haven't been blessed with that lesson. Knowing that the normals, as I call them, live in fear. Fear of death, fear of disability, fear of weakness, fear of their own shadow. The normals are to be pitied." With that Rindyl crossed his arms and hopped to the ground, rolling once and coming to a perfect landing.

Koko's expression became grave. "The concept that those different from us cannot lead productive lives is absurd when spoken in a place like this. These are the ideas we strive to overcome. And many of the most difficult burdens we bear are those undetected by the eye. But enough of this talk. Come along. We will get you fed and situated!"

35

E nouim wondered at the people around them. She felt curious and somewhat uncomfortable, just as Rindyl had suggested most people would be who were new to such things. She immediately liked Rindyl, but was also a little afraid to speak to him. What does a person say to someone without legs? Would she sound insensitive if she acknowledged he was different? He seemed to wear his difference as a badge of honor, but perhaps only people with disabilities were allowed to talk about them. Still, the boy seemed to have tough skin. If he could take Canukke saying he should rather be dead, he could probably handle Enouim's good intentions derailing a bit.

"So, um ... what do you do for fun around here, Rindyl?" *What do you do for fun?* Seriously, she had no better ideas for conversation than that?

He turned to look at her and grinned. "I like to go running." His face lit up, intensely serious.

Caught off guard, Enouim tried to make sense of the comment. Could he have some sort of stilts?

Baird snort-laughed behind her, and Gabor hit him, but

Rindyl cracked a smile and giggled. "Or long walks in the meadows down below. Just kidding! I do lots of things. I like to swim in the river when we go below, and I like to play games, zip line, climb, and teach the younger ones what I am learning in carpentry and leather working."

Enouim felt foolish to have fallen for the trick, but was relieved Rindyl broke the tension. He seemed accustomed to doing so. "Wow, you do both? My brother works with leather. He made me my belt and dagger sheath."

Rindyl paused and examined it. "I love the designs on the sheath. The belt must have been earlier, when he still needed more practice. But yes, I build all the time! I want to build for my friends, whose fingers shake a lot and cannot build, or are otherwise unable to. I think it is a beautiful art, to take what is in the world and create from it. Don't you?"

"I do. I wish I could do it."

"You could. You don't get the shakes, do you?"

"Err, no. I don't. I just don't think I would be any good at it."

Rindyl waved his hand dismissively. "Practice would make you good at it. If you don't want to, that's okay, but just say you don't want to!"

"Do you mind if I ask, um, what is it you are walking, or, going, on?" Ruakh looked at the base of Rindyl's torso. Enouim hadn't noticed before, but Rindyl wore a sort of harness tied into a flattened piece of some sturdy material— leather or rubber, Enouim wasn't quite sure— fitted to the bottom of his torso. His tunic hid most of it, and he lifted the hem to reveal more.

"I call it my shoe. It's a little like a bowl with a flattened bottom, and it keeps me from getting bruised or raw when I'm out and about for a long time."

"He doesn't seem to understand the concept of rest," Koko commented. "Ah, well. We tried."

"Rest is for old people, like you!" Rindyl laughed. "We have had to change it up a few times to keep chafing down, but this one is the best yet. We even made some designs on the bottom of it for traction. You can sign it later if you want. Most of my friends have."

"I'd love to." Kilith gave him a warm smile. Enouim wondered why he hadn't had any children of his own. Maybe he had and just never spoke about them.

Rindyl turned to Vadik. "So, Vadik, how long have you been a seer? Was it since birth, or were you gifted later?"

Canukke's eye brows shot up. "A what?"

Vadik shook his head, looking baffled. "I'm not sure what you mean."

Rindyl furrowed his brow. "You are a seer. A *seer* into the hidden layers of the world. Koko, didn't you say he was?"

"Rindyl, not everyone is as open as you are." Koko reproached him and turned to Vadik. "I'm sorry. It was encouraging to me to discover that you were also a seer, as I am. Some of us at Rehim see and hear what is not, but you and I see what is, though hidden from others. I noticed you could see the Pneuma. The heron. The Pneuma is real, and is indeed here with us. It is a comfort to know your experience with Eh'yeh was taken to heart and that he has blessed your mission. The fact that he goes with you is a credit to your purpose, and encouraging for us as we support you."

"It must be good to know you can be warned of signs of dark Malak ahead of time," Rindyl said. "Our seers often take shifts as watchers."

Gabor turned his gaze back to Vadik. "You've seen other things?"

"Some ... things," he replied tentatively. "I didn't know what to make of them. I thought I was crazy at first. It's why I asked Baird what he could see when we were at the river that night, before the serpent came. It's why I've gauged everyone else's reactions before saying much of my own."

"You keep it to yourself?" Canukke shook his head. "We could have been killed, and you knew something and hid it? Fool!"

"What would you have said? What would you have done if I told you I was seeing things?"

"He's got a point," Ruakh said. "How would we have reacted, without knowing about seers?"

"Better to ask and be thought crazy than not to ask and get us all killed," Canukke retorted.

"He has helped us," Enouim put in. "He's the one that found the stairs to the Nazir, and the door to the Rehi tree."

"You did?" Oloren asked.

"Well, yes," Vadik said slowly. "I couldn't see the whole Nazir society, but I could see signs—shimmers, differences in the light. With the Rehi entrance, I didn't find it on my own, but the heron—er, the Pneuma—showed me where it was."

"I thought Enouim found it." Gabor looked doubtful.

Enouim shook her head. "No, it was Vadik."

"See!" Rindyl said, eyes sparkling. "As worried as you were to see how we are different from you, you aren't all 'normals' either. Maybe you fit in better than I thought."

Vadik looked dreadfully uncomfortable, and Enouim didn't think he wanted to fit into a place of misfits.

"All this time. I can't believe it," Baird said, shaking his head.

"He can't help it, and he did what he could with the knowledge he had," Mereámé said.

"What we see on the outside is not the same as what we are on the inside," Koko said. "Some look able-bodied, strong, warriors of the highest caliber, and yet they fight more demons and listen to more ill voices than any would dare approach willingly even in broad daylight. Others appear weak, deficient, victims of an unfortunate catastrophe, and yet these are the strongest and most free of all. When you saw me, you made assumptions about my character, my strengths, my life. When you met Rindyl, you did the same, but I would stake my life you made different assumptions when you saw him. It is only human to make such assumptions, but they can be misleading. We may find we discount those that would be of most help to us, and put our trust in those not fit to have it."

Oloren grinned. "Well, we certainly are a more interesting party today than we were a week ago! Vadik and Enouim both had secret abilities nobody knew about."

Rindyl turned to Enouim with renewed interest. "What can you do?"

"Weren't we getting something to eat sometime soon? Your food doesn't make us see visions, does it?" Canukke grumbled.

"Oh, you'll be going places you never dreamed of after eating our stuff!" Rindyl quipped. "You'll hear colors and see sounds, and trip over your own feet!"

Koko frowned at the boy. "Rindyl, stop toying with our guests." Though said with reproach, Enouim thought maybe a smile lay beneath the remark. "And stop probing into their personal business. No, there is nothing you might find unusual about our food, except that it is shared among friends who are unafraid to be themselves."

"Your food will be wonderful, I'm sure," Kilith said. "Please, lead the way at your leisure. Thank you for your hospitality. We do not take it lightly."

"I don't know about that—this one could stand to lighten

up!" Rindyl laughed. "Must be tough, stuck on the road with his attitude. But you know what's not tough? Our smoked meats! To die for. Even people who used to want to die say so. But don't worry, they're only kidding."

Enouim thought it a strange thing to say and found it unnerving that he spoke so freely of such serious topics. She felt uncomfortable even hearing it. Still, neither Rindyl nor Koko seemed to mind, and perhaps no one here did. Maybe it was Enouim that could stand to change her perspective.

Koko and Rindyl beckoned them to follow, and they traversed precarious rope bridges and zip lines until they reached a large round structure surrounding another enormous tree trunk. This one was enclosed, and a pulley system allowed them to enter a large room inside the trunk through an oversized door. Enouim wished she were back on Inferno and close to the earth, rather than up here in the highest boughs she had ever imagined.

Ruakh landed with a laugh. "Whoa! Well, that happened. This place ..."

He was right not to end the sentence, because what they saw was difficult to describe. People of all shapes, colors, sizes, and abilities danced around the room. Music was playing, and songs were sung, beautiful voices mixing with the sound of what could have been mistaken for a dying cow. One of the beautiful voices cut out as the woman singing turned her attention to celebrating the cow-sounding noises of a man to her right. The woman laughed and took him by the hand, dancing him around the room and begging him to sing again.

One-half of the room was clear of furniture and being used for dancing, and several tables full of food lined the other half. They made their way to the tables and sat down to eat, Enouim still taking in the sights around her.

A woman pointed at a little boy and said, "Your hair looks

funny. Why does your hair look funny?" The boy smiled and patted her hand as though he understood something she did not. Enouim watched the exchange with an uncomfortable curiosity, and the woman turned her eyes onto her. "You have a strange face on. I like your hair. Your clothes are dirty."

"Thank you," Enouim said, unsure what else to say.

The little boy giggled.

A teen boy ran up to Rindyl and they exchanged a complicated handshake of sorts. "Serete is here! Serete is here!" Rindyl whooped. "Wooooooo! When? Where?"

"Came in an hour ago. He's on his way here now. Dropped off his horse down below."

Several more kids heard their discussion and clustered around them excitedly, all apparently impatiently awaiting this Serete's arrival. Enouim couldn't help but smile as she watched them. A tug in her heart affirmed that yes, this was a beautiful place, and all was as it should be. The tug was so strong, so distinct, that she knew it was Eh'yeh before even thinking about it. The reassurance of his presence not only in this place, but with her, could not have been overstated.

Enouim smiled and leaned over to Vadik, who was grinning from ear to ear and scanning the whole room. Quietly, she asked him, "Where is the Pneuma now?"

"Oh, everywhere," he replied. "Just zooming here and there. Playful, happy, free. I mean, I suppose he's always free, but this is the kind that makes you feel free too just by watching."

"I know just what you mean," she said, a warmth spreading in her chest. In that moment Enouim knew that though she couldn't see the Pneuma like Vadik could, she could experience him just the same.

They ate with vigor and joined the excitement around them. Baird was the first to start dancing, and Enouim laughed as she watched him drag Gabor out of his seat. He went reluctantly, and then drew Mereámé to her feet.

Enouim glanced behind her and saw Canukke against the back wall by the window, arms crossed and shoulders hunched, shifting his feet. She shook her head. Canukke would be Canukke, after all, and no one could change that. A different tug within her suddenly seemed to pull her toward him, but she stood her ground. No, she was enjoying herself. Why get brought down into the dumps with Canukke when she could stand here with Vadik and the others, soaking in the surrounding joy?

Another tug, more distinct and unpleasant, almost as if she had yelled at her brother Pleko and knew he didn't deserve it. But Canukke *did* deserve it. *Deserve what?* the tug seemed to ask. *Everything!* she countered, frustration mounting. *It's his fault he is this obstinate and difficult. If he wants to be sour, let him be sour, but why let one spoiled fruit taint the rest of the bunch?* Enouim turned her eyes resolutely back on the scene before her, with dancing and music and giggles rippling through the air. The air didn't feel the same though. The tug called to her again. *Enouim.*

Frustrated, she moved further from Canukke and stood closer to Oloren and Mereámé, who were watching several children holding hands and running in a circle. Her friends received her warmly, touching her arm or leaning on her in greeting while they shared the moment. Mereámé's musical laugh floated out into the room to mingle with harmonious song.

Why are you running from me? said the tug.

Because I don't want to go over to him. He's difficult and grouchy, and it won't do any good. Enouim folded her arms uncomfortably, but the tug refused to die down.

And who are you to decide what will and will not do any good?

Eh'yeh. His compassion motivated his firmness, and Enouim knew she needed to follow. Maybe she could wait a moment longer ...

"Look at Canukke," Oloren said suddenly. "He's just hanging back there. He's been aloof again lately." The timing of the observation couldn't have been more pointed.

"That one?" said a nearby boy of about ten. "I pity the horse that bears him. I think his soul is sour."

"He may not be easy to like, but he's worth the effort. Everybody is," Oloren responded. After a pause,she began to speak again. "Do you think I should ..."

Just then, Kilith called for Oloren, and she stepped over to him, leaving Enouim with her dilemma.

Enouim took a deep breath, steeled herself, and walked back to lean against the wall next to Canukke. She folded her arms, but said nothing. Gabor cast a funny look their direction, but shrugged and turned away. Canukke looked at her darkly, a hint of confusion flitting across his face, then ignored her.

What am I supposed to say? "Er, hello there," she murmured, half to Canukke and half to herself.

He arched an eyebrow, looking at her as though she had shapeshifted into a freshly muddied pig.

Enouim struggled to picture him as the man with the leaf tucked behind his ear and a child holding onto him. Perhaps that would help. After all, he hadn't tossed the girl off the ledge to speed "nature's course" on its way. Maybe there was good lingering in there somewhere.

"How are you doing over here?"

"Nearly vomiting with joy, now that you've come for idle prattle."

Okay, so if the good was in there, it was buried deep. She tried again. "It's been a full day to say the least."

Canukke let out a long sigh, but this time Enouim thought it emanated from a tired soul rather than annoyance. "These people are not what I had pictured."

"What had you pictured?"

"We are headed *home.*" Was that a catch in his voice? "Home, with no weapon, no army, none of the help we promised them. Even here, after our mission has failed, I see none I could call upon to aid us in an hour of need. If we were to waste these months, I would have spent it on other things. If it was all for naught, I would rather have died beside my countrymen facing the Sumus.

"I am an experienced man, but even I may not have been able to tip the scale against such numbers. I'm afraid we return to the destruction of all we hold dear, and I am not sure which I fear more—finding our people slaughtered for fighting to the death, or returning to find them alive under the thumb of Khoron muu, their fire extinguished and their existence diluted. We are lost."

Enouim's heart sank. Images of her mother and brother mutilated in the streets filtered through her mind, followed by images of her friend Balat, of Canukke's wife and Enouim's confidant Edone, visions of the Mangonel burning. She thought then of the other possibility. Instead of bodies there were shadows passing where once was life, going through the motions as if death had come to the living body. Was a life oppressed worth living?

A lump lodged in Enouim's throat, and a tear slipped down her cheek. She ached for her people, and she ached for Canukke. Beside her stood a defeated man, sent off as the valiant conqueror. He left parading away with a banner of hope and freedom waving in the wind, only to have that hope turned to ash, the freedom as unattainable as that wind. Enouim felt a wave of guilt hit her for worrying about her birth history and weird new abilities when her family was very possibly dead or dying back home. And all along, while she thought Canukke was just being mean, he was seeing the hope of a nation laid waste.

But that hope was not truly decimated. It lived still in Eh'yeh. Still, Canukke's hope had been fixed on a legendary weapon, and that weapon had not lived up to his expectations. And what of Eh'yeh? What was the plan? The company had been sent out from an ethereal glade with little more direction than to *go*. What if there would be no happy ending? No reunions? Enslavement or death, were those really her choices? If so, why had Eh'yeh sent them back at all?

"I don't know what to say," Enouim said softly at long last.

"Words cannot help us now," Canukke answered.

Enouim stood beside him, watching the gleeful scene before them with a brokenness heavy in her chest. When she pulled herself out of her thoughts, she realized she'd been staring at a child who now noticed her and was making funny faces to get her attention. She smiled back weakly and stuck her tongue out. The child rewarded Enouim with a giggle and ran away. When she saw Vadik and Ruakh observing her, Enouim wiped the tears from her face, pushed off the wall, and wandered back into the room.

As she stepped forward, Ruakh leaned over to her and whispered, "Eh'yeh is no fool. Everything he does is purposeful."

"I just wish he had come up with some sort of practical plan before we left."

"Who says he hasn't? Just because he didn't share it with us? No, there is a plan. The stone remains the stone. The power that stopped Morales in the First Morthed War was not the sword Glintenon wielded, nor Glintenon himself, but Eh'yeh fueling him. There is something ahead that must happen, and we are sent to meet it. We simply aren't privy to the details yet. And we're not entitled to have them."

36

Torches were lit as evening light faded, but the music carried on. Food was passed around on plates that floated from person to person across the room and onto tables. Vadik and Gabor sat together at one of the tables, while Ruakh whittled a wooden bird for a young boy. Oloren and Baird danced with a circle of children, and Mereámé fawned over a baby. Enouim couldn't help but smile as she watched her companions. What a lovely lot she'd fallen in with. As her eyes scanned the room, she noticed Kilith had been watching her. He pushed off from his position leaning against a pole and extended his hand to her. Enouim looked up at him in surprise.

"You think too much," he commented, pulling her into the center of the room. "You need a break."

With that, he danced her across the room and twirled her round, Enouim laughing at her clumsy mistakes as she tried to keep up. Kilith was a marvelous dancer, and though no one in her own family danced, she felt like a beloved uncle or perhaps a second father were holding her. Enouim hardly needed to know any steps as Kilith directed and spun her this way and that, until Baird called to him and Kilith spun her right across to Baird. Baird caught her, took her hand, and brought her into the circle of children squealing with delight. Baird on one side, a small child on the other, and Oloren five children down, Enouim lost herself in the joy of that moment.

Heart swelling, braid flying, and feet finding a trustworthy rhythm, Enouim allowed herself to laugh as she hadn't laughed since sitting with Eh'yeh. It was a moment of purity and freedom, like a crisp breeze on a warm summer day, or the sight of a glittering ocean from atop the cliffs of her homeland. Another young girl, perhaps nine years old, tugged at Enouim for her undivided attention, and Enouim acquiesced.

As she took the girl's hands, a thud resounded through the floor, a shout went up, and the room filled with excited clamoring voices. Turning, Enouim saw that a man clad in the travel-worn garments of a ranger had just come ziplining through the wide-open window and landed on his feet. His effervescent-blue eyes sparkled with mischief, reminding Enouim of a younger, more outgoing version of Kilith.

"Serete! Serete!" Young teens and children, including the girl Enouim had been dancing with, swarmed the man was by. He turned to greet them all, his own strong voice rising with those of his young admirers.

Everything in the room paused as the main event seemed to have arrived. Serete's handsome features lit up as he poured his attention onto children who were hungry for it. He gave Rindyl a high five and complimented him on how muscular he was getting, and the boy beamed with pride. When he glanced over the kids heads and caught Enouim's eye, something in her stomach tightened. She had been enjoying taking in the scene, but now felt somewhat awkward. Enouim smiled sheepishly, nodded in distant greeting and, fiddling with the end of her braid, looked away.

Gabor gave her a snarky, knowing look and wiggled his eyebrows. He didn't know anything! It was just a fun scene to see play out, that was all. She stuck her tongue out at him, perched herself on the edge of a nearby table, and reached for a piece of bread.

Serete moved to Koko and clasped his arm in greeting. Above the din Enouim heard snatches of conversation.

"...Came from along the river, upstream. Something is off with the water, and ... the tracks of the tannin were fresh ..."

"... Certainly couldn't have come at a better time ... Kilith, whom it appears you know, is here as well ... dangerous business ... sent from the glade."

Enouim watched, intrigued, curious, but not wanting to be caught staring. Something about this man's presence drew her in. But then, judging from the ring of people surrounding him, this effect wasn't unique to Enouim. And she certainly had no plans to be one of many placing herself in his path.

Serete reached into his pack and pulled out a handful of something Enouim couldn't quite see. "Some fascinating new specimens I found in the river," he said to Rindyl and some others. "I saw it and knew I had to bring some back for you. It's been touched by something—perhaps fire fern, though I've never seen any leaving marks as strong as these on stone. Here, take them."

With great excitement Rindyl and his friends took hold of the stones and passed them around, murmuring together over their new trinkets. "Any new stories?" asked one, looking up from her stone.

"Stories!" called another. "Yes, tell us a story!"

Serete laughed and put his hands up. "Yes, of course. But I only just got here, and the food will all be gone. You know what happens to me when I don't eat, don't you? Give me a few minutes to catch my breath, and then I will tell you all about where I have been and what strange creatures I have come across this time."

Serete extracted himself from the group and angled toward Enouim's table. Quickly she bounced her eyes to another part of the room, not wanting him to notice her gaze. The knot in her stomach intensified, but whatever strange reaction she was having to this man would surely pass over her once he did. Except he didn't.

Serete reached for a piece of bread from the table, then glanced at her, drilling Enouim with cool blue eyes. "What do you think?" he asked.

"Hmm, what? Me?" she stammered, looking up at him. "Erm, of ... what do you mean?"

"You've not been here before," he remarked. "I was here only a couple of months ago, and you weren't here then. What do you think of Rehim?"

Enouim stared at him. Maybe if she waited to answer, she wouldn't feel so uncomfortable. But it was a new kind of discomfort, one she didn't quite want to go away. "It's incredible. And different."

Serete nodded. "There's no place quite like it. I'm Serete."

Enouim laughed. "So I gathered."

"You gathered that, huh? Well, your deductive skills must be extraordinary!" He grinned.

"Oh, sure. I was brought up in the sleuthing business. Investigation is my middle name."

"Pretty weird middle name. Must have been tough to learn to spell as a kid. And what's your first?"

Enouim gave him a sarcastic look. "Wow."

"See what I did there?" He was so proud of himself she couldn't help but smile. She also couldn't help but notice how she couldn't help but smile. *Ugh.*

"Genius."

"So...?"

"Oh, right. My name is Enouim. Nice to meet you."

"You too." Serete hopped up on the table next to her, legs dangling off the edge. "What brings you here?"

"Um ..." How exactly could she sum up their mission? *My people are doomed and probably dying, if not obliterated already. We were sent to save them, met a man instead of a weapon, and are sent back totally clueless with only a couple of people to try to save the whole civilization.* "Hmm. I guess it's a bit of a story."

"Nobody who comes through here is without one. That's how it goes."

"Huh. Well, I guess that makes sense." Enouim paused. How secretive was their mission really? It had been secretive at first, but along the way they'd told a number of people their purpose and to their benefit. And here they were at Rehim, sent directly from Eh'yeh himself to these people, and as safe as she'd been in a while. "I'm here for my family. I'm from um ... I'm from Gorgenbrild."

Serete absorbed the information solemnly. "Oh," he said at last. "I see. Few come to Rehim from that direction. You must be here with Kilith Urul then."

Enouim looked up at him in surprise. "You know him?"

Serete nodded. "Our paths have crossed several times. We share some common interests. I've heard news abroad of Gorgenbrild's ... situation. It must be hard for you, being here."

"It has been." Enouim was struck by how easily her thoughts came to her as she spoke to this man. "I miss home, and I wonder what's happening there. I don't envy their position, but I wouldn't have chosen mine either. I guess it's just as well that I didn't get to choose."

"You were made to come?"

"Well, not precisely. I mean, it was sort of an accident, but

I'm here now, and now I think it was on purpose." Enouim scratched her head.

"Sounds like a story worth hearing. I hope you don't feel like I'm trying to pry. I just would have noticed had you been here before. And I've learned to pick out the newcomers."

"The wide-eyed confusion give me away?" Enouim laughed. "No, it's okay. I'm not sure it would feel right to talk about something trite, or the weather, in a place like this. Anyway, small talk is a necessary evil to survive pleasantries with people you're afraid won't like you."

It was Serete's turn to laugh. "That's true. Why do people do that?"

"So what about you? What brings you here?"

"Well, I suppose that's a long story too. The short version is that I just came from upriver seeking to rectify a problem with the water that the Madzi have not been able to correct. I saw some strange tracks and followed those as well, but lost them some ways northwest of here. My search was cut short by an encounter with Morthed scouts and news of Khoron-khelek in Gorgenbrild. I wish I had pleasant news to share."

Briefly Enouim wondered what kind of problem there could be with the water, but it left her mind when she heard him say there was news of home. Hearing Serete had news, most of the room crowded around him, effectively ending any private discussion.

"What news?" asked Gabor, edging in.

"Has Gorgenbrild been breached?" another voice wondered. One of the Rehi.

"Are they holding?"

"What are their chances?"

"Is this Khoron-khelek really worth the worry? I heard he was nothing but a vengeful boy, with delusions of grandeur too big for his shoes."

This last comment caught attention, and the cluster of people around Serete and Enouim fell silent. The speaker was a well-muscled fellow, absentmindedly twirling a knife in one hand, and wearing a dismissive expression.

"Boy?" Canukke shoved off the wall where he'd been quietly observing and stewing until now. "Boys grow up to be men. A thirst for blood is only assuaged when the last drop is drained. And delusions? Delusions are only delusions to people with stunted imaginations. To those that dream, farfetched desires and ideas are possibilities fueled by fire. Malum Khoron-khelek has been dreaming a long time. That is why we are here."

"I feel sorry for him," said one woman. "Anyone who does horrible things didn't get to that place overnight. He must be hurting."

"Hurting!" Canukke scoffed. "He certainly is. Hurting everyone I care about, as far as I know. And that is precisely what he has to look forward to when I get my hands on him —*hurting.*"

"So ... that brings us back to my news, I should think," Serete said, gathering back the room's attention. "Malum Khoron-khelek has taken Gorgenbrild. They are overrun. His Sumus sent several captured Gorgenbrilder scouts back to the people in pieces, catapulting heads and hands in. Khoron-khelek sent a negotiation party into Gorgenbrild, whom Gorgenbrilders killed and sent back in like fashion. Khoron-khelek continued to press in, binding them to their own cliff until none could pass in or out. He waited like this for months, killing and eating from the bountiful prey in the mountains and sending the scraps to be picked off the bones from Gorgenbrilders as a power play. Any caught slipping past Sumu sentries to hunt were killed, and any Sumu allowing them to pass was also killed.

"Gorgenbrild was forced to begin killing livestock, and as supplies ran thin and psychological warfare ran high, he made his move. Not a month ago Khoron-khelek swept in. He sent another negotiation party, stating that any who surrendered would be assimilated into the Sumu empire and welcomed with joy, but any who withstood would be destroyed. The people of Gorgenbrild met the threat of violence with violence, and I'm afraid the reports are not good. Many were lost."

Enouim's heart dropped, and her eyes pricked with tears. Her mother and brother ... were they dead? What of friends like Balat and Edone?

Oloren shook her head. "We are too late."

"Many were lost, but there are survivors. Gorgenbrild put up an admirable fight, but the Sumus under Khoron-khelek are well trained and far better acquainted with Gorgenbrilder fighting style than the Iyangas were under his father Urgil those thirty years ago. Gorgenbrild was simply no match for their numbers when resources were so low. Survivors now live under the thumb of Khoron-khelek, and as I heard it, dissension is publicly ... annihilated."

"We are doomed," Gabor said glumly.

"There is more yet to be done!" Kilith said. "Tell us, how many?"

Serete took in a deep breath and sighed. "I didn't hear specifics. Five to one? Ten to one? It's not good. For every sentry standing in the open and roaming the streets, there are twenty more in the surrounding mountains."

"How can we get in?" Vadik asked.

"Get in?" said the dismissive man with the knife. "Be grateful you got out!" He flipped it into the table to stab a bread roll, then plucked it out of the table, and took a bite off the roll.

Koko tapped the man's shoulder, and he took a step back. "Perhaps there is yet a way. You were sent by Eh'yeh, after all."

"A month ago, you say? Why, we were with Eh'yeh when it happened!" Baird said.

"And what good did it do us? What good did it do home?" Canukke demanded. "For all his talk ... nothing!"

"How much time did you spend with him?" Ruakh asked, gently but firmly.

"Enough to know a fake when I see one!" Canukke shot back. "Oh, so high and mighty he is, with his golden better-than-everyone standard and his pretentious guards. How powerful he is—so much so that he hides in stunning emerald glades far away from a view of suffering. But he cares, oh how he cares!" His voice bled sarcasm.

Gasps filled the room, and all eyes bored into Canukke, ranging from shock to anger to pity.

"Suffering!" The voice—deep, strong, and lined with the danger of a thousand zegraths' hackles—belonged to Kilith. "One who has embodied suffering itself need not be taught its meaning. One who defined the epitome of deplorable experience, the zenith of human pain, and chose to endure it rather than allow you to fall prey to yourself—insult him again, and it will be the last words you utter. The maker allows his hunger for justice be put on hold for your sake, that you might retain breath enough in your lungs to mock him. Be silent!"

None dared speak.

Canukke looked as though he'd been slapped. He opened his mouth, then shut it. Turning, he wheeled round and stormed out through an open doorway to a ledge outside.

Enouim choked on tears, struggling to regulate her emotions in the crowd. Her home was ruled by a tyrant, the people she loved might be dead, and they had been sent on a failed mission. And if Chayan hadn't tried to kill her, Enouim might very well be dead too. Enouim wondered if Chayan was alive. Surely that much fury could not be easily snuffed out. But then, neither could the collective fire of Gorgenbrild's most brutal warriors, and yet they were defeated. How gruesome the fields must have been, strewn with the spent passions of her people. Enouim shuddered.

If Eh'yeh knew, why didn't he do anything? Why hadn't he told them when he saw them? Why hadn't he prepared them for this, and told them a plan of action? Was it folly to return to Gorgenbrild? Somehow, doing anything else seemed wrong. How could they desert the last of their people? How could they go knowing they would die, or be enslaved themselves? Why wasn't there a plan?

Ruakh's words came back to her then. *Who says he hasn't made one?* Enouim thought of this for a moment. Sumus outnumbered Gorgenbrilders ten to one. There were only nine left in the company, and of those only seven were experienced warriors. What could they do against such an adversary?

Another wave of emotion threatened to take her down, and Enouim wordlessly got up and made for the exit, glaring at nothing and everything, so focused was she on getting out of that room. She needed some air. Enouim walked as though in a dream, her feet and legs carrying her up the stairs in the middle of the room. She didn't want to be around anyone and was relieved to see the stairs open onto the roof, which was open to the world, lit by several torches, and empty.

Grief hit her like a sledgehammer crashing through a barrier. Enouim fell to her knees, buried her face in her arms and wept. She wept for her mother and brother, who were either dead or wishing they were. She wept for Pakel, whose life was lost on a mission destined to fail. She wept for every moment laughing on the road when she should have been torn to shreds. Enouim gripped her knees tight and rolled to her side, curled in a ball, ribs aching and throat tight from sorrow. Tears rolled down her face, rivers of confusion and bereavement and pain.

As the last of her energy sapped from her body, Enouim opened her eyes and looked to a landing across the way, over an expanse of dark forest. Canukke stood there, silhouette outlined in the dim light of the flickering torches, shaking and clutching something to his chest. She squinted to see that he held little Urou, the child who had given him the leaf. All the strength of his pretenses were shattered, and his body sagged. As exhaustion took her, the last sight she remembered was Canukke, weeping bitterly in the embrace of a child.

37

"Up here, I got her!" called a voice. "Shh, she's asleep."

"Good, I'm glad she's okay."

"How long has she been up there?"

"Don't wake her, just bring her down so she doesn't freeze. We'll set up here for the night."

Voices drifted lightly through the edges of her consciousness, and distantly she felt herself lifted from the ground. Strong arms cradled her close to a warm body, and she swayed gently with his footsteps. Serete's soothing voice was close to her ear, and Kilith spoke to him in hushed tones. As she was set down softly, Enouim's body melted into a pile of blankets ready and willing to receive her, her weary mind taking refuge in sleep once again.

Enouim woke slowly to a room full of light. Oloren sat next to her, laughing with Baird. Mereámé spoke to Ruakh, and

Gabor arranged plates on the table. Enouim sat up, wiping her eyes.

Wzzzzzzzz. The sound of the zip line announced someone's arrival through the open window. Vadik swung into the room, clipped onto the rope with a bag of food in each hand. *Thud.* He landed with a smile. "Good morning sunshine!" he said to Enouim. "I certainly expect you to be full of energy today after the sleep you've had."

Oloren turned to her. "En, you're awake! Hi."

Enouim drew her brows together, trying to remember when she had fallen asleep.

Wzzzzzzzzzzz, thud. Serete bounced in on the balls of his feet, laughing, with a large pack on his back and two more bags in his hands. Enouim's heart quickened, but she squashed the feeling as well as she might. What was her problem? She averted her gaze and caught Gabor's eye instead. He winked at her. *Oh no.*

Serete set the bags down, unclipped himself from the line, and greeted the room with a hearty good morning just as Canukke and Kilith walked down from the stairs in the center of the room.

"You set a nice table, Gabor," Kilith said.

"Exquisite artisanship. I've never seen anyone so precise in all my life," Baird teased. "I think he must have spent an hour doing nothing but setting out knives and forks."

"Might as well enjoy it—who knows how long it will be before we can sit at a proper table again," Kilith said. "We'll eat comfortably while we may."

Serete appeared at Enouim's side as she untangled herself from blankets. He held out a hand. "Good morning. Let me help you up."

Suddenly feeling incredibly awkward, Enouim took his hand hesitantly. The group was staring. She just knew it.

Enouim turned her eyes to Serete's deep blue ones. "Thanks," she mumbled.

"How did you sleep?" he asked as he walked her to the table.

"Well, I think," she replied, running a hand over her face. "I'm not entirely sure I'm awake yet."

"It's a beautiful morning," Vadik said. "That'll wake you right up. And the horses are ready for us on the forest floor."

Enouim perked up. "Fern is here?"

"In all his spunky glory," Vadik answered.

"Which one is Fern?" Serete asked.

"Oh, he's gorgeous." Enouim turned to him with excitement but felt her face turn red and looked back at the table. "His name is Inferno, I just call him Fern for short. Big black blanket appaloosa. Can't miss him."

"I believe I saw him on my way in last evening. He looked to be quite a horse."

"We don't cut corners when it comes to horses," Baird commented. "Kalka'an horses are the best of the best, and Inferno is top notch even for us. We outdid ourselves."

Enouim grinned at him and looked back to Serete. She sighed contentedly, grateful to have the heaviness in the air lifted from last night. He smiled back at her. How was he so comfortable everywhere he went? He seemed to be a part of the group somehow, though he had only just met them. Speaking of that, Enouim paused to wonder why he was there with them.

"So did you get kicked out of breakfast elsewhere and got stuck with us?" she asked.

"He's coming with us, didn't you hear?" Oloren said.

"He ... what?" Enouim looked at Serete in surprise.

He nodded. "I spoke with Kilith, and he agreed you could use an extra set of hands."

Gabor raised a glass. "The more the merrier. Die with us, my friend!"

Enouim felt both excited and troubled. The two emotions battled as Mereámé spoke up.

"Speaking of ... I have some hard news to share," she said, swallowing. All eyes turned to her. "I was just talking with Ruakh. I have been wondering where my place is in all of this, now that found Eh'yeh. My father will be anxious to hear of Eh'yeh and all that we learned. Still, it's hard to leave you. I have only known you for a couple months, but already you have become like family." Enouim saw her face fill with emotion, her voice as soft and genuine as ever. "I'm sure you will all miss my physical prowess back in Gorgenbrild, so I'm glad you will be adding another to your number." She smiled. "All jokes aside, I didn't know when to turn back and had thought I would travel with you at least a bit further. But last night I had a dream, and Eh'yeh spoke to me and told me to return to Levav today. One of the Rehi has agreed to escort me through the forest to the plains, where Eh'yeh told me I would find Mayimesh and the rest of the Pyren on their way to Levav."

"Today?" Gabor repeated, processing the information.

Enouim wasn't sure what to say. "We will miss you. I'll miss you," she said. This journey had far too many goodbyes. She wondered how many more she would have to endure before the end. At the same time, Mereámé returning to Levav would keep her safe. Perhaps Mereámé would be the sole survivor of their venture.

"It was inevitable that you would need to return, I suppose," Baird said. "We have enjoyed your company and kindness. Your people will surely be happy to hear from you again, and have their historian write her own piece of history to fill in the blanks there."

Mereámé's face brightened in knowing Baird had understood her.

"We will miss you both very much," Oloren said. "And we wish you the safest of travels."

"Both? No, it's just me."

Canukke turned to Ruakh. "You are not returning home?"

"No, you are stuck with me a bit longer. It appears Eh'yeh calls our dear friend Mereámé home to Levav, and with her the legacy of the Way is safe and the appropriate corrections can be made. I myself feel a pull toward Gorgenbrild, and for better or for worse, I do not believe our paths are yet meant to be diverted."

The rest of the meal was bittersweet, and though they could not linger, they did not hurry either. Enouim wondered at why Mereámé was given a dream with specific instructions when Enouim herself felt like she was running blind. She tried to remind herself that just because she didn't know the plan, didn't mean there wasn't one, and let that be that for now. As for Serete, she wasn't sure why he would change his plans to head toward almost certain death. It made her feel selfish for being grateful that he was there, as his presence was confident and comforting.

Toward the end of breakfast, Koko and Rindyl came to greet them and lead them down the seemingly never-ending series of swaying bridges, zip lines, slides, pulley systems, and stairs. Enouim found Serete close by to help her across many of these, and the rest of her companions encouraged her along. Serete and Vadik seemed to get along particularly well, showing off as they swung from one bridge to another, or leaning out precariously over the expanse beneath them. Oloren yelled at Vadik several times, but it didn't stop him.

After entering a final spiral staircase inside one of the trees, Enouim caught a glimpse of the horses at long last. A window in the side of the tree opened up over a large branch perhaps a foot wide, hanging ten feet off the ground. They waited in a grassy glade, tacked up, supplied, and ready to go. Hardly containing herself, Enouim stuck her head out the window to take in the gilded morning light, the breeze, and the blessed forest floor. Inferno whinnied as he saw her, tossing his head and prancing his feet in place. Laughing with relief, Enouim climbed through the window and out onto the branch. Serete, Vadik, and Oloren looked on and the rest continued down the tree and out the more civilized door.

Clucking to Inferno, Enouim crouched along the branch and crawled further out along it as he trotted underneath her, then she swung herself down and stood upright on his back.

"Monkeys, all of you!" Gabor called, but his tone was light-hearted.

Proud of her little accomplishment, Enouim bowed with a flourish, but as she did so the stallion beneath her started to trot off. She squealed and crouched down, her friends laughing behind her, as she wormed her way into the saddle and reached forward to give Inferno a hug. "I missed you!" she told him, slipping her hand beneath his shining mane. He had clearly been well taken care of during his stay. He tossed his head as if to say he knew how handsome he looked.

Behind her, Vadik and Serete did flips off the tall branch and landed light on their feet. With a joyful cry Rindyl emerged from the window and hurtled himself off the branch. Vadik and Serete caught him mid-flight and set him on the ground. Oloren, close behind, ran down the branch before launching herself onto an opposing branch and down to the ground below. Laughter filled the air, and the warm light fit the mood. Enouim dismounted to reorganize her saddle bags a bit and say her goodbyes to Mereámé.

"I needed you here with me, I think," Enouim said to her.

"Your warmth and sincerity, and the way you listen so entirely, was a beautiful thing to help me get through the last couple of months. Thank you."

"You have been so welcoming and kind to me," Mereámé said. "I'm sure we will see each other again. I can feel it. This is only a pause in our friendship."

The two women embraced, and Enouim had a hard time trying to express everything she wanted to say. She'd developed many wonderful friendships, but Mereámé was so warm and safe, her gentle touch could validate and soothe any experience. Enouim had often been drawn to Mereámé when needing space to process freely. Wiping away a tear, Enouim laughed as Gabor stood awkwardly next to Mereámé for his own goodbye, saying, "I'm ... glad you're not dead anymore. Stay that way, okay?"

Rindyl and Koko gave parting remarks as well, wishing them all a safe journey and welcoming them back to Rehim anytime. "Remember that what you see is only a sliver of what is there," Koko reminded them. "Lean on Vadik as your seer into the hidden layers."

The rest of the company bade Mereámé and their Rehi friends farewell, and Rindyl and Mereámé waved them off. Nine had come into the forest, one had died and been revived, and nine now exited the forest again. Serete took the ninth place, and Enouim wondered if all nine would make it to Gorgenbrild.

Fresh air wafted by, rolling hills spread out before her, and the sun brought a glisten to every blade of grass. Enouim breathed in deep. A new day had dawned, and the hopelessness of night had lifted. Surely Eh'yeh had not sent them from him simply to die. Enouim bent her thoughts toward Eh'yeh. *Okay, a dream would have been nice. It would have been more than nice, and I think I would still prefer it. But if you choose not to send any specifics today, I will do what I can with what you have sent. And right now, you send us home.* Enouim closed her eyes and gave herself over to the rolling motion of Inferno beneath her, the familiar feel of horse and rider, the sound of excited chatter on the road. Could it be she had missed this?

Enouim prayed the sun still shone on her loved ones in Gorgenbrild.

38

Back in the saddle, they traveled west through the forest of the massive trees that characterized Rehim. It was going to be a long way home, and it didn't take long for the group to pass the time by getting to know its newest addition.

"So, Serete ... jumping headfirst into almost certain death," Baird grinned. "Is your home life that bad, or did you just have nothing better to do?"

"Oh, just bored, really," Serete replied. "I could be tracking dragons, charting new land, or sourcing the problems with the river, but I'd miss out on where the real action is."

"I don't know," Gabor said. "Anybody who volunteers to spend this much time with Baird is questionable to me. That's where the real concern for survival comes in."

Vadik laughed. "Because you're so easy to get along with. Serete, you seem like an optimistic man. Get out now before Gabor steals the sunshine from your soul."

"Or before Vadik smothers you with questions just for a good debate," Oloren added.

"He also sees things and doesn't tell you," Canukke said dryly.

"Well if he mentioned everything he saw, he'd be talking all day long," Serete pointed out.

"No ... he *sees* things. Invisible things."

"Invisible is not the same as nonexistent. Sounds like your friend has valuable abilities."

Vadik snorted. "If you think that's something—" Enouim shot him an icy glare, and he nearly choked on his words, but he stopped and smiled to himself.

"Something to share?" Serete asked.

"Yes!" Vadik said. "But apparently not from me. Even though it will inevitably come up in conversation."

Enouim glared at him but tried to hide it when Serete looked from Vadik to her.

"Hmm ... well, perhaps I didn't know what I was getting myself into." He looked at her again, and she felt her face flush.

"And just like that, we are back to certain death," Baird said. "Honestly, why are you here?"

"Sounded like an adventure I hadn't had before."

"Well, we gladly accept!" Canukke said. He seemed in better spirits now that the company was back on the road. "You're insane, but if it channels fortuitously into battle, we will take whatever we can get. Tell me, have you traveled the mountains before?"

"I have. I enjoy learning about anything there is to learn, from land navigation to combat, tactical games, history, and interesting creatures. Whether I am protecting, tracking, or exploring, I am liable to cover a lot of ground. It's the nature of the lifestyle."

"Well, we have some interesting creatures up our way. Have you ever killed a zegrath?"

"I can't say that I have."

Canukke's face took on a satisfied expression.

"But I have followed a few to their dens to observed them," Serete continued.

Canukke sobered.

"You what?" Oloren stammered.

Gabor frowned in disbelief. "You followed them? Without getting eaten?"

"Well, if I had been eaten and still managed to look this good, I would say that's pretty impressive. But if I was eaten in the first place, the zegrath would have gotten the drop on me ... Hmm. Okay, the truth is. I followed them without getting eaten."

"I think the obvious question is how, precisely," observed Kilith, a twinkle in his eye.

"I tried several times to pick up a trail, but zegraths do not often go directly to their dens. They take time doubling back and losing their tracks in rivers. I saw one once, and after it left I went to the place it had stood and tracked it from there. They have very distinct tracks with those massive talon feet of theirs, though not as obvious as they might seem. Luckily it was close enough to home that I found the den, and after I knew what their dens looked like, it was easier to locate them in the future. Zegraths in my experience prefer dens near rivers and on high ground."

"Fascinating," Ruakh said.

"Why would you want to do that?" Vadik asked.

"Why not? I was curious, and who knows when the information might come in handy one day."

"You are a roaming academic," Ruakh noted, nodding.

"Of sorts, perhaps. But I prefer to learn by interacting with the world directly."

"So you just go around trying to answer random questions

for yourself?" Gabor asked.

"Sounds really intellectual when you put it that way. Now I use what I learn to help and protect others, but I suppose you could say that's how I started out, wanting to know what else was out there. I don't have a family I need to be home for, and the travel was an escape."

"I can relate to that," Baird said.

"Of course you can," Vadik said. "If you couldn't, you wouldn't volunteer for dangerous missions. The only one of us that didn't volunteer was Enouim."

"I did eventually!" she chimed in, defending herself. "And I might not be Bondeg's first or second or eighty-seventh pick for high stakes quests, but I have always longed to soak up the world with my own eyes. I dreamed of traveling the trade routes with my father. I read all the old documents I could find. Warriors aren't the only ones enthralled by lands far away."

Serete turned to Enouim. "If you could go anywhere, where would you go?"

"Home," Canukke said curtly. "To a Gorgenbrild that is as I remembered it, safe and without trouble."

Serete's eyebrows rose. "You certainly are a ray of sunshine."

"I don't see the use of frivolity on the eve of darkness."

"Nonsense!" Oloren broke in. "Frivolity is your favorite eve-of-darkness pastime. Once you challenged everyone to a drinking contest and said whoever held their liquor best could lead the charge the next day."

"I never did that."

Vadik groaned.

"I was there," Gabor said. "And that is exactly what happened. We nearly gave away our position the next day because our point man was still hungover as a pelt on a rack."

"That was different. Our people are on the line."

Oloren rolled her eyes. "Two weeks after we lost Lornet you said we needed to lighten up and threw torches at us."

Gabor turned to Oloren. "On my first excursion he added animal blood to my drinking water and let me find it when I got thirsty. He said it was a ritual. It wasn't."

The corner of Canukke's mouth twitched.

"Remember when he told that hostage he would make a victory crown out of the man's entrails, and then laughed when— "

"Enough!" Canukke burst in. "First of all, laughter can be strategic for the good of comrades, and that last one was a tactic that earned us some valuable information."

Oloren looked him dead in the eyes. "Yes, but as you just said, humor is instrumental for the bonding of comrades, and bonding can make the difference between mercenaries and squads. The question is, why does it bother you now? You know you hate it when you are miserable, and other people are enjoying themselves."

"And you hate it when you're wrong," Canukke countered. "You're so stubborn you would die just to be right, and almost did—four years ago on Liombas mountain."

"No, Canukke. No. You don't get to drag that up every time you get angry with me. You always deflect. I'm not doing it today."

Several beats of silence. Enouim involved herself with untangling a knot in Inferno's mane as she rode, stealing glances at her friends as the horses walked on.

"Excellent conversation," Vadik said.

Kilith drilled him a stare.

Ruakh shook his head.

"We will never get home at this rate," Canukke stated. "We

need to pick up our pace." He dug in his heels and spurred his mount into an easy canter.

Baird gave a disgusted grimace, and Vadik rolled his eyes.

Gabor grinned. "I don't know about you, but I haven't had a good gallop in a while!" And off he went.

With whoops and hollers, the others flew down the hill to join him, and the horses tossed their heads in the wind as they relished every hoof beat on the ground. Enouim leaned into Inferno, urging him forward and letting the air ripple past her face and over her shoulders. Serete was closing in, and she peeled off with a laugh, delighting in the maneuvers of her steed.

Kilith and Ruakh slowed first, then Canukke, alone, and the others one at a time. Enouim caught up to Serete, who had managed to pass her for a spell, and slowed Inferno to a walk.

"I love the hills," she said, after catching her breath.

"These are beautiful. Some are more welcoming than others, but these are beautiful."

"Where do you come from exactly?"

"Not terribly far from here, actually. Morthed is northeast of us, and beyond that what you would call the eastern hills. The particular township I am from is called Kalma."

"Do you have any family there still? What led you to be a ranger?"

"Not really. I was raised by my grandparents, and our village is small. There are all sorts of great beasts in the hills, and I was a young teenager when I had to start protecting our home from various creatures. I never wanted to be a ranger, but I did want to learn more about these animals and thought understanding them could help protect us."

"That's how you started exploring."

"Exactly."

"If you don't mind my asking ... what happened to your

parents?"

"They passed away from sickness when I was young."

Enouim paused before speaking again. "That's hard, not knowing your parents. I was adopted, so I don't know my birth parents, but the parents I grew up with were wonderful. My father died when I was eight though, so it was just my brother and my mother after that."

"How did he die?"

"He was a trader, and one day he left and didn't come back. My mother always blamed tribesmen, but I suppose there's no way to know."

Again they rode in silence, listening to birds and a wistful wind. After a moment, Enouim began again. "So Rehim—how did you end up there?"

"I met Rehi Waymakers for the first time when I was ten. Wonderful people. Aside from my grandfather, I had determined by then that adults didn't have any fun. When I met the Waymakers, they came and played games with us and cared about people in a way I hadn't seen before, but the village elders ran them off when they started talking about Eh'yeh. I focused my energies on protecting the village and then left at sixteen, determined to know what else was out there and what kind of meaning life might hold. I've always loved kids, and when I stumbled onto some Waymakers in my travels, we struck up a bond. Now I drop in whenever I'm in the vicinity."

Enouim smiled, remembering his interactions with the children at Rehim. They were entirely taken with him, but the feeling was mutual. She watched him for a moment, deep in thought.

"And how did you come to be there?" Serete asked her. "You said it was a long story. And here we are, with lots of time on our hands. Kilith says the journey will take us two months."

"Are you sure you're ready to hear it? My amazing tale of bravery might intimidate you. I'm quite the conquering hero."

Serete laughed. "So I've gathered from your friends! I'll brace myself. I promise not to see you differently after I hear of your conquests."

Enouim spent the next few hours talking to Serete, telling him of Gorgenbrild, the accident with Chayan, her hasty escape and unfortunate unconsciousness, and waking up in the wagon. She shared her experiences from then until now, reminiscing about all that had happened, but leaving out her strange new relationship with water. Serete seemed to have heard and seen a lot, but Enouim wasn't convinced his promise not to see her differently would be kept if he learned she had gills. Or that she had nearly killed the rest of them with her new abilities, flying them through the river.

Enouim found him easy to talk to, conversation flowing as though they had known one another for years. And no one as attractive as Serete had ever seemed drawn to her before unless they had particularly repulsive personalities. But then, personalities praised in Gorgenbrild weren't her cup of tea. Enouim studied Serete, at ease and comfortable. How did he do that? Bright-blue eyes studied her soul, and when they turned away she caught herself stealing glances. Even so, with death looming low on the horizon, it seemed hardly the time to let her focus drift.

As morning gave way to afternoon, and afternoon wore on into evening, the company evened out their pace and fell into a rhythm. Light began to fade, and the troop dismounted and made camp. Oloren and Gabor were debating whether being drunk or being tired caused the most impairment in battle, and Canukke was jovial and making underhanded comments. Life was back to normal. Whatever that meant.

"I get tired when I drink," Ruakh said. "So I'm not sure

there is much a difference for me. I can never seem to keep my eyes open long enough to tell any other difference."

"You drink?" Enouim asked. "Somehow I didn't picture that!"

"I have, but like I said, nothing too interesting happens."

Canukke broke in loudly. "Once I drank a keg and killed twenty men in battle only shortly after! If anything it made me more lethal. Tame warriors never strike fear into the hearts of men."

"True, but tame warriors don't strike fear into the hearts of their companions either," Oloren said. "Wildness is good when appropriately channeled."

"Is it still wildness if it's channeled?" Vadik asked.

"There are different kinds of wildness," Enouim stated. "One can be wild like a stallion running free, powerful and beautiful in its rawness. Or one can be wild like a pig with its little tail on fire, mucking up any organized thing, destroying anything in its path, and a brute any way you look at it. There are soft wilds, like a flower, and harsh wilds, like fire. But even fire is better contained than it is raging without boundary."

"Some of us call it discipline," Kilith said evenly.

"If I were truly a danger to my own people I wouldn't have allowed it!" Canukke countered. "Not every man can hold his liquor."

"Nor should every man try," noted Oloren.

"Nothing bad seems to have come of it, so I'm not sure what seems to have turned the discussion so sour," Vadik said. "So he drinks—don't we all?"

"The mark of a man is not ceasing all fun, but knowing when to stop." Serete glanced at Canukke. "Like whether to drudge up old grievances or let them go."

Enouim looked from one to the other. They stared one another down.

"Do ... have you two met?" asked Baird.

"No, we haven't," Serete replied. "But it feels as though I've met him a hundred times over."

"You've met me a hundred times, have you?" Canukke demanded. "Well, I'm glad you've had the pleasure. As for me, I've met plenty of people too tall for their boots. Tell me, friend, whose opinion is more valid? Those that work within squads and teams, leading men successfully in and out of battles more times than you can count, or a man who spends more time watching squirrels than analyzing the ways of war?"

Serete's jaw clenched, and he opened his mouth as though to speak but was interrupted.

"Squirrels!" Baird exclaimed. "That's what the two of you look like right now. Squirrels facing off on a tree, about to go round and round in circles."

"Baird is right," Ruakh said. "What good will this do?"

"Maybe we will learn whose face can get reddest," Vadik suggested. "Any bets?"

"I'm sick of this," Enouim declared with a heavy sigh. "Canukke, I've defended your leadership before. I have. Even after all you have said to me, after ditching me in Kalka'an, everything. Because when it comes down to it, you know what you are doing in dangerous situations. At least, that's what I thought, and your confidence carries you most of the time. But then I hear a story like this, or I see you poking at everyone looking for a rise out of people. And you get one. Because the rest of the group can't let things go. And Vadik, you egg it on. Why do you do that? Why do you want to watch people tear each other down? I'm exhausted just listening to you all. I'm going to bed. Please keep any screaming matches to a minimum."

Enouim got up from the ground, dusted herself off, and

walked away to get her blanket out of Inferno's saddlebag. Voices rose behind her and she heard Kilith's strong voice attempt to harness them all, but even he seemed unable to abate the rising tempests.

Yes, everything was back to normal all right. It was going to be a long road home.

THEY TRAVELED due west at first, giving Morthed a wide berth, before bending their course northwest. They left the forest behind and found themselves again in open plains. There would be nothing but grassy flatlands evolving into hills for weeks to come.

Tensions rose over the next several weeks. A heavy feeling dropped over them like a thick foreboding cloud, and none of them seemed able to escape its touch. Conflicts were sparked from the smallest imprecision in packing the saddle bags to the more critical strategy plans being batted around for what to do upon arriving in Gorgenbrild. During one brief respite, they sat in a circle on the grass of an open field.

"Like most of the ideas so far," Canukke said, "this is beyond our means and hardly addresses the greatest need. It is as effective and feasible for the nine of us to accomplish as it would be to lay siege to our own people. Imbecile."

"I am still waiting for your brilliant ideas," Vadik shot back.

"If I've said it once, I've said it a thousand times. The tunnel system is our way in. Every family has one."

"Yes, but not all of them are long enough, and we don't know where they all lead. We would be going in blind, one at a time, with no one to cover us."

"If the tunnels we hope to use haven't been found, and

supposing we can find the outside exits to the ones that are still safe," Oloren added.

"I would prefer to run an operation that gets us inside with a better visual, or at least split up," Serete said.

"Naturally," Gabor said. "If Vadik was found in the tunnel ahead of me, I would rather he die than all of us one after another." He smirked.

Vadik spread his palms. "Clearly we would scout our options ahead of time. And you are very welcome for my noble sacrifice. May your selfishness and cowardice live on forever."

Serete brought the attention back to his point. "Survivors are remaining in their homes under Sumu control. If we can get inside and blend in, we may go undetected long enough to gather intelligence. How many are dead? How many able-bodied men are ready to fight? What access is there to weaponry, and what schedules do the guards keep?"

"This is Gorgenbrild. The women fight just as well as the men," Oloren said, indignantly.

"Fine, how many able-bodied men and women. The intent was clear—how many could join us?"

"Perhaps if we found a clear tunnel, we could smuggle out a few key players to aid us," Kilith said. "There are several men I would give my right arm to have on the outside with us."

"If we are relying on stealth, I do believe my expertise will be worthwhile," Baird said.

Vadik rolled his eyes. "Yes, because Gorgenbrilders are so bumbling when they crash through the forests to hunt, or slaughter entire camps of silent Sumus."

"Your expertise was well displayed in Levav, Baird," Canukke said in a clipped tone. "And that is why we have the pleasure of only your company, and not the other weasel."

"Silas is a good man! If you had treated us as equals we

wouldn't have resorted to such measures!"

"What happened to the other one?" Serete asked.

"None of this would have happened if you had listened to us from the beginning!" Baird insisted.

Canukke scoffed. "Eagles do not listen to the ravings of worms!"

"Says the worm to the worm—or haven't you been paying attention?"

"ENOUGH!" Kilith drilled them all with a cold glare. Enouim wondered if he had ever considered preserving meats with it. "We will not have discord like this among us."

Baird snorted. "Oh, we will have discord all right."

"No," Kilith said. "We will not. This is a volunteer mission, and everyone on it is free to come and go. But as long as you remain on this mission, you will speak cordially or not at all. Life and death, slave or free—what are squabbles and petty comments in light of these? The fool acts younger the angrier he becomes, and I am convinced the lot of you have regressed all the way to toddlerhood. So shut your mouths for a spell and grow up a bit. We review our options in an hour. On the road."

Enouim glanced around at them all. Kilith got up and walked to his horse, mounting and setting off in their chosen direction. Serete stood next, until one by one all got up and mounted, heading out in relative single file.

After forty-five minutes or so of silence, Oloren pulled up next to Enouim and leaned in. "With this easy terrain and fair weather, it should be a pleasant ride, but I think I'd rather the sea serpent over this."

Enouim laughed. "I'm not sure about the sea serpent, but the perasors at least. Men complain about women being petty, but I'm not sure they ever listen to themselves when they make the claim."

Oloren shook her head. "Overgrown children. Kilith had it right. I'm not sure about the sea serpent though—you just might hold your own now. Somewhat of a sea serpent yourself."

Enouim rolled her eyes. "Please, of all the nicknames I could have, don't put me on the same level as that thing!" She shivered. "*Ick*. Just thinking about it gives me the chills. Still, it would have been nice to know what was going on with me back then. Maybe Baird wouldn't have had to save me. But no, there is no scenario in which I am stronger than that beastly creature."

"I don't know, you felt strong to me in the river. Strong enough to dash me to pieces."

"That's what you've always wanted in a friend, isn't it? Someone who almost kills you."

"You might be surprised," Oloren said, smiling. "Most of my friends have matched that description at one time or another."

Enouim laughed again, grateful for the reprieve. "You know, I've been thinking more about the river. It was the most invigorating experience of my life. Maybe with a little practice I could avoid killing everyone."

"That does sound like a worthy goal—enjoying yourself without accidentally dispatching your friends."

"Honestly, though. Now that we're traveling again, I can't stop thinking about it ... and how if I die in Gorgenbrild, I'll never get to flesh it all out and figure out who I am."

"I believe we're going to make it, somehow. And if we don't, I suppose you won't be around to overthink it. Perhaps, death or no death, Eh'yeh will show you more about who you are."

"And where I came from. What is that about? I have so many questions. I don't even know exactly what Madzi are. And I am one! Or, sort of."

"Aha!" Vadik shouted from behind them.

Enouim nearly jumped out of her skin. She hadn't realized he had come up that close.

"Kilith! I don't think we have weighed all our options!" Vadik nudged his horse into a trot to catch up to Kilith up ahead.

"Oh no," Enouim muttered, exchanging glances with Oloren. "Please tell me his ideas do not have to do with me." Oloren and Enouim clucked to the horses and followed Vadik, the rest wondering what all the commotion was about, until nine horses were walking close together.

"... I don't know about that," Kilith was saying.

"About what?" Ruakh asked.

"Enouim's outlandish water antics," Vadik said excitedly. "There is a river just east of Gorgenbrild where Sumus will be making camp. And I don't know what you are talking about. There are nine of us total. Nine. Against an entire army of Sumus. We need any element of surprise we can get, and I cannot possibly think of anything more surprising than this."

"Water antics?" Serete asked, looking at her with a puzzled expression.

Enouim shrugged and shook her head, wishing Vadik would leave it alone.

"She can do some kind of absurd water magic," Gabor explained.

"It's pretty incredible," Baird added.

Serete was still looking at her, and Enouim avoided his gaze. Looking from Enouim to Kilith, Serete voiced his thought. "Madzi?"

Kilith gave him a nod.

Serete's eyes grew wide as he turned back to Enouim.

"Half," Vadik corrected. "She only just found out before Rehim."

"Vadik's right," Canukke said. Enouim jerked her head up. "We can't afford to underutilize any tools in our arsenal."

Kilith looked uncertain and glanced at Enouim. "I'm not sure this is entirely necessary."

"Not necessary?" Canukke scoffed. "In what abundance of options do you find such luxuries?"

Oloren sighed. "I'm sorry Enouim, but we do need to use every last ounce of resources at our disposal."

"You wanted to learn more about it anyway," Vadik said. "Now you get to practice. And I'm not convinced you would be safer on land."

"If you couldn't tell, that was definitely an insult to your honed fighting skills," Gabor added.

"Thanks." Enouim grimaced. "And what about you, Vadik?"

"Me?"

"*Every last ounce of resources.* I haven't heard you volunteering, but of all lookouts, you are our best chance of seeing what's coming."

"Also true," said Canukke. "We'll consider both of our mutant companions when devising our final approach."

"Mutant? Really?" Enouim said.

"Aberration, monstrosity. Does the term matter overmuch?"

"I should think so. I prefer aberration to monstrosity, wouldn't you say, Vadik?"

Vadik grinned. "No—monstrosity is fine by me. Let the Sumus know a powerful monstrosity is about to observe them to death!"

Enouim let an unsettled smile come over her face. "Well, I suppose we have little other choice." She turned to Kilith. "All right then! And what shall the aberration and monstrosity do exactly?"

39

"Yes, what exactly?" Gabor asked. "Splash inordinate amounts of water on them? Put out fires? Dash them against the rocks? Hmm, actually, maybe that wouldn't be so bad!"

"We'll throw them into the river and you can drag them around until they die!" Baird said.

"What can you do?" Serete asked.

Enouim hedged. "Not entirely sure as of now."

"We were trying to get away from thousands of bats and went into the river, and Enouim made some sort of current and dragged us all with her underwater," Oloren explained.

"She can also propel herself through the water incredibly fast," Gabor added.

"There was a lot of water that never made it back into the river," Ruakh said. "And more than a few unhappy bats!"

"Half Madzi and not half bad!" A look of wonder remained in Serete'ss eyes, but the playful twinkle was back. Enouim smiled, unsure of herself. "What else have you learned?"

"Else?" Enouim asked. "I haven't really explored it. The bats were pretty much the extent of things."

"What about ... er, how long can you stay underwater?"

"Oh ... indefinitely, I think."

"Fascinating. Can you make a bubble?"

"Why would we need it?" Kilith asked.

"What are you talking about?" Enouim asked.

"Madzi are guardians of the water, and in these parts, specifically rivers and lakes. The Madzi of the seas are a different sort entirely, but that is a story for another time. They govern water and so can manipulate it in some ways. If any human is granted the unusual privilege of entering the river to meet with Madzi, they create an air bubble the size of a small room to meet in."

"They hold meetings underwater?" Enouim asked.

Serete blinked. "Well, yes. That's where they live."

Enouim tried to imagine an entire society underwater.

"Madzi holding humans hostage is similar," Kilith said. "Few humans have ever been held against their will by the Madzi, as it is beyond their boundaries, but they have overstepped on occasion. The less hospitable Madzi may hold a person deep enough that any effort to escape would cause them to run out of air."

"That sounds like something worth tapping into." Canukke furrowed his brow, deep in thought.

"I thought Madzi were like Nazir," Oloren said. "They are supposed to be caregivers and nurturers."

Kilith shrugged. "Some have taken their duties too far, and are resentful of men, but by and large, they remain nurturing and quiet, keeping out of human affairs."

"Do hostages ever run out of oxygen?" Gabor asked.

"They take shifts to guard and have a rotation schedule for bringing bubbles in and out of the cell to refresh the air supply."

"I'm sorry, but I'm not sure how taking hostages helps us in any scenario," Enouim broke in. "I don't know how to do that, but if I did, why would we take hostages? There are too many Sumus to try to restrain. And even if we did, I imagine I would have to sleep at some point."

"The main thing is finding out what you can do," Serete said. "I think the first step will be getting you into the river. You need to practice. We should be coming to a river in two weeks. You will have time to experiment soon enough!"

MANY MORE SUGGESTIONS WERE MADE, most of which were utterly ridiculous and suggested by Baird or Vadik. Enouim asked if Vadik's ability to see the invisible extended to seeing his own brain to make sure it was there, but Vadik told her that was ludicrous since his eyes were attached to his brain. The company seemed to have become cohesive again, and the two weeks flew by. By the end of it, just as Serete had predicted, Enouim found time to experiment.

Trees cropped up around them until they were immersed in woods once again. As they continued northwest, they heard the river before they saw it. It was much larger than the rivers in the plain or in the forest near Rehim and had a strong current. Gabor, Vadik, and Canukke began competing to see who could skip stones into the river the furthest.

Serete nudged her. "See if you can influence their game."

"How?"

"How did you move us all in the river?" Ruakh asked, over-hearing.

Enouim furrowed her brow. She remembered feeling the force of the water around her, flowing through her. She remembered asking the water, in a way, to bend to her will, and directing it with her hand. Enouim felt foolish, but focused on Gabor's stone as it spun downriver. Nothing. She tried again, this time adding a hand motion that felt entirely ridiculous.

"Try standing in the water," Kilith suggested.

Enouim looked at him quizzically, but then thought perhaps he was right. She took off her shoes, walked to the water's edge and stepped in, laughing as the pleasant coolness of the water welcomed her feet and swirled around them. The water seemed to call to her, beckon her in, and she took several more steps until she stood knee-high.

Enouim refocused on Gabor's latest pebble. She could almost feel the river itself, knowing where the pebbles were just as she would know were one to hit her in the head. The pebble jerked once as it landed on a skip before careening around the bend with the current.

Enouim waded a little deeper, savoring the feel of the water around her, washing the weariness of the road from her body. The current looked strong, but she didn't find it difficult to stand, and Enouim dismissed Oloren's warning from the bank to be careful. It must not be as strong as it looked. She smiled and sunk deeper in until she was up to her neck in coursing waters gurgling at her collarbone. She could feel the ridges on the back of her neck open as if to gasp for air as the water reached them.

Enouim played with the water between her hands, passing small currents back and forth between her palms with gentle extensions of her fingers.

"One, two, three!" Canukke called, and all three men tossed new stones into the river about thirty feet upstream from her.

Now more fully in the river, Enouim felt her sense of it increase. Hands underwater, she extended her index finger toward Vadik's pebble, which was winning, and twirled it in a small circle. The river created a small whirlpool, catching the pebble in a circle and delaying its journey. Confused shouts from the men upstream rewarded her. Enouim grinned and looked back at Serete, who smiled back at her, but she forgot to continue the whirlpool and the pebble sank. Focusing now on Canukke's pebble, she sent water shooting toward it until it was expelled from the river, skipped twice in the opposite direction, and tumbled beneath the surface. Cries from the men rose up again, and this time they noticed her game and came closer.

"How's the current?" Baird asked.

"Not bad," she answered. "And it feels wonderful!"

"I could use some refreshing!" he said, taking off his own shoes. He dipped a toe into the river and gasped. "Wonderful! I should think not! It's freezing in there!"

"No, it's not. Just get in. It's not bad at all!"

"Well, I'm not half fish, I suppose."

"I'm not a fish."

"She's an abberation," Vadik corrected. "Now let's see what you can really do."

They spent the next couple of hours playing in the river. Enouim was thrilled to discover how the water responded to her—fleeing from her outstretched fingertips and rushing toward her palm when she pulled her hand into a fist toward herself. She could move up and downstream easily, since she didn't have to fight the current, but rather directed it to carry her where she wanted.

As the day wore on, the company had to keep moving, but they instructed her to stay in the river as they walked along the bank while she practiced. Ruakh started throwing sticks for her to retrieve or send back through the water, and she learned to manipulate larger objects from further distances. Other times she maneuvered quick turns and experimented with how fast she could go underwater. Inferno galloped along the river watching her, following her as she zipped up and downstream.

By the time Enouim finally came out of the river, the rest of the group was thoroughly immersed in strategy talk once again. She had been out for a whole fifteen minutes to catch her breath and dry off when she nearly wished she was back in the river to escape the debates.

"No rivers run directly through Gorgenbrild, so it would have to happen on the outskirts, where Sumus will likely be encamped," Gabor was saying. "Bows and arrows could help us pick them off from a distance, but we don't want to arouse suspicion too early."

"I'm sorry, but does your quiver regenerate with arrows?" Baird said. "No? Neither does mine. Even to think of using archery for such a long period of time requires far more than we have with us. Which is why we have to steal some first. Sumus are legendary archers and will have quivers upon quivers of arrows."

"Archery would get us distance coverage to protect our entry, but using it would blow our cover," Canukke said. "We need to sneak in, learn the lay of the land, and fight our way out."

"Suicide!" Serete said. "Getting information will be important, but fighting our way out would be futile. If Gorgenbrild could be defended from inside, it would have been by now."

"You underestimate our people."

"Apparently not, or they wouldn't be in the position they are in. Gorgenbrilders are excellent fighters, but no match for the numbers they face now."

"This was already a suicide mission." Gabor sighed. "I'm not sure how you haven't accepted that yet."

"Any mission worth going on is worth dying on," Canukke said. "And we will carry it through."

"*Is* it worth dying on, though?" Baird asked. "The way I see it, we are nine people headed into an army with endless supplies and full control. Perhaps we should seek allies first."

"We cannot waste another moment," Canukke answered. "Our families could already be dying. Time is not on our side."

"Nothing is on our side!" Baird shot back.

"What of Kalka'an?" Kilith asked. "They have aided us before. Would they assist us?"

Baird shook his head. "I don't know. No conglomerate of tribesmen has amassed like this before. When Malum's father Urgil Khoron-khelek united several tribes to create the Iyangas, Kalka'an rode with Gorgenbrild and won victory, but by no comforting margin. Malum seems to have done what his father could not and is more ruthless and fatal. He has brought warring tribes to peace in greater numbers than ever before. Our people still feel the losses of the Liombas-Katan Campaign. I fear there is little left we can do for Gorgenbrild, and many there may reject any help as futile."

"What are you saying?" Enouim asked. "This is all pointless, and we are all going to die?"

Baird paused. "Maybe."

"We can outwit them," Canukke said. "We were chosen for this reason. Small numbers have defeated larger forces before. Let us make history! No one who sits back and complains that a task is impossible ever gets the job done. Those that forge ahead, believing in the cause, define what is possible. We will go to our people in Gorgenbrild. They will not be abandoned in their hour of need by the very warriors they elected to defend them. No, we will come to them, bringing fire as we come."

"Still, no one who valiantly challenges the limits of impossibility and fails ever lives to tell about it," Baird pointed out.

"Aren't you afraid?" Gabor asked Canukke. "What if it is all for naught?"

"I am afraid only of doing nothing."

"What if there is no one left to die for?" Vadik said.

"There are survivors," Serete said.

"There *were* survivors, last you heard," Vadik corrected. "Through the grapevine, I might add."

"By the same token, perhaps things aren't as bad as they seem. Exaggerations by Sumus wanting to spark a fearsome reputation?" Enouim suggested.

"Spark!" Vadik said. "I would say it has burst to full flame."

"It was once Gorgenbrild with the fearsome reputation!" Canukke shouted. "Gorgenbrild is the land of the brutal warrior! A place where war is as breath to the lungs, and violence as natural as sunlight. A force to be reckoned with. One Gorgenbrilder is worth twenty Sumu slime. May Glintenon see us through to the end, as our cause is just and their end is sure."

"Should such a place be saved?" Serete pondered. "Surely there is more there than a thirst for blood."

"It is a place of honor," Kilith said. "Honor and truth, valiance and bravery. And, yes, bloodthirst. Vengeance. Wrath. Judgment lives in the mind of every Gorgenbrilder from childhood. But there is more to us than that."

Enouim's head went into a tailspin. Were they deserving to be saved? Would Eh'yeh truly aid such a mission, or did he send them to die as they deserved? Something wasn't sitting right with her, but she couldn't place it. She thought of her mother and brother, of Edone, and her friend Balat. There was good in Gorgenbrild yet. Still, the culture of vengeance was the framework of their society. Enouim's stomach turned sour.

More shouting brought her back to the present.

"And what do you know? You have been unraveling since Eh'yeh!" Baird scoffed.

"Eh'yeh! And what has he done for us since then?" Canukke demanded. "I have more experience than all of you combined, and yet you would set yourself up as leader over us? Go home, child. This is no place for over ambitious prepubescent boys."

"The wit of Kalka'an is an art and a finesse that Gorgenbrild only dreams of while tripping over spilled ale."

"Finesse! Your glorious plans killed Pakel!" Canukke shouted.

"Killed—how dare you," Baird whispered, face reddening.

"Baird has been loyal to us!" Vadik yelled back.

"Loyal," Gabor muttered. "Is it or is it not true that Pakel would be alive if it weren't for him?"

"Since the day I set foot on this journey with you, I have been an outcast," Baird said. "Untrusted, underappreciated, and undermined at every turn. I thought we had moved past all of that, but here you are, blaming me for your problems when your people were too busy killing each other to consider dangers beyond your borders. You will excuse me for being part of a civilized society! If anyone could lead us into Gorgenbrild, it is someone who doesn't think like a Gorgenbrilder!"

"You know nothing about us! How could you think to lead us?" Gabor retorted.

"Too far, Baird!" Oloren added. "You remove our humanity without a thought, and forget we have been your friends these months!"

"I was born for this, and yet you waltz in pretending to know everything at a glance," Canukke declared. "Were you hand selected to lead? No! You were an afterthought, sent along to spy on us and take the weapon were we to find it!"

"I should lead! I am of Gorgenbrild and more than capable, without delusions of grandeur," Vadik said.

"You? You were on my list right after a blind bird flying through a forest!"

The voices blended together.

"We need someone who can take charge."

"We need someone with a level head!"

"We need an adult," Serete called out.

"Stop!" Ruakh said.

Kilith leaned back and crossed his arms.

"Tension!" Oloren yelled. "I would say *attention*, but, well, considering the circumstances ..."

Everyone turned and looked at her, dumbfounded.

"We haven't had clear leadership since before Eh'yeh, if I'm being honest," she said. "We can't move forward without it."

"Kilith was named," Enouim said.

"Everyone is strained and on edge," Ruakh said. "Think for a moment about why we are where we are. We are walking into a nearly hopeless situation, building our anxieties until they spill over onto each other. Oloren is right, we need clear leadership or all is lost."

"I'm not sure we do," Baird said. "I cannot put my life in the hands of those who do not trust me. Nor should you allow me to continue with you when you consider me a liability."

"Maybe so," Gabor said.

"What? No," Enouim exclaimed. "They were angry! You are valued here!"

Canukke guffawed, and Enouim glared at him. Gabor crossed his arms.

"He brags about his stealth, yet he jumped out of a canoe and dashed through Levav in plain sight, getting caught almost immediately," Canukke drawled.

"He was stealthy enough to take your precious wristband without your knowledge," Enouim said. Canukke looked up in surprise. "That's right, it was Baird, not Silas. And it was Baird that returned it to you, also without your knowledge. He saved me from the sea snake; he fought with us against Canus and his nomads. He has been with us every step of the way and borne all of your resentments. I blamed him for Pakel too, but I was wrong. Not everything is as simple as it seems."

Enouim looked around the group, scanning. Canukke's eyes were hard, Gabor's angry. Vadik shifted his feet. Serete seemed to be sizing everyone up, taking in the situation. Kilith wore a pained expression but said nothing. Why did he say nothing? Ruakh's mouth was parted, seeming to be at a loss for what to say. Oloren was withdrawn, quietly brooding.

Baird looked at her softly. "I think no more can be done here."

"We need every set of hands we can get!" Enouim pressed.

"Perhaps these hands are better suited to Kalka'an."

"This is so sudden. You've argued before and gotten through it."

"I've been thinking about this for a while. This is simply the push to show me the direction I must take. They are right —I left on a mission for the Ecyah Stone. We found Eh'yeh, and I have information to share with my people. They should know what we found. And though I have been willing from the beginning to follow it through to the end, I fear without trust I will do more harm than good. I will return to Kalka'an."

"Don't go," Vadik said. "We will work it out."

"Friend," Baird said, "I hope we meet again. But this mission is no longer mine."

40

The morning came in bright, oblivious to the company's troubles. Kilith, Vadik, Oloren, and Enouim all spoke to Baird, but he did not change his mind.

"The extra hands are not worth the danger that mistrust poses," he said. "My loyalties must now return to my own people, though my heart remains with you and my thoughts with your journey. May we meet again."

After this he gave Enouim his remaining ethanine in a pouch, bid them farewell, and left quickly on his horse. Oloren was hurt and angry, both at Baird for his decision and at Canukke and Gabor for causing it. Enouim felt much the same, but was more sad than angry with Baird. She worried that he was right and their mission was hopeless. And what if, even at their best and most unified, they would only die with honor?

The next several weeks passed with an unshakable somber tone, each member caught up in personal thoughts. With Baird gone, the tension did not dissipate but seemed instead to have been fueled. The forest changed from mostly flat to rockier and steeper. Great mountains loomed above them, lush and green, with two peaks rising above the others.

"Look!" Vadik said.

Kilith nodded. "The mountains Liombas and Katan, upon which the last valiant campaigns against tribesmen were fought. Never did I think I might ask for those days to be returned to us."

"We will be there in less than a week," Ruakh said. "And poor odds or no, if we are to move forward, the issue of leadership must now be addressed. The strain we have carried since Baird left us is as tangible as it is dangerous. We have several perfectly capable warriors with us who could lead, but a moment of indecision or dissension in Gorgenbrild could be the death of us all."

"I have been the leader of this mission since its beginning, when Bondeg and Twedori first thought of it," Canukke said. "Long before we set out, I was at its head. Some of you seem to be bitter toward me, but that is none of my concern. I do not see the value of wasting what little time we have left discussing questions we know the answers to."

"True leaders listen to the warriors under them," Enouim said.

Ruakh held up a hand. "We have to consider ability, experience, knowledge of the terrain and culture, knowledge of Sumu fighting tactics, as well as leadership style."

"I am comfortable with leading a squad," Serete stated, "but I am not familiar with the terrain closer to Gorgenbrild nor the culture into which we are walking. And this is not my fight. As it stands, I would gladly follow Kilith into battle."

"Kilith!" Canukke spat, eyes wide, jaw clenched.

"Canukke has been with us this long. Shall we not let him share the plans he had for the return?" Vadik asked. "Would it not dishonor him to take his position now, when he has been hand selected by our leaders back home?"

"Bondeg and Twedori approached Kilith also," Enouim reminded them. "And he has been our leader since Eh'yeh. Canukke is a skilled warrior, but his pride and insecurity are a problem. He began unraveling with the Nazir, and Eh'yeh was his undoing. Kilith has been our faithful leader ever since. Do not forget it was Kilith whom Eh'yeh gave instructions to in order to bring us to Rehim."

"You give your trust to the judgment of Eh'yeh, a man who has never seen Gorgenbrild?" Canukke exclaimed.

"No," Gabor said. "We give it to a man who is not a man, and whose breath gives life to the dead. And this man selected Kilith, who *has* seen Gorgenbrild. Though were Eh'yeh to appear in the flesh before us today, I would abandon Kilith's wisdom for Eh'yeh in a moment."

Kilith nodded. "I have held my peace for long enough. I have watched Canukke lead, and have followed and consulted long with him. Canukke, you are integral to our mission. You always have been and always will be. Bondeg and Twedori spoke to me at the beginning, and I have been in the planning process since its inception just as you have. Your strength in battle will not be laid aside, and we would be remiss to leave you out of any significant endeavor. It is our privilege to have you with us. Simultaneously, I echo some of the concerns of our friends in regard to your leadership at this stage. I will take us into Gorgenbrild. Based on experience, as we split into groups, Canukke and Serete will be leaders of teams. There are eight of us left. We will need more than one leader in the days ahead."

Enouim nodded and thumbed the scar on her collarbone. Canukke was upset, but after speaking with Kilith and Oloren seemed resigned to his role as co-leader of sorts with Kilith.

They had discussed for hours their final approach to Gorgenbrild, and a rough plan had begun to take shape. Enouim was nervous about her part in it. Her combat skills since leaving home were greater than the average, but questionable against experienced warriors, and her abilities with water were only helpful while she was actually in the river. As such, she would only be able to use it in the outskirts and the Sumus's camps rather than Gorgenbrild itself. Enouim rode next to Serete as they started up the mountain. He seemed surprisingly calm.

"This is insane," she said, shaking her head. "We are days away from Gorgenbrild with no plan, no numbers, no allies. Baird has left us, and I fear for the commitment of the others. Our families and friends may yet live in Gorgenbrild, but what good are we to them? Eight of us, against so many. It is impossible! What do you think? What should we do?"

He shrugged. "We'll figure it out."

"That's it? That's all you have to say?"

A nonchalant nod. "We will."

Enouim stared at him. This was not an acceptable answer to her. We'll figure it out? That's exactly what she was trying to do! And if they never discussed it, how would they ever figure it out? What if he just assumed a constant state of *we'll figure it out* until the moment of decision passed and the battle was upon them? Disaster! Disaster would ensue, that's what.

But then, Serete wasn't stupid. Surely he couldn't mean that. What else could he mean? Did he just mean they would talk about it later? How on earth he could live like that, not knowing the fullness of the plan but content nonetheless was utterly confounding to her.

Serete took her mind off their fates for a while, sharing memories of home and childhood. He told her riddles and jokes and lifted her out of her thoughts. Soon they had to move more cautiously and quietly, with a wary eye out for tribesmen scouting the woods.

They progressed this way for several days until they approached Gorgenbrild, and when they were only two hours away by foot, Kilith turned and spoke quietly. "From here we split up. As discussed—Oloren and Gabor, with Canukke around the south tunnels. Vadik and Enouim, with Serete trying the southwest tunnels. Ruakh, with me, to scout Sumu positions on the perimeter and surrounding camps."

"Remember the signal, and keep the ethanine powder close," Canukke said. "Anyone who does not make it out will be left for the sake of the mission. Watch each other's backs, and be on high alert. Utter silence from here on out. Meet at the rendezvous point in twenty-four hours with whatever you can find. Do not be late. Let's move."

ENOUIM'S HEART POUNDED, and her breathing was shallow as she scuffled along on her elbows in a narrow dirt tunnel. They had untacked the horses and hidden the supplies, leaving the horses well enough behind and as hidden as they could manage. Enouim was taking up the rear in the tunnel, with Serete in front and Vadik's boots in Enouim's face. The first tunnel they had come to, one Vadik was aware of, had been blocked. Some explosive seemed to have collapsed it, and the next was packed with rocks. Gratefully, the only other tunnel Vadik knew of remained untouched, and they made their way through it now. It seemed narrower and more crudely made than most Gorgenbrild tunnels, and Enouim wondered how old it was. It certainly wouldn't provide for a swift exit, so stealth was paramount to their escape.

All hint of light vanished as the tunnel wound round and

finally opened up enough to crawl on hands and knees. Enouim had a twig of some sort trapped in her boot, and shook her foot several times to free it, but it only sunk further down into her shoe. Shortly the opening narrowed again and finally opened to what Enouim guesstimated was a dirt vestibule about three feet high and four feet across. All three of them knelt in this space and paused, listening to whatever may be beyond them. They heard nothing except their own breathing. Hands began to pat at the walls and ceiling, and Enouim did the same, searching for the exit. In a moment of panic Enouim wondered if there wasn't one, and they had gone all that way only to find the entrance sealed off.

Vadik tapped her and she jumped at his touch, then turned his direction and saw the faintest sliver of light revealed to one side. He pushed the dirt wall gently and it swayed open a crack, enough to see that their position was part of a rock wall on the other side. Enouim pressed her eye to the crack and saw they were facing an open space in the center of Gorgenbrild. They must be in a space between the outer wall of Twedori's dwelling, and a false wall on the inside of the home. Sumus swarmed the area, twenty easily seen in a glance.

Serete brushed dirt away from the inside of the swinging panel and found a notch in the stone to pull it closed once more. Feeling around again, he took a small pebble on the ground and scraped away some of the dirt caked onto the inside of the panel. Enouim realized he wanted to see out without the entire door standing open, but the panel, made of stone bricks, would be perhaps two inches thick. Remembering the stick stuck in her boot, she reached down and retrieved it, then handed it to Serete. Ever so carefully and quietly, he worked at the dirt between the stones until a pinprick of light came through, then he passed the stick to

Vadik who did the same, then handed the stick to Enouim until each had a peephole beyond the wall.

Just as Enouim put her eye up to the hole she had made, she heard the distinct creak of a door and nearly jumped out of her skin. The door was no more than five feet from where they crouched and most certainly connected to the outer wall of which their panel was a part. Two men held torches on long poles to illuminate the dimness of dusk. They walked forward and tapped their poles twice on the ground. A gong sounded —one, two, three, four—and Gorgenbrilders stepped from the shadows into the open space.

They came like half dead forms, pale and gaunt, faces drawn. The shadows they emerged from settled underneath their eyes, and it seemed to Enouim that they themselves were shadows of who they used to be. Where was the fire of their souls? Where was the light in their eyes, the rage, the wild?

A Sumu man stepped forward between the lights with all the confidence of a king of kings. Enouim could only see him at an angle, as he faced mostly away from her and toward the crowd. He was not a tall man, perhaps no taller than Enouim, but his muscles rippled in arms that could likely snap her in half. A voice called out, "Hail the lord of the mountains, ruler born of the stars, Emperor of the East!"

So this was the mighty Malum Khoron-khelek. The man stood in a long silence as he observed the people standing before him. In the face of such hopelessness, the man's voice rang out powerful and clear. "A great new age has begun. Things have been hard. Your people have suffered. You have been starving; you have been hurt; you have felt the anguish of great loss." His voice rang out in the emptiness and hung in the air.

"Yet no more! When you cling to the old ways, they condemn you. You see what they have gotten you. Grief, sorrow, pain! Why must you do this to yourselves? As long as there is a *your people* and a *my people*, you will forever feel the unforgiving heel of the emperor upon your necks. But is not this what you would desire of your leader? My people are always protected, always well cared for, fought for to the bitter end. My people are never left to die when a new threat appears, as you have been. Desolate and alone, you have wasted away. Yet no more!

"I tell you what I have long told my men: if at the beginning you only ever do what is easy, you will eventually face much hardship. Well, I tell you, it is difficult to go against the pressure of friends and family telling us to do or say a certain thing. It is difficult to leave behind a legacy of murdering one's own people and open your eyes to a generation of peace. Here I am, ushering in this new day, and yet after all these months I still find resistance. And so the easy way out now turns to bitterness.

"Times are changing, and with it, we must adapt. Let go of the old, and put on the new. Lean into a bright new world of promise. Obedience is not so high a price for life. A new day has dawned. Let the old, who chain you to this condition, pass away."

As he said this, two Sumu soldiers dragged a man, bound hand and foot and badly beaten, out into the center. He seemed only half-conscious and moaned as he collapsed on the ground. One of the soldiers held a sword out in both hands as if to offer it to the people.

"This must happen to purify you, my people. This man, he has done nothing for you! Did he save you? Did he stop the iron fist of the Sumu Empire as it swept through Gorgenbrild? No!"

Khoron-khelek walked over and yanked the man's head back by the hair. Enouim sucked in a breath. It was Bondeg.

His face was bruised and one eye was swollen shut, but there was no mistaking the familiar face of the community leader. Khoron-khelek released Bondeg with a flourish. "And what does it mean to protect your people? Will you do what he could not? There is no honor in this man. He has not truly tried to protect you, or he would have either died in the effort or saved you all this trouble and allowed a peaceable union. Remove this plight from among you! Here at dusk, as we have done these past months, we are reminded by ritual that the old shall expire, and the new day, the new era, shall be established. With the sun comes new blessing. It is not I that afflict you, my friends, but those parasites who seek to bring you down to die with them in their folly, in the name of nationalism. You are the future, but how can a future be established on faltering ground? No, this new dynasty is built on a solid foundation, and weakness will be eradicated for the sake of our future.

"You hinder my blessing! I long to gather you under me as friends and comrades. Why this needless waste? I have never lied to you. But you lie to one another! We tell you we offer safety, food aplenty, and position for standing up for your people in the name of a Sumu Gorgenbrild. For it is only this Sumu Gorgenbrild that offers life as a possibility. Where is the courage? Where is the honor among you? May the brave rise up and take their rightful places among us! Why make us do these things? Come! May the man or woman who loves his land most stand first."

Enouim held her breath. Silence hung in the air as the men and women of shadow watched the spectacle. No one moved. No one spoke. No discernible expression could be seen on their faces. Why? No fear, no sadness, no anger. Numbness. Fury rose in her chest, competing with fear and an overwhelming sadness and helplessness. The injustice of what she was seeing burned in her heart, and the reality that she could do nothing about it rent it in two.

A full minute went by, Khoron-khelek simply watching and waiting. Two minutes. "I do not like to be kept waiting," he said in a warning tone, like a mother whose child had stepped out of line. Another thirty seconds, and a man from the crowd broke free in a frenzy, rushing the guard with the sword. For a moment Enouim was sure he would be killed on the spot, but at the last moment the man took the sword from the guard, whirled it in the air and brought it down on Bondeg's neck with a blood-curdling shriek. Enouim drew back in horror, shutting her eyes and begging to shut out the sounds assaulting her ears.

"It is done!" said Khoron-khelek with a grim smile. He put an arm around the man, who was heaving and seemed utterly beside himself. A tear slipped down the man's grimy cheek, and he ran a hand through his disheveled hair. Malum spoke again. "Tonight, my friend, you feast, and tomorrow, you taste the privilege of Sumu unity. Tonight!" his voice shattered the night in a great command, and he raised his fist in triumph. "The old dies, and blessing is ushered in with the morning! A meal comes in the morning for all of you, in honor of this man, a true patriot! May you all love your people and your land as this man does. Sleep well, my people!"

nouim trembled as she pulled away. Not only had Bondeg been murdered before her, but Khoron-khelek said it was a daily ritual. For months they had killed a resisting Gorgenbrilder at the end of each day. No wonder the people looked as if they walked in a fog. How else could they survive such horror, if not to shut out the world entirely?

Enouim rocked back on her heels and heaved a tormented sigh as a tear cleared a path down her dirty cheek. Hopeless. What could they do against so many? Serete and Vadik were still watching outside intently. She heard a dragging sound, and shut her eyes again. She didn't want to see it.

Vadik tapped her, and Enouim looked at him in the dim light coming through the pinpricks in the wall. He motioned that they would be going out, and for Enouim to stay put. She would watch and wait. Maybe for hours. Enouim nodded, then looked out again. Sumus had begun to disperse, but several remained nearby. Khoron-khelek went back inside Twedori's house, where he seemed to have staged himself. The message was clear: there was new leadership in Gorgenbrild. Enouim wondered if Twedori had been kept alive for a ritual killing, or been killed on the spot when the Sumus first swept through.

Serete reached for the panel, but Enouim shot her hand out and gripped his arm. She motioned furiously at the dirt wall behind them. Their hiding place was attached to Khoronkhelek's new headquarters! They would be seen. Serete leaned forward and placed a hand on the back of her neck, drawing her close to speak in her ear. "We'll be okay. Don't move unless you have to. Be safe." He took one more look through the panel and rolled out. Vadik waited several minutes before following suit.

Enouim sat in the dark, her heart beating like a thousand drums. At first her thoughts came so quickly that she could hardly focus on any, and she sat in a daze of confusion. Slowly the moments turned into minutes, and she began to identify the thoughts assaulting her consciousness. *We'll be okay?* He can't promise things like that! He doesn't know. Is my family okay? Is anyone? Who is this monster, and what has he done to my home? She felt like a stranger, at a loss in a distant land, a shadow of what she knew. Enouim leaned forward to look out once more. Night was closing in.

Few people were out now. Sentries patrolled at intervals, and the occasional Gorgenbrilder passed by, but for the most part all was quiet. A form crossed in the torchlight, and Enouim caught her breath. It was her mother, Qadra! Surely it was! Was her brother alive? How were they faring? She could wait no longer. Enouim paused for the sentries to pass once more and then swiftly pushed open the panel and rolled out, closing it softly behind her. She sat for a moment with her back against the rock wall, hidden by shadows, as the sentries made another pass.

Her movements needed to be smooth, she reminded

herself, but her heart rate was not level enough to cooperate. Too fast and she would be noticed, out of place. Breathe. Enouim bade her time, sitting against Khoron-khelek's headquarters, steadying her heart rate. If she waited too long, her mother would be gone.

Enouim lifted the hood of her mantle over her head and rose, moving forward as languidly as she could manage. Enouim turned the corner and picked up her pace, but her mother was gone. Enouim headed toward her house, and saw a man standing at the doorway of one of the homes as she walked. He turned, letting his thumb brush against the frame around the door as he did. It was Vadik, and the powder he left behind was ruddy red, like clay.

It was the signal—that house was unable or unwilling to assist them. Enouim made brief eye contact with him and continued walking, the two ignoring each other. She wondered what he thought of her abandoning her hiding place so soon. Still, she was grateful someone knew she was alive in case they beat her back to the tunnel.

Footsteps approached, and Enouim ducked around the bend and dropped to a lower level as another Sumu marched by. She saw none of her countrymen out and about anymore, and Enouim wondered if there was a curfew of some kind. She hugged the wall and clung to shadows as she made her way to her home, and tears stung her eyes at the relief of seeing it. There was only one young goat outside, no pigs, and no garden she could see. How was her mother faring on so little? A light was on inside.

Enouim opened the door to slip inside and stopped cold. Her mother stood backed against a wall in the hall facing the doorway, holding a blanket out to a strange man. Qadra looked up, eyes wide, and Enouim jumped back outside just before the man turned to see her. A Sumu tribesman was in her house.

Enouim dashed to the side of the house. What now? Another tribesman approached, and Enouim dropped into the goat's pen against the house in the shadows. If the Sumu inside came to investigate, she was done for.

"What was that?" a gruff voice demanded from within the house. The Sumu outside her house passed by, but the one inside sounded closer to the door.

"Just the goat, I'm sure," her mother responded. "Probably got out again. Please, rest. I will check on him."

Enouim held her breath, and the goat came to nuzzle her hands. It was skin and bone, poor thing. Enouim wrapped her arms around it and held it close, stroking its fur. Qadra appeared at the doorway, looking out. Drawn she looked, Enouim thought—older than she remembered.

Her mother turned, saw her sitting in the darkness and came to fall on her knees beside her, crushing the goat between them as they embraced. After a moment, Qadra whispered frantically in her ear. "You can't stay here! I told them you were dead. They took your room. They have infiltrated every home in Gorgenbrild. They will kill you!"

"You told them I was dead?"

"I thought you were—you fled from Chayan and were never seen again. She swore honor, that her vengeance would not surpass the transgression, but then you disappeared completely. I feared the worst. Glintenon! He smiles on us even now." Qadra hugged her again.

"Mother, I have been searching for Eh'yeh."

Qadra drew back and looked at her, searching her eyes. She didn't understand.

"The Ecyah Stone. It's a long story—I accidentally ended

up on the mission with Canukke Topothain after Chayan chased me down and have been with them ever since."

Qadra clasped her hands together in silent praise. "So many questions. What adventures. There you go, following after your father after all. Well, I will stand in your way no longer. And the stone?"

"Yes! It is—well, it is not what we thought it was. He is a man, mother, greater than anyone you have ever known!"

"A man! Why, he must be terribly old by now. Perhaps legend has mistold it. Perhaps ... oh, never mind. We don't have the time. But this man, he comes to save us?" Qadra whispered, hope flooding her face. Enouim nodded. "Does he have an army?"

"He ... well, I don't know," answered Enouim honestly. She hadn't considered this before. She had seen the Malak guards, and certainly there were no fiercer warriors than they. But an army? And her mother expected a different kind of army than any she could describe from Eh'yeh.

"He sent us back to you. He knows everything that has happened. There are nine ... well, eight of us." Enouim's stomach soured as she realized Baird was no longer with them.

"Eight!" Qadra shook her head, and all trace of hope extinguished from her eyes. "Eight! He is a fool, or worse, and he sends you to die with the rest of us. No! Do not let this man win, Enouim. Leave now, while you still can—if you still can. No one knows you are here. Most of the tunnels are blocked, but ... how did you get in? Get out, get out now. Don't look back, Enouim. They will kill you."

"But mother, I—"

"Qadra!" A harsh voice cut the air, coming from inside the house. "Was it the goat?"

Qadra stood abruptly, and Enouim passed her the goat

when she reached for it. "Yes, I have him," she called back, voice breaking. "His foot was stuck. I'm coming now."

Qadra looked deep in her daughter's eyes, taking her in one last time. "Go now," she said. "Our time is passing. Get out, and do not look back. Be careful. Be free. Get out." And with that her mother darted back into the house, goat cradled in her arms, as a light rain began to fall.

ENOUIM SAT IN THE DARK, listening to the rain. Her mother didn't want their help. She had given up. Qadra was a Gorgenbrilder. Never to turn, never to abandon the fight. Relentless, resilient. But the fire had gone out.

Unsure of what to do, but knowing she couldn't stay there forever, Enouim got up and headed back toward Twedori's house. Her mind was in a tumult, and as she walked she was only dimly aware of the steps before her. Enouim pulled her hood closer around her face and ducked her head as the rain rose from a soft drizzle to a driving downpour. She quickened her pace and hugged the buildings and walls as she went.

She turned a sharp corner and ran straight into a solid frame. Enouim looked up, startled. An equally startled tribesman stood before her, but his face quickly recovered and turned to flint. "Who are you?" he demanded.

Enouim's eyes widened, and she opened her mouth to speak, but no sound came out. It was just as well. What could she have said?

"Where do you think you're going? No one is to be out at this hour," the man growled. "And yet here you are." The man leaned forward to examine her in the rain, gripping her upper arm. "I don't recognize you. Why have I not seen you before?"

"Please, I ... er ... I got turned around." Enouim rolled her eyes at herself. A toddler could have been more convincing.

The man's eyes narrowed, and his grip tightened. This was insane. Insane! In a panic, the only thing Enouim could think to do was to double down on the crazy. "My goat!" she exclaimed, tossing her hands up in the air. "My goat is mad at me! He ran away! Oh, what ever will I do? My best friend! My favorite dinner! My family! He's all I have left!" Enouim clutched at the man's leather breastplate, bulging her eyes out at him as far as they could go. The Sumu leaned away from her, looking confused. "Have you seen me? Have you seen him? Have you taken my goat?" Softly Enouim began to sob, sinking to the ground. Suddenly she stood and raised her voice at him, furious. "You took him and ate him! You ate my son! How could you do this to me, after being friends for so long?!"

Caught off guard, the tribesman loosened his grip, and Enouim kneed him in the groin and fled. A grunt from the man behind her was followed by heavy footsteps. She didn't have long. Enouim flew around another corner and leaped up a short wall to the level above, running on the soggy sod as quickly as she could manage. She slipped on the wet grass of an abandoned horse pasture, and drew the knife from her boot before staggering forward.

A thud warned her the Sumu tribesman had made the leap and was on her heels. Enouim veered left, running along the edge of the pasture on top of the rocky ledge, and as the wall rose with the ground, the houses on the level below stood at the same height as the pasture. She heard another shout and knew the chase had not gone unnoticed. Enouim jumped from the wall to the roof of a house and ran along it to the end. The tribesman followed, and Enouim looked for a way down.

She was on top of Bondeg's house, the exact spot she had

been in six months before, except a Sumu tribesman was on her heels in place of Chayan. Enouim twisted as the man ran toward her and with a flick of her wrist let her knife fly. The knife sunk into her pursuer's neck ten feet from her, and he kept coming for one final long leap as the momentum of the knife drove his head back and his body continued forward. He swayed and slipped down the roof and over the edge, crashing to the ground below.

Enouim whirled and used the window ledge she remembered from the Chayan incident to drop down to the ground. She ran to the man. Blood poured from his neck and washed away in the rain as he spent his last moments aspirating his own blood. She couldn't leave him in the open. Enouim peeked through the window. Nothing. Enouim grabbed his wrists and tugged the man around the corner to Bondeg's door and opened it.

The table Enouim had hidden under remained exactly where it had been before. Enouim lugged the man through the doorway and over to the small table and felt for the knob underneath it. The trap door swung open. The tribesman lay still now, and Enouim snatched a cloak draped over the table to mop up blood on the floor before draping his hands over the hole to keep the trap door from closing, closed the door to Bondeg's home, and climbed into the hole. Standing four feet deep with her head poking out, Enouim took hold of the man's forearms and pulled him into the small space after her, letting the trap door swing closed to shut them in.

Sitting in the dark once again, Enouim's chest felt like it might explode. Her breath caught in her lungs as she sat with her back against the dirt wall, the dead man draped in her lap. She had killed him.

Someone ran by above her outside the house, but no one entered. Enouim closed her eyes. What now? If she was caught, she would be executed either on the spot or in ritual, in front of all of Gorgenbrild. If she wasn't caught, what would they make of the man's disappearance? Who would be blamed? Did anyone see her enter the house?

Out of pitch blackness Enouim heard a rustling sound down the tunnel. Her frantic heart stood still. She wasn't alone. She felt along the dead man's body and up to his neck to retrieve her knife. She winced and tugged, but it didn't move, so she propped the Sumu up in front of her as a shield. Another movement in the darkness. Silence.

Her breath came quickly. She couldn't see her own hand in the darkness, much less whoever crouched beyond. The rain continued to pound outside, unaware of the tension below. Finally Enouim could take it no more. *If I'm going to die anyway, I might as well get it over with.*

"Who ... who's there?" she asked. She had hoped to sound commanding, but her voice wavered.

"Enouim? Is that you?"

"Who are you?"

"It's Gabor. It's me. You're okay."

Relief flooded through her. "Gabor! I've never been so glad to hear anyone's voice in all my life. What are you doing down here? This tunnel only leads to the outskirts by the cliff."

"Well, maybe once it did. Not anymore. It's an underground meeting network. There's a meet going on right now, but we heard the noise when you entered the passage and I came to investigate. I'm sure they will all be glad to hear they aren't going to be found out and slaughtered tonight."

"Well, don't speak too soon. A tribesman chased me and I—"

"Zegrath's teeth. You were followed?"

"Yes, just outside. He's ... he's dead, Gabor. He's in here with me, dead. I'm holding a corpse between us right now."

Realizing the truth and sudden absurdity of what she'd just said, Enouim released the body abruptly, and it fell to the side against the wall. "My knife is still in his throat."

"Get it out. You'll need it yet, and we are running short on weapons of all kinds. Get it out and let's go. I'll come back to get him, just move him out from under the trap door."

"Ugh. Do I have to?"

"Well, gee, Enouim, do you want to live?" Gabor hissed. "Hurry!"

Enouim rolled her eyes in the darkness but did as she was told. She ran her fingers up the corpse once more, gripped the hilt of her knife with both hands, and yanked it free. Enouim clambered over him and dragged the body out from under the trap door, further into the passage.

"Where are you?" Enouim swung her hand out blindly in front of her.

"Here, I'm right ... *aghhh*!! Your hand is wet. Did you get Sumu blood on me?"

"Well, *gee*, Gabor, what do you think? Let's go. I'm claustrophobic in here as it is. Please tell me this new meeting room is wider than three feet across."

"Oh, it is ... but I wouldn't get your hopes up for a palace or anything. Follow me."

Enouim followed Gabor down the tunnel, and after a few minutes he paused and took a turn off to the side. Soft, indiscernible voices drifted out to them as they continued down into the new tunnel, until finally they were dumped out into a room about twenty feet by fifteen feet with wooden support beams. In it twenty or so Gorgenbrilders circled around Canukke as he spoke.

"We need more numbers! How many of you know someone who could join us when the time comes?"

"We are divided, I am afraid," answered one. "It's hard to

know who is friend or foe. Khoron-khelek murders any openly resisting him, or forces one of us to do it publicly. If you speak to a neighbor, he may share our desires for freedom, but fear death."

"Worse still, he may consider it a moment to better himself and turn you in for a meal and more comfortable lodging, or status," another put in.

Canukke shook his head. "This is not the Gorgenbrild I know. The Gorgenbrild I know is built on loyalty and strength, and an honor that would not be parted from it even in death. How has one evil man stolen your valiant essence? My friends, now is the time to rise up!"

"There are those of us who would, if there were enough of us to make it anything but suicide," remarked a third.

A murmur passed around the group.

"We tried it, didn't we, last time? And the time before that?"

"What have we to lose?"

"We've already lost too much. Perhaps Khoron-khelek will hold to his promises and we can earn a life worth living. As barbaric as he is, he has been true to his word so far."

"Listen to yourselves," Canukke exclaimed. "Where are my countrymen? Where are the warriors that fought by my side against these tribesmen time and again over the last decades? If you are not warriors of honor, you cannot claim yourselves of Gorgenbrild. And if you are not of Gorgenbrild, who are you of? The Sumus? Are you tribesmen, too, blown about by whatever your abhorrent authority tells you is true? Well, I say never! Never to turn! Gorgenbrild! Reignite the fire in your souls!

"I would die valiantly a thousand times before I would waste away a hollow old man. I hear your frustrations, your fears. But do you know what I fear? I fear existing without purpose, under the thumb of a grotesque man drunk on his own grand illusions. I fear losing myself. If I die, I will die a man of honor! Who are these tribesmen to challenge us? Did we not drive them back ten to one in the campaign of Liombas-Katan? Simmet, tell me ... how many men did you purge from the earth that day?"

"Twenty-three!" Simmet responded proudly. "But I did not come close to your number, if I recall!"

"Twenty-three! Cokar, what was your number?"

"Twenty-six, no mistake," Cokar answered, nodding.

"Twenty-six! You speak of numbers, my friends, but we are not a ten-to-one people. We are a twenty-to-one people on a rainy day! Some have lost hope, you say. Some tuck their tails and turn themselves over to the whim of that tyrant. If they do not know how to respond, let us show them. If there is no safety in words, let us prove ourselves in action. Give hope now to the hopeless, and as the tide turns, see who is willing to join us then! But we need leaders! And who better to lead than a warrior of Gorgenbrild? Fight with me again!"

Cheers went up from the modest crowd, before someone shushed them to keep volume down.

"You have come too late, friend," said a man on the other side of the room. Enouim couldn't see his face, but his voice was raspy and worn. "It will take more than a few inspirational words to get Gorgenbrild out of the clutches she has fallen into. You say all we have to do is rise up, but it is madness! On Liombas-Katan, we were well supplied and prepared. Now weapons are scarce, and those we have are carefully hidden. Our physical strength wanes even as our minds struggle to cling to hope. You are a worthy fighter, Canukke, but it is not enough. These months you have been gone, we held out hope that you might return borne on the crest of Glintenon's will, with the Ecyah Stone as the bane of our enemies. But you come empty handed! You should have stayed gone. Let those who wish to leave organize their escape, and those who wish to live remain."

Enouim spoke up. "Glintenon stands with us still." All heads in the room turned toward her. "And he is sent by Eh'yeh—Ecyah himself. We do not come home in vain. Our visible strength is dismal, but as Vadik could tell you, the greatest strength is often invisible."

"Perhaps there is simply no spark left to ignite in some of us, visible or no," said a woman standing in the middle of the gathering. "What fire could burn in these conditions?"

"What fire!" Canukke cried. "It is not the fault of the fire that you failed to fan it into flame. No, the fire is roaring, and ready to be let out of its cage. How long will you pretend to be a demure little bird when you have always been a zegrath? What zegrath deigns to be kept as a pet? It is indecent! It is against the laws of nature! They have pulled a tooth, but they do not have our hide, and our claws and spikes are as deadly as ever. You want a fire? I will give you a fire. Swear to me that when you see it, you will take me at my word and rise to fight —if not under me, then under Glintenon himself. Swear it!"

Nodding, more murmurs.

"My people," Canukke said, shaking his head. "The oaths of men of valor are not taken in secret. We fight to live a life worth living or we die in the effort and reclaim our honor. We defend our people, our land, our personhood! Never to turn! For what were you born if not this moment? This is the day our children's children will establish in the memory of all generations to come as the turning point, the day when Gorgenbrild lived up to its name. Never to turn! Swear it!"

"By Glintenon!"

"My sword!"

"Sworn!"

The room seemed to have picked up an electric current, and Enouim felt goosebumps prickle her flesh as she saw the ragged, hopeless lot before her brighten and steady their resolve. Gabor appeared behind them with Enouim's downed Sumu and a ripple of bloodlust seemed to have taken hold of them all. With a tribesman killed, the status quo was already tipped, and if something didn't happen soon, ritual killings might increase in hopes of exposing the killer.

Cokar produced a knife and flung it into the Sumu's lifeless form. "Never to turn!" Cheers.

Simmet walked up and plunged his own knife into the corpse. "May he be the first of many!"

Enouim grimaced. She looked down at the knife she still held and wiped it on the dirt to clean it, then on her clothes. She wanted no part of blood for the sake of blood. Only to survive.

42

The meeting carried on into the early morning hours. Canukke told Enouim to get some rest, and the plan would be explained again back at camp. She needed no further urging, and had curled in the corner and nodded off. She woke to Gabor gently shaking her.

"Time to go, Enouim," he said.

"What? Go? It's not light out yet," she mumbled, rubbing her eyes.

"Yes it is. You're underground, silly. Time to go."

Enouim bolted upright. She was underneath Gorgenbrild. There had been a meeting—where was everyone? Canukke held up a dwindling torch next to one of four exits from the room, gesturing them forward.

"Gabor, you first," he instructed. "Enouim, you're next, and I follow. No lights from here on out. This tunnel leads to the outskirts, and then we will have one more tunnel to go."

Gabor climbed into the tunnel, and Enouim clambered after him. When they came to the end of the tunnel, Gabor pressed on the side of the wall and it swung outward. Gabor peered out, then disappeared through the opening.

Enouim worked her way up to the opening on her elbows, and saw it dumped out straight into the wall of someone's bedroom, several feet from the ground. Enouim marveled at the many creative passageway options Gorgenbrild afforded them by sprawling across so many different levels of terrain.

Gabor held his hand out to her and helped pull her out of the tunnel and into the room. Once Canukke followed, Gabor closed the tunnel entry again and Enouim saw that a weapon display case hung in that space. It was empty now, and Enouim assumed Khoron-khelek had either emptied it or the owner had hidden the items from sight.

Canukke strode across the room and ducked through the open window without pause. Enouim began to follow when Gabor gripped her wrist and gestured her to wait. After a couple minutes, he let her go and nodded. Stepping forward, she dipped her head through and crossed to the other side of the street, scanning for Canukke.

She saw him some thirty paces away, and slowly began making her way in that direction. There were a few people out and about, tribesmen and Gorgenbrilders alike, making as little contact with each other as possible. Enouim, Canukke, and Gabor continued on, keeping distance between the three of them but always within eyesight.

Up ahead, Enouim saw Canukke's broad form suddenly duck out of view between two houses. Enouim quickened her pace and looked around the corner. Canukke was nowhere to be seen. Glancing back and seeing Gabor, Enouim ducked in the row where she had seen Canukke disappear. She glanced in windows, and down the road. Nothing. Enouim turned around to look how close Gabor was. He would know what to do.

Except that Gabor wasn't there. Enouim spun around, panicked, and saw a Sumu tribesman had taken interest in her antics. Leaning against the wall of a house, he straightened as he watched her. It was only then that Enouim realized there was no good reason for a Gorgenbrilder to be so intensely focused now that they were overrun. No one looked quite so motivated anymore, much less at this hour. Enouim looked back at the tribesman, then tried to pass him by on the far side.

As she did, the tribesman pushed off the wall and took several steps to block her passage. "Where are you going so quickly?"

"I lost my ... goat," she answered, eyes still on the ground. Clearly all her behavior could be blamed on goats now.

"Your goat? There are hardly any left. If it's been out long, someone else has taken it by now. Head on home."

"I'll do that. But I've already been in circles. Home is this way." Enouim gestured beyond the man.

"No one can pass this way."

"Why not?"

The Sumu examined her closely. "Everyone knows this is a restricted area. The better question is, why didn't you know that?"

"I forgot, that's all. Turned around by the goat."

"I saw no goat."

"Neither have I! That's the problem," she reminded him.

He narrowed his eyes. "I don't recognize you. Come with me."

"I have to get back home! Look, I'll let the goat go, but I have to leave now. I'm sorry I lost my bearings, but I won't do it again."

"Ah, so we are bargaining now?" scoffed the Sumu. "I said come with me."

"What for?"

"What for! It doesn't matter. What matters is that I—stop!"

What he said didn't matter much to Enouim, though. She wheeled and fled. The nearest clear tunnel was in the opposite direction, through the restricted area to Twedori's house. Going around would take too much time. To make matters worse, Gabor and Canukke were still missing.

A shout behind her was followed by another, alerting her that she was already outnumbered. Enouim rounded the corner and dove through an open window. She rolled to a stop, footsteps pounding toward her. A bed was made up on the floor, a doll made of grass beside it. Beside the bed was a small table with a Sumu mantle draped over it. A tall crate of blankets sat in the corner. Enouim pulled out the blankets and climbed into the crate, pulling the blankets on top of her as quickly as she could. A baby whimpered nearby, and two sets of footsteps brought the whimper into the room with Enouim.

"If they find you, all three of us die," said a woman's voice in hushed tones. "You, me, and the baby."

"I don't understand. Did they ..." a man's voice trailed off, gruff with emotion.

"You were never good with numbers, were you?" hissed the woman. "She's two months old. Two. You've been gone for seven. Do the math."

"Why would you hide this from me?"

"Hide it!" exclaimed the woman, her words steeped in contempt. "You were distracted. All about the next adventure. Too wrapped up in the next badge of honor, or the bottom of a glass of meade to see what was at the end of your nose! I was sick for weeks, and you never took notice. I let you believe whatever you wanted to believe. It was better that way, Canukke."

Enouim's mouth dropped open from under the blankets. She knew this woman's voice. It was Edone.

"Please ... can I?" Canukke asked. Enouim couldn't see, but imagined him reaching out to the baby.

"I think you'd better not," Edone sniffed. "You could be dead tomorrow. And if you spend another second here, she will be too. We all will."

"No one saw me. Edone ..."

A pause. Enouim felt incredibly uncomfortable being privy to such a private moment. Still, she knew they had even less time than they thought. But what could she do? Just pop out of the blanket box with news of her latest caper?

"Someone ran by. Something is going on. It's only a matter of time."

She had to say something. Enouim reached up to claw the blankets out of the way, so abruptly that the crate tipped and spilled her out onto the floor. Canukke and Edone gaped at her, frozen. The baby in Edone's arms smiled.

"Err ... hello, Edone. Canukke?" Enouim stammered.

Edone gasped. "Enouim?"

"We have to go," Enouim said to Canukke. "Sorry. I ... did something. People looking. Gabor missing. You disappeared! And we apparently aren't supposed to be ..."

"Get up," Canukke growled, face turning to flint. Just like that, he closed himself off and again became the warrior. He turned to look again at Edone, softening as he took in the sight of his wife and daughter.

Allowing himself no more, Canukke snatched the Sumu mantle off the table and shrugged into it. Canukke gripped Enouim's wrist in a tight vise, and she winced as he pulled her to the window. "You will stay close. You will say nothing, and you will do everything I tell you. If I tell you to fall on the ground, you drop like a sack. If I tell you to run, you run like your life depends on it—because my every word is life to you, you understand?"

Enouim stared at him.

Canukke put his face an inch from her nose and spoke again. "Do. You. Understand?"

Enouim nodded.

Canukke gave her a short nod, then looked out the window again. He glanced back at Edone one more time. "I will come for you." With that, he stepped out the window and dragged Enouim behind him. Outside the window, he pulled Enouim in front of him, gripping her left elbow with his left hand, and putting a knife at her back with his right.

"Crouch a little," Enouim hissed. "You're too tall for a Sumu."

"A quick enough glance and we'll make it," he whispered, but he bent his knees as he shoved her forward.

They came to the end of the row, passing where Enouim had met the Sumu soldier before. Canukke was moving at a clipped pace, and she stumbled to keep her feet. As they rounded the corner, she saw several tribesmen scattered about, one guarding a barred wooden cage four feet wide and six feet tall. A woman stood inside it, leaning back against the side with her arms crossed. She looked up as Canukke and Enouim passed, and Enouim's eyes widened. It was Chayan.

Their eyes locked for a moment as they passed, but now instead of hate Enouim saw fear. Chayan's glance drifted from Enouim's face to Canukke's hooded form, and recognition flooded her expression. Looking ahead, Enouim saw they were almost there—rounding one more corner to the right would lead them to Twedori's tunnel. Still, there were now eight tribesmen milling about between them and where they needed to go. The guard by the cage had let them pass, but now another Sumu approached.

Just then Chayan reached through the bars and yanked the guard back toward her, wrapping her arm around his neck and choking him from behind. Shouts ensued and the men ran to the cage. Enouim heard a thud as something heavy hit the ground. She tried to turn back and see what was happening, but Canukke's knife dug into her back and his grip on her elbow tightened.

"This is for us," he hissed. "Make it count."

Canukke pushed her ahead of him as they turned the corner, and more shouts and the clash of steel proved that somehow Chayan was still fighting from within her cage. Three more tribesmen ran past them as they reached the tunnel. In the commotion, Enouim and Canukke managed to slip inside without attracting attention.

Enouim paused in the passage, afraid for Chayan. What would happen to her? But it was out of their hands.

"Go!" Canukke demanded.

She went.

THEY MADE it back to the rendezvous point, where Ruakh and Kilith were waiting with the bows, arrows, and other weaponry they had scavenged. Enouim and Canukke went to check on the horses, hiding them as best as they could and caking mud on the distinctive white markings on Inferno's hindquarters. No Gorgenbrilder or Sumu horse had them.

There was no good way to get the horses into Gorgenbrild, so all they could do was untack them, take as many supplies as they could manage, and hide the rest. By the time Canukke and Enouim returned, Gabor and Oloren had made it back. Gabor let Canukke have a piece of his mind for disappearing. He'd watched Enouim wandering about looking for Canukke, but knew better than to follow suit. When he saw that the guard had run by empty handed, Gabor found his way back on his own.

Knowing they couldn't stay out in the open, Gabor climbed a tree at the rendezvous to keep an eye out for Serete and Vadik while Enouim created an air bubble in the river and floated the rest of them to the bottom. The river ran through the woods just east of Gorgenbrild and continued on southeast the way they'd come. Enouim sat cross-legged inside the bubble on the cold, wet ground at the bottom of the river, listening to the others strategize.

"... still, at this point, I wonder if it's not a better idea to smuggle out as many as we can," Oloren was saying. "Then make the assault from there. If we die, we die; this way at least some of our people may survive. Once a true rebellion breaks out, Khoron-khelek will slaughter everyone rather than continue the games he has been playing."

"It would attract too much attention." Ruakh shook his head sadly. "I think that may be as quick a road to death as any."

"We got eight people in and out successfully," Oloren answered. "Perhaps we can get just enough out to assist us."

"Serete and Vadik aren't back yet," Canukke reminded her. "But it is true, eight people is less than ideal for launching an assault. There are several men I would want by my side, but of those willing to join us, we still need a number of them waiting inside Gorgenbrild."

"Ruakh and I brought back far more bows and arrows than we have manpower for," noted Kilith. "I think we can make it appear we are a larger force than we are."

Enouim squeezed her eyes shut for a moment, focusing on the feel of the river around her. She pressed a hand to the earthy river bottom, still wet. The river coursed by them, sure and steady, consistent, predictable. She wished life was more like that. For a moment Enouim allowed herself to breathe in the tranquility of the river, a calm that may well have an expiration date. Who knew what tomorrow would bring?

As her thoughts began to wander, Enouim felt something nudge her, but she didn't pay it any heed. Suddenly Canukke gave a disgusted yell, and Enouim's eyes snapped open. He was sopping wet.

Oloren laughed. "Stay with us, Enouim! You started to drift, and the bubble wavered and plopped the world's biggest raindrop right on his head!"

"When you startled and opened your eyes, the bubble widened and resettled," Ruakh added. "Looks like it requires a little more focus."

"Sorry," she said, grimacing at Canukke's expression.

"He'll get over it." Ruakh grinned.

Kilith couldn't help but smile.

"That is good to know though," Oloren said. "You will need to pay attention so we don't get swept away out of the blue."

Enouim nodded. Just then she heard a dull splash—she felt it, too, in a way—and saw Gabor swimming down toward them. Placing a hand on the wall of water beside her to increase her accuracy, Enouim pulled a bubble down from the surface to envelop him as he swam, and carried him down to join them—all while sitting peacefully on the river floor.

Gabor was dumped rather unceremoniously into their circle, and he looked at her in wonder. He shook his head, but seated himself, and gestured toward the surface. "They're coming now."

Enouim closed her eyes, hand still on the edge of the waters. Two more forms stepped into the water, and she carefully divided the river on either side of them. She heard Vadik yelp, and then Vadik and Serete walked right down the riverbank and to the river bottom, Enouim allowing the river to close over the bubble, like a tunnel. Soon all eight were sitting in a circle together, recounting what had happened in Gorgenbrild. Canukke said nothing of his daughter, and Enouim respected his wishes.

"You weren't supposed to leave the passageway," Vadik scolded Enouim.

"*Unless I had to,* you said," Enouim corrected.

"And you had to?" Serete asked.

"Er ..." Enouim paused. Okay, so technically she didn't *have* to. "I mean, it was right next to the Sumu headquarters. Not the safest of places."

"She went on a killing spree," Gabor added. "Turns out she's Gorgenbrilder through and through!"

"You *what*?" Vadik and Serete exclaimed at once.

Enouim jumped, and the bubble around them wavered.

"Careful, boys, or you'll drown us all," Canukke cautioned dryly.

Enouim regained her composure. "Okay, first of all, it was hardly a spree. I left because I saw my mother and needed to make sure she was okay. And I only killed one person. It was either him or me, and I did not enjoy it. I would very much like to have this whole ordeal over with to avoid killing people in the future."

"Hardly people, these tribesmen!" Vadik spat.

"They certainly have the brains for a successful takeover, though," Serete said. "And their numbers are nothing to sneeze at. We are too few, even with the bloodthirsty swords of a hopeful handful inside."

"Kilith, what was this you mentioned about making it seem like there are more of us than there are?" Oloren asked.

"The bows and arrows ... we brought rope too, and a few other things. I think we can booby trap them to fire from multiple directions at once. The trick will be that each rig will only fire once, since it will be impossible to reset the traps on the move. But maybe that is all we need ... enough to draw attention and distract."

Ruakh began drawing in the damp dirt, laying out the Sumu camp. "Meanwhile, we set up here and here," he said, emphasizing these on his map in the ground. "The surprise and confusion will give us an advantage. But we will need more than a few bow and arrow tricks to get things going."

"The Sumus need to be thrown in as great a disarray as possible to offset our numbers and give us a chance to send the signal inside." Gabor began drawing Gorgenbrild itself, marking tunnels with the small stones and bits of plant life around him. "At least two of us need to enter Gorgenbrild and fan out to send the signal and rally the people—three really, if we want a real shot at this. And three should truly be more like sixteen, but I suppose we must work with what we have."

"A big enough distraction, and we can skip the tunnels altogether and take horses," Oloren suggested. "We just need one or two of us in the trees to provide cover."

"That will spread us too thin," Serete said. "Perhaps we can wrangle their horses once we are inside."

"Where am I supposed to be?" Enouim asked. The thought of being left to fend for herself in hand-to-hand combat made her nauseous.

"Despite your remarkable achievement of surviving last night, your strength is in the river," Canukke said. "Upriver from here, it runs right through their camps. That is where you will take up your position."

Enouim breathed a sigh of relief. The river was her safety.

"We brought more knives for you, too," Kilith said. "You have good aim, so we'll strap you with as many as we can. We may set booby traps or light fires or any number of things as distractions from our small force, but you are the greatest weapon we have at our disposal. You can course through water at breakneck speeds, and you have power over anything in the water. Part of our responsibility will be to give you material—whatever we dump in the river will be yours to play with."

Enouim smiled. "I can do that."

"You said you wanted all this to be over so you wouldn't have to kill anyone, but it's not over yet," Vadik said. "You need to be willing to do what it takes. The mission might be doomed already, but if you fail to give one-hundred percent, you may as well dig our graves."

Enouim's eyes widened.

"No pressure," Gabor laughed. "You'll do what it takes in the moment. You will be fine."

She swallowed, suddenly unsure of herself again.

"Don't worry. We won't leave you alone," Serete added.

"I still think we need to find a way to get the horses into Gorgenbrild—at least enough to rally everyone together," Oloren said. "And we need more than a few fake arrow shots or even Madzi magic to disguise the fact that there are only eight of us."

Enouim thumbed her collarbone, then ran her hands along her belt. She touched the edge where she had memorialized Pakel, and thought of all there was still left to lose. She wondered what Baird was doing now, and if he had made it back safely to Kalka'an. Her hands traveled across her belt to finger the small pouch at her waist.

When she spoke again, she spoke in sync with Serete: "I have an idea."

43

"You first."

"No, go ahead."

"Well, it's pretty simple really." Enouim tugged the pouch off her waist and held it up. "Ethanine. Could we sneak it into their food supply?"

Vadik laughed. "Perfect! How much is there?"

"I don't know—this much?" Enouim tossed him the pouch.

He took it with glee and peeked inside.

"It won't take much to knock them out if it's ingested," Serete noted, nodding. "Where did you get that?"

"Baird gave it to me before he left."

"Figures—Kalka'aners love their plants and potions!"

"How do we get it in their food?" Oloren asked.

"Sumus make large batches of soup in their main camp," Kilith said, "and then have dried meats and whatever they hunt. The main camp supply would be our target, if we can get to it."

"We can kill them quickly on our way in, once the ethanine puts them to sleep," Gabor said. "Or even afterward if we give them enough. It lasts a long time."

"We're going to kill sleeping Sumus? That doesn't seem right," Enouim objected. "Why can't we just leave them lie and capture them or something?"

"Doesn't seem right, eh?" Gabor said. "You know what else doesn't seem right? Tribesmen slaughtering people. Eight morons against an army. No way we can capture that many anyway. We need to even the odds."

"They're animals, Enouim," Canukke agreed. "Dying in sleep is too good for them."

"I don't think we should be part of a mass slaughter." Enouim turned to Serete. "What was your idea?"

Serete grinned. "What greater distraction is there than a zegrath tearing through camp?"

"And you are the zegrath whisperer, are you?" Gabor asked.

"Pretty much," Oloren said. "He has studied them and can track them to their dens."

"Even if you found one, how could you make it go where you want?" Vadik asked.

"Pups," Ruakh said.

Serete nodded. "Exactly. Zegrath pups stay in the den while mom goes out to hunt. If we take the pups, mom's incredible sense of smell will lead her in all her fury to precisely wherever we drop them off."

Canukke smiled. "I love it."

Enouim frowned. "What if the mother is in the den when we get there?"

"Run." Gabor smirked.

"Zegrath hunting is hardly a spectator sport, so we won't all be going. We'll be quieter if we take only as many as we need.

Still, zegrath pups take some wrangling. Litters are usually one to three pups, and we may only take two if there is a third. Two men per pup is still a handful. Kilith, who do you want me to take?"

"Canukke, Gabor, and Oloren can go with you," Kilith said.

"What? Why can't I go?" Vadik demanded.

"You and Ruakh can focus on the ethanine plan," Kilith answered, "and any other powder or plant related tricks you have in mind. Enouim and I will go over strategies for the river."

"We are going to have to move quickly once the pups are in hand, if you are able to find any," Ruakh reminded them. "Our horses are still exposed and could trigger an alarm if found."

"So to review ..." Kilith paused. "We have booby trapped bows and arrows to set up and trigger, ethanine to sneak into meals, and zegrath babies to catch and let loose in the camps. Two or three of us need to go into Gorgenbrild, either by foot or by horse, to start the revolt from inside. Enouim will be causing an uproar in the river through the camps, and several of us will accompany her there. Enouim, perhaps you can smuggle some of us further upriver so we can attack from the north as well, rather than just the south and southeast. The thinner we spread them, the better off we'll be. They will not be expecting opposition from outside—much less from the north. On these bare bones we will make our final stand. For Gorgenbrild! Never to turn."

———

"I HAVEN'T HAD much time to practice," Enouim said to Kilith, as they discussed what the battle might look like from the river. The two of them had climbed a tree to talk out of sight while Ruakh and Vadik went off in search of useful plants.

"You can do this," Kilith reminded her. "It's in your blood, so let your body take over when your mind doubts. And if you get hurt, you can't stop. There is no giving up—giving up is death."

A rustle down below was followed by an ear-splitting screech.

"We got them," a voice called.

Enouim looked down through the branches to see Canukke with a dark, furry bundle slung over his shoulder, and Oloren grabbing at its talons to tie its feet together. The thing was writhing and hissing, and plunged its talons into Canukke's back. Canukke cursed and slid it to the ground, lifting its two forelegs into the air to hold it steady in one hand, and plucking a quill from his shoulder with the other. The zegrath pup looked about two feet long, not including the tail. Serete and Gabor had a second pup peeking out of a saddle bag carried between them. Each had a hand on the top of the bag, struggling to keep the pup inside.

"Careful, the teeth are razor sharp," Serete said to Gabor. "It could tear through that bag any minute."

"Teeth," Canukke exclaimed. "I think the teeth are the dullest part of the creature. The quills and claws are like knives."

"Talons," Oloren corrected.

"Claws, talons—what difference does it make? They are sharp, and somehow worse than an adult zegrath!"

Enouim and Kilith descended from their tree just as Vadik and Ruakh reappeared.

"Anything good?" Gabor asked.

Vadik shook his head. "Not what we were hoping to find. There isn't much in the area that could make any helpful compounds."

"We brought back tree sap though," Ruakh said. "It's flammable."

"OW!" Gabor swore, wringing his hand and looking incredulously down at the saddle bag.

"We don't have much time," Serete reminded them. "The pups will whimper, and mom will come calling. We certainly don't want her finding them with us instead of the Sumus."

The eight of them set off toward the main Sumu camp, splitting up shortly before reaching it. Vadik, Canukke, Oloren, and Gabor set off eastward with a zegrath pup, bows, arrows, and supplies to rig up triggers for them. Enouim, Serete, Kilith, and Ruakh continued further north with the ethanine and the other pup, following the riverbank as closely as they could. As Kilith had explained, they would drop off the pup and the ethanine, and Enouim would escort them further north at the bottom of the river.

The four of them moved as silently as possible, Ruakh and Serete taking turns wrangling the zegrath pup. Serete had been carrying it in the saddle bag until the bottom of the bag slit open and gave way. He wrapped the quilled tail in as much leather from the bag as he could and draped it over his shoulders, careful to keep the soft underbelly against his skin and secure the taloned feet with both hands.

Snap. Enouim froze. The sound had come from the woods to her left. Serete ducked behind a tree and gestured their silence. He motioned beyond them, and held up two fingers. Enouim's stomach lurched. She tried to focus on her breathing, but couldn't help thinking instead about how ridiculous it would be to come all this way and die before even starting their plans. They were within earshot of main camp, and had seen several tribesmen already on the way in, but none so close.

Enouim glanced in the opposite direction—the river was fifty yards away as it wound down the mountains in the direction from which they'd come. Too far to be of any use. Enouim looked up at Serete and saw the zegrath pup struggling against his hold. He grimaced as the creature bit his hand. The frustrated pup began to thrash and let out an angry, piercing screech. Enouim's eyes grew wide.

A beat of silence.

Thud. An arrow hit the tree trunk Kilith leaned against, missing him by an inch. Lurching forward, sword in hand, Kilith swung at the first tribesman, closing the twenty feet of distance in a flash. Ruakh spun his staff and engaged the second, and Serete reached for his sword before the pup dug into his neck.

"They've got it handled!" hissed Enouim. "We have to go!"

Serete looked longingly at Ruakh and Kilith, each engaged in battle with an adversary, but nodded. Serete and Enouim took off in a low run up the hill and over a ledge toward the main camp. Serete grunted and Enouim turned to see the pup had climbed up and over his shoulder, dangling off him. Serete sheathed his sword and used both hands to grip the hind legs of the pup and wrestle it back into his control.

Enouim saw the tents up ahead, and a swarm of Sumus milling to and fro. She ducked behind a thick tree and ushered Serete over. Enouim grasped at the pup, careful to avoid the quills on its hackles and tail, and carefully separated a talon stuck in Serete's leather belt. Firmly placing the pup's hind legs on the ground, Enouim and Serete each awkwardly held a taloned front paw so that it seemed to stand upright between them.

Enouim offered it a dried piece of meat from her pack, but the pup gnashed its teeth at her. Enouim drew back, holding her arm out so that its forelegs were too far extended for its short snout to reach. "What now?"

"We need to get further in before letting him go," Serete said.

"Without getting caught."

"Precisely."

Behind them they heard another crunch, and Serete and Enouim whirled just in time to see Kilith and Ruakh pulling themselves up over the ledge, each wearing a Sumu mantle over their clothes.

Ruakh grinned. "What a beautiful family," he laughed, taking in the sight.

Enouim blushed as she realized what he meant, the two of them holding the baby zegrath up like a toddler. The pup hissed and sputtered, clicking his teeth together as it tried to reach Serete's hand.

Ruakh tossed the ethanine pouch up in the air. "You wake them up. I'll put them to sleep."

Serete nodded, eyes bright. "Let's go."

Enouim and Serete walked their waddling charge across to the next tree and paused. A cluster of tents stood not thirty feet from them, and a smoking cauldron was set in the open area beyond the tents.

"What now?" Enouim whispered.

Serete motioned to Kilith for his Sumu cloak, and Kilith took it off and tossed it. Serete set the shredded saddle bag aside and wrapped the pup in the cloak so that it was a wriggling bundle of cloth. He caught it up in his arms and nodded to Enouim. "Pull up the bottom of that first tent there, at the edge. We'll sneak up to it and let him loose in there. Once the pup distracts everyone, Ruakh and Kilith will empty the ethanine into the cauldron."

Enouim dipped her head and started forward. Ruakh and Kilith bore away to their left to wait for their distraction, drug the soup, and make for the river. Snaking their way among the trees, Enouim pulled her hood up over her face and ducked behind the tent. She heard voices inside.

"The rat killed four of them before they got to her," said a voice. "Four! And she was in one of *your* miserable holding cages! Riddle me that. How does a caged woman kill four of your guards?"

A second voice muttered despondently in reply, but was cut off by the first. "And yet you ask for more responsibility. Well, friend, you are certainly responsible for your own neck. Remember that when Khoron-khelek has it sliced clean through."

Enouim smiled. Chayan was a force to be reckoned with.

"She dies tonight, by my hand, in the sight of the people," the other said, speaking up.

Enouim's smile faded. Her eyes hardened, and she pulled a knife from her belt. Enouim knelt at the base of the tent, slit the fabric, and swiftly lifted it as Serete tossed the bundle of fur into the tent. A horrendous screech mingled with a cry from the men, and Enouim heard the sound of steel unsheathed right before a small gray streak escaped out of the opposite side of the tent and into the heart of the camp.

Serete gripped her arm and motioned her to follow him toward the river. Enouim glanced back long enough to see the camp in an uproar, as the Sumus scrambled to catch the zegrath pup. In the middle of the chaos, one man with a Sumu mantle and a staff nonchalantly passed by the cauldron. Enouim turned and ran after Serete.

Enouim and Serete leaped over low bushes and brambles, around trees and through the woods to the river. Enouim waded in while Serete stood a few yards off to keep watch for their friends, shifting his weight impatiently. Presently Kilith and Ruakh came sprinting toward them, the sound of crashing and yelling drifting past them to the river.

"Time to go!" called Ruakh.

An unearthly shriek shattered the air, and Enouim shuddered. "Mama zegrath came not a moment too soon," Kilith explained, panting. "Get us out of here. To the north!"

Enouim closed her eyes and felt the river rise around her, surging at her request. She stepped further in until she was completely submerged, and sent the river like branches to wrap around each of her companions. Careful to trap some air around them in bubbles, Enouim extended one hand ahead of her northeast, and with the other hand she reached back, closing her fist to bring her three friends behind her as the river caught them up and thrust them forward against its natural current.

Her heart pounded in her ears against the *woosh* of the water. The fuse was lit, and there was no going back now. In this moment Enouim began to imagine all the ways she could die. Perhaps she would be shot by an archer she had not seen, or sliced in pieces. She might be captured and beheaded in front of her mother and brother. What was the use? Eight fools against so many!

Enouim wished Vadik were with her. She would ask him if he saw the white heron, and he could assure her that Eh'yeh had not abandoned them. It was Eh'yeh who sent them, after all, wasn't it? At first they sent themselves, but now they had been sent by someone greater. Surely that counted for something. *Eh'yeh, I am not gifted in combat, and I am the least qualified person for miles. I can't do this alone. I'm afraid.*

As she sent out those words in her mind, she felt an ethereal tranquility cover her like a blanket. Enouim's thoughts had been in disarray, but now a courage she did not know lay claim to her soul. She closed her eyes again, allowing her feel of the river to guide her course, delighting in the peacefulness of that moment and the glorious experience of rushing through the river. It was for this that she was born.

Enouim glanced behind her and saw Kilith, Ruakh, and

Serete being pulled along by her currents, smooth as butter. They traveled undisturbed until the river grew shallower and Enouim was forced closer to the surface.

A muffled yell behind her caused Enouim to twist. An arrow parted the waters inches from Ruakh's head. Alarmed, Enouim turned and sent a tower of water up out of the river to knock the archer off his feet.

Turning again, she saw she had inadvertently released her friends from their air bubbles and they were spinning off in the river. Enouim's eyes widened, and Kilith motioned for her to bring them up. The game was up. Ready or not, the time was now.

44

"Three, two, one!"

At Canukke's signal Gabor pulled a thin rope, releasing a volley of arrows from their bow and arrow rigs in the woods. On the other side of the camp, Oloren and Vadik followed up with shots of their own, and four tribesmen fell. The woods were alive with panic, as the zegrath pup had been released only shortly before and the Sumus were still chasing it. Now in response to this new threat, they took defensive positions throughout the camp.

"They have us surrounded!" shouted one.

"Idiot!" hissed another, as Oloren picked off the first speaker from her position in a tree.

Canukke nodded at Gabor and gestured toward six horses tied nearby. Gabor dipped his head and darted toward them. Canukke, Oloren, and Vadik provided cover fire and drew numerous blind shots from their enemies in retaliation.

Gabor untied the horses and swung up on one with Canukke close behind. Kicking the horses, they tore through the camp, slashing as they went. Vadik lit the tip of his arrow on fire and shot a supply wagon.

Canukke bore down on a tribesman aiming at Vadik, pulling at his horse at just the last moment for a quick turn into his adversary—except his horse turned swiftly in the opposite direction. He swore and tried again, pulling the horse in a circle, and looked up in time to see Oloren's knife sink itself into the Sumu's neck.

"What's your problem?" she demanded. "Never been on a horse before?"

Gabor yelled from his horse as he careened through a tent. "They're trained all wrong! I can't get him to stop!"

Two tribesmen mounted and pursued Gabor at top speed. Vadik threw his spear into one of them, who fell from his horse. Gabor clung to his steed and pulled right to avoid a wagon, but his horse peeled off left in response. He swore. The sound of steel on steel rang out behind him, as several more Sumus gave chase.

As Gabor galloped off into the distance, Canukke brought his horse in a tight circle and experimented with directing his mount. He swung at another Sumu, but the man jumped back just out of range. Just then a tribesman fifty feet off came out of a tent holding the zegrath pup triumphantly in the air, leather armor scratched in every conceivable place. His jaw dropped and so did the zegrath, taking off and darting under Canukke's horse. The horse reared and shied to the side, and the pup shrieked an ear-splitting call. An answering call shattered the air, starting in a high scream and plunging into a guttural snarl that rattled the bones.

"The mother's here," Vadik yelled, as he thrust his sword through his opponent. "Go, go!"

"What about you?" Oloren demanded, fighting back-to-back with him. "I'm staying until you're out!"

Meanwhile, Gabor crashed through the trees on his horse. At the sound of the zegrath, his horse had bolted with a new fervor that Gabor could not reign in. He tugged at her head, but to no avail. The animal careened through the forest, a thousand arrows whizzing by Gabor's head.

A great many tribesman rose from their places, shouting, but then he was gone, galloping into a new clearing. A tribesman still chased him, but Gabor's mount was faster. An arrow slit the sleeve of Gabor's mantle and he grimaced as the sting of the arrow's edge bit his flesh.

In the new clearing he saw nearly a dozen horses clustered together. There were many men, but despite the racket around them most were asleep. Those that retained consciousness lay about as if in a stupor. Gabor glanced beyond the clearing and caught sight of a great cauldron. Ethanine! Ruakh had done his part.

Gabor reached above him to a branch and pulled himself up, letting his horse fly by without him and narrowly evading the scimitar of his pursuer. Gabor dropped to the ground and beckoned to the tribesman. The man took in the mysterious scene around him and his eyes narrowed as he fixed his eyes on Gabor.

The tribesman felt for his next arrow and found his quiver empty; Gabor whirled his sword in a flourish and grinned. The tribesman lifted his scimitar in the air and drew his tongue across its edge.

"Let me show you the taste of a real blade, scum!" Gabor taunted.

The tribesman snarled and slid from his horse.

In the other part of camp, the zegrath still rampaged against the Sumus. The pup bit the boot of a tribesman, and as the man tried to shake off the pest, the zegrath mother bore down on him and slashed through his throat. She took him by the neck and shook him, tossing him aside like garbage and snarling, her quilled hackles raised, dark eyes flashing.

Oloren and Vadik made a break for the other side of the clearing to join Canukke as the mother attacked another Sumu. Canukke straightened on his horse and freed his sword from the chest of his foe.

"We need more horses," he said. "Ours are too far away."

"I see the heron." Vadik pointed. "Go that way."

ENOUIM DUG her hands deep into the river surrounding her and gathered the waters around Kilith, Serete, and Ruakh, driving them up out of the river so that they landed squarely on their feet on the bank. In a flash they were fighting, blades and staff moving with the grace and speed of a hummingbird's wings. Twenty, thirty, fifty tribesmen ran toward them en masse. As skilled as they were, three men couldn't fight off the whole camp.

Enouim raised a great tower of water and sent it barreling down on ten of the men near the bank, knocking them off balance and landing three in the river. The men running toward them froze for a moment, eyes wide to take in this impossible sight. Enouim sent one of the three in the river flying downstream, and with water wrapping around their ankles like fingers she plucked the other two out of the river and flung them into their companions.

"Stop this!" Enouim cried. "Turn back now and you will not be harmed!"

A tribesmen snickered, and Serete shot her a look. *It's no use.* She had to try. The sneering tribesman lifted his saber and charged Ruakh from behind. Enouim's heart dropped. Ruakh, occupied with two more men, was unaware of the new threat.

"Please, stop! Don't die for Khoron-khelek's greed!" Her

pleas fell on deaf ears. They would not stop. She had known it was a vain hope. But if they only turned ...

Enouim rose high in the air and flung a knife into the heart of a man approaching Ruakh, just as Ruakh shoved one of his adversaries into the river with his staff. Enouim pulled the Sumu toward her and up into the air, slashing at him and taking his saber and knives before depositing him back into the water and ushering him downstream with his comrade.

She turned and threw her new knives into her opponents. The Sumus recovered and began drawing bows and arrows, firing at her as she spun in the air, ducking and twirling above and below the surface of the water. Serete, Kilith, and Ruakh quickly caught on to her strategy, dumping tribesmen and ammunition into the river to keep her well supplied.

Soon the tribesmen drew back from the water's edge and kept out of her range. Looking about, she saw a supply wagon, but it was twenty feet from the bank. If she could reach it ...

Enouim dodged a volley of arrows and sank back into the river, disappearing beneath the surface and pulling away downstream. She gathered herself and extended her arms over her head, shooting forward toward the wagon's place on the bank and diving deep just before the water's edge. The river surged over the bank, knocking one man off his feet, but the wagon did not move. She came again, full throttle and a plunge—but again the wagon remained. Enouim sent the river like long tentacles up and out toward the tribesmen. One of them slashed uselessly at the water with his sword.

"Enouim!" Kilith yelled, as he fought off four tribesmen at once. He used one as a body shield and maneuvered his attackers to deal with one at a time. "We need horses. And another surprise. Let's try upriver before word spreads."

"It may already be too late," Ruakh said, as he watched a Sumu sprint off toward Gorgenbrild.

"Catch!" Serete ran back to the bank and leaped into the river.

Enouim enveloped him in a bubble and let the water absorb his impact, bringing him gently back to the surface. "Let's go then," she urged, dunking Serete into the water as an arrow whizzed by where his head had been.

He sputtered. "Hey!"

"You're welcome!"

Ruakh and Kilith jumped into the river and Enouim swept them upstream and out of range of the archers. She pulled a bubble down into the river as they traveled underwater and converged them all into one. "I don't think we can keep doing this."

Ruakh shook his head. "The element of surprise didn't get us as far as we were hoping. It's still only three of us, and the bank is too far from where we need to go."

Kilith nodded. "Drop us off beneath the surface and draw fire a bit further up. We will slip through, find horses, and ride in from there."

Enouim dipped her head and shot forward, extending one hand before her and one behind to draw her companions along. At a bend in the river, she looked back at her friends. This was it. They nodded to her, and she slowed them down and released them underwater near the bank. Serete somersaulted backward as the bubble imploded, and Kilith and Ruakh drifted off in different directions. She didn't have long to cover them before they would be coming up for air.

She rounded the bend in a flash and looked up in time to see that the river had narrowed and a wooden footbridge was above her, with the shadow of a Sumu crossing it. Enouim sank down into the river, pulling the water around her in a bubbling mass, roiling with power as it awaited her command. Like an arrow leaving the string, she sprang from the river and barreled through the bridge, knocking the tribesman into the river. Shouts erupted and a flurry of motion met her eyes before she fell once more beneath the surface.

Enouim drew herself down and flung the flailing man from the river depths up and out as if an invisible giant had plucked him up and tossed him aside. Screams drifted down to her through the water. She waited a beat. Two beats. Nothing moved.

The apprehension was tangible, as the men on both sides of the bank breathlessly watched the water. The shock and mystery of her attack had caught them off guard, and she relished their confusion—once she rose, the game would be on.

And this game was bloody.

45

Canukke let out a savage cry as he brought his sword down on his adversary's neck. The sheer passion and force felt as though it should have shorn the man in two, but the sword clove through the neck at an angle and reverberated as it hit the sternum. Canukke kicked the man off his sword and ran him through, turned, and drove his elbow into the face of an attacker to his right.

They had stolen into Gorgenbrild after one final distraction. Gabor had found several more horses, and Gabor, Oloren, and Vadik each had one before Canukke set fire to tails of the others and loosed them in the direction of Gorgenbrild. Between the ethanine, the zegrath, and the horses, they found an opening and made their entry. Vadik mixed powders together and set off a cloud of yellow smoke to signal the Gorgenbrilders waiting inside, so that fighting had already broken out by the time they charged in.

Canukke shoved aside another limp form. A just end to these barbarians. Merciful even. Every last one of them deserved to be hamstrung, gutted, and burned alive! If only he could take his time, dole out to them the punishment they had earned ... still, in lieu of that, slaughtering them in great numbers would pacify him.

Slipping to the left, Canukke avoided the sword stroke of a new opponent and countered with a basic hook to the head and sword hilt to the temple. Thirty years ago a weaker conglomerate of tribes had called themselves Iyangas, but they were all the same. Urgil Khoron-khelek had swept down the mountains and threatened them then, and the fate of Canukke's father at their hands should be the fate of them all. It was no small sadness to Canukke that Malum Khoron-khelek had murdered his own father, Urgil, before Canukke could do the honors. Now he would spill Malum's blood, and so end once and for all his grotesque bloodline.

Canukke flipped his sword round to meet another Sumu saber and glanced up at the scene around him. Their approach had been successful, and the Gorgenbrilders had made good their promise to rise up on the signal. Once the first wave of rebels had started the fight, those more timid joined in with relish. But the fight was now hours underway and their strength was waning. Sumus converged on Vadik and Oloren, and there was no way out. The two were back-to-back fighting off swarms of the enemy. Oloren's strokes were strong, but less frequent. Vadik began to stoop as he fought, and Canukke saw him sway with fatigue.

Fresh tribesmen poured into the space around them, and Canukke swore as he twisted to meet yet another blade. The fight had burst with energy at the start, but the tribesmen were hardly inexperienced buffoons; they regrouped well and had countered effectively. They had been making their way toward Twedori's house where Canukke hoped to find Malum, but their endurance was waning. The candle was burning from both ends, and they were running out of time.

Canukke fought his way to Oloren's side, shoving off her

attacker. "Something big needs to happen, and fast. We can't keep going like this!"

"We aren't alone," Vadik called, gesturing briefly up at the sky before dealing another stroke.

"What do you see?" Oloren asked.

"Malak. Conand and Fetrye. And two others—one with us, one against us. Glintenon! Perhaps it's really him!"

"What good does it do us if they fight each other up there?" Oloren grumbled.

A great bellow rang out, and Canukke looked up. There before him was a mighty man of the tribes, still some distance away, slinging a great black scimitar. Khoron-khelek.

Oloren looked up from her latest adversary to see a tribesman angling for Canukke, and Canukke distracted. She leaped into the opening between them and parried the blow with her sword in her left hand, crashing into the assailant. Steel rang against steel as they clashed again and again. Oloren saw her chance and seized it, thrusting forward to cut him down. She swung her sword down and reached up once more for a final strike.

Just as she did so, she felt a tug on her sword arm, and a moment later searing pain exploded from her arm. Her sword was on the ground, and glancing down she saw her arm just below the elbow was sliced almost completely through, hanging by a thread. She cried out in shock as the pain hit, clutching her left arm with her right and sinking to her knees.

Thrown out of his reverie by Oloren's cry, Canukke turned to her aid. Alarmed, he looked for her attacker, but was clubbed on the head from behind. Canukke was sent sprawling to the earth beside Oloren. He twisted back just in time to see a tribesman bearing down on him.

As the tribesman stepped over Oloren toward Canukke, Oloren pulled a knife with her good hand and jabbed upward into the man's stomach. Canukke looked at her, eyes wide, and sprang to his feet. She winced again, grabbing at her injured arm. Injured was an understatement. If she sneezed, she might lose it entirely.

Canukke gathered his feet under him as the Sumu raised his saber, and kicked his exposed stomach, driving him back. He stepped into the opening, positioning himself over Oloren. Canukke glanced down at her. "You save my life, I save yours. That's how it works."

Oloren grinned wearily. "I saved yours twice."

Canukke couldn't help but smile. Oloren had always been a warrior worth her salt. Happy to repay the favor, Canukke fended off attacks as she began fumbling with her belt with her free hand.

"Vadik!" Canukke yelled.

Vadik looked up, and the blood drained from his face as he took in the situation. If they weren't quick, Oloren would bleed out. Vadik reached them and took over the fighting long enough for Canukke to undo Oloren's buckle and yank the belt free from round her waist, tossing it at her before engaging another Sumu. Oloren began to turn it into a tourniquet near the shoulder just above where her arm was nearly cut through, but she wavered, woozy. She tried to tighten it, but her tugs did little as her strength left her, and her hand relaxed as she lost consciousness.

Cokar, one of the men from the meeting in the tunnels, made his way to them with two other men. Canukke was too heavily engaged in battle to help her, but fought with an anxious edge to his mind. Vadik lost his weapon and had his man in a headlock. He reached down to break the man's neck, but the Sumu tucked his chin tight into Vadik's ribs and swung a knife at him with a free hand.

Vadik dodged and moved his right hand from the man's

chin to the back of his neck, flipping the man onto his seat facing away from Vadik. In a flash Vadik stripped the weapon away, stabbed him under the arm, and stepped back to let him bleed out in the next few seconds. Finally free, Vadik turned to Oloren to see Cokar tightening her tourniquet.

Canukke released himself from his latest victim and raised his eyes once more to the tribesman emperor. The great Sumu was charging toward them. Unyielding ferocity lit his eyes, a fury carrying him forward on the crest of an impregnable darkness of soul. His leather armor fit a body built of nothing but sinew, strength, and hatred—the body of a man who had lent his life to the worship of power and destruction.

Malum Khoron-khelek.

He carried a scimitar in one hand, and ran with no shield. He had never needed one. *He will need one today,* Canukke thought to himself. Canukke glanced back to see Oloren in Vadik's capable hands, and knew there was nothing more he could do for her here. This was the moment he had been waiting for.

Canukke drew himself up, taller but certainly no heavier than this pillar among men. Still, all the hatred of this man could not compare to the resentments in Canukke. Across the battlefield the two men locked eyes, and Canukke broke into a run.

Bodies were strewn over grass and gravel, and Canukke dodged Gorgenbrilder and Sumu fighters alike as he ran. Though the battle still raged, Gorgenbrilders were outnumbered five to one in the square outside Twedori's house. If they were going to fail, and Canukke die, he would bring Malum Khoron-khelek down with him.

One of the Sumu warriors called out to Malum, but he ignored him. Again the man called out, and again he moved on unheeding. A third time the man called to Malum in urgency, nearly stepping in his path, and the great leader reluctantly slowed his pace. The Sumu spoke low, gesturing frantically to the east. Malum's stony face soured to an even deeper displeasure as he listened. The Sumu looked to the east, then back at Canukke, and Malum's gaze pierced him through. Conflicted for a moment, Malum cast Canukke a fated look and turned east.

Canukke's stomach dropped. This hurricane of a man had just been dispatched to the river. To Enouim.

Canukke turned to follow, but a pounding commotion behind him pulled his attention. He pivoted to see a cloud of dust above the stone and thatch houses ... and beyond the rise, horses.

ENOUIM FLUNG herself into the air out and let her knife fly. It found purchase in the neck of an archer on the west side of the river before she sank back into the water. Only two knives remained. She had again tried to dislodge a supply wagon from its perch by the bank into the river, but to no avail. It was closer to the bank, but with enemies on both sides of the river she had been fully occupied. The bridge was out, and no one on the easterly side dared cross the river with Enouim guarding it. Gorgenbrilders had begun spilling out into the surrounding woods, and among them Ruakh and Serete had found their way back and were fighting on the Gorgenbrilder side of the river, as the tribesmen focused on finding a way to take her down.

It had been a bloodbath on both sides, and Enouim had managed to wash significant portions of the carnage into the river for her to use, but now she was running on empty despite the ongoing battle below her. She beckoned a tower of water shooting her high up into the air again. She flung her next knife at an archer on the eastern side, but even as she spun she saw an arrow leaving his string—she was too late. In a panic she released the water holding her up and fell, but her speed and trajectory carried her over the bank and out of the river. She dropped fifteen feet to the earth at an angle, absorbing her impact in her best break fall yet; still, the force of the hit rippled through her body. She wavered, dizzy, and her head swam.

Enouim lay for a moment in confusion, pain radiating up her left side where she had fallen. Wearily she looked up from the ground and saw the thick muscled frame of a man barreling toward her. It was Malum Khoron-khelek, captor of her people, and every brutal fiber of his being was fixated on her thin frame. She lurched for her final knife—only to find it had been pitched far from her when she fell.

Forty paces off, Khoron-khelek slowed from a run to an intimidating stride. Thirty paces. She searched the ground for something, anything, that she could use. The ground was littered with bodies, blood, and weapons, but none close enough to help her. Behind her the river was too far to be of service—she had fallen twenty feet away—and the corpse of her felled archer lay between her and the bank. The supply wagon sat broken and useless just behind her, with nothing but spilled foodstuffs left adorning it. At a loss, Enouim snatched up a rock and flung it in Khoron-khelek's direction.

She gathered her feet under her, retreated to the battered supply wagon, and yanked at one of the spokes of the wheel. Nothing. In vain she stomped at its base with her foot, and still he came. Enouim kicked wildly at the spoke, and on her third strike it came loose and she slung it with all her might just as her enemy came in range. Malum leaned out of reach, swung forward with his blade in his right hand, and struck her with the butt of his sword on her upper right arm before she could recover.

The power of his swing sent her flying to the ground, landing again on her left side. A shock ran through her and pain shot up her right arm where she had been hit. Malum strode toward her and lifted his scimitar to deal her a final blow. Unable to wield a weapon with her injured side, Enouim leaned on her right and reached up with the wooden spoke in her left.

With a *whack* they met, and as they swung again, Enouim struggled to back away and regain her footing. They met again. On this second hit, Enouim heard a *crack*, and on the third, the spoke splintered and broke. With her right hand on the earth for balance, half-sitting, Enouim grasped a handful of dirt and threw it in her opponent's face. Malum stumbled back, covering his eyes, and Enouim seized the opportunity.

She leaped to her feet and saw the corpse of the archer she had killed only four feet to her right, two knives still strapped to his thigh. Enouim feigned a trip and rolled over the body as Malum recovered. In a rage he came for her, swinging at her as he crossed the corpse, and she jumped back. He raised his weapon once more, and Enouim lifted her hands to protect her face. It was the wrong move. Khoron-khelek sliced her left side as she exposed her torso.

She gasped, her left hand clinging to the wound. With her right hand she plunged the archer's knife into Malum's forearm, and he dropped his weapon. He roared and brought his fist down hard across her face, doubling her over as he followed it up with a kick to her waist. Enouim crashed to the ground.

46

No sooner did Enouim's back smack the earth than Malum was on top of her, straddling her and pinning her to the ground. He held his injured arm close to his body and pounded her repeatedly with a left fist twice the size of her own. Enouim lifted her hands over her face, warm blood trickling down her brow. The hits kept coming, and Enouim's vision blurred. Her heart pounded in her ears, her strength sapped. She had little left against this monster of a man.

With nothing left to lose, Enouim grabbed for the knife still lodged in his forearm and latched onto it with her left hand. It wouldn't budge. She reached over and gripped it with both hands, yanking the blade embedded in his arm. Malum arched back in pain, steadying himself with his left arm on the ground by her head. When the blade still did not pull away, Enouim reached up with her right hand and raked her fingers over his face and eyes, digging them into the tender tissues as hard as she could.

He bellowed as blood poured down over his eye, obscuring his vision, and for a moment pulled up away from her. With the extra space Enouim seized the knife hilt with both hands and ripped it free. She shoved the blade at his face, but he gripped her hands in a vise. Adrenaline laced her fatigued muscles, and he wrested the knife from her hands and threw it beyond her reach. Rearing back he went to hit her again, but Enouim redirected his blow and let his own energy follow through to take him beyond her so that he fell on his chest.

Malum reached for the knife he had tossed just moments before, but Enouim struggled out from underneath his legs, slipped the archer's second knife out from its hiding place in her boot, and made a slit across the tendon of his ankle. With difficulty Enouim stood, heaving from exertion, left hand again clutching at the wound in her side.

Malum attempted to get up from his kneeling position, but trembled as he tried to put weight on the ankle she'd cut. Still favoring her left side, Enouim stood over him and, holding her hands together, used every last ounce of strength she could muster to pull herself back and swing at his head with all her might. With a guttural cry she whirled into him, her momentum carrying her through so that they both fell. He collapsed on impact and lay facedown in the dirt, and she tumbled in a spiral so that as she hit the ground, her legs were flung over his body.

Enouim edged away from him warily, leaning on her right arm for support and scooting backward. He wasn't moving, but she doubted he was dead. Maybe he was even pretending to be dead to get her closer. Enouim kicked at his feet. Nothing.

For the first time, Enouim took a moment to take stock of her surroundings. The fight was still going on around her, but no one seemed to pay her any notice. The woods around them seemed to have thinned of warriors, though many lay slain on the ground. Ruakh danced his staff in and out among three attackers about fifty yards to her left, but they looked spent. One leaped back and simply stared at Ruakh for a moment, unsure of how to engage next.

Thirty feet from Ruakh was Serete, who had just disarmed a tribesman and kicked him in the face. He stumbled back, and Serete took the opportunity to plunge him through with his own saber. Still tribesmen outnumbered Gorgenbrilders by the river. Two Sumus finally saw her and started running. Enouim let out a long sigh, doubtful she had anything left to give. Perhaps this was how she would meet her end.

She scanned the ground for her knife and labored to pick it up near Malum's fallen body. She stood next to him, watching the two Sumus come for her, unwilling to expend the energy to meet them. They would be upon her soon enough.

Just then, forty horsemen riding appaloosas swept through from the direction of Gorgenbrild. The men were sturdy, tattooed warriors. Kalka'an!

Baird had come to them.

Baird himself she did not see, but his fellow cliff dwellers did him justice as they galloped in with a vigor that refreshed her spirit. Enouim's would-be attackers were overtaken and killed in moments, and the clamor that filled the air was alive with victory as Gorgenbrilders rejoiced. In the dwindled battle by the river, Kalka'an provided the numbers needed to beat back the tribesmen.

Her despondency lifted, and with her immediate danger removed, Enouim returned her focus to Malum Khoron-khelek, unconscious at her feet. Enouim carefully rounded him and looked down upon his face. He was breathing, so he was dangerous. He was a malice, a blight afflicting the world with a silver tongue and a bloodstained sword. Ever since Malum murdered his own father at a young age, he had been hardened—a soul without tenderness, a heart without conscience, a killer without honor.

She was well within her rights to kill him. The harm he had done not only to her people but to her personally was untenable. She thought of Pakel, a needless loss; the flat, emotionless eyes of everyone she ever knew as they watched Malum execute friends, family, and community leaders; the declaration he made that they deserved such treatment; the dead littered around the forest where she now stood.

A new question came to mind as she looked down at him. *What is honor?*

The question surprised her. Honor was respect. Honor was knowing the boundaries of right and wrong, and having the self-discipline to adhere to them. Honor was bestowed upon those with qualities deserving of praise.

And who determines right from wrong? Who determines which qualities are deserving of praise?

Enouim studied Malum's face, streaked with blood and sweat. She thought for a moment that these likely defined the last few decades of his life—toil, pain, survival. He was a young man, maybe thirty years old. He must have been ... what, maybe ten when his father was betrayed by his right-hand man? How must that have shaped his life?

It doesn't matter, a voice inside her seemed to say. *You are avoiding the question.*

Of course it matters! She raged back, angry at the voice. *If I'm not going to kill him, I want a good reason. I want to know that somehow it makes sense that he is the way he is. That somewhere in his twisted mind, there is rhyme and reason for all this suffering.* A hot tear trailed down her dirty cheek. The faces of Kenan, the kindly guard from Levav, and Pakel, cycled through her mind again. Her mother Qadra's hopelessness. Bondeg. Then in rapid fire the faces of the dead filed through her mind, from the nomads in the desert to Mereámé's sweet face, before she had been resurrected, and all those Enouim had killed in the past twenty-four hours.

Who are you to determine his deserving end? Who determines right from wrong?

Enouim raised the knife with a sharp inhale, trembling as she stood over her enemy, trying to shut out the voice that demanded an answer. This was the question of the last seven months, really. She had always been one of the few peaceful sort in Gorgenbrild, keeping out of trouble the best she could and avoiding the brutality typical of her society. It was not considered wrong to kill so long as there was provocation. But who was to say what provocation warranted death?

And then there were Baird and Silas. In Kalka'an, there was a new way of doing things. It wasn't a way she agreed with ... after all, the "wit" and "strategy" so highly esteemed by Kalka'an were really deceit and manipulation, and such underhanded practices were disgraceful to Gorgenbrild. At least her people were up front about their dealings—honorable. To do otherwise was cowardly, though Baird had not seen it that way.

Yet Baird had come back for them in their hour of need, and brought with him a willing cadre risking their lives. Even now the cheers wafting toward her from Gorgenbrild indicated the rest of Kalka'an were sweeping through. Surely this loyalty was evidence of an honorable man! But Enouim could no more say Gorgenbrild's way was better than Kalka'an's as Baird could say Kalka'an's way was better than Gorgenbrild's.

Levav had suggested that motivation and attitude of the heart determined right and wrong, denouncing standards of Gorgenbrild and Kalka'an alike. But being different did not make them more credible. Why bother if the source was only another Enouim or another Baird, no more credible than they?

A tightness in her stomach prodded her with the answer she had known all along, but was unwilling to acknowledge. Malum Khoron-khelek and his united conglomerate of Sumus had a code as well, and if no standard could be reliably measured against another, she had no right to be angry. But she was furious and devastated all at once.

That's because I placed those emotions there, said the voice. *It is right for you to feel. It is wrong for you to kill in anger.*

Enouim nearly cried out, *SAYS WHO?* but didn't dare. She knew who. The voice was not hers, but Eh'yeh's, and he was the only one with the authority to declare what was and was not.

Canukke and Ruakh's conversation after the encounter with the sea monster floated back to her.

"Humans without dignity do not deserve the title."

"It seems you place yourself in that category, then. You forfeit your own title when you lower yourself to animalistic impulses. There is a better way, one that doesn't come at the cost of your humanity."

Her shoulders slumped forward and she closed her eyes, weeping softly. She fell to her knees, her knuckles white with the fierce grip on her knife. She dropped it. Khoron-khelek stirred, and she jumped.

Serete and Canukke, whom she had not seen near the river until now, came running up to her. Both froze as they took in the scene, then Serete stepped to her side and Canukke kicked at Khoron-khelek.

"GET UP!" he screamed, disappointed to find the villain unconscious. "Look me in the eyes as I take your life!"

Enouim, suddenly filled with a strength that had abandoned her before, leaped between Canukke and Malum. "No!

He is mine. He came here looking for me, and I am the one who defeated him. We will take him to Gorgenbrild and show them he is conquered. Alive."

"We will take them his head!"

"You will take them nothing!" Enouim's tone was ice. Seeing his stricken face, she added, "You will lead him in and secure his ties. You will ensure no other hand destroys him. But you will keep him alive until daybreak, and I will address the people."

47

Enouim thumbed the scar on her collarbone. She wasn't quite sure what had come over her when she stood up to Canukke about killing Khoron-khelek. And she had been equally surprised that it had worked. Serete and Canukke were finishing binding and gagging their hostage.

The remains of the conflict could yet rage into the night, but the freshness of the Kalka'an horses, and the renewed vigor and brutality of the Gorgenbrilders had managed to turn the tide. Aided by the cliff people's knowledge of powders, explosives were set in many of the tunnels, including the one in the wall by Twedori's house—effectively destroying the Sumu command center. It was still the land of Gorgenbrild, and every stone and blade of grass was known to them.

"Get him to the river," Enouim heard herself say, surprised at the authority in her voice.

Canukke crossed his arms. "The fight is over in this area, and there are still enough warriors around to protect us. We should wait here until Gorgenbrild is clear, and take him in."

Enouim scanned the forest. Gorgenbrilder and Sumu

bodies littered the ground, and Gorgenbrilders now sought out their injured countrymen. Two of them knelt over a friend twenty paces off, glancing up at Malum's still form every spare moment. One looked frightened, but the other ... well, the look in his eyes made Chayan look tame.

"I don't think it's a good idea to be around so many people," Enouim said. "Even of our own." She jerked her head in the direction of the two men tending their friend, and Serete followed her gaze.

"They're not the only ones. People are beginning to recognize our prisoner. We're getting looks from all directions, and the whispering has started."

Canukke put his hand on the hilt of his sword and lifted his chin as three men to their left progressively searched bodies closer and closer to where Malum lay.

"I hate it when people stare." Enouim clenched her jaw and raised her voice toward the trio. "Can I help you?"

"Is that who I think it is?" one of the men replied.

"The infamous Canukke Topothain," Enouim answered, hedging his real question.

"No, not him. The Sumu. It's Khoron-khelek, isn't it? Is he dead?"

"Who wants to know?" Canukke called back.

"Pinet Horomat, at your service."

"It's a pleasure, Pinet. It is indeed the emperor himself. He breathes ... for now."

"Are you sure that's such a good idea?" Pinet stepped closer, and his focus shifted from Canukke to Malum. His breathing quickened and his fist tightened on the sword at his side.

"He cannot be allowed to live," said the second. "He's slaughtered our people time and again, and has proved impossible to catch. What if he gets away?"

"He won't," Serete said, drilling the man with a cool glare.

Pinet glanced between Canukke and Serete. "Khoronkhelek has wronged us all equally—any of us has the right to his blood."

"Is that so?" Ruakh asked. "Did you fight him hand to hand? Sustain injuries from him? Defeat and capture him?"

Pinet scowled. "I suppose Canukke did all that, eh? He holds highest rights? The Canukke I've heard about would have wrought swift justice, not watched him peacefully slumber."

"Not me." Canukke pressed his lips together, as if contemplating whether he really wanted to say his next words. He nodded at Enouim. "Her."

"Don't toy with us," one of them said with a scoff. "She could hardly fell a rabbit."

"Isn't she the tavern girl?"

"The tavern girl! The coward who ran away from Chayan?"

"I guess Chayan didn't kill her after all."

"I heard she fled the mountains entirely."

Great, she hadn't been as invisible as she thought as a tavern girl. Everyone knew her as the worthless wimp. Enouim's gut pinched, and she swallowed. Her eyes glistened, but she blinked hard. Crybaby would *not* be added to their description of her.

The men edged closer still, eyeing her with interest. Canukke slid his sword from his sheath. "Back them up, Pinet. Didn't you say you were at my service?"

Pinet's eyes were black as pitch. "What are you going to do with him? Gorgenbrild has a right to know he has been defeated. And he cannot be allowed to live."

Enouim squared her shoulders. "We go to Gorgenbrild at daybreak. Tell them to expect us. Tell them Enouim Cokanda holds highest rights to his blood."

Serete leaned down to whisper in her ear. "What are you doing?"

"I have a plan." A half-baked plan, but a plan at any rate. "There's something we need to do."

Malum stirred, and Enouim jumped. Ruakh whacked him in the head with his staff, and he slumped back into the dirt. Enouim arched an eyebrow at Ruakh, and he shrugged, a small smile on his lips.

"We need to move him," Serete said so only they could hear.

Ruakh nodded. "To the river."

Canukke swung his sword. "Enouim, lead the way. You are our protection in the river. I'll cover the rear."

The entire forest was watching them now, perhaps thirty Gorgenbrilders and Kalka'aners. Enouim strode toward the river, walking backward to face her people. "Not a hand but mine shall shed his blood. Daybreak. In the square outside Twedori's house."

Enouim waded into the river and extended her fingers into the rippling water, swirling at her will, awaiting her command.

"Where are you going?" Pinet demanded.

"She's the water witch!" someone exclaimed.

"She's a hero. She's the one who took out the bridge."

"Impossible."

Enouim shut her eyes against the endless commentary on the bank and breathed in deep as the cool water beckoned her. *Come play.* Behind her, she felt the forms of her friends and her enemy as Canukke, Serete, and Ruakh brought Malum into the current.

"Come on, Enouim," Canukke said. "Give them a show."

Enouim's eyes snapped open, and she called to the river, sweeping the four men deeper into the current and wrapping them in a protective bubble of air. She plunged them beneath the surface, the gills on her neck welcomed in the river, and she carried them off downstream. Nothing filled her ears but the rush of water. Nothing filled her sight but underwater plant life, a few startled fish, and the twists of the river ahead. Enouim wondered what life for Madzi was like beneath the surface. Surely it was simpler.

Sploosh.

Something large hit the water above her, and something inside her said, *look up.* An unconscious tribesman sank into the water, his hands and feet tied, a large rock strapped to his feet. This was not merely a casualty of war. This was unsportsmanlike. Unnecessary. Cruel. Anger built in her chest, her hands began to shake, and with every fiber of her being she knew there were more. *Save them.*

Enouim recognized the tug on her heart and caught the falling Sumu in an air bubble of his own before carrying him to the surface along with her friends. Ruakh steadied himself in the shallows and ran to the bound tribesman, turning him over and bending to his aid. Serete and Canukke held Malum between them. He was disoriented but coming to, and blinked at Enouim with astonishment. Dried blood decorated long scratches across one eye, somehow making him look even fiercer. Enouim wondered what it was like for him to wake up inside a river when the last time his eyes were open, he was in hand-to-hand combat with her upstream. On dry ground.

She shrugged off the thought and twisted to face land. It was not far from where Ruakh had drugged the soup cauldron. She marveled that the drug lasted so long. Ten Sumus lay bound and gagged in the same manner as their companion, and a dozen Gorgenbrilders stood over them. Eight of the bodies breathed. Two were dead. One was torn open with entrails staining the ground, and the other had too many slashing and stabbing wounds to count. Nausea washed over her.

The Gorgenbrilders jumped back, shouting, then whooped and hollered as they laid eyes on Malum Khoron-khelek in the hands of their hero, Canukke Topothain. They looked at Enouim with wild admiration and shock.

Enouim hardly registered it. "What are you doing?"

One of the men lowered his dagger. "Did you want a turn?"

"No! This is not the way! This is not Eh'yeh! What honor is there in ripping men apart as they sleep?"

"We were going to be more creative with them when they woke up, but they are only just starting to come out of it. We got tired of waiting. Do you have a better idea for that one?" The speaker indicated the Sumu Enouim had saved from the river.

"Yes, in fact, I do." Enouim snatched the man's dagger, ran at the Sumu struggling to sit up next to Ruakh, and sliced through his bonds.

"Hey! You can't let them go free!"

"I'm not letting them go free. You want him in the river, I'll put him in the river. Somebody give me parchment and pen."

"Who goes to war with parchment and pen?"

One of the men called to another further off, and he disappeared in the forest. Moments later he returned with twenty more Gorgenbrilders carrying more bound Sumus. Parchment and pen was found and delivered to Enouim. Enouim stepped back into the shallows, careful to stay in the bounds of the river should need arise.

"Almost all of them speak the common tongue, don't they?" Enouim asked.

"Yes," Canukke answered. "They use it with each other since there are multiple languages between the smaller tribes Malum joined together."

Enouim nodded. Three of the bound tribesmen had woken and were surveying the scene with silent alarm. Enouim gestured toward them. "Move a muscle, and all my friends will fight over who gets to kill you first."

Shouts of approval rang out from the Gorgenbrilders. Enouim glanced back at Malum. "Same for you." She twisted a finger and a whirlpool swirled around his torso like liquid ropes. His lip curled, but he did not move.

Enouim gestured to her compatriots. "Where are the rest of the tribesmen? There were more. A lot more. Bring them to the river."

"Even the dead ones?"

"Are these the only ones left alive?"

"Yes. There was some debate about whether to burn, drown, or dismember, so we were saving these."

Bile flew up her throat. Enouim grimaced and swallowed its bitter taste as hard as she could. It was evil. How could Gorgenbrild blame the tribes for their brutality? Gorgenbrild was evil.

"Just these then. To the river." Enouim turned back to the river and a tear slipped down her cheek. Malum's expression was unreadable as he took her in, but Ruakh offered her his hand in support. She squeezed his hand, then dropped it. Now was not the time to look weak. She wiped her face and turned back to her people.

"What can you do?"

"Dash them to pieces on the rocks!"

"Drown them!"

"Water warrior!"

Eight of perhaps fifteen tribesmen were awake now. Enouim wrote a note on the parchment and tucked it inside the leather breastplate of one of the tribesmen. He spat in her face. His captor slugged him in the gut, but said nothing. She directed the hostages all be placed in the river and their hands and legs freed. Enouim bent all her focus on the fifteen enemy men. This would be the greatest challenge to her powers yet.

She leaned close to Serete. "Watch my back. I can't focus on anything else." Serete nodded and placed a hand on his sword hilt.

Enouim shut her eyes tight, feeling the forms of the men through the tendrils of water around them as the river reached up like vines to cover them. Gorgenbrilders on the bank cheered and the Sumus let out terrorized screams as she pulled them down into the river depths in a bubble and shot them upstream. They had come from the north, and to the north they would return. Far away.

For several minutes her concentration bent on swirling her captives up, up, upriver, round curves, and further and further away. She flinched as one of them hit rocks on the side of the river about a mile away. He likely died on impact. Enouim felt her control wane the further the men were carried, and at long last she dumped them on the bank on the eastern side of the river. She heaved and sighed.

"Are they dead?"

"There has been death," she hedged. More celebration.

Enouim rested briefly and conferred with Ruakh, Canukke, and Serete, and it was decided that Serete would go with this group to route any surviving enemy and carry the news of Malum Khoron-khelek's capture to Gorgenbrild. Serete would gather news and return in the early hours of the morning while Enouim took Malum, Canukke, and Ruakh to the river bottom. It would be safer there for now.

Enouim would retreat to the river with her powerful charge in tow and stay the first half of the night there, then sleep on the far side while Canukke and Ruakh watched over Malum. Canukke had begged her to let him take Malum's head, or at least his right arm and sword to show the people and parade about the streets.

"It would relieve their pain and encourage them. It would prove that their oppressor was captured," he had explained.

But Enouim had shook her head. "It would add blood to blood, and they would drown themselves in it. Let the crimson of this night seep into the ground ... they have won the battle today. It is enough. If they do not believe we have him now, they will believe tomorrow when they see him."

Still, she had allowed Canukke to take Malum's sword, a black scimitar with ornate golden inlay in its hilt. "There is none like it. This will ease their minds for the time being."

Enouim brought them all to the bottom of the river in a bubble, safe and removed from prying eyes until it was fully night. Bitterly, Canukke surrendered the scimitar to Serete to take into Gorgenbrild. Canukke could not bear to leave Khoron-khelek, and took seriously his duty of keeping him alive—if for no other reason than in hopes of killing him later himself.

48

Canukke held a torch lighting the bubble, and Enouim, Canukke, and Ruakh sat in a circle with Malum on the river bottom. A fish darted by in the water next to them, swerving to avoid the narrow tube of air and torch smoke leading up to the surface. Malum stared at Enouim with shock. She hadn't known his beady eyes could get so big. His surprise wore off and he lunged for Canukke, but Enouim let the water come into the bubble and catch Malum up in it, toying with him until his face turned blue. She dumped him gasping and spluttering back into the bubble, and he struggled little after that.

They spent most of the night at the river bottom, only coming up to allow Enouim a few hours' rest before daybreak. Baird had found and fetched Inferno for Enouim, and met her early at the riverbank.

"I've never been so happy to see you!" she cried, throwing her arms around his neck.

He laughed and gave her a big bear hug. "You thought I would leave in a huff and then forget all about you, eh?" He winked.

"Well ..." Enouim eyed Canukke darkly.

Canukke reached out and clasped Baird's arm. "An honor to have you join us, friend. I misjudged you. I owe you a debt."

Baird dipped his head. "Kalka'an and Gorgenbrild have always been friends. No reason to let that die now. Speaking of which, everyone is dying to see the two of you."

"The ... two of us?" Enouim stammered, glancing at Canukke with uncertainty.

Baird nodded. "Oh, news of you has spread. Canukke has always been their conquering hero, but today a new hero is born. They even have a few nicknames circulating about. Water warrior, river fury, lady of wrath ..."

Enouim scrunched up her nose. "What?!"

Baird shrugged. "They need some finessing. But they are excited to see you, and what you're promised to bring them." Baird tipped his head at Khoron-khelek, who glared back at them.

The time had come. Within an hour, twenty Gorgenbrild and Kalka'an warriors arrived to escort them into Gorgenbrild. Enouim mounted Inferno and they turned the horses toward home. She released a heavy sigh and surrendered to the rolling motion of Inferno's walk, caressing his neck. She looked up at the beautiful azure spread across the sky, swathed ever so lightly in dreamy white wisps. If only her heart could be as tranquil. *Eh'yeh, help me.*

Enouim rode in front with Canukke abreast, Baird and Ruakh at the flanks, and Serete behind. Gagged and arms bound, Malum Khoron-khelek rode a horse in the middle, surrounded by them all. Canukke and Baird had protested this, Canukke suggesting he be tied and dragged along behind the horses on the ground, and Baird suggesting he be strung up between two horses and left to hang the whole way in. Enouim vetoed this and stated that he was a leader and would be treated with more respect than that. She did, however, request an older, slow animal for him to ride in on. Even with bound hands, he could easily maneuver the horse with his legs.

The animal they chose was a truly haggard creature, ribs showing, gray coat unkempt, and head hanging low as he walked. Enouim felt pity pull at her heart and thought it wrong to pair such a good-willed animal with the likes of the villain behind her. The poor thing reminded her of Pinky. Still, it must be a horse he came in on, and better this one than a more able-bodied specimen. If Malum made a break for it and miraculously broke free of his escorts, they would quickly overtake his horse.

When people saw them coming, shouts erupted from the buildings ahead, and ten more Gorgenbrilders and Kalka'an men rode out to join the escort, Gabor at the front. Enouim let out a heavy sigh as she looked at her home. Smoke carried high into the air from burning bodies, and explosives from the night before had damaged many houses. Pastures once filled with well-fed horses were empty, and the comforting sounds of sheep and goats were missing. Still, the alternating green and gray soothed the ache in her heart.

Enouim arched an eyebrow at several rangers among the Gorgenbrilder and Kalka'an warriors. Baird had wrangled up more than his own countrymen! Kilith spoke to them quietly, giving orders to men around him and dispersing them in various directions as Enouim led Malum Khoron-khelek's processional.

She scanned the survivors lining the street. An older man, gaunt and bent, gaped at her with awe. His big brown eyes were curious, innocent, weary, hopeful. But as his gaze passed beyond her to Khoron-khelek a shade of hideous hatred fell across his face. He snarled and spat.

They passed rows of houses, bloodstained cobbles, and her many expectant countrymen. Whispers washed through the people, who lined the street and fell in behind them as they passed. The people were all on foot, only Kalka'an men and a few choice Gorgenbrild warriors on horses. Horses would likely be a great commodity for days to come, with so many starved, stolen, or killed by the Sumus.

They were nearly at Twedori's house and the open square when an arrow flew through the air. Enouim ducked and turned. Tribesmen! They had come for their leader. As she turned, she saw the arrow glance off Baird's shield as he raised it to block. Murmurs in the crowd rippled down the path, horses pawed, and Baird reared his horse in protest. Enouim glanced back in the direction of the arrow. A Gorgenbrilder perched on a house two houses down. There were no tribesmen. He had been aiming for Khoron-khelek.

Among the stir and the scuffle, a clattering came from behind her, and by the time she turned again, Khoron-khelek had managed to gather his feet under him on the horse. Still gagged and hands bound, he leaped onto Ruakh's horse. Sky shied in a sidestep into the stone wall to her right, and Malum pulled his arms under him on the hindquarters of the horse and threw his still-tied hands over Ruakh's neck. Ruakh whirled his staff behind him and struck Khoron-khelek so that they both fell from the horse. In an instant Malum was accosted again, gag freed from his mouth, hands bound in front rather than behind, but held on the ground by Ruakh, Serete, and Gabor.

Chaos erupted as the people began to scream, "Kill him! Kill him! Spill his blood for the blood of our sons and daughters! Spill it for our pain! Spill it for our land! String him up in pieces for the birds to feed on his carrion flesh!"

The people pressed in, and Enouim's squad pushed them

back. Anger boiled in her chest. Did they really believe they were so different from the Sumus? Canukke positioned himself next to Khoron-khelek, still mounted, surveying the scene. Enouim pushed Inferno forward between Malum, Canukke, and the crowd.

"Enough!" she called. But the people ignored her. "Enough!" she called again, raising her voice. Exasperated, Enouim reached down and drew Canukke's sword from his side, thrusting it into the air and screaming with all she had, "ENOUGH!"

The crowd settled, and their eyes fixed upon her. She heard whispers of *water warrior* filter through the audience.

"People of Gorgenbrild! I thought you braver than this," she said in a loud, clear voice. She let her words fall and watched as confusion and tension filled their expressions. "Yes, I am your water warrior. I am also daughter of Rotan and Qadra Cokanda. My father was as Gorgenbrilder as they come. You sent away this sword"—Enouim thrust Canukke's blade into the air again—"and knew what you were asking for when you sent it.

"You asked for savagery; you asked for conquest; you asked for a hero to snatch a legendary weapon and return to overthrow any who dared approach our doorstep. And your champion, Canukke Topothain, delivered!"

Cheers. Canukke inclined his head, but turned a curious eye on Enouim.

"You did not ask for your bartender to entangle herself in military matters, and believe me, neither did I. But we don't always get what we want. And it is good for you that we don't, or some of you may not have been standing here with us today. You asked for deliverance, and you have it. You asked for safety, and it has been restored to you."

Whoops and hollers thudded in response, and a chant broke out. *Water warrior! Water warrior! Water warrior!*

Enouim gestured to Khoron-khelek. "This man is but a man! And you are but men and women yourselves. Our code demands blood for blood and bone for bone—unless a stronger man sees retaliating against the weak as a waste of effort, the slight too small a thing to bother with—the mercy of strength. This is an honorable, acceptable response to an altercation. And do you find yourselves so equal with this man that he warrants such attention?" Enouim searched their faces. They were angry, but attentive ... and surprised. This twist on their logic piqued their interest.

"Malum Khoron-khelek is a leader with his own code. If we judge them on our code in our land, do we expect them to judge us based on their code in their territory to the north? What is a code worth? And yet even our own code lowers us to his level, his depravity. You say he is an animal, and so you become animals yourselves. Have you no humanity?"

She continued. "If Gorgenbrild is full of beasts, what complaint do you have? If composed of humans, where is your heart? A man who believes he is an animal will certainly never learn otherwise if he is always treated like one. I left you as a bartender, and I return as your water warrior. In the same way, we went in search of the Ecyah Stone and found that it brought more life than it did death. And he judges what is man and what is beast."

"Bring us the stone!"

"Kill him with it!"

"Send him where he and his kind belong. Death! Death!"

Enouim sighed. They heard nothing. They understood nothing. They could not comprehend Eh'yeh in this moment. She hadn't really expected them to, but hoped they would at least be open to it. Perhaps she could show them just a piece of Eh'yeh. Gorgenbrilders had never been much for talk, unless over drinks recounting their violent escapades.

She held up her hand. "It is my right to kill this man!"

Cheers, agreement.

"He came looking for me and attacked me. All of you he has hurt, capturing Gorgenbrild and afflicting it, but I too am of Gorgenbrild and he did these things also to me. And he tried to take my life with his own hands!"

They shouted their support.

Enouim dismounted and faced Malum Khoron-khelek. His eyes were dark, body tense, shoulders drawn back in arrogance. The muscles of his arms flexed in the grip of his captors, and his visage contorted in utter disdain. She walked forward and passed the sword in her hand back to Canukke.

"Shall I?" he asked eagerly.

Enouim shook her head.

"You could hardly hold your own in battle against a rabbit," Khoron-khelek said, and the condescension dripped from him like butter. "Your people are deceived."

"You're right. You are the better fighter, and I never claimed differently. But it was not you or me controlling the outcome last night."

Khoron-khelek raised his voice to the crowd. "You think holding me will save you? You think this water wretch is worth anything? I will never surrender, so kill me and see how many I take with me! Each one of you deserves to die—that is why I came! My spirit shall return with the strength of a hundred thousand Sumus. Kill me, and I only grow stronger. You return your loyalties to your weak— "

Enouim didn't let him finish. She crossed her arms in front of her chest in an "X" and stepped forward, pressing into his chest. Audible gasps from the audience escalated into a roar that drowned out anything else he tried to say. In the midst of his vitriol, she offered him the mercy of strength.

Malum's face twisted into a disgusted scowl, and he spat in her face. His beady eyes bore into her soul, and a sneer replaced his scowl. He spoke in a threatening low tone that only she and the two holding him could hear above the din. "You are nothing and no one. You are not even one of them. They will learn soon enough."

Her heartbeat pounded in her ears, but she leveled her stare back at him and allowed her own expression to soften. It was not of Eh'yeh to match his sentiment. The two of them were far more alike than she wanted to admit. Enouim gazed at him intently, studying the hardness in his exterior, and wondered how exhausting it must be to carry such great anger for so long.

Enouim bowed before him to honor his title as emperor of his people, and urged Canukke to take him away. The people were in chaos, shouting, screaming, fighting among one another after watching the unthinkable unfold before their eyes. As Canukke lead him away, their wrath was again fixed on their oppressor, their captive, Malum Khoron-khelek.

"Time to go," Kilith said in her ear, stepping behind her out of the sea of humanity and taking her arm. "From the dirty looks you're getting, Khoron-khelek is not their only target."

49

Kilith hurried her into a large home to the side, Twedori's house. They entered the large foyer where one door lead to a formal dining area and a kitchen, one to a grand meeting hall, and one to bedrooms. Though the furniture was as ornate as Gorgenbrild could produce, the walls had been stripped bare, so that only hooks and tattered Sumu garments hung where swords and vessels of trade once hung proudly on display.

Kilith took no time to marvel at the house, marching her down the hall and into the meeting chamber, where a long, carved table stood with matching chairs. To Enouim's surprise, Oloren lay at the near end of the table, surrounded by Vadik and two men Enouim didn't know. The chairs on this end had been pushed back against the wall, and light poured in from the hall and foyer, though the chamber had none of its own.

"This is the safest room in the house," Kilith said. "Stay here." With that, he turned and left, leaving Enouim standing in the entry gaping at her friend.

Oloren lay on her back on the table on a linen sheet

soaked with blood. She wasn't moving, and the ghastly pallor of her skin made an eerie contrast from her usual caramel complexion. Enouim stepped forward hesitantly, and gasped —her friend's left arm was missing below the elbow.

Vadik stood by Oloren's head, holding her right hand, as the other two crushed leaves and mixed substances together in bowls. One of them began pouring something over the stump where her left arm should have been. Oloren jerked up with a cry, and just as quickly fell back on the table with a thump, eyes closed again.

Enouim's lip quivered. "Is she going to be okay?"

Vadik looked up, eyes misty. "She's strong."

A beat of silence. "That's not what I asked. Vadik?"

The man still crushing leaves to Enouim's left looked up, and passed a glance between them. "She is a true Gorgenbrilder. So far she is doing well, but the window for infection has not yet passed ... and there were many particles embedded in the wound when she was brought to us. We are cleansing the wound and applying poultices to ward off infection, but we will see. If she is lucky, her arm is all she will lose."

A loud crash caused them all to jump, and Enouim's mind returned to the chaos outside. The yelling and screaming continued, and people pounded on the door and windows. Enouim stepped back through the passage and peeked around the corner into the foyer. Ruakh was there, leaning against a large chest he had placed against the barred door. Five other men stood at the ready.

"I am supposed to keep you away from the door," Ruakh told her. He smiled, his eyes soft. "Good speech."

"Lot of good it did. They're out for blood."

"You touched a nerve in the heart. This passionate of a response shows how deep the nerve ran. It is better than apathy. Your words made an impact. How they respond now is not up to you."

Enouim sighed. He was right. He seemed often to be right. "Where is Malum?"

"Canukke and the others took him to the dungeons. The explosions collapsed most of the tunnels, but there is one cell left in the underground dungeon and only one way in and out. He should be safe there, for now."

Enouim nodded, chewing her lip. "And my mother; have you seen her? Is she okay?"

Ruakh looked back at her in surprise, then in sadness. "Who is your mother?"

One of the men nearby spoke up. "I saw her at your little charade. She was fine. If she heads indoors, she should stay that way."

"How ...? I don't know you," Enouim said skeptically. She didn't appreciate the disapproving tones in his voice. "How do you know my mother?"

"Everyone knows you now," said another. His eyes were softer than his friend's.

Ruakh spoke again. "The people want us to know they're angry. Their energies are mostly following Khoron-khelek, and I do not envy Canukke and Serete's responsibility to safely contain him. But they will wear themselves out. We will keep our heads down today and let them sleep on it."

SUNRISE KISSED the hills with a gentle greeting, flooding the morning with hope and life. By the time Enouim awoke, the sun had already ascended high into the sky. She opened her eyes and blinked in the light, trying to remember where she was. She found herself on a bed draped in furs, with three other beds made up and lying empty in the room. Many hooks decorated the wall, and Enouim imagined that quite an arsenal of impressive weaponry once hung there.

A shadow passed over the window in the hall. Enouim froze. Someone stood just outside it, unmoving. Was she a prisoner here? What had happened in the night? She passed a hand over her eyes. No, she was all right. They had taken Twedori's house as their own headquarters and let the day wear on and wear out all the frenzy of the morning. Next to the bed lay a fresh set of clothes. Enouim glanced down the hall. Seeing no one, she quickly changed under the blankets and rose from her place, letting out a deep sigh.

She walked down the hall, past two empty bedrooms, and into the foyer. Voices came from the dining room, and she followed the sound to a long table with benches. To her delight, Oloren, Gabor, Vadik, and Serete all sat at the table.

"Oloren!" Enouim exclaimed. "How are you feeling?"

"A little lighter, thanks," she answered, lifting her stump and wincing. Two clean socks covered the bandages on her arm. "I'm sorry to have missed your speech. Sounds like quite the event."

"How is it out there?" Enouim asked, sliding into the bench next to Oloren and reaching for an apple in the center of the table. "It sounds quieter. That has to be a good sign."

"Good morning, sleepyhead." Serete greeted her with a smile. "Gorgenbrild is divided. Most are still bent on killing Khoron-khelek, and the guards stationed with him are nearly giving in. A few have really been pondering your mercy of strength."

"But most just don't understand it," Gabor said. "And Canukke is struggling with it himself. I think he's almost killed Malum a hundred times."

"I'm surprised he hasn't," Enouim answered honestly. "Is he there now?"

Vadik shook his head. "He was here earlier, to see Oloren. Couldn't shut up about the mercy of strength. Kept wondering why and how it could help matters. He went after his woman though. He's with her now, I believe."

"Ooh! Did he tell you? Do you know?"

"Know what?" Serete asked.

"How can we know if we know, if you don't tell us what *you* know?" Vadik prodded playfully.

Enouim paused. How could Canukke not have mentioned his daughter to them? "That he ... uh ... you know, family stuff."

Vadik gasped facetiously but then smiled. "Yes, we know. Crazy. I'm not sure I picture him a father of a girl."

"What's that supposed to mean?" Oloren demanded. "Girls are tough. I could beat you all to a pulp even still. After breakfast, maybe I will!"

"Tough, maybe, but as it turns out—less handy," Vadik said with a smirk.

Oh, put a sock in it." Oloren rolled her eyes."

"I can't! You stole them all."

Enouim laughed, and the rest joined in. Perhaps life would slowly return to normal now they were home.

A pounding came at the door. Serete and Gabor jumped up, instinctively placing themselves between the doorway and the table.

"We aren't children," Oloren muttered, but Gabor shushed her.

Gabor and Serete crept to the foyer, and Enouim heard a long slide as they moved the heavy chest from the door. The bar lifted, and a beat of silence followed. Whispers. A low creak let them know the door had opened, and Gabor called back. "Enouim?"

She got up cautiously and rounded the corner. There before her stood her mother, still gaunt and thin, but with a light in her eyes Enouim had dearly missed at their last meeting. Tears streamed down her mother's face as she reached for her daughter, and Enouim ran to her.

"I thought I would never see you again," Qadra managed through tears after a long embrace.

"I'm okay. We're okay," Enouim said, choking back tears of her own.

Qadra pulled back and searched her face. "How grown you are, little one," she said, and a fresh tear slid hot down Enouim's cheek. "You must tell me everything!"

Enouim pulled her mother into the dining room, where she filled two plates with food and hastily introduced her friends to her mother before scampering off to her room with Qadra in tow. Enouim sat cross-legged on the bed and poured out everything that had happened.

At the end Qadra held up her hand. "I still question this man Eh'yeh's intentions, sending nine against an army. How could you trust him so readily?"

"Mother. Mereámé was dead. She is alive now. I'm not sure what else I can tell you, other than the fact that we spent time with him there, and ... well, if you knew him, you would know."

"So it's true. You left for the Ecyah Stone, and came back empty handed. And yet you ... you were the weapon all along!" Her eyes widened with awe.

"No, I was not the weapon. I learned some things about myself, but it's still just me—and had it all been left in my hands, we would all be dead."

Qadra shook her head. "So modest. A hero, Gorgenbrild's

finest. No matter what they say about you, almost all agree you saved us."

"What do you mean, no matter what they say?"

Qadra paused. "I ... er, well," she said slowly, "some question your loyalty. Some say you are not of Gorgenbrild, that you have deceived us. A few know about the Chayan situation, and say you are a coward, but obviously you have outweighed the wrong to Chayan with victory. They are fools. The rest say you are a hero. And so do I."

Enouim had nearly forgotten about Chayan. An uneasy feeling settled on her chest. *You need to face Chayan.* Enouim shook off the thought.

"And what of the mercy of strength?"

"A powerful insult." She nodded approvingly. "It was a greater blow to let him live with the knowledge that even a young girl like you considered herself stronger than he, and not worth the effort of killing. But don't you think he is too dangerous to leave alive?"

"I meant no insult." Enouim shook her head. "I meant it in truth. I offered him mercy, the best way that our culture would allow. It is acceptable to do so."

Qadra's eyes narrowed, but then she waved her hand. "No matter, it's all over now. You are safe and sound. Gorgenbrild is saved because of you, and we can rebuild. You know, the Mangonel was never destroyed."

Enouim blinked. Did she really expect her to go back to serving mead at Mangonel Mornings? "I can't go back there now!"

"Oh ... well, of course not. Not now. Now you could do whatever you like. Perhaps be a horse breeder like you dreamed of as a girl? Heaven knows we will be needing plenty more of those now. And that Kalka'aner stallion you brought with you is quite the specimen."

Enouim gaped at her. Why did her childhood dream, her teenage dream, her dream up until this year, sound like such drudgery? She couldn't stand the thought of Inferno being cooped up for use as a stud horse. He was built to fly! He should be galloping over mountains and through rivers, chasing down the horizon, forging ahead with the wind in his mane.

And so should she.

"I can't stay here forever."

"Nonsense! Gorgenbrild will be safe now. We're vulnerable, yes, but the Kalka'an men are graciously willing to stay and help protect our borders while we rebuild. We will be bigger and better by the time any tribesmen attempt to trifle with us again, and their numbers are drastically cut down. They are scattered."

Enouim shook her head slowly. "That's not it. There is more out there for me than divvying up lunch to travelers or breeding horses for their adventures. *I* am the traveler now. Don't you see? I walked the trade routes of my father, and surpassed even his distances. I saw things—*saw* things! It can't be unseen or untraveled, and I am not the same person I was when I left."

Her mother's eyes brimmed with tears, and guilt rose up like a tidal wave. Enouim hurried to catch it. "I mean I am ... but I'm not." Enouim scratched her head. *You need to face Chayan.* She hurried on. "But, Mother, Gorgenbrild will always be my home. And I won't be going anywhere right away. I am a Gorgenbrilder through and through, daughter of Rotan and Qadra Cokanda, the greatest parents in all the world."

Qadra's countenance brightened, and with it, Enouim's heart. Still, she questioned what she'd just told her mother. She may have been raised in Gorgenbrild, but she was less

Gorgenbrilder than her people hoped. And though it made her feel out of place, she was glad of it —glad to be free of paralyzing hatred and anger that weighed down the soul. And although she didn't know where her next adventure would come from, she knew it would come.

Enouim. Do not run from me. You need to face Chayan.

Enouim sighed. Whatever the people thought of her, she had been brought up in Gorgenbrild, and she'd violated its cardinal rule. Why would Eh'yeh have her honor such an absurd standard? The culture of Gorgenbrild was wrong. Anxiety filled her stomach with sour butterflies, but she knew what she must do.

It didn't have to make sense. If Eh'yeh asked, the answer must always be yes.

50

Three men stood in the entrance to the dungeon where a locked gate should have been. The hinges had been blown off in one of the explosions, but a single half-collapsed cell remained usable for the tribesman emperor. Enouim wiped sweaty palms on her tunic and bit her lip as she walked toward Chayan, who was fully engaged in an argument with the guards.

"Your water warrior *forfeited* highest rights to his blood! Any of us can now carry out what she could not!"

The first guard, a man Enouim recognized as Simmet, shook his head. "She didn't forfeit them. She pardoned him."

"That was not within her rights to do."

"Our orders come from Kilith Urul, as do yours. Until Quarot recovers enough to confer with Kilith and Canukke, Khoron-khelek lives. I'm sure he will be appropriately disposed of at that time."

Enouim hesitated. Maybe now was not the best time.

"Water warrior!" The second guard acknowledged her with a dip of his head, rapping his right fist to his left shoulder in deep respect. Enouim's breakfast suddenly did not quite agree with her.

"Have some respect for yourself," Chayan sneered. "She's a tavern girl."

"I've never seen a tavern girl save a nation before," Simmet said. "It doesn't make her a saint. But she has a lot of supporters. I'd watch yourself if I were you."

The second guard looked eagerly at Enouim. "Are you joining the leadership of Gorgenbrild? What do you think should be done with Khoron-khelek? You are the one who captured him, after all."

Chayan snorted and took a swig from her flask.

Enouim grimaced. "Um ... I actually came to talk to Chayan."

Chayan choked on her drink. "What?"

Enouim swallowed. The four Gorgenbrilders gaped at her as though she'd lost her mind. Perhaps she had. "In private?" Her voice squeaked with as much authority as a mouse in a zegrath's claws. She cleared her throat and tried again. "In private."

Chayan crossed her arms. "I don't think so. I have nothing to say to you."

Enouim surveyed Chayan's guarded pose. She might be butch in front of the guards, but her eyes were curious.

"Well, that's obvious, because if you did you would have come and found me by now. But I'm the one with something to say."

Chayan lifted her chin. "Say it."

The guards glanced uneasily from Enouim to Chayan and back again. People passing by slowed down to watch the interaction. The longer she took, the more of a spectacle this would be.

Enouim pursed her lips. "Right, okay."

Chayan arched an eyebrow.

Enouim put her hands on her hips and took a deep breath. "If it weren't for you covering for us, Canukke and I never would have made it out of our scouting mission alive. We never would have launched a successful attack, and we would have lost. I never meant to hurt you, and it isn't fair that someone unqualified like me took your place going after the stone. I can never give that back to you. The last words you said to me those months ago were, *your bones belong to me.* I don't want to turn this into some sort of show, so I won't do it now, but tonight I'm giving you the chance to do whatever you feel you must."

Chayan blinked back at her, dumbstruck. "What's the catch? You think you can face me now that you have powers? Let me guess, we're meeting at the river?"

"No. We'll meet on the east side of Gorgenbrild, at Sefer's Knoll by the cliff. You're stronger and faster than I am. I won't get away from you there. And there's no river on that side."

Chayan's eyes narrowed.

Simmet's lips parted, but no sound came.

Enouim gave a short nod. "I'll see you at dusk."

FOR THE NEXT FEW HOURS, Enouim steered clear of anyone who might talk her out of meeting with Chayan. She hadn't told anyone her plan, but Serete found her meandering the outskirts an hour before dusk.

"Everyone is talking about your meeting tonight."

"What? I haven't told anyone! I didn't even tell you."

"You told Chayan in front of three guards. Everyone saw you talking to her. It didn't take long."

Enouim sighed. "Fantastic."

"Your mother sent me to check on you. This meeting sounds like a bad idea."

"Thanks. But it wasn't my idea."

"Eh'yeh?"

"I think so."

Serete raised an eyebrow. "You *think* so or you *know* so? If you just *think* so, it's possible you're being an idiot. If you *know* so, then I guess there's nothing left for me to say."

"I'm pretty sure it was Eh'yeh. I wouldn't have wanted to do it on my own." Doubt washed over her, and a chill ran up her spine. What if she was wrong? What if she was going to her death for absolutely no reason? *No, that thought was not your own. It might not make sense, but somehow, it'll work.*

Serete stayed with her until it was time, and they walked together to Sefer's Knoll. Enouim gasped as they came into full view of the meeting point. A crowd of people waited, and in an open circle in the midst of them, Chayan swung two broadswords in a flourish.

"I'm beginning to think this was a bad idea," Enouim whispered to Serete.

"You're coming to that now, are you?" Serete nudged her. "I'm just kidding. If Eh'yeh brought you here, he must have a reason. And if anything goes sideways, I'll be right here."

"You can't interfere with the exchange."

"If she breaks an arm, I guess I'll do my best to restrain myself, but I won't watch her kill you. I'm not a Gorgenbrilder. I'll do whatever I please."

The two of them approached the crowd and chants broke out, one side chanting *water warrior* and the other, *water witch*. Chayan swung her swords again and lifted one in Enouim's direction. The people roared.

Serete melted away into the crowd, and Enouim's heart hammered. Her fingers trembled, and the empty dagger's sheath at her belt taunted her. She'd purposefully left her dagger at home so that she couldn't change her mind on her approach. *At least if you die, you won't regret it long,* she thought. *Eh'yeh help me.*

The crowd parted as Enouim entered the ring in the center of the mass of people where Chayan paced like a hungry zegrath.

"Chayan, Chayan, Chayan!"

"Water warrior!"

"River witch!"

"Coward!"

Chayan lifted her swords to the air and let out a war cry that sent goosebumps across Enouim's flesh. Chayan lifted a huge, muscled arm to point the end of her blade at Enouim's chest. "Where is your weapon?"

Canukke stepped from the crowd and offered Enouim a scimitar. Malum Khoron-khelek's scimitar, its famed black and gold markings glinting in the evening light. Chayan faltered, and a hush fell over those assembled. Enouim met Canukke's gaze, and his eyes were as soft toward her as she had ever seen them. She felt his concern, his fear, as two people he cared for faced off against each other.

A gentle wind wafted through her hair, and Enouim felt a blanket of unexplainable calm. She glanced beyond Canukke and saw Vadik. He glanced at something invisible in the air and gave her a small smile and encouraging nod. Enouim took the scimitar and Canukke returned to the crowd. Chayan took in the scimitar and looked at Enouim with wide eyes.

Enouim leveled a stare at Chayan and swung the scimitar in as beautiful an arc as any practiced warrior. She whirled it downward and burrowed it into the dirt so that it stood on end at Chayan's feet. Enouim knelt before her adversary.

"Pick up your weapon," Chayan growled.

Enouim raised her eyes to meet Chayan's, and when she spoke, her voice was low and steady. "I said I would offer you my bones. And I intend to make good on that promise."

Surprise flitted across Chayan's face, and she paced back and forth before Enouim. She threw one of her swords into the dust inches from Enouim's knees. *"Pick up your weapon!"*

Enouim maintained eye contact but said nothing.

Chayan crossed the space between them and stooped until she was nose to nose with Enouim. "Why are you doing this?"

"The brutality of our people is little better than the Sumus. I will take no part in unnecessary violence. There is a better way, but I will let you do what you see fit."

Chayan straightened. She paused, unsure of herself, and glanced behind her at Canukke. They shared some unspoken understanding, and Chayan twisted back to Enouim.

"Enouim Cokanda, I don't know why you didn't kill Malum Khoron-khelek, but it was not cowardice." Chayan threw her final sword to the side, pulled Enouim to her feet, and crossed her arms into an *X*.

Gasps rippled through the crowd as the most unlikely of Gorgenbrilder's warriors offered the mercy of strength. Chayan completed the gesture, picked up the Sumu emperor's scimitar, and ran a finger down its sparkling blade. She lifted her voice for all to hear. "I have offered Enouim Cokanda the mercy of strength! I declare now in the presence of all of you that, though her decision with Khoron-khelek may be misguided, it was made with honor. Without her our people would still be subjected to his reign of terror, and the debt we owe her as a people is greater than any outstanding debt she may owe any individual. If man or woman takes issue with the water warrior, let them take it up with me."

Chayan pressed the hilt of Malum Khoron-khelek's scimitar firmly into Enouim's hand and wrapped her own calloused fingers over top. She lifted Enouim's fist with the scimitar high into the air, shouting, "Water warrior! Never to turn! Gorgenbrild forever!"

Shock reverberated through Enouim's bones as the sea of people before her hoisted their weapons in the air, echoing back Chayan's words.

"Water warrior!"

"Never to turn!"

"Gorgenbrild forever!"

51

Three months after the great battle, Enouim walked the paths of her homeland, relishing the light breeze toying with her hair and the soft light of evening. Somewhere a sheep lowed, a promise of a future where resources would again be plentiful. Few sheep or goats had avoided death or pilfering at the hands of the Sumus, but several had been saved, and some the Sumus had stolen had been recovered. Even so, much of the Sumu camps were burning when Gorgenbrilders came upon them, and little had been left behind. Traders had already been sent out to surrounding areas to barter weapons and other goods for stock animals.

On her left, a family rebuilt the stone wall of their home, two parents and three small children all carefully working to lay the stones. One of the children cried out and pointed at her as she passed, and the family looked up. The smallest child hid behind her mother's skirts, and the father smiled and waved with the older two children. The mother glared at her with a piercing, accusing look. Enouim smiled weakly and offered a wave before turning away.

Three nights after Sefer's Knoll, a quarrel had broken out over what to do with Khoron-khelek. The guards fought with one another, as did a mob of Gorgenbrilders outside, and finally Chayan had pushed her way through to his cell. In the dark of night she had stabbed him to death ... only to find the next morning that it was indeed a tribesman but not Malum Khoron-khelek. No one knew what had happened, and half the people blamed Enouim. The other half blamed her indirectly, for not killing him when she had the chance.

All along her walk through Gorgenbrild people stopped and stared, muttering or whispering to one another. The sentiment had mostly been positive after Chayan's mercy of strength, though somewhat confused, but she became more controversial again after Khoron-khelek's disappearance. Sometimes people smiled and praised Enouim when she passed, some asked her about her powers, others only glared with disdain, and a few hurled insults. Enouim wanted none of it.

She rounded the bend at the edge of the residences and found what she'd been looking for—her favorite spot to get away, a little way off from any buildings, overlooking the cliff. She picked up her pace, and as she drew away from Gorgenbrild, her heart grew lighter and her breath came easier. As she drew closer, she noticed Canukke's strong frame leaning against one of the few trees clustered together there by the edge of the cliff. She had hoped to be alone.

Enouim walked up the gentle slope and stood at the top of the cliff next to Canukke. Neither said anything. Swaths of dreamy pinks and oranges dressed the sunset for a glorious departure, doubled in the reflection of the ocean far off. Enouim wished she could see Yadara again, her gentle spirit painted with these brilliant colors. A light wind wafted

Enouim's hair away from her face and she closed her eyes, letting out a relieved, contented sigh.

She sat and hugged her knees, gazing out over the horizon. After several minutes, Canukke sat down next to her against the tree, arms crossed. Enouim glanced at him, but he was still looking out over the cliff. He seemed deep in thought, brows furrowed, as if working out all the problems of the world. Not wanting to pry, she looked away from him and back over the cliff.

"She's beautiful, you know," he said at last.

Startled, Enouim looked up. "Hmm?"

"My daughter. She is the most beautiful thing I have ever laid eyes on, if you can believe it. And I have seen much beauty."

Enouim stayed quiet, but the corner of her mouth twitched. His rough exterior had softened somewhat since the battle, and he had spent every free moment with Edone and the baby.

"I am a great warrior of many exploits. My strength and experience are unmatched in Gorgenbrild. Yet still I cannot protect her from the evil polluting Yatzar." He drew a deep breath. "If I cannot protect her, no man can."

Enouim paused, then spoke slowly. "Perhaps no man can."

"What kind of father does that make me?"

"I think it makes you the human kind."

Silence settled into the air around them. She listened to the breeze rustling the leaves of the trees and breathed in the salt air. Enouim felt her heart beating in a low, constant rhythm, reminding her of the life she possessed. But she didn't really possess it, did she? It was borrowed. There were no guarantees in life, and she was human too—without control over her destiny. But she was now convinced that her destiny was in safe hands.

"I had a dream," he continued. "Back in the glades with Eh'yeh. I had pushed it aside pretty effectively until your little stunt in the Battle of Mercy." Accusation laced his tone, but when she looked at him, his face was soft.

"Did you? So did I. And Gabor."

Canukke shrugged. "Perhaps we all dreamed there. In the dream Eh'yeh was somehow dying in my stead, and his blood entangled and entrapped me, condemned me, drowned me. I knew I would be free and safe if only I surrendered to it, but I fought it. I didn't want to give in."

"What did you do?"

"I didn't. I woke up at the last second before I choked to death on his blood. What is the purpose of such a dream?"

Enouim paused. "I think you already know. You can't hold onto control forever, because it doesn't work. As Kilith said to me once, would you rather follow something that works, but doesn't make sense, or makes sense, but doesn't work?"

Canukke nodded. "Eh'yeh has been pulling at my sword for a long time now. I think ... I think soon it will no longer be mine, but will belong to him."

Enouim smiled. "It is the freest you will ever be. We are all drowning in something or other."

"I will not return to his glades now. Perhaps one day. But my place is here in Gorgenbrild, to rebuild and to lead, and to patch together the shambles of my family as it should have been. I have ... I'm afraid I have not been a good husband."

She sobered, thinking of Edone's bruises. "I know."

A tear slipped down Canukke's cheek. He had not bidden it, but neither did he wipe it away.

"Things are starting to return to normal," Enouim said, "though I'm not sure what normal is anymore. I'm beginning to think the new 'normal' will never quite be the same."

"I think you're right. But I am not sure how much of the

difference is because of difference in the people, and how much is because of difference in us."

"True. They see me differently now, and it can't be undone. But it is just as well. I see them differently now too." She sighed. "The people see me as a foreigner at best and a traitor at worst, staring at me everywhere I go. Some claim me as a Gorgenbrilder through and through, a hero, but that's even more disturbing than the glares."

"They hardly saw you at all before this. You were no one. Now that you are talked about, there will be strong opinions from a hundred different angles. But it's not about you. If everyone agreed, it might mean something, but the fact that they all squabble about it tells a different story. You have been the catalyst of change, but only time will tell what sort of change it will be."

"I'm not sure I want to be here long enough to find out. Gorgenbrild has become a weight to me."

Canukke nodded. "I have a feeling you won't be spending the rest of your years the way you spent them up until now. Oloren is already itching to get going on some venture or other, restless as ever despite her surgery. It seems you two may be cut from a cloth more similar than I expected."

Enouim laughed. Oloren's amputated arm had developed a serious infection and required another amputation surgery, so that her left arm now ended in a short stump just below the shoulder. She had lost none of her spunk in recovery, and was raring to go. "I would be at least as afraid to cross her now as ever before."

"More so, I think—she's always been small, and now she's even smaller. Leaves all that fire in her tiny little frame even more concentrated." He smirked.

"There you are!"

The voice took them both off guard, and Enouim jumped.

She turned to find Serete sauntering toward them in his familiar long, confident strides. Her heart warmed to see him, and she smiled. The evening light shone favorably upon his handsome features, and she found herself distracted for a moment, taking him in.

"I have news," he said excitedly, lighting himself next to them with the springing energy of a child.

The corner of her mouth twisted. She couldn't help herself. "What kind of news?"

"Oh, the best kind. Adventure." His eyes twinkled. "I've heard reports of something big in the waters to the north, something that has been frightening all the prey animals away, and with them the main food sources for surrounding areas. The rivers have been 'behaving strangely'—your guess is as good as mine as to what that means. And there are rumors it's headed this way."

Her heart sunk. "You're leaving?"

Canukke laughed, and Enouim shot him a glare.

Serete raised an eyebrow. "I just told you about an exciting adventure—focused on rivers—and all you can say is 'you're leaving'?"

"Well ... aren't you?"

Serete smiled, a little dumbfounded.

Canukke snorted. "You aren't going to send this poor man off all alone, are you? Please."

Enouim blushed. "Oh."

Serete paused. "Well? What do you think?"

Enouim's heart pounded. It sounded like salvation. A getaway, with less chances of dying than her last venture—but who knew? It was an adventure, after all. A smile slowly made its way across her face. Starting fresh, seeing the world. "What else do you know about this mission?"

"Oh, a few details, not much. Rangers often operate on rumor to get going."

Enouim laughed. A year ago she never would have dreamed she would be in this position. But that was a year ago, and a lot had changed since then. She wondered what would change this time. She turned to Serete, eyes bright. "When do we leave?"

The End.

PRONUNCIATION GUIDE

Characters

Enouim – *En*-new-ihm

Chayan – Shy-ahn

Bondeg – Bone-deg

Quarot – Kwar-aht

Pleko – Play-koe

Qadra – Kah-druh

Malum Khoron-khelek – Mal-uhm core-on keh-leck

Pryan – Pry-on

Twedori-- Tweh-dore-ee

Canukke – Kuh-newk

Edone – Ee-doe-n

Balat – Bahl-aht

Pakel – Pah-kell

Oloren – Uh-lore-en

Vadik – V-add-ihk

Gabor – Gabe-or

Kilith – Kill-ith

Baird – Bare-d

Silas – Sigh-lahs

Kenan – Kee-nah-n
Banor – Bah-nore
Javen – Jah-ven
Jenulia – Jen-oo-lee-uh
Ruakh – Rue-ah-ck
Len – Lehn
Mereámé – Meer-ah-may
Eh'yeh - Eh-Hyeh
Canus – Can-uh-s
Amun – Am-uhn
Mayimesh – My-eem-esh
Iamwë- Ee-ah-m-weh
Poleia – Pole-ay-ah
Yadara - Yuh-dar-ah
Nyeur – Nye-your
Laskallel – Lahs-kah-lell
Fetrye – Feh-tree
Conand – Cone-and
Nymrenil – Nim-wren-ill
Rindyl – Rinn-dull
Koko – Koh-koh
Urou – Oar-ooh
Serete – Seh-ret-tay

Places

Gorgenbrild – Gore-gehn-brild
Kalka'an – Cal-kah-ahn
Levav – Lev-ahv
Iyangas – Ee-yah-ng-ahs
Sumus – Soo-moo-s
Morthed – More-thed
Rehim – Reh-heem

Creatures

    Zegrath – zee-g-wrath

    Tsiza – T-sieze-uh

    Perasor –pair-uh-soar

    Tannin – tah-nin

ACKNOWLEDGMENTS

To my husband George, thank you for supporting me in this and every other endeavor, for loving me unconditionally, and for being such an incredible man.

To Lo, Kendria, Derrick, Melissa, and George: thank you for letting me pick your brains to create round characters that remind me of each of you on some level. Thank you for the significant roles you have played in my life, and for being the type of people I would want along for the ride as I debut my first novel. You were generous with your time and gracious in your encouragement!

To Mr. Clifton Abercrombie, Ms. Jessica Maupin, and Ms. Janine Koehnke at Warrior Success Academy: a special thank you for your dedication to excellence in the training of Krav Maga martial arts, as well as your enthusiasm and encouragement not only in my physical training, but in my writing. You have gone above and beyond to assist in making fight scenes believable, from choreographing to consulting.

Finally, and most importantly, I acknowledge my Creator for loving His creation so much that He shares the thrill with us, that we might create as well.

ABOUT THE AUTHOR

E.A. Winters is the author of *The Forgotten Stone* and *The Blood & Flame Saga*, writing fast-paced epic fantasy stories that keep you turning pages long into the night. She was born and raised in Raleigh, NC and currently resides in Lynchburg, VA. She writes with a chai or hot chocolate close at hand, and deftly fields being Tigger-pounced by her toddlers at home. When she's not writing, she enjoys board games, escape rooms, and general family time with her husband and two boys.

ALSO BY E.A. WINTERS

Blood & Flame Saga

Book 1: Dragon's Kiss

Book 2: Broken Bonds

Book 3: Noble Claims

Book 4: Crimson Queen

Made in the USA
Coppell, TX
16 July 2023

19237482R00310